A
MURDER
OF
CROWS

A MURDER OF CROWS

Riftborn * Book 5

STEVE McHUGH

Podium

GLOSSARY

SPECIES

Ancients: The oldest, but not necessarily the most powerful, members of the rift-fused. They ensure that there are checks and balances between rift-fused and humans.

Eidolons: Living embodiments of rift power that reside as caretakers of a riftborn's embers. Can change shape to most animals as needed. Are always two for every riftborn's embers.

Fiends: Animals that die on Earth close to a tear and are brought back to life from the power of the rift. Comes in three kinds: lesser, greater, and elder.

Practitioners: Those born inside the rift. Can create constructs along with using the rift to imbue writing and potions with their power.

Primes: The rulers of Inaxia, the capital city of the rift.

Primordials: Creatures that live inside the Tempest in the rift.

Revenants: Those who died on Earth as human, close to a tear, and were brought back to life by the power of the rift. There are ten different species of revenant.

Rift-fused: Anyone or anything given power by the rift.

Rift-walkers: Can create tears between the rift and Earth at will.

Riftborn: Those who were mortally wounded on Earth as human but were taken into the rift and gifted incredible power. Can move between Earth and the rift using their embers.

GROUPS

Guilds: Seven groups of powerful rift-fused who ensure that humans and rift-fused live in harmony.

Investigators: Police force of Inaxia.

RCU (Rift-Crime Unit): Multinational agency that investigates crimes committed by and against the rift-fused.

Talons: Guild members trained in secret to remove threats to their Guild.

PLACES

Agency: Largest Lawless City in the rift. On the border of the Vastness.

Crow's Perch: Prison city in the rift, run by the Queen of Crows.

Embers: The pocket dimension used by riftborn to travel between Earth and the rift, as well as to heal any physical wounds the riftborn has sustained.

Harmony: The area surrounding the Tempest.

Inaxia: Capital city of the rift.

Lawless City: City in the rift that lives free from Inaxian rule.

Mercy: A place no one wants to admit exists.

Nightvale: Settlement in the rift.

Plainhaven: Largest settlement inside the Vastness.

Rift: Dimension attached to our own that allows incredible power to flow out from it through tears between dimensions.

Tempest: The maelstrom of power at the north of the rift.

Vast Death: Otherwise known as the Vastness. Large area of the rift which is considered the most dangerous.

PREVIOUSLY IN RIFTBORN

I have been alive for over two thousand years, and in that time, I have come across many people whose only interest is in power and how much they can claim for themselves. But I've rarely met someone quite like Callie Mitchell.

Born inside the rift, she was a practitioner, which is, when you boil it right down, just a human with an exceptionally long lifespan and an affinity for making things using rift energy. A rare occurrence within a place that is known for the impossible. She banded together with a group calling themselves the Blessed—a terrorist organisation which wanted to overthrow the government of the rift's capital city, Inaxia—and set about figuring out how to gain as much power for herself as possible.

In keeping with her personality, and unfortunately for the other members of her organisation, she betrayed them, allowing herself to be exiled to Earth so that she could continue her experiments on the rift-fused who lived there. Over the decades, revenants, riftborn, and rift-walkers all fell victim to her machinations.

I'd stopped her from creating monsters more than once over the years, and managed to force her underground. After several years, her past, and I, caught up with her, and she attempted to sway me to her cause.

Eventually, Callie found a way to tap into the Tempest—the source of power within the rift, far to the north, hidden under the mountain range that cuts through the area, and protected by the indigenous group of creatures who lived there, the primordials. While I tried to stop her, she stepped inside the Tempest, the core of rift power beneath the mountain, and discovered that this sapient creature, with the power of a god, did not like her trying to use it. Instead, the power of the Tempest vaporised her before me. I thought at the time it was the end of dealing with Callie Mitchell and her plans.

It turns out that I was far too quick to celebrate.

Not long after Callie's supposed death, my old mentor and friend Neb went missing while in the rift. I journeyed deep into a part of the land that few attempt to traverse in an attempt to rescue her, only to discover that Callie, for some unknown reason, had been resurrected by the Tempest itself, in addition to giving her an unprecedented portion of that power, allowing her to go out and fulfil its own plan of healing the rift.

Callie carried out her own plan by messing around with the link between the rift and Earth, causing chaos with riftborn being unable to move freely between the two, and the creation of a large number of fiends on Earth, which I was pretty sure Callie did to keep those who might get in her way busy.

It was obvious that Callie's mind was beginning to fracture, and she murdered the imprisoned Ahiram, one of twelve Ancients who'd been isolated and held in stasis for trying to rule the world and the rift centuries ago and having tried to bring about the downfall of his brothers and sisters. Each Ancient was linked to another, but no one knew who, a reason which ensured, for everyone but Ahiram, that they didn't try to kill one another for centuries. As Ahiram died, severing his link with an unknown Ancient somewhere out in the rift or Earth, one of the surviving Ancients would lose their connection to the rift and would slowly, over months or years, lose their power. It would end with them losing their life, as the power that they'd taken from the rift would return to it.

Meanwhile, Callie used the chaos that she had created to escape. The chaos in question was a new Guild called the Vipers, who once belonged to Ahiram and were led to believe that Callie was there to free him, which she did—but not in the way they expected.

So, that was it. One dead Ancient, an old Guild that my allies and I had to destroy before they killed more innocents, and one missing Callie Mitchell, who could have been anywhere, doing who knows what.

I hadn't seen Timo—the Ancient who lived in Plainhaven—or Neb since what happened in the rift. I didn't harbour any ill feeling toward either of them, a difficult thing, considering Neb had withheld information that, if we'd known, might have stopped all of the chaos from happening. Also that the Ancients, as a group, willfully hid the fact that they had imprisoned Ahiram for thousands of years and then buried their heads in the sand about what might happen if he woke up.

There's a curse that I've heard all my life, which is "May you live in interesting times," and frankly, I was beginning to think that I must've angered a particularly furious deity to have to live for so long in such an interesting time.

A
MURDER
OF
CROWS

CHAPTER ONE

Callie Mitchell wasn't one to do things by half-measures. She was a smart and capable woman who was never going to stop with the death of just one Ancient. Maybe she'd changed tactics, though. Currently, there was a guerrilla-warfare campaign against Inaxia, killing several Guild members who were sent there to keep the peace, along with soldiers and anyone else who got in their way.

No one knew exactly who was carrying out these attacks, although the prevailing opinion was that it was the remains of Viper Guild, possibly with Callie Mitchell's direction, but with no proof, we had no clue as to where to look for those responsible. The rift is a big place, and if you want to hide and never be found, it's easily done.

The whole time the attacks were happening, the remaining Ancients did very little. Ancients are good at lots of talk and no action. That ended a week ago when two of the three Ancients who lived and worked within Inaxia were assassinated, along with several Guild members sent to protect them, and two of the Primes.

The Primes were the de facto leaders of Inaxia, although how much power they had when it came to the Ancients was up for debate. They were, in my humble opinion, mostly out for themselves and about as useful as a glass hammer, but they didn't deserve to be murdered for it.

That got the Ancients wanting to do things very quickly. Although *quickly* is a relative term when the Ancients are concerned. A conclave was arranged, essentially a meeting between the remaining eight Ancients in a place they all considered to be neutral. The rift was out, mostly because none of them could be convinced that it was a safe place. Earth seemed to be the best option.

The conclave of the Ancients was to be the first time that the now eight remaining Ancients were to be in the same room for centuries, if not longer.

Ji-hyun, my friend and head of the eastern USA branch of the RCU (Rift-Crime Unit), was given the job of arranging it, simply because she was trusted by everyone involved to dislike them all equally. Or at least, that was the general impression I got when she spoke to me about it. Truth was, she was neutral because she didn't much care about the political or financial machinations of a bunch of people who had been playing the same games for longer than many of us had been alive.

For some reason, I'd been given the unenviable task of finding a location to host the meeting. Somewhere that everyone could agree on. Or, as it turned out, that they all disagreed on to approximately the same level.

I picked the New Forest in the South of England for two reasons. One, I knew the place fairly well, and two, the Horsebrook estate where the meeting would take place was at least a kilometre's distance from any towns, villages, or hamlets in the area. It was also big enough that the Ancients and their entourages could each have their own space.

I didn't want to have anything to do with the conclave. I wanted to hunt Callie Mitchell down, figure out what the hell she was doing, what game she was playing. She wasn't really Callie anymore. At least, I didn't think so. She'd been vaporised by the power of the rift and had returned quite different from the Callie I'd remembered. If nothing else, she was definitely a lot more helpful, especially having killed Ahiram. That didn't mean I thought she deserved to live—whatever game she was playing, I didn't trust it. Ji-hyun had convinced me to leave Callie for now and concentrate on keeping the Ancients alive until we could figure out what the Viper Guild had planned beyond "kill everyone in charge."

The conclave was to be kept secret from the vast majority of rift-fused who lived either on Earth or in the rift itself. It wasn't often all the Ancients gathered in one place, and from a security perspective, the less people who knew about it, the better. The only people I knew who were aware of it were Ji-hyun and a few trusted RCU staff in Boston, and Ravi Gill, the relatively newly appointed head of the UK RCU. Despite the fact that Ravi was human and therefore squishy, he'd worked for the MI5 before the RCU had been given its own autonomy, so he knew the risks, and he knew how to make sure to keep himself and his people safe. Having worked with Ravi previously, I trusted him to both be competent and also not try to kill any of the people coming to the meeting.

I'd arrived in England two weeks before the conclave was due to start, and spent those weeks with Ravi, vetting everyone who had been hired and then cross-referencing everyone with intel about which Ancients hated one another and ensuring there were no known pre-existing connections between them. We managed to make sure that everyone working the conclave wasn't about to try and kill the Ancients. Unfortunately, when it came to figuring out which Ancient hated which, we had a slightly more complex time. Mostly because, it turned out, the answer was almost all of them. It was tedious and dull work but necessary. We couldn't have someone try to stab an Ancient with a steak knife because of some long-held grudge, or, as was more likely, the personnel of two Ancients fighting in the car park. Unfortunately, we weren't allowed to vet anyone the Ancients were bringing with them, so we just had to trust that the Ancients weren't trying to kill one another.

Of the eight Ancients who'd be arriving, only five of them lived on Earth. One in the UK, two in the United States, one in Russia, and one in Egypt. The other three lived in the rift itself. In fact, the only Ancients who had been attacked so far had been those who lived in the rift, which probably went some way to getting everyone to decide to have the conclave on Earth.

Lists of those traveling with the Ancients were sent, along with detailed requirements: anything from a room facing the morning sun to what wine should be in their room. One of them wanted a cat in their room. That one was rejected. No one wanted to deal with live animals in the establishment. It was like dealing with the riders of the most tedious celebrities of all time.

Two weeks of mind-numbing work, going through the lives of hundreds of people: staff, Ancients, the few entourage members we were allowed to look into, and anyone else involved in the event, before it was all signed and agreed. Every one of the Ancients had gotten their way—except for the cat.

Two days before the whole thing started, a tear happened in the sky above the estate.

I stood outside of the massive building with Ravi beside me, looking up at the mass of purple, red, and blue swirling above our heads. While the embers had mostly been fixed now that there weren't people continuously trying to weaken the fabric between the rift and Earth, that fabric had remained in its weakened state. The massive tears in the sky were less frequent but still caused a lot of problems for anyone having to deal with whatever was created after they appeared.

"Maybe we'll be lucky?" Ravi asked, not convincing anyone, least of all himself. Ravi was just over six feet tall with brown skin and a slight Cockney accent. He wore jeans and a thick black hoodie; a holstered Glock sat at his right hip, and a rift-tempered dagger at his left. The Glock was rift-tempered too, but the bullets were standard, meaning they didn't always take a charge, but they also didn't blow up the second you pulled the trigger.

I looked over at him. "I think we can assume we won't be."

"How long do we give it before something bad wakes up?"

I looked out across the massive front lawn and parking area, over the field in front of the estate behind us, to the trees at the beginning of the drive, next to large steel gates. Several armed guards were already stationed there. I wondered if any fiends created tonight would cause a problem for the guards, if they'd try to attack the estate or, worse, one of the villages.

The New Forest had its own, albeit small, RCU station, but it was in Lymington, and there was little chance they'd get to the closest villages before something decided that humans were tasty treats.

"I'll go check the local area," I said.

"You need a hand?" Ravi asked.

I shook my head. I still carried my primordial bone spear, my knuckledusters, and an assortment of knives and daggers. So long as the fiend was lesser or greater, I'd be fine. If it was an elder fiend . . . well, I'd probably still be fine, although almost certainly not happy.

Since I'd been with Callie Mitchell under the mountain in the Tempest—the most power-saturated place in the rift—my own power had started to change. Callie had informed me that I was evolving, or words to that effect.

It meant I was able to track large amounts of rift energy, which was pretty much exactly what a tear was. On Earth, that equated to the fact that I could track the creation of fiends. It wasn't an exact science, and it had to be within a few hundred metres at most, but it had proved useful more than once in the last few months.

I'd wanted to spend time trying to figure out what else touching the centre of the rift had done to me, but I simply hadn't the opportunity to go away somewhere quiet and figure it out. The world was still total chaos—and I didn't see that changing anytime soon.

Ravi threw me the keys to a nearby 4x4 Range Rover and I set off out of the estate and along the dark country roads of the New Forest.

You have to pay attention when driving somewhere like the New Forest. The roads rarely have markings and are usually just about wide enough for one car at a time. There are few lights on the roads too, and at night, if you're not careful, it's not unheard-of for people to take the wrong corner at the wrong speed and end up in a ditch. Or wrapped around a tree. Or both.

Thankfully, it wasn't raining, so that meant I didn't have to factor slippery roads or mud into the equation.

I drove along the country lanes until I reached a crossroads with signs pointing to the villages in the south and east. The north pointed back the way I'd just driven, and apparently, there was nothing worth notifying people about to the west.

I stopped the car at the junction and left it running with its hazard lights flashing, while I stepped out into the cool night air. The tear had snapped shut, leaving the sky looking like tiny pinpricks of light in a blanket of darkness. I looked around the various roads and stopped when it came to the west. The darkness had a slight shimmer of indigo to it. That wasn't good—a clear indicator of rift magic.

Getting back into the Range Rover, I switched off the hazard lights and drove down the westerly-heading road. I drove at a steady speed, well under the speed limit, the road before me becoming more and more solid indigo with every passing metre. After a short distance, I spotted a detour off to the side of the road. I stopped outside of it and peered into a trail bathed in increasingly purple light. It was big enough to take the car, so I turned down it at a crawl, keeping aware of just how easy it would be for a fiend to leap out at the car.

When the trail turned off into a large field, I stopped the car on the side of the road and got out. The indigo glow was all around a metal gate that had been torn through as if it were paper. I stepped by the razor-sharp shards of metal that protruded out at all angles, and noticed the blood that covered several of the larger pieces. The fiend that did this had been hurt.

I crouched down by the mud next to the gate and studied the prints. The creature was large, its print bigger than my hand. I couldn't tell exactly what it was, although I was pretty sure it wasn't a bird, sheep, cat, or horse. Not a cow or deer, either. That didn't leave a lot of animals in the area. It looked a little like a bear paw, although that was impossible, considering bears had been extinct in the wilds of England for well over fifteen hundred years.

I was grateful for my sturdy boots as I trudged across the wet field, climbing the steep slope up to its summit. Once there, I got a good view of the whole area. What I thought was a large field was actually much smaller, surrounded by large hedges, with the only exits being the one I'd just walked through and a small kissing-gate. The gate was designed to let people but not livestock through, which, considering the lack of livestock, probably wasn't an issue.

Unfortunately, the thick hedges hadn't been designed to stop a fiend from running through them, and next to the kissing-gate was a large hole.

I ran across the field, removing my spear as I did. The purple trail showed that whatever the fiend was, it was trying to get back to the forest behind the field.

I moved out of the field and into the forest as an animal let out a shriek of pain. There was a second and third squeal and then nothing.

The trail was easy to follow, and it didn't take long for me to creep through the forest to find the fiend gorging itself on a deer.

Lesser and greater fiends are created when energy from the rift comes through a tear and touches a recently deceased animal on Earth. It reanimates the corpse while giving it a host of new and usually unpleasant attributes.

The thing before me had been a badger. It still had the black-and-white fur, although it was now bisected with six armoured plates down its back, like a stegosaurus. Its tail was also five times the normal size and tipped with a large black barb. It dug in to the deer with six-inch claws, making quick work of flesh and muscle, practically shovelling the meal into its oversized maw.

Considering how UK badgers normally only eat bugs or fruit and the occasional hedgehog, the fact that this fiend had taken down a deer was not good news. The badger was the size of a large deer itself, and with its added need to constantly feed now that it was a fiend, it wouldn't stop with only the one kill. It needed to be removed as a problem.

The badger turned toward me, its newly acquired sabre-tooth fangs dripping with the gore of its recent kill. It roared, which was a noise I'd never heard from a badger before and would like to never hear again.

I stood, stepping out of the vegetation I was in, as the badger moved around in front of its kill protectively.

I took another step toward it. I wasn't particularly worried about the badger killing me or even seriously hurting me, but this creature had already died once and been brought back to life. I didn't want to have to cause it any more pain than necessary to send it into oblivion.

The badger scuffed the loose dirt in front of it, as if daring me to attack first. I stayed where I was and waited. It was early in the morning and there was no one out; I had time.

Apparently, the badger didn't, as it rushed toward me, moving faster than its bulk would suggest possible. It swiped at me with its claws, but I'd already turned to smoke, moved up above it, and re-formed, falling down, with my spear tip aimed at its skull.

The badger looked up at the last second, and I drove the blade of the spear into its exposed gums. The badger's jaw snapped shut, and I rolled to the side, still holding on to the spear as it sliced up through the side of its nose. I turned back to smoke as the creature screamed in pain, re-formed on the ground beside it, and drove the blade of the spear up into its throat.

The badger died shortly after, and I waited with it until it had passed on, its blood spilling out across the ground. When it was dead, it dissolved quickly, leaving only the blood on the ground as evidence of our fight.

I walked back to my car, popped the boot, and removed a bottle of water and a cloth, washing the blood from my arms and hands as well as the blade of my spear. Removing my phone from my pocket, I noticed a dozen messages all from Ravi, and called him.

"I assume you're not dead, then," he said with just a touch of irritation. He'd had a very long two weeks, and I got the impression that he was close to snapping at someone. Hopefully, not one of the Ancients.

"Badger fiend," I said. "It's dead now, but not before it killed a deer. You found any more on your end?"

"Thankfully, no," he said, his irritation having dissolved. "You heading back?"

"Yeah, I'm going to my room and going to sleep. Tomorrow is going to be a long day." I ended the call and leaned up against the Range Rover. I wasn't looking forward to the conclave of the Ancients. Of the

Ancients I'd met, and I'd met nearly all of the surviving nine at some point, I liked four of them. At a push.

I looked up at the sky and let out a long, weary sigh. There were going to be arguments; I was sure of it. I just hoped that I could keep them all from trying to kill one another.

CHAPTER TWO

Sleep came easily, which was one of the more surprising things I'd encountered in the last few months. It appeared that whatever connection to the rift I'd attained, I found myself sleeping better and feeling refreshed upon waking. If that was the best benefit it had, I would take it.

My room in the estate was big enough for a double bed, an oak wardrobe, and a matching bedside table, along with a chest of drawers, upon which sat a large HDTV. I had an ensuite bathroom with a tub big enough to fit three quite comfortably, and I'd found myself enjoying a long, hot soak after some of the more arduous days I'd had since arriving in England.

I showered, hoping the hot water would remove the lingering anxiety of what was to come, before getting dressed in a charcoal suit, white shirt, and newly polished black boots. I put some vanilla-scented beard balm through my increasingly bushy beard. It needed a trim by someone who knew what they were doing, but I hadn't really had the time for it the last few months.

By the time I was done, I looked in the mirror and figured it would do. According to Nadia, my hair was long enough to go into a man-bun, to which Drusilla, my . . . partner, for want of a better word, told me she would cut the bun off while I slept. Seemed fair.

There was a knock at my door as I placed my Raven Guild medallion around my neck. I opened the door, revealing Ravi, who was similarly smartly dressed, although his navy-and-red checked suit was probably something I'd never be able to pull off.

"You ready?" he asked.

"I still don't like the barrier around this place," I told him. "I think it should be extended."

The barrier was designed to ensure that anyone within it no longer had any access to their powers. It essentially turned every rift-fused into a human, and it was a feeling I disliked. The barrier worked due to a generator inside the house, which projected the barrier about a mile in all directions away from the house.

"Lucas, it's fine," Ravi said. "The only people who have access are me and my team, and I trust them."

I picked up my spear, placed it back on my bed, and settled for the knuckleduster in my jacket pocket and the knives in the belt at the base of my spine. I doubted I'd need either, but you could never be too sure when it came to the Ancients.

"Does it ever feel weird that the Ancients have so much control and power but aren't actually in control?" Ravi asked as we strolled through the second-floor hallway of the estate.

"Constantly," I said as we started down the staircase to the side of the estate that contained the kitchens and staff quarters. "Some, if not all, maintain a level of power in rift politics. Three of them sat in with the Primes in Inaxia before two of them had been murdered, leaving only Attia as the surviving member of that trio. Neb has Nightvale, Timo Plainhaven. Noah has at least half a dozen members of Congress and senators as people who would like to keep getting his contributions. The other five are mostly involved with various governments, that we know of, on Earth or the rift. One of them has her own city. Second-largest in the rift, so people tell me. It's called Asteria."

"Like the ancient Greek goddess?" Ravi asked as we walked through the busy kitchen, the smells of cooking making me want to stay and taste everything.

"Yes," I said, pushing open the exterior door. "She named it that because it's the island that fell from heaven, or something along those lines. It's farther south-east than Inaxia, across one of the rivers. Takes a few days to get there from the capital city."

"You been before?" Ravi asked as we walked across the tarmac driveway that could easily fit two dozen cars.

"A few times," I said. "The Ancient's name is Theoris. She seems to think things through before making decisions, which some of the other Ancients could learn from. Her people seem happy and satisfied, but becoming a citizen means relinquishing any links to Inaxia, which a lot of people aren't willing to do. She's Egyptian, as in ancient Egypt, when pharaohs ruled. Rumour has it she was the wife of a wealthy merchant, and they were murdered when he crossed the wrong group. No idea if that's true."

"What about the others?"

I stopped walking and thought about them. "You've read the files on them, I assume."

"I have, but I want your opinion," Ravi said. "Which you keep putting off giving me."

I smiled. "Ah, yeah, well my opinion might be slightly skewed, due to the fact that I have issues with the Ancients as a concept and individually."

"I'll take that into consideration."

I looked across the drive to the entrance, where more guards than usual patrolled. There were two dozen moving around the exterior estate, and another dozen inside.

"Okay, fine," I said. "You know my feelings about Noah, Neb, Timo, and now Theoris. There's Ahiram, who, as you'll know, is very dead thanks to the work of one possibly insane Callie Mitchell."

"Who was meant to be dead," Ravi said.

"Yeah, that would have made things much easier," I replied. "Instead, she seems to have bonded with the rift itself and is now . . . well, strange. Anyway, moving back to the Ancients, there's Cal, who was a Roman senator and thinks very highly of himself. There's Eztli, who took an Aztec name but is from the Olmecs. I don't know much about him, but I don't think anyone else does either. He's . . . reclusive. I hear he's actually a reasonable and thoughtful man, but I can't be sure.

"Attia, Asiah, and Saul are the three who worked with the Inaxian government before the latter two were killed. They were . . . fine, I guess, but they were also quite happy to keep a clearly corrupt government in power, so what do I know.

"Fă Zi is an arsehole who thinks he's a king and that everyone else should think he's a king too, and Hesansh is someone who never stopped wanting to fight people. I think I've met both of them twice, at a push, and had very little interaction with either. Their reputations are certainly enough to know I would rather not spend time with either. That's all twelve of them, although obviously Ahiram and the two who died won't be here."

"And of the nine who live, you like four of them?" Ravi said. "How many do you trust?"

"Oh, none," I said. "Even the ones I like have a tendency to keep their secrets and only tell you what they think you need to know, Neb included. They're a frustrating bunch of people."

"Any of them likely to start a fight?"

"Hesansh," I said, thinking about it. "From what I hear, he hates pretty much everyone."

"I'm beginning to regret volunteering to do this," Ravi said with the sigh of a man who wished he hadn't gotten up this morning.

"After a few hundred years of dealing with them, you become more accustomed," I said.

"I'm human," Ravi pointed out.

I clapped a hand on Ravi's shoulder and gave him an understanding expression. "In that case, just be grateful that one day, you'll be long dead and never have to deal with them again."

"Unless I become riftborn or a revenant," Ravi pointed out.

"In which case someone somewhere clearly hates you," I said with a chuckle.

Ravi walked off back toward the house to do his job, while I remained outside and basked in the quiet that I knew for a fact was soon going to be obliterated. I hadn't been at the last conclave, but I had been around at a few in the past, although I'd never been considered important enough to be around when the dignitaries arrived. I longed for those days of anonymity.

I returned to the house, grabbed food, the book I was reading, and coffee, and went back outside, taking a seat in a wooden gazebo that sat just outside of the main building and driveway. I looked across the large field to the woods that surrounded the area, knowing there were highly trained RCU agents roaming them. This whole endeavour needed a veritable cornucopia of people looking out for any tiny thing that might be out of place, or a threat, or may annoy a seriously powerful person who could probably make their lives difficult. My life was, of course, already difficult, so good luck to them in making it worse.

There were several Guild members from a variety of Guilds— though no Vipers, obviously—also helping out with the security. All had been vetted by Ravi to make sure that none of the various factions were going to start throwing punches the second they saw each other.

I'd found my current read in a library within the city of Plainhaven, one of the largest populated places inside the rift. The book was titled *Secrets of the Ember* and postulated several theories about the embers of a riftborn. Including some that I had considered myself. Should the breakneck pace I was experiencing ever slow down, I hoped to try a few of the ideas out myself. It had been a long time since I had considered experimenting within my embers, and the book had given me many ideas, although a few of them would require the willing assistance of a human near death. Which might not be the easiest thing to find. Few people want to be a guinea pig when questions about the outcome of what you're asking them to do are met with a shrug and a hopeful thumbs-up.

After an hour of peace while I ate my toast and rhubarb jam and drank three cups of coffee, the sound of a large-engined car rumbled to life nearby, and a convoy of black Range Rovers drove up the road a few hundred feet in front of me, at the edge of the nearby field. Six cars in total drove by me, moving to park at the entrance of the estate. "And so it begins," I sighed.

I squinted at the horizon as a dark blob appeared there, moving at speed. A helicopter.

Remaining where I was, I watched the helicopter get ever closer, until it was joined by another some ways behind it. I wondered if every Ancient would be using their own helicopter to get to the conclave, and really hoped not, considering they'd been asked to only allow for time to be dropped off with their entourages, so as not to congest the area.

Nadia walked into the gazebo and took a seat opposite me. She was five-foot-five with olive skin and short dark hair, and was someone who didn't give off the impression she was a member of the highly trained RCU. She wore a black vest top, a pair of navy combat shorts, and white Nike trainers; she didn't much mind the cold weather, as her chains wrapped around her body. I'd used to wonder how chained revenants stood being able to see so many possible futures all at once, and the truth was, they didn't. They usually went insane or lost themselves to the visions and decided to start making sure certain paths didn't happen. Usually by murdering a bunch of people.

Nadia was different; she was sometimes a little bit out there and would occasionally say something that in an alternative timeline would maybe make sense, but she kept herself in check by never allowing herself to spend too much time seeing the possible timelines. For a while, she'd been my shadow, thinking that I was where she needed to be, although she couldn't say why, but she seemed content to know that I wasn't going anywhere and she didn't need to constantly watch out for me.

"I've been told not to be there when they arrive," Nadia said, placing a glass of water on the table and lying back on the seat beside me. "For some reason, they think I can't be subtle . . ."

I grinned at the thought of Nadia meeting a bunch of self-important egotists.

"Why are they all arriving at the same time?" Nadia asked as the helicopters got ever closer.

"Stupidity," I said. "In not wanting to be considered to be the last and—therefore—not as important. They couldn't agree to come separately. Despite four of them being killed, the majority of them still think they're untouchable. They won't even say if any of them have lost their connection. Four of them are dead and they're still protecting their stupid secrets."

"These people all suck," Nadia said. "Even the ones deemed nice are just near-immortal assholes."

"You like Noah," I said. I did my best to ignore the sounds of people exiting cars inside the grounds beside me.

"I do," Nadia said. "But he's not in those cars; he's in that."

I followed her finger to a second helicopter that was a short distance behind the one that was landing in the nearby field. Several RCU agents were already on hand to help people get out of the modified Bell helicopters. There would be more people arriving over the next hour, and I was grateful I wasn't going to be part of the introduction.

"You don't like some of them either," Nadia said, regaining my attention.

I finished off the dregs of my coffee and placed the mug back on the table. "I do not," I said. "Some are more tolerable than others."

"But?" Nadia asked.

"But, they're all out for themselves," I said. "Even Neb has her plans and machinations that she doesn't share with anyone. I like Timo, too, but again, she's an Ancient, so I always make sure I keep that in mind."

"You think this little get-together is going to help figure out how to deal with Callie and whatever plan she has for the rest of them?"

I shook my head.

"You think putting them all in one place is like signalling a giant beacon?" Nadia asked.

"It crossed my mind," I told her, and looked over to watch as one of the Ancients and their entourage walked across the field toward us while the second helicopter landed a little distance away from the first. "However, they do need to get together and figure out what to do to stop whoever is killing them."

"Callie."

I nodded. "Her in particular? No. But probably people she's working with."

"The Viper Guild?" Nadia said with more than a hint of anger.

"There's not enough of them left to do it alone," I said. "Which means they've got new recruits from somewhere."

"What if one of the Ancients is working with Callie?" Nadia asked. "Maybe this is all a trap."

I glanced her way and smiled. "Another thought that had crossed my mind, but these . . . Ancients wouldn't be dissuaded. Some think this is a defiant show of power for those who would dare come after them. Like I said, stupidity. This whole thing could have been done over video calling."

"Which one is that?" Nadia asked, nodding toward the tall, muscular woman who strolled purposefully toward us, while a standard-bearer walked behind, a dark red flag depicting a roaring brown bear in front of a round green shield fluttered in the wind.

"After what happened in Inaxia," I said, "I'm still surprised that Attia agreed to come."

"Probably safer here than there at the moment," Nadia said.

"Oh, yes," I answered grimly—wondering at what fresh hell this was going to cause.

"You are Lucas," Attia said, pointing a long finger at me. It was the first time I noticed that every single digit on each hand had at least one ring on it, all gold, all with jewels of various colours and sizes in them. Her wrists were adorned with several golden bracelets and bangles on each.

"I am," I said, not getting up.

Attia, one of those who had supposedly been assassinated in Inaxia, walked toward us as her four accompanying guards tried to keep up with her long stride. She stood at the base of the gazebo as one of her guards—a young-looking man with tanned skin and an expression of irritation on his face—glared at me. "You look like you've seen a ghost."

"He doesn't like you," Nadia said looking at me with a grin and pointing at the guard glowering at me, showing her usual tact and diplomacy.

"You stand and show respect for our Ancient Queen Attia," the man said.

"Hush, now, child," Attia said to the guard, who nodded, although his outraged expression only grew. "You were there when our brother Ancient died."

I nodded.

"When this Callie Mitchell murdered him," Attia went on.

"I was," I said, wondering where this was going. I wish I'd brought a weapon with me.

"Ahiram used to be the best of us," Attia said softly. "His death was long overdue. But it also brings about a dangerous question."

"How did you survive the attack?" Nadia asked.

Attia turned to her. "I was not in Inaxia at the time. I was traveling to Plainhaven; I wished to see the fort where one of my kin died, to see if I could find the answer to a question that is burning in all of our minds. It was a decision that saved my life."

"You wanted to know which one of you he was bonded with?" I asked.

Attia nodded. "None have come forward to claim their loss in power," she said. "And none will. It would show a weakness that none of us can afford."

"Now another two of you are dead," I said. "So, that means it could be that three of the survivors has lost their connection to the rift. It would be too much to hope that Ahiram was bonded to one of the two who were murdered."

"I hope our losses will change things," Attia told me. "But I doubt it."

I nodded in agreement.

"I just wanted to meet you," Attia said. "You have been a name I've heard about for some time now."

"We've met before," I said. "Hasn't been for a long time, though. I was with Neb at the time."

"Ah, Neb," Attia said. "Will she be here?"

I shrugged. "Neb has never felt the need to tell me what she's going to be doing."

Attia laughed. "That sounds like Neb." She looked over at Nadia. "You are this man's protector."

Nadia nodded.

"A chained revenant?" Attia said in the tone of someone who wasn't entirely sure what to make of that.

"I am," Nadia told her.

"Do you see anything that we should be concerned about?" Attia asked her.

"Every single day," Nadia said grimly. "It's hard to tell the bad from the good anymore."

"This will be an entertaining few days," Attia said. "We are not a group who is open to trusting one another easily. I would say that with Ahiram dead, there may be some among our number who might wish to take advantage of the uncertainty. Today may turn out to be a deeply interesting experience."

"I'd rather it was a deeply quiet one," I said.

Attia laughed again. "You and me both, Lucas. I wish you both a good day."

I nodded a goodbye and Nadia waved as Attia bowed her head slightly and walked away, her entourage following behind.

"That was weird," Nadia said.

I watched the Roman Ancient walk away. "Yes, it was."

"She didn't bring up that you're a Carthaginian," Nadia said. "That's a good thing, right?"

"I think the time for holding grudges because of a war over two thousand years ago has probably passed," I said. "I'd hope so, anyway."

"She thinks something bad is going to happen here," Nadia said. "Why come if she's so sure?"

"Because if she's wrong and she doesn't come, she may miss out on opportunities for knowledge or power," I said. "And if she's right, she might miss out on an opportunity to remove anyone she sees as a problem."

"You think she'll kill someone?" Nadia asked. "Or that she had her other Inaxia Ancients murdered?"

"She is the only Ancient ruler of Inaxia now," I said. "Maybe she's looking to extend her influence away from its base, spread out across the rift. It's possible that the death of Ahiram has started a sort of Cold War between the other Ancients. Some of them wouldn't say no to more control."

"The Ancients aren't meant to control anything anymore," Nadia said.

"Yet here we are," I told her as another series of cars drove by and a third helicopter landed.

"Lucas," Nadia said, her tone making me look over at her.

"You okay?" I asked as more Ancients and their people walked by us, barely giving us a glance as they continued on to the grounds of the house.

Nadia smiled and nodded. "It's nothing. Just not used to having so many people in the same place who all want nothing more than to see the others fail, but none of them actually doing anything about it. Usually, people like this try to murder one another in an elaborate game of cat and mouse."

"It's still early," I told her.

"There's another one coming," Nadia whispered.

I looked over as Theoris walked toward us. She wore a tailored dark navy suit and high heels, which clicked on the path as she walked along it, her people staying some distance back from her. A blood-red teardrop-shaped gem hung on a golden chain around her neck, which she quickly tucked behind her blouse when it became visible.

Theoris had olive skin and long, dark, curly hair that fell over her shoulders. Neb had once told me that she was the living embodiment of elegance, and I couldn't disagree. She was also a dangerous woman who had ruled her own city far from Inaxia for centuries, a feat in and of itself.

"Lucas Rurik," Theoris said, her tone suggesting nothing one way or the other about how she felt.

I bowed my head in greeting. "Theoris, I hope the trip treated you well."

"It did," Theoris said. "However, I want to know why you didn't stop that madwoman from murdering Ahiram, and why you're not out there right now looking for my kin who died in Inaxia. Assassinated."

The question caught me off guard. "Callie Mitchell has bonded with the power of the rift itself," I explained. "Stopping her from doing anything she wanted would have been like trying to stop a hurricane with the power of positive thinking. And I would be looking into what happened if I'd been asked to. The guards in Inaxia are doing that, and they do not appreciate outsiders."

Theoris stared at me for a moment before looking over at Nadia. "Have your chains told you anything, revenant?"

"Nadia," she corrected, bristling for the first time.

"Nadia," Theoris repeated, her tone full of calm pleasantry, although there was no smile on her lips nor friendliness in her eyes.

"No," Nadia said. "Nothing."

Theoris smiled for the first time and nodded as if that had been what she'd expected.

"Are you being awkward?" a familiar voice asked.

I looked over as Noah Kaya strolled toward us. As usual, the tall, broad-chested Ancient wore a colourful suit, this one a deep purple, and an easy smile. He was one of the few Ancients I actually liked, and one of our friends, Hiroyuki, trusted him, so that was a good enough reason to feel like he was one of the few Ancients who weren't just out for themselves.

"Noah," Theoris said with a genuine smile as she embraced her fellow Ancient.

"Let me introduce you to the others," Noah said as Theoris placed a hand on his forearm and allowed herself to be guided away. "I'll see you shortly, Lucas."

I raised a hand in greeting and mentally made sure to remember to thank Noah later.

"She's intense," Nadia said when we were alone again.

I nodded. "I think this gazebo is becoming a place we should leave before more of their brethren decide they have questions."

Nadia stared off after Noah and Theoris.

"You okay?" I asked her.

Nadia looked over at me, smiled, and nodded. "Yeah, it's probably nothing."

"No, go on," I said, fully aware of how many of Nadia's visions had come true over the years.

"I don't see her in my chains," Nadia said. "I've seen glimpses of Ancients before, of being here, although no, I don't know what's going to happen next. But Theoris isn't in any pathway of the chains I've looked down. It's like she's not here."

I looked over to Noah and Theoris as they stepped into the house grounds and disappeared from view. "That's weird."

"It is," Nadia said. "But it's happened before. With you, for one, when you went into the rift. Maybe that's all it means, that she goes back to the rift and stays there. Her city is there, so it could just be that in the chains I've looked down, she never bothers to come here. It's just weird, is all."

"Keep an eye on her," I said. "Just in case your weirdness feeling turns into something we need to deal with."

"I'll keep an eye on all of them," Nadia said, leaving the gazebo. "This much power and influence in one place is a recipe for egos to overcome common sense."

I walked with Nadia back to the house and really hoped she was wrong. That this conclave would be completed with the minimum of fuss, but it was unlikely. For a start, whatever gods of fate I'd managed to piss off during my lifetime weren't going to let such an opportunity go by. I just hoped that whatever it was they had planned was something I could deal with without the usual explosions, deaths, and general level of total chaos.

CHAPTER THREE

The room in which the conclave was taking place was some kind of game room. It had a full-sized snooker table, a dartboard, and several arcade games, which I'd quite enjoyed my time with. Everything had been cleared out for the meeting, including the snooker balls and cues. Leave no weapons for people to grab in haste or anger.

All that remained were a dozen chairs around a long wooden table, next to several large windows overlooking a tranquil garden at the rear of the property.

The first chair went through a window forty-five minutes after the conclave started, which, if I was honest, was about thirty minutes longer than I'd expected. I owed Hiroyuki twenty quid.

I'd been sat at a small table outside the far end of the room, next to the garden. There were two RCU agents with me, both of whom were in various states of nervousness.

For several of the more tedious moments of the meeting I studied the flowers that were close by. One rose bush had several months to go before it bloomed, and I wondered if the meeting would still be going on when it did.

The RCU agents sprang to their feet as the chair smashed through the window, sailing across the lawn and impacting a stone vase, taking a substantial chip out of it, judging from the noise. I sighed, got to my feet, and casually followed after them toward the sounds of raised voices. The petulance of the powerful.

"I will not be spoken to like a child," a tall, slender man with brown skin and long black hair said. He wore a burgundy suit and ran a hand through his dark beard as he pointed at the smashed window. Callinicus. The Byzantine general who never really stopped preparing for a war that he'd always seemed desperate to fight.

"You just threw a chair through a window," Neb said calmly from beside the man. "Hardly the actions of an adult."

Callinicus pointed a long finger in Neb's face. "You will not—"

Neb's hands moved quickly to grab hold of the digit, twisting it around as several guards from both her and Callinicus's contingent shouted warnings at the pair. It was hard to unravel the mass of voices at that point, so I just ignored everyone, gaining a few weary glances in the process, and stepped through the smashed window into the game room.

"Neb," I said softly. "Let him go. Please."

She released Callinicus, who glared at Neb, then me, then decided to rub his sore hand.

I looked out of the window at the two sets of guards. "Show's over; can someone grab that chair, please?"

One of the RCU agents passed me the chair through the ruined window, and I placed it back beside the table, motioning for Callinicus to reclaim his seat, which he did after grumbling for several seconds.

The two sets of guards continued to argue among themselves, and it was pretty clear that at some point, someone would offend someone else's ego and it would all go to shit. "Hey," I shouted at them. "Go somewhere else, *separately*, and calm the hell down."

The guards from Neb's contingent, who mostly knew me, although I couldn't have remembered their names if I'd tried, nodded an apology in my direction and walked away. Callinicus's people glared at me until their master waved them away, and only then did they obey.

"You have no authority here," Callinicus snapped as I surveyed the eight Ancients. Three dead, and Hesansh, who had elected to send an emissary in his place with a message that had read *Fuck all of you los-ers*. Unfortunately, that was not paraphrasing.

"I honestly don't care," I said, noticing the weariness in my voice. "One of your number is dead, murdered by Callie Mitchell because she thinks the rift wants her to. Two more have died at the hands of a group who may or may not be the remnants of the Viper Guild. These are serious threats, and I would hope you would all behave like serious people to deal with them. Or just let yourselves get picked off one by one, your choice."

Several people opened their mouths, presumably to object, and I carried on regardless. "I don't care if what Callie believes is true; I care that *she* thinks it's true. Three of you are dead, which means if they weren't connected to each other, which would have been far too con-venient, then at the very *least* one of you here is dying—if not three of you. I don't know who, I'm almost certain *you* know who you are, but the deaths of your brothers and sisters have set in motion your even-tual loss of power. And if you think you just need to deal with these fighters in Inaxia, you need to think again. I very much doubt Callie is going to stop anytime soon, so you need to work together to ensure that you are all on the same page."

"She's one woman," Callinicus snapped. "I will crush her."

"Have you not been listening?" Timo said wearily from the end of the table. "She has the power of the rift."

"So do we," Theoris said.

"Some of us won't for much longer," Neb pointed out. "We have no way of knowing who is bonded with whom. It's stopped us from try-ing to kill one another for thousands of years. What if Callie knows and she uses it against us? What if she starts to pick us off one by one? Ahiram had an army of his . . . Vipers with him."

The word *Vipers* was spat with some . . . well, venom.

"We have our own armies," Fǎ Zi said from the opposite end of the table to Timo. Even with such few words spoken, he still man-aged to sound like he felt only disgust at having to lower himself to being there. He also wore a cloak made out of peacock feathers, which might have been the most on-the-nose item of clothing a man had ever worn.

"She will go through them," I said. "You all took pieces of power from the rift; she is the rift. Honestly, we're not even sure what her abilities are. She possibly knows the future, at least in part. It looks as if she can teleport, seemingly at will, and she has a very real urge to kill you all. The fact that she hasn't done so yet should concern you all. We don't know if this second group are working on her orders. The fact that Hesansh elected to not bother coming at all isn't a great start."

"The man is little more than a thug," Fǎ Zi said. "An uncontrolled lout who spends his time drinking and fighting."

"Do we even know where he is?" Eztli asked. I hadn't actually seen him arrive, and he'd been silent throughout the entire proceedings.

"Unfortunately not," Theoris said. "I looked for him but found nothing. I believe he's in the rift; I can't say more than that."

"We are better off without him," Callinicus said. "So, where do we go, then?"

"Inaxia," Attia said. "We should all go to Inaxia. We have guards; we have multiple ways to stop an incursion. The surviving Primes will aid us."

"You want us all to go to Inaxia, where two of our kin were recently assassinated?" Fǎ Zi said, with far too much of a smile on his lips. "Do you think we're all stupid?"

Yes, I very much wanted to say.

"You have another plan," Neb said to me.

All eyes turned my way. I did have a plan; I just hadn't considered all of the variables yet. I also hadn't thought it all the way through, so what I really had was the shadow of a possible plan.

"I trust you," Noah said kindly. "If you have a plan, I would hear it."

"I'm going to go to the Tempest," I said. "I want to see if there's a way to actually remove Callie's connection to the rift. I don't know if there is a way, but at least it's a plan. And right now, we don't know anything, so it would be more information than we currently have. In the meantime, I think you should all stay here. Or at least somewhere

where we can keep an eye on you, and your people can keep an eye on you, and you might be safe."

"I will not be leaving my city," Theoris said. "I cannot just up sticks and abandon my people because Callie Mitchell might come knocking."

"This is why we do not involve underlings in our plans," Fǎ Zi said bitterly.

"It's a good idea," Neb said thoughtfully.

"Of course you would think that," Callinicus said. "He's your boy."

It took every ounce of willpower I possessed not to punch him in the face.

Neb got to her feet, glaring daggers in Callinicus's direction. "If you insult Lucas, you insult me. Is that something you want to do, Callinicus?"

The tall man held Neb's glare for several seconds before nonchalantly looking my way. "Do what you will."

"I'm going to go to Inaxia with Attia," Neb said.

"I'll be joining them," Timo said. "We need to make sure Inaxia isn't destabilised, and there's a chance that we can figure out who these assassins are; it might lead us to whoever is behind them. Be that Callie Mitchell or some other entity working with her. You said that Callie wasn't really Callie, the last time you saw her."

I nodded. "She was not all quite there. There were flashes of who she used to be, and, if I'm completely honest, I'm not entirely certain *who* she is now."

The group quickly descended into people talking over one another yet again.

"This gets us nowhere," Noah said, interrupting the din. "Let's break for an hour, go get some rest, food, and come back. We need to put aside our nonsense or we might well be picked off one by one."

I left via the shattered window as three very unhappy-looking men appeared with tools to clear away the debris and presumably sort out a new window.

"You probably want to wait until they've gone," I told one of them. "Just in case."

He nodded a thank you and let out a long sigh. It was hard work, dealing with Ancients.

I went to reclaim my seat at the end of the garden and, after about ten minutes, was joined by Hiroyuki, who wore a smart black suit, although he carried no visible weapons. His silver pendant hung around his neck, proclaiming him to be a member of the Silver Phalanx, the bodyguards to the Ancients. Each of the ten there would have their own members of the Silver Phalanx, and each member would give their lives to protect that of their Ancient.

"So, it's not going well," he said, taking a seat beside me. Hiroyuki was shorter than me by several inches and had long hair on top of his head that was always in a ponytail, with his hair shaved around the back and sides. He'd actually been a samurai during the Sengoku period, and while he was no longer one of their number, he still held on to some of the lessons he'd learned as one.

"It is not," I agreed. "Though it's going better than I thought."

"How bad did you think it would be?"

"I figured one of them would be dead by now," I said.

Hiroyuki laughed, realised I wasn't joking, and frowned. "That isn't funny."

"Wasn't meant to be," I pointed out. "They all hate each other. Or at least they hate half and they distrust the other half. Each one of them has maybe two other Ancients they trust. Maybe. At a push. I genuinely don't know how they ever managed to get anything done."

"I'm not sure they ever did," Hiroyuki said. "Noah said you have a plan, though. To go to the Tempest and look for a way to break Callie's connection. You think the primordials might know of a way?"

"It's a rough plan," I said. "I don't know who knows what, but it's all I've got, and it feels like it's better to do something. The primordials are the closest link to the Tempest we have, and the Tempest itself gave Callie some of its power. If it can be communicated with, and I got the feeling there was some kind of intelligence there the last time I was in its presence, maybe it can be reasoned with. It's that or sit on our hands and wait for Callie to make the first move."

"You think she will?"

I nodded.

"Yeah, me too," Hiroyuki said. "I was hoping you'd say otherwise."

"Sorry to disappoint," I said with a wry smile. "So, did Noah send you here to talk me out of the plan or join me?"

"Join you," Hiroyuki said. "He wants to know if the primordials will help. We don't really know what they might say or do."

"They're the only things I know that have a deep connection to the core of the Tempest," I said. "They stay in the Tempest; they live their whole lives there. They die there. The power of the rift starts in the Tempest."

"Occasionally, one tries to break out," Hiroyuki said. "We still don't know why they do that, either."

"No," I said. "We really need to find out if they can help. And the last time they were there, they didn't eat me, so I'm going to guess they've decided I'm either accepted or not worth the bother."

"Or are very stringy," Hiroyuki said.

"Or that," I agreed. "After the mountain exploded, I spent time in the Tempest with Valmore. I'm pretty sure he'll help me."

"Will he help the Ancients, though?"

I shrugged. "I was under the mountain when the rift energy took Callie before she resurrected and became this weird version of her that walks around now. I felt that power, Hiroyuki. I thought at the time that it was almost like it was alive. It reached out and took Callie. If the rift is alive . . ."

"If," Hiroyuki said. "That's a pretty big if."

"If," I repeated. "Maybe we can figure out what it wants. Why it resurrected Callie. What the whole point was of killing Ahiram. She was all very vague about needing his death to happen, that she can see where it leads, that she *needs* it to go in a direction, but we don't actually know what that direction is."

The Ancients returned from wherever they'd gone and set about arguing for several more hours, although by the end of it, they'd at least come up with an agreement to all behave until this situation was resolved. That meant no one was going to act against the others. No trying to take advantage of the situation to gain more power or wealth. There weren't even any more broken windows, which I took as some sort of moral victory on their part.

As they'd said earlier, Timo and Neb were going to go back to Inaxia with Attia in the hope that they could figure out who had assassinated the two other Ancients. And, if there were any links to Callie, find them before it was too late. Noah was going to use his connections on Earth to see if he could look into who might be responsible for the assassinations.

Theoris was the first to decide she'd had enough and wanted to get back to her little slice of power in the rift. And with nothing else decided by the rest of them, the only actual decision they made was that the conclave was over.

Although I got the impression that several of the Ancients only used the time of the conclave to try and get leverage or information on the others, it was good that half of them were willing to work together for a common aim. Considering that aim was survival, I figured more of them would be interested, but I saw no point in involving myself any more than I already had, considering I now had a plan of my own.

There was no way to open a tear into the embers from the House or the surrounding area, because the barrier which had been put in place made it impossible. It meant they all had to leave the same way they arrived and go back to the rift when they were far enough away from the House and surrounding area. That meant helicopters and cars.

Noah had left first, taking one of the cars that had been provided for the Ancients, instead of the helicopter he'd arrived in.

Theoris opted for the second of those two modes of transport.

Unlike the arrival, where they all decided to descend at once, the Ancients actually had the foresight to not all leave at the same time, so Ravi and his people only had to deal with one at a time, while several others complained about *waiting*. How the Ancients ever got on long enough to achieve anything would remain a mystery to me forever.

I sat back in the gazebo with Nadia and Timo as Theoris spoke to her people, occasionally glancing back our way. Fă Zi and Callinicus sauntered over to Theoris and started to loudly complain that she was taking her time.

Neb brought us a pot of tea and several cups, placing them on the table between us.

I poured tea for everyone, distributing milk and sugar as taste required, and sat back to watch the show.

"Several of the others will be leaving within the hour," Neb said, blowing on the hot beverage before taking a sip. "I guess we failed."

"What had you hoped all of this would achieve?" I asked.

"Something," Neb said. "Anything. Although at least now I know where the other Ancients stand. We know who we can work with and work around."

"We have a plan of sorts," Timo said. "With us two, Attia, and Noah's help, we might be able to head this off before anyone else dies."

"It's not much of a plan," I pointed out.

"It's a start," Nadia said.

"None of you admitted to having lost access to your power," I said. "At least one of you must have."

"After all this time, we don't trust one another," Timo said. "If it helps, it's not me."

"Not me, either," Neb said. "And I'm aware of how much I like my secrets, but on this I'm truthful."

"You know who it is?" Nadia asked.

"If I had to guess?" Neb asked.

I nodded.

"Callinicus," Timo said. "Probably Attia, too. I think she's terrified of going back to Inaxia alone. Callinicus is an imbecile, but he backed down from Neb a lot quicker than I expected him to."

"I saw that too," Neb said. "My guess would be the same."

Fă Zi, Callinicus, and their respective entourages had retired to the building, which allowed Theoris and her own people to continue preparations to leave. After a few minutes, the sounds of the helicopter filled the air, and I looked over to see it take off. It flew across the forest toward wherever it was that they deemed a safe extraction point.

I was lifting my cup of tea to my lips when a massive explosion shook the gazebo. I looked over to see the helicopter fall out of the sky as burning wreckage. A second explosion happened inside the house, and I turned to see black smoke billowing out of one of the upper windows as whatever fears I may have had about what was coming next came to fruition.

CHAPTER FOUR

Nadia ran toward the house as I sprinted to the wreckage of the helicopter. Like every other rift-fused at the conclave, we no longer had access to our abilities due to the cordon around the area suppressing them. I ran through the invisible barrier, feeling my power pop back to life inside of me, and continued on for another hundred feet toward the wreckage.

Any hope that there might be some survivors vanished the second I got close enough to feel the heat from the closest crash site. The helicopter had hit a large oak tree, obliterating it, before crashing into the tarmac of the private road.

I quickly scouted the area, making sure that there were no further attacks coming from the direction of the forest. When I was sure, and as the sounds of sirens filled the air, I ran back to the house, where I was met by Nadia, who looked less than thrilled.

"What happened?" I asked her.

"Some of Fǎ Zi's and Callinicus's people turned on them," Nadia said. "Killed them both, tried to go after Attia, but she escaped. Ravi's people managed to kill them. Neb and Timo are helping out."

"Their own people killed them?" I asked.

Nadia nodded. "It was a mess. Eight people dead, another six who were killed by Ravi's RCU after the two Ancients were killed. What happened with the helicopter?"

I looked back at the still-burning wreckage as the Fire Brigade arrived, along with several RCU agents.

"Do you think that Theoris's people turned on her too?" Nadia asked.

"I have absolutely no idea," I said, feeling numb.

"Because otherwise, I don't think anyone survived that crash," Nadia said.

I glanced over at my friend. "Hopefully, some of them managed to get out, using their embers. We were past the cordon, so they should have been able to if they could open it in time."

The next hour was a blur as the fire brigade were called, and they extinguished the flames. As I said to Nadia, I'd hoped that the riftborn among them had been able to get out to their embers in time, or at least that as the first pangs of pain had hit their bodies, they'd been forcefully removed there, but the bodies inside the helicopter suggested no one had gotten out. We presumed one of the charred remains was Theoris, but without some kind of genetic sampling, it was impossible to say who was who.

I managed to get into contact with Hiroyuki, who said that Noah and his people were already back in America, having used their embers. They were in Noah's compound and were making sure that it was safe.

I told him to double up on all security and hang in there, then hung up the phone.

"You okay?" Ravi asked as he came to stand beside me.

I shook my head. "Not really. Lots of questions. How long before you can identify everyone?"

"Hopefully in a few hours," Ravi said.

"They wouldn't let us check the people they were bringing with them," I said.

"It looks like they turned on their own Ancients," Ravi said. "This was planned well in advance. There's going to be a lot of questions. Especially considering how me and you spent all of our time making sure this place was safe."

"This is a mess, Ravi," I said. "Three more Ancients dead. That's now six, and we still have no idea how many people are working with whoever is doing this."

"If everyone on that helicopter died, excluding the Ancient, it's nineteen dead," Ravi told me. "Nineteen people died to kill three Ancients."

"Whoever is doing this isn't bothered about the odds of their people surviving," I said, and left everyone to do their job. I returned to the gazebo in the hope that Timo and Neb would walk by. It took an hour for them to return, both of them looking tired and despondent.

"They were set up," Neb said, tossing a small metal device onto the table with a *clunk*.

It was three inches long and looked like a battery pack, although it was charred, warped. "The heat?" I asked, lifting the small handle and finding nothing inside.

Timo nodded as she sat beside me.

I turned the item over and stared at the markings. "I have no idea," I said.

"You remember the barrier around the prison?" Timo said.

"The one where Ahiram was?" I asked. "Yeah, it was like walking through treacle. It slowed you—"

"The markings are the same as what was used to create the barrier," Neb interrupted. "It's obviously smaller. The markings in the prison were etched into a hundred different places, so it was much larger, but otherwise, same shit."

"No one could use their power because the bubble slowed them all down. But wouldn't it have slowed the explosion, too?" I asked.

"These were behind two of the seats," Timo said. "Possibly they were behind all of them; the wreck is too far gone to know for sure. My guess is this stops your reaction speed just enough that an explosion would kill you before you could open your embers."

"So, it's possible that the same people who betrayed Fǎ Zi and Callinicus put those devices on the helicopter," I said.

"We've told Ravi," Neb said. "He's going to look into it, but whatever was inside these was destroyed. Unfortunately, right now it's all we've got to go on. You still heading into the rift?"

I nodded. "Going back to Boston first; want to debrief Ji-hyun and see Drusilla."

"We'll be at the Crow's Perch," Neb said. "It seems to be the safest place to go, considering how many times people have tried to murder my great-granddaughter and been thwarted. Attia will be with us; we'll go down to Inaxia together once I'm sure we'll get there without people trying to kill us. More than usual, anyway."

The Queen of Crows—Darice—had survived two assassination attempts that I knew of and was both beloved by her people and feared by everyone else. One day, her luck might just run out, but I had to admit that she was one of the most capable people I'd ever met when it came to staying in one piece.

"If I find out anything, I'll let you know," I said.

"You know that with three more of us gone, there's potentially three more living Ancients who are about to lose their link to the rift," Timo said. "At some point, it's going to get out that the Ancients are dying. That might lead to panic among the rift population."

"Let's hope we figure this out before it comes to that," I said. "I'm hoping the primordials will be able to help or at least point us in the right direction."

"The primordials hate us," Neb said.

"You stole the power from the one thing they were meant to protect," I replied. "Of course they hate you. You're little more than thieves and interlopers to them."

Neb was quiet for a moment. "We didn't even know what we were doing. None of us could remember how we came to be within the Tempest or how we gained its power. I still can't remember. All I know is that the primordials hate us for it. I don't think they're going to be willing to help us." I got the impression there was more she wanted to tell me.

"Maybe not," I told her. "But if the rift still has a connection to Callie, and if she is behind all of this, we might be able to figure out how to stop her. She said she needed Ahiram to be dead for the next part of what she saw to come true. She's never been one to care too much about collateral damage, and she was single-mindedly focused enough when she was human, or practitioner, which is as close to human as someone gets who was born in the rift. It might be a long shot, but we don't have a lot of choices that aren't."

"It's not me you have to convince," Neb said.

"I know," I told her.

Neb and Timo said their goodbyes and left me alone in the gazebo as daylight faded and dusk gave way to night. The lights of the RCU lit up most of the front of the area, and a quick search of national news headlines told me that no mention of it had reached the general populace yet. Probably for the best.

I remained there for some time, until Nadia arrived and sat beside me, resting her head on my shoulder for a moment. "I'm staying," she said. "They have a chained here, but I think this might be too much for them to deal with."

"What are they like?"

"Young, odd, male," Nadia said. "I don't think they've been a chained for long. They used to be a cop, which may or may not help. I think he only joined the RCU because he wasn't sure what else he was meant to do with his life. I figured I could help."

"Good idea," I said with a slight smile.

"I didn't see this happen, Lucas," Nadia said with a frown. "In all of the chains I travelled down, in all of the things I saw that could happen, I never saw this. My chains are muddled now. I can't see anything clearly; all I see is me. Everyone else is cloudy, as if something is coming that I can't foresee. That scares me."

I looked down at Nadia. A woman who had faced death, faced monumental challenges to her very soul, and passed them. Or at least managed to cheat well enough that it looked like a pass. For her to be afraid was something new.

"Be careful, Lucas," Nadia said as she left the gazebo. "I don't think whatever is happening here is over yet. Callie doesn't seem like the kind of person to do half a job."

Ravi arrived a few minutes later, with several RCU personnel. "We need to take a statement from you."

"Not a problem," I told him. "Do you want to do it here or do you have a room in mind?"

The room they had in mind was the office of the hotel manager. They kept me in there for several hours, making me go through the events of the day, asking me questions, trying to trip me up. It was all standard stuff, and I expected nothing less.

When they were done, I was allowed to go get some rest. I dragged myself to bed, where I immediately fell asleep. I woke to moonlight streaming in through the curtains I'd forgotten to close. I showered, got changed, and made sure I had everything I'd arrived with before leaving the building.

I left the house and walked out of the main gates, by the gazebo, and down toward where Ravi and his team were still working.

"You heading off?" Ravi asked me as I watched a group of people in white forensic outfits go through the debris on the ground, the helicopter having presumably already been collected during the day. Large spotlights illuminated the whole area, giving everything a slightly ethereal look to it.

"They find anything else?" I asked.

"Nothing conclusive yet," Ravi said. "The remains of the victims and helicopter have been taken to our office in London. I'm off there myself later, so whatever I find out, I'll let you know."

"Thanks, Ravi," I said shaking the man's hand. "I wish this had been a more pleasant visit."

"You and me both," he said.

"Has everyone gone?" I asked.

"There are no Ancients still in the vicinity," Ravi said. "They left as quickly as possible, although I can't say I blame them. I have a meeting with our Prime Minister tomorrow to explain how this happened, and I'm hoping I have some actual answers by then."

"No one blames you, Ravi," I said, and removed the item that Neb had given me. I looked down at it and passed it to Ravi. "I assume you saw this before Neb took it."

Ravi nodded. "Found two more on the helicopter. We checked CCTV cameras in the vicinity and found footage of two of Fǎ Zi's people gaining entry to the helicopter. It looked like they were trying to put their own bags on it before Theoris arrived and told him that she was leaving first. That's when we think they placed the devices on board."

"This was supposed to be secure," I said.

"Would you like to hear some worse news?" Ravi asked, removing something from his pocket and passing it to me.

I looked down at the Guild medallion showing an owl.

"We took it from one of the bodies of the attackers," Ravi said. "All of them had Guild medallions on. Any chance the Owls are making a play for power?"

I stared at the medallion for several seconds. "I haven't heard anything, Noah would be better placed to ask. He's had more dealings with the Owls than I have. I haven't really had any dealings with any of the Guilds since the Ravens were destroyed."

"Maybe a visit to Noah is in order," Ravi said. "If you're going back to the States anyway."

I nodded. "This sounds like a *Strangers on a Train* situation. You kill my Ancient and we'll kill yours. The Ancients were all vetted, but they refused to let us check the people they were bringing. That was the assassins' way in. Could be that one of them had a word in the Ancients' ear, made them think they were being told how to behave, and so the Ancients pushed back a little. Not letting us check their people, daring to question their loyalties. This isn't on you, Ravi."

"Feels like it is," Ravi said.

I understood; if I'd been in his shoes, I'd have felt the same way. "Be careful, Ravi," I said with a smile.

"You too," Ravi replied, and went back toward the group working on the road. Once out of sight, I opened my embers, revealing the old houses inside, the swirling mist covering the pathway. I stepped inside, shutting the tear quickly behind me. This was only the beginning.

CHAPTER FIVE

The architecture of my embers, much like those belonging to all riftborn, was a combination of different styles from periods of time in history I'd lived through. Up until a few years ago, they'd all been mostly one type, Carthaginian, but something had changed over time, and more and more architecture from other periods had started to show up. Now they ranged from Carthaginian buildings, Roman villas, Victorian townhouses, to more modern-style structures. The mishmash of buildings had been jarring at first, but I'd gotten used to them.

The shadowy visages of people from my past that patrolled the embers were something I'd never get used to. There seemed to be less and less of them as time went on, although if I was caught out at night, they would still hunt me down and try to destroy me.

A large grey stallion trotted up to me, a small sparrow perched atop its head. "Lucas," the horse said with a slight neigh at the end. It bowed its head.

"Casimir," I replied, bowing my own head.

The sparrow leapt off Casimir's head and landed on my shoulder. "Maria," I said with a smile. "Just passing through; I need to get back to Boston."

Casimir and Maria were my two eidolons, creatures of pure rift energy that stayed inside my embers and protected it from external threats. On occasion, I'd taken one of them through to Earth or the rift, but it was dangerous to keep them out of the embers for any real length of time.

"No *Hello, how are you?*" Casimir asked. "Just right down to business."

"Hi, how are you?" I said with exaggerated cheerfulness. "Three more Ancients and their people have just been murdered. Looks like the Owl Guild were involved. I need to get back to Ji-hyun and let her know, and then maybe talk to Noah. If the Owls are working with Callie, or the Vipers, or whoever, I want to get ahead of it."

"That's a lot," Maria said, breaking the uncomfortable silence that descended.

I nodded.

"What else?" Maria asked.

I wasn't entirely sure if my eidolons were able to know what I knew, although it seemed like it happened more after I'd spent the night in my embers. Time in the embers moved differently from the rift or Earth, and spending several hours inside the embers might only be minutes in normal time. It was another thing in an ever-growing list of things that took time to get used to.

I told them both everything that had happened in England while we walked along the stone-paved street, the mist swirling around my ankles.

Despite the fact that Casimir and Maria had male and female names, which I had given them, neither of them were actually male, or female, or anything else for that matter. They were beings of pure energy and thus had no actual genders. And seeing how they weren't actually biological beings, just power that formed a physical shape, they didn't have any biological sex, either. I'd only given them names because it felt like something I should do. Over the years, some people I'd spoken to about my eidolons had found it weird that I used *they/them* for the pair, and I cared approximately zero percent about their opinion on the matter.

"I don't know what's going on," I said. "I don't know who's behind all of this. I'm thinking Callie, but I need proof. I need to know there's

not a new power trying to make a play. I would've said it was one of
the Ancients, but seeing how they're all being killed off, I just don't
know anymore. Why would an Ancient risk killing the others and losing their own connection to the rift?"

We reached a large, three-storey Gothic building after a few minutes of walking. I stood at the edge of the stone fence that surrounded
it, and looked up at the windows, all of which were fogged over. "This
is new."

"Embers change over time," Maria said.

I walked up the path to the door and opened it, revealing the tear
beyond. I turned back to Casimir and Maria. "Thanks. I'll be back
soon."

Both nodded, and I stepped through the rift into the bedroom I
shared with Drusilla on Peddocks Island, just off the coast of Boston.
It was a place that had once been an American fort but had fallen into
disrepair over the years. It was now the RCU Headquarters for the
entire East Coast of America. Ji-hyun had taken the job of director of
the RCU without really wanting it and had ended up transforming the
entire organisation into something that was effective at both helping
people and keeping them safe, and yet she also managed to not fall into
the trap of wanting more and more power. The people who don't want
the positions of authority really are usually the best people for the job.

"Drusilla," I called out, leaving the bedroom and taking the stairs
down to the living room. "Dru."

When there was no answer, I left the house, stepping into the darkness of night, and took a moment to get used to the fierce wind that
whipped across the island as if it held a grudge. I walked the short
distance to the Drusilla's forge next door. Her riftborn power gave her
an affinity for working with metal, and she made some of the most
impressive pieces I'd ever seen—including the short spear that I carried on my back. The forge had once been the downstairs for her living
accommodation, but as I'd spent more and more time on the island,
we decided to renovate the house next to the forge. She'd turned the
upstairs into more of a storage area.

The sounds of hammer on metal reached my ears well before I opened the door to the forge, taking a moment to acclimatise to the heat that rushed out.

"Dru," I said, stepping inside.

Drusilla stood at her furnace and turned to me. She was, as always when working alone, naked. The heat, the splashing of anything that might burn someone else, didn't bother her in the slightest, but she said that wearing heatproof clothing stifled her creativity. Honestly, I'd never once complained.

Her newly dyed red hair was pulled back in a ponytail that stopped about halfway between her shoulder blades. She had piercings up both ears, along with a silver hoop in her lip and a stud in her nose. Her bellybutton was pierced too, with a turquoise gem sat where last had been nothing.

"That's new," I said, pointing to the bellybutton.

Drusilla smiled, removed the heated steel, and plunged it into cold water, leaving it there as she crossed the room and kissed me softly on the lips. "This is a nice surprise." She placed her arms around my neck, interlocking them, and pulled me back in for another kiss, which I was only too happy to allow.

"It's not a good thing, unfortunately," I said.

"What happened?" Dru asked, all playfulness evaporated in an instant.

I told her what had happened.

"We need to get to the RCU," she said. "I'll get some clothes on and meet you there."

I nodded. "I missed you," I said as she ran off.

"Of course you did," she said with a smile. "I'm awesome."

I left Drusilla to get ready and ran across the island to the RCU building. The automatic glass doors slid open, and I continued on into the reception area. "I need to speak to Ji-hyun," I said to a young man who I didn't recognise.

"She's very busy," he said conversationally as he tapped something on the screen in front of him. "Do you have an appointment?"

The lady beside him noticed me and immediately recognised me, as her eyes went wide and I nodded a hello.

"No," I said. "I'm—"

"And you are?" the young man interrupted.

"Lucas Rurik," I told him.

I saw the gears whirl inside the man's brain as the woman beside him looked like she wanted the ground to swallow her whole.

He looked up at me, staring at the Raven Guild medallion that hung around my neck.

"She's on Moon Island," the woman said, when it became clear that the man's career was flashing in front of his eyes. "I can message her and get her here."

"Please," I said. "I'll meet her out front. Is Dani Sosa here?" Dani was a rift-walker, someone who could move between the rift and Earth with relative ease. While she was admittedly still young, she'd decided to join the RCU and had been with them for a while now. It turned out the job was something she was very good at and enjoyed.

"Also on Moon Island," the receptionist said.

"What's going on?" I asked.

"I can explain," a man said as he exited from around the nearby corner, where the lifts all sat.

"Gabriel," I said with surprise, walking over and giving my old friend a hug.

Gabriel Santiago was a spined revenant, and a cleric with the Church of Tempered Souls. It was the only church that dealt with the rift and those created by it. Since riftborn and revenants had become common knowledge many years earlier, the popularity of a church that actually told you about a possible afterlife—the rift—and how some people who die or nearly die come back as revenants or riftborn had continuously grown. He had a church in New York State, a few hours away, and I wondered why he'd left his home.

"It's good to see you," Gabriel said, sounding tired. "We should go outside and talk."

I followed Gabriel outside, hearing the whispered *I didn't know* from the receptionist behind me. Poor bloke.

I said nothing as I walked with Gabriel down to the helipad, where he took a seat on a bench that overlooked the ocean between where we were and Moon Island, where, apparently, Ji-hyun was.

"Gabriel, what's going on?" I asked.

"You remember that a lot of Guild members had been sent into the rift?" he asked.

I nodded. After the appearance of the Vipers and Callie, the Guilds closed ranks, bringing back members from around the world to their various home bases. They expected an attack, and small task forces were sent into the rift to help track down the remaining Vipers. The rest of the Guild members sat quietly in their home bases, awaiting word from those who had gone into the rift.

"Well, over the last few days, we've heard rumours that those Guild members who went into the rift are uncontactable," Gabriel said. "As in they've gone missing."

"How many?"

"Several dozen," Gabriel said. "Maybe twenty to thirty percent of the Guilds. A lot of dangerous people."

"The Owl Guild?" I asked.

"Some," Gabriel said. "Then we lost contact with a Falcon Guild compound about a day ago up near Vermont. Ji-hyun was going to send some agents to check it out, but last night, there were a bunch of attacks on RCU offices all across the country, so it was all hands on deck. A young woman tried to gain access to the RCU facility on Moon Island; when she was told no, she tried to force the issue. She attacked the agents there, hurt a few of them before she was put down. She did not let herself get taken alive. We found an Owl medallion on her."

"There were Owls in England who are responsible for the attacks there," I said. "It's possible that it's a Guild gone rogue like the Vipers, making a play for more power. It's also possible that the enemy infiltrated the security of the Ancients to assassinate them. I need to speak to Noah. He was the one who was working with other Guilds over the years. He might have been the only Ancient on Earth who was."

"There are only six Ancients left now," Gabriel said. "Someone really wants them all dead."

I mentally went through the remaining Ancients: Neb, Timo, Attia, Eztli, Hesansh, and Noah. Half of them dead in such a short space of time.

"Where's Nadia?" Gabriel asked.

"Still in the UK," I told him. "Working with Ravi."

The unmistakable sound of a helicopter flying toward us caught my attention and I looked up as it came closer, the image of the wreckage of the one carrying Theoris that I'd seen fall from the sky, filling my mind. When the Black Hawk helicopter landed safely nearby, I let out a slight sigh of relief, and a second Black Hawk landed beside the first.

The sliding rear door to the first helicopter opened and Ji-hyun stepped out into the night, followed by Dani and Zeke, while Ji-hyun's guards left the second helicopter and ran over to her.

"Take the night off," Ji-hyun told them as she spotted me and waved. "I'll be fine."

The guards looked a little nervous about the idea, but she was the boss, and she was a powerful riftborn, so the odds were pretty good she would be okay.

"Lucas," Ji-hyun said, as Dani and Zeke both hugged me in turn. "You scared the poor receptionist, I hear." She looked over to Gabriel and back to me. "What happened?"

Drusilla caught up to us as we all stood on the helipad. I told everyone a quick version of events.

"Fucking hell," Dani whispered.

"Look, why don't you go get some rest, see Dru, and I'll talk to you in the morning," Ji-hyun said. "Or if something else blows up. Whichever comes first."

I stared at my old friend.

"Lucas, we have this," she said. "We're really good at our jobs. Let us do them. Go spend some time relaxing. You can go into the rift tomorrow and see if the primordials will help. We'll do a check on the other Ancients and Guilds, too. Maybe Noah and some of the other Ancients will send people to help."

"Good idea," I said. "I want to talk to Noah myself. I need to go see him, find out what he knows about the Owls."

"We've got this," Dani said. "I'll call Noah and Ravi, too, get an update. You need some rest, Lucas. You need to let us do stuff."

"Okay," I said, "but if anything else happens—"

"We will contact you," Ji-hyun said.

"Did you manage to get your agents to look in on the Falcon Guild?" I asked.

Ji-hyun shook her head. "Not yet; it's one of the many things I need to look into when you go away. Lucas, before you ask another question, it's been a hell of a day, and people need rest. That includes you, my friend."

Dani smiled.

"You too, Dani," Ji-hyun told her without turning around. "That's an order."

Dani pulled a face behind Ji-hyun, which made me laugh, but she nodded when her boss turned to her.

I walked back to the house I shared with Drusilla and we went upstairs to bed, spending some time getting to enjoy one another's company before we both showered and actually got to sleep. It felt like I'd had no sleep at all when someone knocked on the door.

"I'm beginning to get déjà vu," Drusilla said from beside me. "People always come knocking at stupid hours."

I glanced over at the clock on the bedside table next to me. It said *2:36*. I sighed, got out of bed, and pulled on a T-shirt and pair of jeans, leaving Dru to lounge in bed as I made my way to the front door, which someone was still knocking on and ringing the doorbell.

I opened the door to find Gabriel stood there. His face was ashen; he held out a mobile phone, which I took from him, my mind racing to come up with new possibilities as to what was happening.

"Yes?" I asked.

"Bonjour," the voice said with some enthusiasm, his accent also French. "You don't know me, but I know you. My name is Christopher."

"Congratulations," I told him. "Why does my friend look especially worried?"

"I told him why I wanted to speak to you," the man said. "You have friends in New York. Bill and George Hawkins. An adorable married couple, even if I do say so myself. They appear to be entertaining guests at a private function at their bar, the Stag and Arrow. If you are not at your apartment in the next two hours, I'm going to walk into that establishment with a loaded semi-automatic weapon and kill everyone there. Keep the phone with you. I'll call soon. Good-bye."

The phone felt heavy in my hand as I stared at Gabriel for the second it took my brain to catch up to the news I'd just been given. "Get me to New York. Now."

CHAPTER SIX

Within five minutes, I was sat in one of the Black Hawk helicopters flying toward my home in New York City. Drusilla, Gabriel, and Dani all accompanied me, and Ji-hyun put in a call to have Bill and George protected until I could get there.

We tried to track and trace the number of the phone used to call me, but that was a no-go. They had used a burner phone and pinged the signal all over the country. It would take hours of work to get even a rough idea of their location. It wasn't a huge deal, considering I was more concerned about my friends.

The passengers were quiet as we soared over the East Coast landscape, while I wondered who had the power and influence to go after not only Ancients but members of the Guilds. Were these things even linked? I had to believe they were; it seemed far too much of a coincidence that their attacks in England and now the threat to me happened at the same time.

Ji-hyun had her people contact Noah again and keep him informed of what was happening. He was probably safe in his compound, but I couldn't be a hundred percent sure of that. Not anymore. I asked her to get hold of Ravi and Nadia, too, and she assured me that she would. Nadia and I were the only two remaining Raven Guild members. I'd given her the medallion after what had happened in the rift with Callie.

Nadia had been using my apartment as a place to get away from everything. While she loved working with the RCU, being around people was sometimes a bit too much, and so she spent time at my place, which was close to the Stag and Arrow.

The thought of Bill and George getting hurt made my heart ache and, in turn, the anger rise inside of me. Bill and George Hawkins had been a staple of my life when I'd lived in the area. Their bar was a safe place for the riftborn and revenants to go and feel like they were welcome. For someone to threaten them . . . well, I was going to ensure they regretted it.

"Lucas," Drusilla said, pointing out of the window. "Isn't that your building?"

I unbuckled my seatbelt and moved to the opposite side of the helicopter, looking out of the window at the black smoke which poured out of the building where my apartment was. The fire department were outside, ushering people away from the devastation.

"That can't be a coincidence either," Dani said. "Someone does not like you."

I didn't dare speak, and continued to stare at the destruction as the helicopter landed in Prospect Park. The building appeared to be intact, until you got to the sixth and top floor, where it looked like someone had set off a bomb. Parts of the walls were missing in what had been my apartment, and I saw no remaining windows.

I was already out of the helicopter before it landed, sprinting toward the Stag and Arrow to make sure my friends were safe. My home was torched, but stuff could be replaced; people, not so much.

I stopped running as I reached the edge of the park and saw that there were six RCU agents outside of the bar, as Bill and George served them cups of tea and coffee. I crossed the road as Bill saw me and waved.

"You okay?" Bill asked after he'd hugged me, while his husband came over to get his own hug. "It's been a while."

"Are you both okay?" I asked, looking between them.

"We're fine," he said. "The RCU has done several sweeps of the area, and we are safe. Besides, I'm not about to let some . . . *phantom* call terrify us. We are not helpless little lambs."

I looked down at my phone; we had very little time before the threat was carried out, and the sense of relief that I felt at seeing my friends safe was palpable. "You should both stay inside the bar," I said. "It's safer."

"We saw that," George said, pointing across the park to the billowing black smoke. "To be frank, I don't think we were the target."

I was about to reply to George when my phone rang. I looked down at the number and didn't recognise it but answered anyway. "Christopher."

"You are in New York," Christopher said. "Glad to see you can follow orders."

"You blew up my apartment," I said. "I assume that's why I'm here."

"Stay out of our business, Lucas," Christopher said. "You saw what happened in England. You do not want to be in our way. This is your only warning. From one Talon to another."

"The Owl Guild, I presume" I said. "You're their Talon?"

"I am," Christopher said. "Although I guess it would be more accurate to say I *was* their Talon. There is no such thing as the Owl Guild anymore. Like I said, this is just a professional courtesy. The next time, I wait until the bar is full, and I kill every single person in it. You should go check on your home, see if you can salvage anything. You don't get another warning." The phone went dead.

I looked up at Bill and George. "Neither of you are staying here. No arguments; you're now in protective custody."

George Hawkins, the lawyer, raised a hand to argue.

"No, George," I said before he could. "I know what you're going to say, and I agree with you. And ordinarily, I would be fine with you just staying here. But the person who just blew up my house is a Talon, and there's a pretty good possibility that there's a rogue Guild out there. Or at least the remains of one. And I can't stop them if they're going to threaten your lives. I'm aware that neither of you are lambs, but this isn't a normal threat. These people are killing Ancients."

"What?" Bill asked.

I nodded. "It's complicated, and a long story, but three Ancients died yesterday. Possibly at the hands of the same person who just threatened your lives. This isn't the time to be a hero. This is the time to please do as I ask, so that I can keep you safe."

George and Bill shared a glance, before George nodded. "Thank you," he said.

I let out a sigh of relief. "No, thank you."

I spoke to the RCU agents and told them to process George and Bill, to get them back to Paddock Island, where they would be safe. Or at least safer.

I left the pair of them and the RCU agents with Dani and made my way back through the park to the mass of people watching as my home continued to smoulder. Drusilla and Gabriel were talking to those in charge of the area. As I joined them, I spoke to several of the police and then fire personnel, explaining who I was and why I was there. Thankfully, no one was seriously injured. The fire chief explained that they had received a tip-off from a Frenchman about an explosive device within this building. They arrived to find the building was already on fire.

They'd tried to put the fire out, but the moment the building was evacuated, the apartment . . . my apartment had exploded. The police, or fire department, or whoever it was who investigated arson were now involved, and I'd been assured that the culprit would be found. They wouldn't be, we all knew that, but they had a job to do, and part of it was to assure me of something they couldn't possibly deliver.

The smell of burning hung in the air. I couldn't even tell what had been burning to make the smell, but I was going to guess everything. Several people from the fire department were still hanging around, and Gabriel went off to talk to them, returning a short time later.

"They would not recommend you go up," he told me. "Or anyone, for that matter. They can't state with any level of certainty that there's no more danger, and they don't know how bad the structural damage has been."

"Okay," I said.

"I told them you'd be fine," Gabriel said. "Said Drusilla and Dani were RCU agents, and that they would take responsibility for it."

I nodded.

"Be safe," Gabriel said.

Drusilla and I stepped into the foyer, which had its lifts out of order, so we took the stairwell up to the sixth floor. The smell of burning was stronger there, and the hallway had some smoke damage to it, although it was nowhere near as bad I as I expected.

I stood in front of what had been my front door and was now shards of wood. It littered the inside of my home. I stepped into the soggy flat. Every step was accompanied by a small splash, or a squelch, depending on what the item was I'd stepped on. The sprinklers had either come on or been destroyed, resulting in some pipes bursting, flooding the whole place.

"Oh, Lucas," Drusilla said, picking up a warped photo frame. The photo itself—which had been of me and a friend of mine, Isaac, before he'd died and been taken into the rift as a revenant—had been incinerated.

"I wonder if there are a few locusts in here," I said. "It looks like the people who did this were trying to get all of the plagues in one place."

I walked through to the bedroom, or what was left of it. Almost everything I'd owned was in there. Anything I needed on a day-to-day basis was in Drusilla's home back on Peddocks Island, but I'd a lot of sentimental stuff here. I'd told myself that I would have time to collect it all, that it wasn't going anywhere. The duffle bag that had contained the other Raven Guild medallions was back on Peddocks Island too, as I hadn't wanted to leave them far from me for any length of time. A small, good thing is a sea of shit.

I walked out of the bedroom, glancing down what had once been a hallway, and into the next room. It had been my second bedroom, which Nadia had taken as her own. She owned little, and what she did own usually went with her wherever she went, but she'd started to talk about decorating, and it felt like she might actually have found somewhere to call her own. Or, at least, feel comfortable enough to relax in. She was going to want blood for this, and I couldn't say I would blame her.

"Lucas," Drusilla called out from back toward the front door.

I wandered back along the burned-out hallway and found Drusilla inside the front room, a metal box in front of her.

"What's that?" I asked.

She looked up and shrugged. "It's got your name written on one side." She turned it around to show me. "It was in the corner of the room and not touched by the fire. It's not yours, is it?"

I shook my head. "Someone put that here after the fire."

Drusilla nodded. "You want to open it? Might be dangerous."

I looked around. "Not like they can do more damage to this place."

She flipped the lid to the box and took out a second box about the size of a shoebox, although it was made of mahogany. She unfastened the small bronze clip and opened it, revealing a black velvet pouch.

"This is a lot of effort," I said, picking up the pouch. "It's got some weight to it."

I opened the pouch and tipped the contents into the wooden box. They were Guild medallions. Over a dozen of them. All Owl. "I think the Owl Guild is officially disbanded or destroyed," I said, and looked up at the sky above me. Parts of the metal beams were showing; the force of the blast had been focused upward, tearing through my home without really endangering anyone else.

"We should leave," Drusilla said, picking up the box and carrying it.

After one last look, I left the flat and made my way back outside, where I found Bill and George, both of whom were talking to Dani and Gabriel as a large number of RCU agents hung back.

I noticed that the fire department had left. "What happened?"

"I told them that the RCU would be taking over the investigation," Dani said. "Have I mentioned that I have a badge and people listen to me?"

I managed a smile despite myself.

"She should not have a badge," Bill said in a mock whisper. "She was here with Nadia the other day, and they both tried to tell me I had to legally give them my best tequila, and that it was for the good of the nation."

Dani gave the smartest salute I'd ever seen someone give.

Bill looked back at her, pointing one finger in her direction. "Also, I am not a fastidious queen."

Dani held her finger and thumb a small distance apart.

George burst out laughing, followed by Dani and Bill.

I started to laugh, and felt a little bit better about everything, although nowhere near enough to not want to find Christopher and feed him his own tongue.

RCU agents came over to escort Bill and George.

"Stay in touch," George said, giving me another hug.

I hugged Bill again and said to them both, "I will. When this is done, I'll come over and eat all of your bacon again."

Bill smiled. "See that you do."

I watched them walk away and felt sad that it might be some time before I would see either of them again.

"Nadia and I will keep an eye on them," Dani assured me. "She's already on her way back from England and messaged to ask if you were okay. I think she might be a little angry."

"Join the club," I said. "I'm going to see Noah and his people. He might know more about this Christopher character. Hopefully, he'll be able to point me in the right direction."

We all got back into the Black Hawk and took off, flying across New York as the skies darkened. Rain was coming. Hopefully not until we were back in Boston. Riding in a helicopter as you fly through a storm is not an experience I enjoy.

The journey from Brooklyn to Long Island wasn't a long one, although by the time we were flying above multi-million-dollar houses, the weather had well and truly decided to turn for the worse. Rain pelted the Black Hawk, and the nearby ocean repeatedly slammed against the beach with some force. The area was probably lovely when it didn't look like Poseidon himself was waging war.

Noah's mansion was at the far end of the row of houses, with thirty-foot-high walls surrounding a house that had enough land to have its own helipad, tennis courts, and at least half a dozen small buildings spread over a considerable amount of what I was sure was prime real estate, should he ever decide to sell.

The Black Hawk landed and shut off the power as Hiroyuki and other members of the Silver Phalanx stood wait outside, all in dark suits, several carrying visible guns.

I opened the door and looked behind them at the white house with the slate roof. "How many bedrooms is that?" I asked Hiroyuki.

"Nine," he said. "I heard about your Brooklyn apartment. I'm sorry."

"I think we have a problem," I told him. "Noah home?"

"In his office," Hiroyuki said, before saying hello to everyone else.

I followed Hiroyuki through a set of open patio doors and into what looked like some kind of living-room area, if by *living room* you meant *the coldest place on Earth.*

"Are the floors made of marble?" Drusilla asked.

"Yes, the entire downstairs has marble floors," Hiroyuki said, pointing to the grey fabric sofa and chairs.

Everyone took a seat as I looked around at the bare white walls and the multitude of clay models that sat on plinths next to the bay windows which overlooked the garden and nearby beach. There was one extra-large painting of soldiers in a boat. It looked to be a stylised version of Washington crossing the Delaware.

"I painted that one myself," Noah said from behind us as he entered the room. He wore a burgundy smoking jacket and black trousers, along with leather slippers. "I made all of these clay statues, too. It's somewhat of a hobby of mine."

"To remake old paintings?" Dani asked.

Noah shook his head. "Not especially; this one was just for fun, but I liked it so much, I decided to keep it. But you're not here to talk to me about my art."

"I have to admit," I said looking around, "this isn't what I thought when I think of you."

Noah laughed. "This is where I have guests who don't know me," he said. "Only my art, nothing that might give away too much. I usually have meetings here. I don't even use this part of the house anymore. The marble is cold; it's not so much a home as it is a statement. Come on."

We all exchanged confused glances as we followed Noah out of the room where welcoming went to die, and down a long corridor to a set of double doors, which opened into a second living room. This had wooden floors and a large black sofa that a family of five could have lived on. There was a TV so big, I didn't even want to guess how long it had taken to get up on the wall.

The walls were covered in portraits of various people I couldn't identify. "My family, friends, people I love," Noah said. "People I liked. Never went in for photos. I know I'm exceptionally old, but I just never found I enjoyed it. Paintings, though, they capture the soul like nothing else. The connection between painter and subject is something wonderful. Most of these are from memories of people long past. People who I knew before I became an Ancient, or people who meant something to me along the way."

I stopped by a portrait of Hiroyuki in full samurai armour, although without the faceplate, which was in one of his hands, while the other rested on the end of his sheathed katana. If someone had said it was a photo, I'd have believed them. "Bloody hell," I whispered.

"I will take that as a compliment," Noah said with a smile and slight bow of his head. "You know, I really do have a lot of respect for what you tried to achieve in England. The fact that you got so many of us in a room together is a miracle in itself."

"Neb and Timo did the inviting," I said.

"Yeah, but it was your idea," Noah said. "In fact, if it weren't that, of the surviving Ancients, three of us can vouch for you, there might have been more questions about your own involvement in the attack."

I stared at Noah for a moment, mentally counting to ten to calm down.

"You've got to be shitting me," Dani snapped, before I could.

"I am not suggesting anything untoward," Noah said. "I think some of the other Ancients came to respect you after that, but I think a few might fear you."

I laughed. "Fear me?"

"You have shown time and time again that you will stop at nothing to ensure the right thing is done. That your loved ones are protected, and that those who threaten them are dealt with. Some of my brethren would find your stubbornness a hindrance to their own plans. I would be careful in future."

"You think an Ancient is behind the attacks?" Drusilla asked.

"I think it's a reasonable thing to suggest," Noah said. "It is possible that one would align themselves with Callie. But you did not come here to discuss my theories. Hiroyuki said your home was attacked."

"Christopher," I said. "The Owl Guild Talon. You know him?"

Noah looked around the room. "I do. One second." Noah left us alone and returned a moment later with Hiroyuki.

"What's happening?" Drusilla asked.

"Hiroyuki," Noah said. "I'll rejoin you all shortly."

"Christopher Dubois," Hiroyuki said as Noah left the room. "The Owl Guild Talon is an exceptionally dangerous individual. He may have a personal issue with me."

"May?" Dani asked.

"I helped train him," Hiroyuki said. "Before I really knew him, the more I grew to be aware of him, the less happy I was with his temperament. He applied to get a job here as a Silver Phalanx member, and I had Noah quash it. Christopher was . . . upset."

"He became a Talon instead," I said.

"What can he do?" I asked.

"He gets inside people's heads," Hiroyuki said.

"Mind control?" I asked, concerned we were adding a very big problem to the list of very big problems.

Hiroyuki nodded. "Although it's more suggestions, persuasion. He removes inhibitions in those who already want to do something but can't quite take the jump themselves. When I knew him, mind control was not on the table. It's possible he's gotten better with his powers, though."

"That is not good news," I said as Gabriel's phone, which I still had on me, rang again. I answered.

"What did I tell you?" Christopher asked as I put him on speakerphone.

"You're bugging this room," I said, looking around.

"I told you to stay out of it," Christopher hissed. "I told you as a professional courtesy. I held back because of it. I held back to see what you would do, to check if you got the message. Apparently not."

An explosion rocked the building, and I looked out of the window as gunfire peppered the thick, bulletproof glass of the patio door beside me. Assailants dressed all in black with masks began walking up the garden toward us, as Noah's security team engaged them in battle.

CHAPTER SEVEN

I opened a door into a hallway with glass windows down one side, overlooking a large front garden and driveway. More masked men were making their way up toward us; one of them saw me and opened fire at the windows. I moved back, but the windows were made from the same bulletproof glass as those in the rear of the house. Thank gods for Ancients who want them and their people to stay in one piece.

Drusilla, Gabriel, Dani, and I ran on down the hallway, as Hiroyuki went to deal with the insurgents. We burst through the wooden door at the opposite side, where Noah was leaning up against a wall, holding a spear with a large, bladed head in one hand. The blade was slightly curved and covered in blood. There were two dead men at his feet; both wore dark suits which did little to hide the stab wounds that cut through them.

"Lucas," Noah said. "I do not think I'll be running."

I thought of my own spear, glad I'd taken it with me, and noticed the bloody wound on his shirt, blood that appeared to be dripping steadily onto the floor.

"What happened?" I asked.

"I believe these people are all here for me," Noah said, "and maybe for you."

"You're still bleeding a lot," Drusilla said. "You're an Ancient. Shouldn't you be healing by now?"

Noah pointed to a bullet on the floor, beside a seriously damaged grand piano. Dani picked it up and passed it to Drusilla.

"Lucas, this is primordial bone," she told me, passing me the bullet that was about the size of a 9mm although in more of a spiral shape, with grooves cut into the sides of it.

"How did someone make a bullet out of a primordial bone?" I asked.

Noah coughed, spitting blood onto the floor. "I have no clue but they got me with three. All in the gut. My body is having a hard time healing from it, Lucas."

"Go into your embers," I said.

"I can't," Noah said, holding my stare. "Something is stopping me."

"Shit," I said looking around. "Look, can you all try to find a small device, about a few inches long, made of metal? It seems to stop people being able to access their embers. If these people brought one in with them, maybe it's in here."

"We'll check," Dani said.

"I'm going after Hiroyuki," I said. "Try to keep Noah from brawling with anyone else."

"You need help?" Drusilla asked.

"Won't say no," I told her.

"We'll keep him safe," Gabriel said, taking the spear from Noah's hand.

I left the room with Drusilla and ran down the hallway toward the sounds of fighting. "Don't get hit by anything made of primordial bone," she said.

"I know," I said softly, removing the half-spear from my back; the primordial bone and steel blade had served me well in killing. If someone else had found out that primordial bones could be used to kill the rift-fused, and that included riftborn and even Ancients if they received enough damage, there could be problems ahead.

I turned the corner and ended up in a large open dining area with an adjoining kitchen. Hiroyuki was fighting several of the black-clad assailants. Three of them lay dead in the room, and the remaining five were holding back.

I tried to turn to smoke, to billow in and stop them, but I couldn't. "Shit. No smoke," I said.

Drusilla removed two curved daggers from sheaths on her hip. I'd seen her fight with them; she was a level of dangerous that few ever master. "We'll just have to do it the old-fashioned way, then," she said with a grin.

One of the assailants came at me with a broadsword, which I easily avoided. "No guns?" I asked, spotting the holes all around the kitchen. There were several discarded firearms on the floor.

"That's helpful," Hiroyuki said, avoiding the swipe of one man's sword and driving his katana up into his chest, tearing it out just above the shoulder in a shower of blood and gore.

"We need more room," Drusilla said as she punched her knives into the neck of one assailant before kicking his lifeless body back into a friend.

I moved out of the room, back into the hallway behind, avoiding the swipe of a broadsword, stepping inside the man's guard and stabbing the short spear up under his throat, into his brain. I twisted the spear as I pulled it free, making sure that the wound was fatal, no matter who, or what, he was.

I moved aside from the dead man as he fell, ducking under the hammer attack from another man and responding with a stab to his gut that he managed to deflect, the black armour on his torso keeping him from getting disembowelled.

There was a noise as small windows nearby were smashed and objects were thrown in.

"Grenades," Hiroyuki shouted, diving over the kitchen counter. Drusilla was already near the entrance and dove back out of the dining area as I was slammed into by one of the masked men and driven through the glass window beside us as the grenade exploded.

A piece of shrapnel cut into my bicep as I hit the gravel outside, the man who had run into me landing heavily on top. I prepared to fight him, but the man who had collided with me had taken the full brunt of the explosion and had a three-inch hole in the side of his head where something had struck him.

I pushed him away and received a kick to my head. I shoved the body of the dead attacker to my side as this new problem kicked again, this time only connecting with his dead friend. I rolled back onto my feet. My arm hurt, and I looked over to see a five-inch piece of bone, not mine, jutting out of my triceps.

I tried to grab the piece of bone, but the new attacker took his opportunity to launch over his dead friend and take me to the ground. He wrapped his massive arms around my head and proceeded to either try and choke me out or twist my head off like a bottle cap.

A second later and I was beginning to lose focus. I tore the bone fragment out of my arm and slammed it into the attacker's knee, causing him to grunt in pain but not actually let go. He smashed my face into the ground, but I refused to release my own grip. I dropped the small, sharp bone fragment and instead pushed my thumb into the hole I'd made in his knee. It was two inches deep, and judging from the scream that erupted from the man's throat, it was quite painful. Good.

I twisted in the attacker's grip and stamped down on the inside of his ankle, which snapped from the force. I pushed him away, and he fell over the remains of a flowerpot, landing in a flower bed and smacking his head on the pale bricks that surrounded it.

I walked over toward my attacker, still feeling groggy from the effects of having my head kicked with some force, and kicked the assailant back to the flower bed when he tried to get up. He went for a dagger in a sheath at his hip, but I dropped my body weight knee-first down onto his chest and heard bone crack from the force. He let out another scream, his hand clamped around the hilt of the dagger. I took hold of his hand, pulled his arm up, removing the dagger from its sheath, and broke his elbow. That got him to release the dagger.

There would have been times when I wanted answers, when I needed to know what was going on and who was behind it. This was not one of those times. I took the dagger and plunged it up under the attacker's chin, feeling bone crack from the force as blood poured out over my hand. I left the dagger there and staggered back, tried to turn to smoke and failed. I looked around and spotted the small metal device on the floor near where the dead assailant and I had fought. I removed the dagger from the dead assailant, wiping the blade on his clothes before picking up the device, which opened, and light blue water trickled out.

The last time I'd seen something like this had been a Callie creation. She had packed the near-frozen water inside containers with primordial bone last time, which made them rift-energy lightning conductors. There were no pieces of bone inside this time, but there was something carved into the back of the metal inside the container, which began to disappear as it was opened.

It felt warm as it ran over my hand. It was the same rift-fused water that sat around the prison in the rift, the same that was used to create weapons that removed access to the rift for any rift-fused that touched it. That killed them if they stayed in contact for too long. The water began to heal my wounds the second it touched my skin.

My immunity came from the fact that along with Callie, when she had been taken by the rift, I had been touched by its power. It was something I still hadn't managed to wrap my head around, but it had changed me. Made me more powerful for one, made me more attuned with the powers of the rift.

I dropped the small device on the floor and wondered how, this time, the devices were made to stop access to someone's power. Maybe the dissolving writing inside had something to do with it. Another question, one I had no time to dwell on at this time.

The window at the far end of the front of the house exploded outwards as two people smashed through it, rolling across the broken shards as they grappled with a gun.

I started toward them and got halfway when I felt something slam into my side, lifting me off my feet and throwing me across the paved driveway. I hit a metal post and dropped to the soft green earth next to the driveway, noticed I was bleeding badly from a wound in my side.

I looked over at a horned revenant that strolled toward me, blood dripping down from its horn onto its face. It grinned, showing long fangs that protruded up against its upper lip. It looked like some-one had taken the minotaur and decided to inject it with all of the steroids.

"So, you can use *your* power," I said, wincing as I got to my feet.

"I am going to rip you in half," the minotaur told me.

"Cool," I said. "Quick question before you do."

The horned revenant looked down at me; its breath smelled of meat and blood. It had eaten someone or a part of someone. I didn't want to know which.

"This isn't a Q and A," the horned revenant said. "But I'll tell you what, seeing how you're all going to die. You get one question."

I nodded. "Very magnanimous of you. How'd you get your people inside the house to help with the attack? Noah and his Silver Phalanx would never let in rift-fused they didn't know."

"Humans work here," the horned revenant said, grasping me by the shoulder and pushing down, forcing me to one knee. "The chef, the cleaner, the gardener, it doesn't matter which one it was; all you need to know is that we've been planning this for years now."

"The Owl Guild," I said.

The horned revenant let out a belly laugh.

I jabbed the dagger up into the side of the horned revenant's thigh; I twisted the blade and tore it out of the revenant's leg. Blood gushed out of the wound, covering the ground around us as I moved to the side and stabbed the horned revenant again and again in its side and back. The beast fell to its knees and I jumped on his back, plunging the dagger into his neck over and over again until it fell to the ground dead.

I looked back at where I'd seen the two people crash through the window, and only one stood triumphant in whatever had transpired between them. Drusilla stepped out of the broken window and over to Dani, who crashed to her knees, the knife in her hand tumbling to the ground.

I ran over to them, dropping to my knees beside Dani as she stared at her hands, which were slick with the blood of her enemy.

"Dani," I asked softly, taking her hands in mine.

"I've never stabbed someone to death before," Dani said in a far-away voice.

"Better him than you." Drusilla said as she took Dani's hands from me and helped the younger woman back to her feet, walking her back into the house through the broken window. Gabriel appeared in the window, looking out at me as I got to my feet.

"Are they all dead?" I asked.

"I think so," Gabriel said. He had a nasty cut on his forehead and a second one on the back of his hand.

"Are you okay?" I asked him.

"Not even a little bit," he replied, sitting himself down heavily next to Dani on one of Noah's expensive sofas.

"They only had a few bullets," Gabriel said. "Hence the swords and stuff. They knew we couldn't use our abilities and thought it would be enough. A lot of the blades are primordial bone."

"Where is Hiroyuki?" I asked no one in particular as I stepped through the shattered window into the living area. The primordial-bone problem was one for after I made sure everyone was okay.

"He's sitting in the kitchen," Gabriel said. "I checked in on him; he's got a nasty wound to his leg and another to his stomach, but I think he'll be okay."

I felt relief flood through me at the thought of my friend being okay after what we had all been through. "And Noah?"

"He told us to leave him with his guard," Gabriel said. "Last we saw, he had six Silver Phalanx members with him. He was in bad shape, though."

It was turning into another very unpleasant day in what had become an increasingly large number of unpleasant days. "Gabriel, you and Drusilla go check upstairs and make sure there aren't more of these bastards waiting to ambush people. Dani, are you going to be okay sat here?"

Dani looked up at me and nodded once. "I'll be fine," she said softly.

I patted her gently on the shoulder as I walked by, back toward the house. The dead littered the ground, and it appeared that whilst

Noah had lost many of his people, those who attacked them had fared worse.

I stepped through the broken window, glass crunching under my feet, and walked through the bloodstained house in search of anyone who might still need help. I reached the kitchen and found Hiroyuki sat on the floor, a pool of blood around his legs. Gabriel had wrapped a bandage around the wound on Hiroyuki's leg.

"You know you don't have to sit there, right?" I asked him.

"Gabriel said that if I moved, I might reopen the wound," Hiroyuki said with a wince. "The one on my stomach is healed almost; two different attackers, two different blades, two different wounds."

"The one on the leg from primordial bone?" I asked.

Hiroyuki nodded. "It feels like ice; no normal blade does that. Wouldn't stop bleeding, wouldn't let me heal. I'm glad Gabriel was here; otherwise, I could've had some serious problems."

"Glad you'll be okay," I told him. "Have you seen Noah?"

Hiroyuki shook his head.

"I'll look for him," I assured my old friend. "He was pretty hurt the last time I saw him, but he's strong, he had a retinue of Silver Phalanx guarding him, and he's an Ancient, so hopefully, he'll be okay."

Hiroyuki let out a long breath and nodded slowly.

I moved the glass from a nearby cabinet and filled it with water before passing it to Hiroyuki. "Small sips," I told him.

"Thank you," he said softly, holding the glass as if it might break from his touch.

I left my friend where he was and exited the kitchen, continuing on through the building until I reached the conservatory at the rear of the property. There were dead bodies littering the ground: the retinue of Silver Phalanx who'd been tasked with protecting Noah. A job they'd given their lives for. The conservatory doors were open, leading to the expensive and well-maintained garden. But that was not what I was immediately drawn to. Noah was inside the conservatory. And he was not alone.

The stranger wore a black mask, the eyeholes covered in a dark mesh. He was about my height and stocky. He wore charcoal-grey leather armour and a long black cape, the hood of which was pulled up over his head. A long beard stretched down to his chest, dark in colour and matching the long hair that spilled out around the hood.

His hands and arms were massive, and he looked as though he was someone who lifted rocks and threw them around for fun. Whoever was behind the mask had killed six Silver Phalanx members to take Noah. The one thing I knew for sure was that the newcomer was a formidable opponent.

He held a long spear in one hand and a sword in the other, both covered in blood. The blade of the spear rested against Noah's throat, and I knew from the look of it that it was made of primordial bone. The stranger stared at me silently as I entered, radiating anger. I instantly knew that he was more dangerous than anyone that I had fought since the attack had begun.

"Christopher?" I asked.

The stranger shook his head.

"You know there's no way you can kill Noah and get out of here," I said. "The second you move, you die."

The stranger removed a pouch that had been tied to his belt and threw it at my foot. It landed with a heavy thump, the noise of the impact making it known that whatever was inside was metallic.

I did not look down at the bag as it lay against my foot. I felt the bag move and something spilled out of it, but I dared not see what it was.

"You can look," Noah said. "If he was going to kill me, he would have done so by now."

I continued to stare at the killer before me. "No," I said. "This is what he wants me to see, isn't it?"

The killer nodded once.

"You want me to see my friends die?" I said.

The killer nodded again.

"I don't even know who you are," I said. "Why don't you take off the mask and show me?"

There was a laugh from behind the mask, although it had no real humour in it. For a moment, I thought that the laugh might bubble over into manic cackling, but the killer controlled himself.

"You should just tell me yourself," I said.

"You can't stop what's coming," the killer said, his voice slightly muffled behind the mask.

"And what might that be?"

"Soon," the killer said. "Look."

Despite the overwhelming urge to look down and take whatever had fallen over my foot, I resisted. I maintained eye contact as much as possible with a person in a mask.

I hoped that someone would come; I hoped that there would be a rescue on the way or cavalry riding to help. But unfortunately, life rarely works out that way. "So, what do we do now?" I asked. "We are clearly at an impasse, and I have no wish to sit here all day and wait for you to realise that you have lost."

"Lost?" the killer asked, sounding amused by the idea.

There was a tear behind the killer as his embers opened. I expected him to jump back through, getting away, living to fight and kill another day. I did not expect him to throw his sword at me. I managed to dodge to the side, but I was not fast enough to close the distance between us before he had driven his spear blade into Noah's throat, and stepped into his embers, which snapped shut behind him.

Rage filled me, just for a moment, but it was quickly replaced with grief when I saw Noah collapse on the floor of his conservatory. I rushed over to him and screamed for help, trying to put my hands around his throat and keep his blood from pumping between my fingers. It was a pointless endeavour, yet I would not let him die without trying to save him.

But that didn't matter. Because he died anyway. I slumped back on the floor, my hands and arms covered in the blood of an Ancient. Noah had been a man I had not always trusted but whom I had liked. Gabriel was the first one to reach me, followed by Drusilla and Dani.

Gabriel went straight to Noah, but he quickly realised there was nothing he could do. Drusilla dropped down beside me, taking my hands in hers and talking to me softly, asking if I was okay.

I shook my head.

"Oh, shit," Dani said.

I looked beside Drusilla and saw that Dani was crouched down by the velvet bag that had spilled its contents over my foot. She picked up several of the medallions that had been in the bag and showed them to me. Each one had a different bird as part of their medallion. Each one belonged to a different Guild.

"It's not just the Owls," I said as the horror dawned on me. "We need to get in contact with the Guilds."

CHAPTER EIGHT

By the time the fighting was all done, Noah's Silver Phalanx had lost nine of its twelve members, along with eighteen personnel who worked for Noah and his people. The attackers had numbered double that, and none of them had survived apart from the masked one who escaped through the embers. It turned out that four of the people who worked for Noah betrayed him. They were all dead, and nothing of value was lost.

The attackers had come with primordial-bone weapons. While primordial bone doesn't immediately kill riftborn or Ancients, doing enough damage with it will, and making sure that those who were hurt couldn't heal definitely would. Whoever had sent them knew what they were doing, but they also knew that whoever they sent were probably not going to make it out alive.

We found one of the small devices that stop riftborn from using the powers on Noah. It had been dropped into his pocket, making him all but defenceless. And with his power cut off, he wouldn't have even been able to access his embers to escape.

Hiroyuki and the surviving members of Noah's Silver Phalanx took the news of Noah's death badly. There were lots of discussions involving revenge and hunting down those responsible wherever they might be and delivering swift and bloody justice.

No one tried to stop them; there was little point in trying to stand before the sea of rage without having it bear down upon you. In their position, I would have felt the same. In fact, in their position, I had felt the same, and it had taken me a long time to feel anything else.

Many of the survivors stood around the lounge, as I had placed the pouch with the sixteen medallions onto the glass coffee table between us. Most in small groups, huddled together, whispering their thoughts of vengeance.

Some of the medallions had spilled out onto the glass. They were made of primordial bone and could have been used to create weapons if they had someone who knew how. Instead, they were used to send a message.

"Ji-hyun is sending her people," Dani told us. "They should be here within thirty minutes."

I stared at the Guild medallions. Sixteen dead Guild members from across the Guilds.

The deaths of so many Guild members brought back awful memories that I thought I had buried. The crushing sadness and anger threatened to overwhelm me, and I felt as if I might need to run and never stop. It was either that or find someone to hurt. Neither seemed like a particularly healthy way of dealing with the problem at hand. There was one part of this whole ordeal which kept coming back to me. An unpleasant thought I just couldn't shake.

"Why me?" I asked.

Everyone turned to look at me.

"What do you mean?" Hiroyuki asked.

"Why did Christopher contact me?" I asked. "Professional courtesy is a bullshit reason. He had me running from Boston to New York, and he was mad that I got back here. He told me to stay out of it. It's almost the exact thing I expect someone to say to me if they wanted me to do anything but. It's like waving a red flag at a bull. Threatening my friends and then telling me to stay out of someone's business is a good way to get me involved in their business. Christopher is a Talon. A man who Hiroyuki trained. Was he a moron when you trained him?"

Hiroyuki shook his head. "He's smart and capable. He does his research; he's not someone who rushes into something."

"So, there's little chance that he just decided to call me and give me a heads-up," I said.

"You think he's been told to keep you busy," Drusilla said.

I shrugged. "I don't know. I told everybody in England that I was going to see the primordials in the Tempest. That I was going to talk to them to figure out a way to stop Callie from whatever her plans are. That should've been the first thing I did, but then the Ancients were murdered and Owl medallions were found on their killers. That all changed my plans. Then my friends get threatened, my home destroyed, I'm left gifts of Guild medallions. All things that would make me want to keep investigating despite someone telling me not to. If he wanted me out of it, why leave me a parcel of medallions in my home? Why have that brute throw me more?"

I studied the medallions before looking up at the crowd that had gathered around them. I caught the eyes of Hiroyuki, who still looked pained from his wounds. One of the Silver Phalanx members passed me a medallion that had skidded off onto the floor. I nodded a thank you and placed it back into the velvet bag. I closed the drawstring and stared at the bag for a moment before picking it up. It felt heavy, and the idea of having lost so many Guild members made my heart hurt.

"Anyone know of a Guild-member meeting place close by?" I asked. "Might be worth paying them a visit to see what's going on."

"I can find out," Dani said, taking her phone and leaving the room.

"You just said that someone might be pulling your strings to look into these Guild members," Hiroyuki said. "If you know that, why not leave? We can deal with this."

"I know," I told him. "But if it leads me to whoever is pulling the strings, it'll hopefully get me answers. Besides, I want to see for myself if the Guilds have turned on themselves, or if they're being wiped out like my Guild was."

Dani returned and passed me a piece of paper with an address on it. "Falcon Guild," she said. "Last known contact put them there. Ji-hyun said there was a phone call to their Talon two days ago. She was going to send people to check out their compound in Vermont but hasn't yet.

Everything has just been crazy. Last contact with the Talon said nothing was out of the ordinary, though."

"Yes, I remember, Gabriel told me." I said as I stared at the address, before putting it into my phone to check directions. "Can you get Ji-hyun to send agents there? We'll meet them at the location."

Dani nodded. "Already arranged. She's sending a group there and a second one here."

I studied the location. "It's in the middle of a forest. It's a compound of some kind."

"I will wait here for Ji-hyun's group," Gabriel said from the doorway. "There are injured people here, and they need to know what's going on."

"Can I assume you'll be paying them a visit in Vermont?" Drusilla asked. "Because if that's the case, I'll be coming with you."

"Me too," Dani said, leaving no suggestion that there was another option.

Hiroyuki looked between his comrades before glancing back at me. "I think it would be wise if I stayed here," he said eventually, sounding as though he would like to do anything but. "My friends need me. And I am wounded. Primordial bone cuts deep and bypasses our power; I can still feel the pain in my leg."

I placed a hand on my friend's shoulder and squeezed slightly. "I will let you know when I find something out. Whatever it is, whatever the outcome, I will tell you what I find."

"Kill them," Hiroyuki said softly. "If these people had any hand in what happened to Noah and what happened to my friends, kill them."

I looked around the surviving members of what had been Noah's personal security force. They had failed. It wasn't a pleasant thing to suggest, which is why I didn't say it out loud, but they all knew it. You could see it in their faces, you could see it in their mannerisms, you could hear it in the tone of their voices. They had failed and Noah was dead. I only hoped they didn't blame themselves the same way I had when my Guild had been destroyed.

I left Noah's estate to find the helicopter that I had arrived on, still on the helipad next to a refuelling truck. It was in good condition, which was surprising, considering the amount of damage that had been done to the building and its surrounding grounds. The pilot was nursing a wound in his shoulder, although it didn't appear to be anything serious.

"I hear Noah was killed in the fighting," the pilot said grimly.

I nodded and passed him the piece of paper with the address on it. "We need to go here," I said. "Are you injured too much to fly?"

"Not at all," the pilot said, taking the piece of paper from my hand and reading the address. He passed the piece of paper back to me and said, "That is in the middle of nowhere. You want to land a Black Hawk helicopter in a Guild compound out in the woods?"

"Yes," I told him. "Is that going to be a problem?"

"No," the pilot said. "The bird is ready to fly; it didn't sustain any damage during the fight, although these bastards definitely tried. Hence the shoulder. You going alone?"

"Absolutely not," I said.

As if they had heard me speak, Drusilla and Dani arrived at the helipad, with Dani putting her phone away. "I messaged Ji-hyun," she said by way of explanation. "Zeke and Nadia are going to meet us at this address. The latter only arrived back in the States about twenty minutes ago. She is grouchy. The boss is also sending an attachment of RCU agents. Ji-hyun says that none of you, us, are to get killed."

I turned to the pilot. "So, now there's a lot more than just me."

The pilot moved his arm up and down as if testing it to make sure that it wasn't about to cause him undue pain. He nodded as if satisfied with the level of discomfort that the hole in his shoulder caused.

"Does that need looking at?" I asked him.

"It's just a bullet wound," he said, as if that was the most normal thing in the world. "Got grazed by one of those little primordial-bone bullet things. Didn't stop bleeding; still hurts like an absolute bastard, as I said. We were refuelling when we got hit. Luckily, they hit me and not the fuel pipe."

"Let's see," Drusilla said firmly, ensuring the pilot realised that this was not a suggestion.

I walked off to look around the helicopter and make sure that there hadn't been any unforeseen impacts where primordial-bone fragments had hit it. The last place I wanted to be after the previous few days was in a crashing helicopter.

As I walked around the rear of the aircraft, Dani caught up to me. "Are you okay?" I asked her as I checked the rear rotor blade.

Dani raised her hand and moved it from side to side in a *so-so* fashion. "Been better."

"Look, I'm sure they won't, but it might be an idea to contact your brother in Boston and get him to move over to Peddocks Island." Her brother worked for a nonprofit organisation helping newly created riftborn adjust to their life after humanity. He was a good man, and it had taken him some time to get over the fact that his sister had wanted a front-line seat in the fight against people who might do us harm.

"Already done," Dani said. "The second all of this shit hit the fan, I messaged him. Told him to go and stay with a friend. He's never going to stay at Peddocks Island; not entirely sure he will ever actually trust the RCU. Even if I'm working for them."

"Good job," I said.

"My parents didn't raise a fool," Dani said. "Besides, if there was an option, I would join him. But I can't just leave all of you to deal with this alone, making things worse with every single step and decision."

I turned back to look at her and found that she was grinning. "It is true—without you, we do get into a lot more trouble."

"See, that's exactly what I mean," Dani said with a slight chuckle. "Do you actually have any clue what part of the helicopter you're looking at?"

I tapped the side of the helicopter and nodded sagely. "Yeah, all of this looks good."

Dani laughed and then immediately looked sad. "Feels like I shouldn't really have fun at the moment."

I walked over to her and she hugged me. "It's okay," I said softly. "You're allowed to feel things other than pain and sadness. Especially at a time like now. It sucks because you feel like you're disrespecting someone, but you're not. You're just dealing with a horrible thing by finding joy where you can. It takes a really long time to get used to the idea."

"I liked Noah," she said softly against my chest.

"Me too," I replied. "We're going to find the people who did this, and we're going to make sure they can't do it to anybody else."

"It feels like all we're doing at the moment is losing," Dani said. She pulled away from me and wiped her eyes with the backs of her hands.

"I know," I said. "You just need to know it doesn't feel like that all the time. That things will get better. And that we are all here for one another."

"And if you ever need to talk," Drusilla said as she walked around the rear of the helicopter, "we are here for you."

Dani hugged Drusilla. "Thank you both," Dani said.

"How's the pilot doing?" I asked.

The window of the Black Hawk opened, the pilot's head poking out, looking down at me. "I have been given a full bill of health," the pilot said proudly. "We should really get going before we get there and it's dark."

Before we could get in, Gabriel joined us, informing us all that he was coming. Ji-hyun was already en route to Noah's compound, and Hiroyuki was happy to take charge of the surviving members of the Silver Phalanx. He carried a large black bag and placed it in the back of the helicopter, between the seats. He opened it, showing the number of rifles and handguns that were inside, along with several bladed weapons. None were made of primordial bone, apart from a couple of the daggers that we had taken from the dead attackers. But the rest of the blades were made from rift-tempered steel, which was good enough that Drusilla gave a thumbs-up after checking it all.

It wasn't long after that that we were all in the air, flying toward the address that I'd been given. In all the time I'd been a member of the

Raven Guild, I could have counted on one hand when I'd been welcomed into the territory of another Guild. It wasn't that they all hated or distrusted one another; it was just that it was better for Talons to keep their distance.

I had no idea how long the flight took; I wasn't really paying much attention to it. The conversation was sparse, which I was grateful for. I needed the time to think about everything that had happened and about everything that might still happen.

I looked out of the window as the pilot said, "We are two minutes out. How hot do you think we need to go in?"

I messaged Nadia and asked how far out she was. The reply was almost instant. *We're already here. Waiting for you before we go in. This place gives me bad feelings. Hurry.*

"We go in hot," I said, retrieving a rift-tempered dagger from the bag and checking that my primordial-bone short spear was in place on my back. Time to get some answers.

CHAPTER NINE

By *hot* the pilot clearly meant *land in the middle of the compound*, next to a second helicopter. Apparently, he'd been in contact with the pilot who had landed and found no one there. Which, honestly, I found more concerning than I would've done if we'd been under fire.

The second the Black Hawk helicopter touched down in the middle of the large compound, Drusilla opened the door and the four of us piled out. The compound itself was a sizeable area of land with twenty-foot-high wooden walls where guards could patrol. There was a guard post, for allowing more mundane forms of transport in and out, and a small car park where four identical Ford SUVs sat.

Several RCU agents nodded in our direction as they stood guard near the entrance to the compound. Hopefully, they weren't going to have to deal with whatever else might turn up to cause our day even more horror. They were several large metal-worked falcons that hung throughout the area; apparently, stealth was not the aim of this place.

As we walked through the land of the compound toward the main structure a few hundred feet from where we landed, I got a good look at our surroundings. There were several small buildings, all of which had RCU agents walking in and out, several of whom waved in our direction.

There were vegetable patches, and a small apple orchard in the distance, and I wondered if this whole place was some sort of self-sustaining compound used in times of trouble. There were Guilds who were more insular than others, and while I hadn't had a lot of run-ins with the Falcon Guild, I hadn't expected to find something like the set-up I found myself in.

Nadia stood waiting for us at the front door of the large manor house at the far end of the compound. Nadia carried no weapon that was visible; she wore no armour. She stood in jeans and a T-shirt, drinking a can of Coke and eating a protein bar. She waved at us with the protein bar–holding hand and took another bite.

The brick building had a grey slate roof and appeared to be a fairly new construction. All of the windows on the front-facing part of the building were shuttered, giving the building the kind of view I'd expect someone to walk out of waving a shotgun and telling people to get off their lawn.

We stopped beside her as she finished chewing her bite of bar. "You took your time," she said to all of us.

"Anyone in there?" Drusilla asked.

Nadia shook her head. "Done a sweep of the ground and first floor, and something definitely happened here. Second floor and attic are being done right now. Not gone into the basement yet; figured you'd like to be here for that one."

"What *something*?" Dani asked.

I stepped past Nadia into the house entirely unsure what I was about to witness. There were RCU agents inside, who nodded a greeting as I walked by. The front door opened directly into a living area, with a set of stairs to the right that led up to the floor above. What had once contained several ordinary items, such as a sofa, coffee table, and TV, now contained a mass of stuff. Broken stuff for the most part, lots of which had bullet holes. The wall behind where a black leather sofa had once sat looked like something out of the Saint Valentine's Day massacre.

I picked up a pair of light blue latex gloves, putting them on. It wasn't that I didn't want to leave fingerprints; I just didn't want to get blood all over my hands.

Glass covered the floor, making every step a loud crunch. I walked through the only other door to a kitchen-diner area, which had looked nice in the estate-agent photos. And now resembled something out of a war zone. Blood stained every surface.

Zeke walked through the back door of the house. "I think we missed all the fun," he said. "Although, obviously, *fun* in this case is very subjective. Whatever happened here was fast and nasty." He tossed me a small item, which I caught in one hand: a primordial-bone bullet.

"They came here to kill them all," I said, turning the bullet over.

"We found that in the wall," Zeke said. "It looks pristine."

"They don't break easily," I said, tossing the bullet back to him. "Any chance you found survivors?"

"Nope," Zeke said.

"Nadia says you haven't been into the basement," I said.

"No, not yet," Zeke confirmed. "It has a metal door with a card reader, and I have absolutely no idea how to get in without breaking it. I don't know what happened here, Lucas, but there's a lot of blood, a lot of broken stuff, and no dead people. My bet is all the bodies are in the basement."

I walked through to the kitchen-diner, which was in about as much of a sorry state as everything else. The entire floor was covered in shattered crockery, some of which was splattered with bits of blood. There were more bullet holes in the walls, ceiling, and floor. I looked around, trying to figure out just how the attack had taken place.

"Whoever was here was surprised," Drusilla said from the doorway behind me. "From what I just heard by talking to the agents here, they haven't found anything to suggest they fought back."

"All the dead are missing," I said, before pointing to the metal door which presumably was the entrance to the basement. "There's no blood leading to that door. No smears on the floor, no droplets. There's blood in all of these rooms, and destruction, and no dead people."

Nadia stepped into the kitchen, a sour look on her face. "There's a lot of blood upstairs," she said. "The agents up there found blood-slicked beds, bullet holes, and little else. They were surprised at night, ambushed, killed, and their bodies were removed. They found one of these as well."

I took the small device from Nadia's hand, turning it over, and passing it back. "These were in the helicopter of the Ancient who was killed. It cuts off someone's ability to access the rift, makes us human. My guess is the primordial-bone bullets were just in case. They wanted to make sure everybody was dead and that they stayed that way."

My hand turned to smoke. "It's not working."

"Must have a limited time," Nadia said shaking it, finding something rattled inside. "Or it's broken."

I stepped up to the door and rapped on it with my knuckles. "Sounds pretty solid."

"We haven't found the key card yet," Dani said as she came to join us in the kitchen.

"I'm going to turn to smoke and go beyond it," I said.

Dani's expression changed from confused to presumably wondering whether or not I had lost my mind. "Absolutely fucking not; have you lost your mind?" she asked, leaving no doubt about what she'd been wondering.

"It is, in theory, a good idea," I said to her.

"In theory, lots of things are good ideas," Dani said. "Some of those things which seem like good ideas blow up in people's faces. Like, for example, flash-frying a turkey at Thanksgiving. It seems like a good idea, and if it works, it's wonderful, but if it doesn't work, you've just burnt down your house."

"I'm not going to burn down my house," I said.

"I'm more concerned about you burning down this house," Dani said. "Mostly because I'm stood inside this one."

"I'm just going beyond the door," I said.

Everyone turned to look at the door.

"Look, we just need to get in there," I said. "We can't stand around here and wonder what is inside. I assume you found no other way to get in?"

"We lifted the floorboards and the room at the rear of the property, and found nothing but concrete and metal," Nadia said. "Whatever is in that basement, they did a really good job to make sure you couldn't get in there without going through this door."

"This seems like a terrible idea," Dani said. "Just want to reiterate that point."

Nadia placed a comforting arm around Dani's shoulders. "It'll be fine," she assured the younger woman. "He's done much dumber things, and they've worked out mostly okay."

Dani looked at Nadia as if she'd grown another head. "Mostly okay? Mostly. How does that word make it feel better?"

Nadia shrugged.

"If we're done discussing this," I said.

"If there's anything behind there that's dangerous," Nadia said.

"You leave immediately," Dani finished.

Drusilla stepped up and kissed me on the lips. "Go do your thing; we'll wait."

I was just about to turn into smoke when Zeke poked his head into the room. "You need to come see this."

We followed him back through the house up the stairs to the second floor, where a ladder sat in the middle of the hallway, leading up to the attic above. There was a lot of blood on the wooden floor, and it had smeared all up the sides of the ladder. I was grateful for the latex gloves. Zeke took the ladder first, placing his gloved hands carefully, with everyone else following as quickly as possible.

The attic was large, but it was full of boxes and old furniture. The floor was slick with blood, and it took some effort to step between the congealing pools as I made my way across the attic to two rooms at the end. The doors to both were open, revealing several bodies.

I stood at the doorway of one room and looked down at the casually discarded bodies in the room. The smell was horrendous, and I was suddenly grateful that it wasn't hot outside. Whoever they had once been, they had been dead for some time.

Zeke crouched down next to one of several RCU agents and, between thumb and forefinger, picked up a Falcon medallion that was in a pool of blood.

"These people were massacred," Drusilla said. "Why drag the bodies up here, though? There must've been a plan to this, although I can't begin to think what it was."

"We've got something," an agent shouted from the room next to the one we were in.

Drusilla went to find out what it was they discovered, and returned a moment later with a white card in a Ziploc bag. There was a bloody thumbprint on the card, but otherwise, it looked completely unremarkable.

"Is that a key card?" Dani asked.

Drusilla nodded, passing the bag to her. "Anyone want to guess what it opens?"

Zeke stood and took the bag. "The RCU will go and open the door, we will check it, and then you can come and see what's inside. That should stop whatever it is that Lucas thinks is a good idea."

"I'm beginning to think you all are under the impression that all I do is insane things," I said.

Nadia let out a little cough.

We left the RCU agents to do their job and went back down to the entrance to wait for whatever the RCU were going to find in the basement. It was an excruciating experience for someone who had never been blessed with an abundance of patience.

We moved out of the way as body bags were brought in for those who had been found in the attic. The Guild members had died in their beds, had died sat on the sofa, watching the telly. There'd been no resistance that I had seen, and I imagined that the attack had been quick and deliberately done in such a way. The who and why it had been done were questions that we still needed to answer, although it now explained why no one had been able to get hold of the Falcon Guild for several days.

After what was probably only minutes but felt like hours, Zeke returned. "You're going to want to come and see this," he said.

"You found someone alive?" Dani asked.

Zeke shook his hand from side to side. "That really depends on your definition of *alive*."

CHAPTER TEN

I t turns out that the word *alive* really is subjective.

The person had been found around the corner at the bottom of the staircase beyond the door in the kitchen. By the time we descended the thankfully lit stairs and reached the team of medics there, I wasn't sure that their attempts to keep him alive weren't in vain.

The basement was a large empty room with a platform at one end, stacks of wooden folded chairs along one blood-splattered wall. In the corner were racks of weights, wooden weapons, and several punching bags. Next to the folded chairs lay two bodies, one of which was partially buried by them.

There was a bloody broadsword on the floor between the bodies and the man being worked on by the medics.

"They fought back," I said.

"One had a bladed weapon," Zeke said, pointing to the broadsword. "I think this place was used as some kind of training gym and meeting room."

"I assume they couldn't use their powers either?" I said.

Zeke nodded and passed me one of the small devices that stopped people from accessing the rift. It was empty inside.

"I already broke it," Zeke said. "Powers should work down here now."

I turned my hand to smoke, just to prove to myself it was true, dropped the device on the ground, and stamped on it. "I really hate these fucking things."

"We found a second one," Zeke said. "It's in the corner. These things have a small distance to work. Only a few feet. It's why they put one on Noah to kill him."

"He going to live?" Dani asked the medics.

"Not sure," the medic replied as she shocked the man's heart with a defibrillator. "It's been several hours since this happened. That device was next to him."

Dani picked up the compact device.

"It must have a small area of effect," Drusilla said. "It didn't stop Lucas from using his power upstairs."

"It probably cost him his escape," Nadia said.

"So, is he one of the people who attacked this place, or is he one of the people who are meant to be dead?" I asked.

"He had this on him," Zeke said, passing me a Viper Guild medallion. "He was wearing it around his neck."

"So, bad guy," I said. "Sent down here to check for people."

Zeke looked up the stairs and nodded. "That's our best guess. There was a fight, and at some point, the attic door was closed, locking them all down here. No one could find a key card, so the plan changed. He got stuck here."

"Collateral damage for your own team," Nadia said. "That's pretty cold."

The man coughed.

"Fucking hell," Nadia said.

"Are you going to torture him?" the medic asked, looking back at me.

"Why me?" I asked. "Also, no. Torture doesn't get results. I would like to talk to him."

"Give me twenty minutes and I'll get him alive enough to talk to," the medic said. "I'd rather I didn't go to this trouble for you to kill him again, though."

"I promise," I said.

We all left the basement and went outside the house. More RCU agents had arrived, and the whole place was swarming with them, most of whom I'd never met before. Drusilla, Nadia, Zeke, and Dani were clearly the de facto people in charge, so I let them do their jobs while I waited for my time to talk to the prisoner.

After twenty minutes, Dani returned to me as I sat on a nearby wooden bench, and said, "You can't kill him."

"I don't plan on killing anyone," I admitted. "I plan on getting answers out of him. As a rule, dead people aren't that great at talking."

Nadia left the building and signalled for me to come over, which I did, although Dani accompanied me. "Seriously," she whispered.

"Not killing anyone," I repeated.

"Personally, I think you should rip his arms off and beat him to death with them," Nadia chimed in.

"Nadia," Dani said softly.

"That seems like a fair way of dealing with it," Drusilla said. "Although it would be good if we could get some answers before he meets his maker. And I assume you won't be letting anybody else talk to him until you have."

"I promise I will not kill him," I said looking between the three women in front of me. "But I think I know who he's working for, and I think that out of everybody here, he's fully aware of who I am."

With the conversation having clearly concluded, I returned to the medics in the basement, both of whom also reiterated that they would very much like me not to kill the person they had just saved. I was clearly beginning to get a little bit of a reputation. I couldn't say it wasn't earned.

"Riftborn or revenant?"

"No idea," the medic told me. "We put the other device next to him. It'll stop his power, but it'll stop yours, too."

I nodded that I understood as I looked over at the man who was laid up against the platform at the far end of the room. He was hand-cuffed to a metal pole which ran the length of the ceiling to the floor; he looked to be quite uncomfortable. Good.

Had he been on his feet, the man would've been taller than me. He was thinner, though, almost skinny, with a mop of blood-crusted dark hair and the expression of someone who hadn't expected their day to get a lot worse than being stabbed with a broadsword.

"Do you feel like telling me your name?" I asked him.

The man said nothing.

"You are Viper Guild," I said. "We found the medallion around your neck."

The man continued to say nothing.

"I'm going to search you," I told him. "If you try to do anything to stop that, I am going to hurt you. That is going to piss off the medics that just spent a lot of time keeping you from dying. I really don't want to have to hurt you. But I will. Do you know who I am?"

The man nodded.

"By reputation or by fact?" I asked.

"Reputation," he said. "You are Lucas Rurik. Surviving member of the Raven Guild. I will not stop you from searching me. But I will not give you information to help you."

Seeing how that was about the best I was going to get, I nodded a thank you. I searched him quickly, which was more difficult to do than I would've liked, considering he was sat on the floor, and only found two things of interest: a Falcon Guild medallion in the pocket of his black combat trousers, along with a mobile phone. Pushed the button on the phone and found there was only one number in it. A burner phone. I didn't recognise the number and put it to the side for a moment as I looked at the medallion.

"Did you take this from one of your victims?" I asked. I tried not to let the anger leak out of my voice, but I failed.

"I am of the Viper Guild," the man said.

"That's not what I asked you," I told him.

"That is all I am going to say," the man pointedly said.

"Here's what I think happened," I said, walking over to the wooden chairs and picking one up. I carried the chair back over to the chained-up man and placed it beside him, taking a seat. "I don't think you arrived here to kill these Guild members. I think you were all already here. I think you killed your own Guild. The Falcon Talon who spoke to Ji-hyun the other day, who we couldn't get back in contact with, is he one of the victims or was he one of the perpetrators?"

"I have nothing to say," the man repeated, looking away.

"It won't take long to find out," I said. "We have all the bodies; it's just a question of figuring out who they are. You are not the Talon; I know that much. Because you're too fucking stupid."

The man's head snapped toward me, rage burning across his face.

"Before you say something stupid," I said, "be aware that I only told people upstairs that I wouldn't *kill* you. Taking your fingers won't kill you."

"Torture is not an efficient tool for getting information," the man said with more smugness than he should have in his current position.

I shrugged. "I have no intention of torturing you. But if you remain quiet, then you have no value, so you die. It's as simple as that. Maybe I'll let Hiroyuki and his Silver Phalanx members know you're down here. I'm pretty sure they could find a use for you."

The man looked beyond me to the stairs.

"No one is coming to rescue you," I said. "No one is coming to help. There's no white knight on a steed, no angel coming to save you from whatever is about to happen. I ask questions, you answer them or I kill you. Slowly. Painfully. You really need to understand the predicament you're in. And it's not a good one. You have no leverage."

The man spat on the floor beside me.

I picked up the device, opened it and poured the contents onto the prisoner's bare chest. To me, the liquid was a warming balm, but to anyone not connected to the rift, it had a more extreme and immediate reaction. The man screamed like a banshee as the bright blue rift-infused liquid burned his skin as it trickled down the flesh of his chest and around to the side of his ribs.

When it was gone, scorch marks ran down the prisoner's chest.

"We done playing now?" I asked, my hand turning to smoke. "Because my next trick is to push smoke into your body and turn you inside out."

I let the man consider it for a moment, and a few seconds later, he nodded once. There was still some fight in his eyes, but he knew when he was beat. "The Falcon Guild Talon was the one who hurt me. His name was Frank; he was better than I thought."

"Your name," I said.

"Ken Cyrus," he said. "I was a member of the Falcon Guild."

"You turned on your own kin," I said with disgust. "You murdered your own Guild members, your brothers and sisters, and you did it in cold blood. Ambushed them in the dead of night, when they were resting, sleeping. When they couldn't fight back."

The man nodded.

I considered my next question carefully. "How many of the Guilds are involved in what's happening?"

Ken nodded again. "All of the Guilds have members who are loyal to someone beyond the Guild itself. When we joined, after a period of time, some of us joined a hidden faction within the Guild. Usually, from what I've heard from people in other Guilds, it was led by the Talons, although that wasn't always the case. We were told that at some point in the future, we were going to help to usher in a new world order but that the blood of those who would stand against us would need to be shed. That some of our own kin, our own Guild brothers and sisters, would need to be sacrificed because they would not understand.

"So, we lived with them, trained with them, fought beside them. We did this for years, for decades, until the time was right. Sometimes, we would ask a Guild member to be brought into the fraternity that we had created, and sometimes, that didn't work out and they needed to be removed before they could tell people what they had discovered. I heard that the Ravens were not to be trusted, that they were too closely linked to Neb. Their elimination was a consequence of this."

As horrified as I was by the information I was being told, I needed more. "This new world order that you want to create, it rests on the back of the dead Ancients, yes?"

The man nodded.

"Who was behind it all?" I asked. "If you've been here for decades, whose orders were you waiting for before you could start these crimes?"

"I don't know," he said. "Only the Talons and their most trusted personnel knew. All I know is that we were going to eradicate those who would stop us. The Ancients have to die to bring about a better world. Without them, we will be given the power we deserve. The fact that you can't see that, that you can't see just how much power they have stolen for themselves, means you are blind to what must be done."

"Where is Christopher Dubois?" I asked.

"I have no idea," he said, his eyes moving ever so slightly, unable to cover the lie.

"Don't make me ask twice; we were getting on so well," I said.

Ken stared at me for a moment. "Once we had dealt with our own Guilds, we were all to go into the rift. It's why only riftborn could be members of the fraternity."

"And you don't know why?" I asked.

Ken shook his head. "Only those in charge knew exactly what we would be doing after this."

"I've been told he can control people's minds," I said. "Any chance he did that to you?"

Ken's expression darkened.

"You've considered it," I said.

"He would never," Ken said, iron in his tone. "My Guild would never allow it."

"The Vipers left you here to die," I told him.

"I knew what might happen when I signed up to this," he said like a good little cult member.

"Knowing what will happen and actually having it happen aren't the same thing," I told him. "It still must sting that they left you here to die. They're probably off celebrating the victory of murdering their friends. They must all be very proud of killing people who couldn't defend themselves. Can I assume that this is the same the world over? That wherever the Guilds are, loyalists would've been killed?"

Ken nodded, although I saw the trepidation in his face. Probably wondering whether or not being honest was going to get him killed quicker. "Like I said, we've been working on this for decades. Waiting for the right moment to strike. I am sorry that our Guild brethren had to be sacrificed, but they would not have understood. Revolutions require sacrifice; they require a hardness of soul and spirit—a vision. Some people don't have that."

"But you do?" I asked. "But Christopher does? You ever heard the name Callie Mitchell?"

Ken paused for a moment, and I knew he was trying to figure out whether or not he should lie. Eventually, common sense appeared to win out. "Yes," he said, that one word making it sound as if he had nothing else to say on the matter.

"Callie Mitchell has been alive a really long time," I said. "She was born in the rift, so while she looks and acts human, she's a little bit more than that. She's a practitioner. She doesn't have any power as such, but she lives a very long time. An exceptionally long time. And she only ever uses plans that she has worked on for a long time."

Thoughts buzzed around my brain as possibilities of an idea began to form. "I'm going to guess that before Callie started wandering the rift, killing comatose Ancients, she was involved in whatever plans you people have. She wanted to take control of the rift, that was her aim, and the Ancients would have stopped her if she'd been able to achieve it. Or, at least, she assumed that. And if she'd made a move against the Ancients back then, several of the Guilds would have become involved. Their members were spread out. She didn't want to activate this plan until everything was in place, but she died before she got the chance to. And then she was reborn, not quite as herself. But between my last seeing her and now, something has changed."

"Okay, let me see if I have it straight," I said. "The Guilds had their people stay in compounds like this, while about thirty percent of every Guild went into the rift to work to track down the Viper Guild. That's the official story, correct?"

Ken nodded.

"So, what really happened?" I asked.

"The guild members who went into the rift were all given our viper medallions. Once we were there, we waited until they were given the word, then we came back at night when everybody was resting, or sleeping, or unaware. Each of the Guilds dealt with their own people."

"And you murdered them all," I finished for him.

Ken nodded again.

"So, you're working with Callie?" I said.

Another nod, although not quite as convincing.

"There's someone else," I said. "I was wrong, and you didn't correct me. It's not Callie's plan."

"I don't know," Ken said. "I've heard the name Callie mentioned, but I don't know."

"There can't be many Vipers left," I said, feeling synapses in my brain firing, giving me more ideas about what was happening as little pieces of information came together to fill in the void. "So, you have seen Callie?"

"No," Ken said. "We were not permitted. The only people who got to talk to Callie were the high-ranking members of each Guild. I am not one of them."

"Some of you were sent to kill Noah," I said.

"Owl Guild," Ken said. "They volunteered. And before you say anything else, it had to happen. And I'm not going to feel sorry for doing what needed to be done to ensure that when the time came, we could make this world and the rift better."

I turned and walked out of the basement, ascending the stairs as Ken shouted, asking what was going to happen to him. I didn't want to answer, because if it were my choice, I'd just cut his throat and be done with it. But I'd given my word.

I found everybody outside. One of the RCU Agents informed me that Ji-hyun was landing soon with a contingent of her people. It was good news. This whole mess was going to be up to the RCU to fix, however they felt the need to do so.

I grabbed a bottle of water and a protein bar from a hastily assembled station just outside of the manor house, thanked the person giving them out, and took a long drink before eating the bar.

"You look like you need a shower," Nadine said.

I finished the water, tossing the empty bottle into the recycling bin which had also been brought out. "That is one way of putting it," I told her.

I waited around for a while as Ji-hyun wanted a briefing on what had happened, and I took her down to the basement so that she could talk to Ken. The long and short of that talk was that Ken was not going to have a pleasant time of it. I'm pretty sure by the time she was done telling him where he would be spending the rest of his life, however many thousands of years that might be, considering he was riftborn, it was going to be in the deepest, darkest prison imaginable. That's if he wasn't executed, because sometimes, there were people who just didn't deserve to breathe the same air as everyone else.

Drusilla and Zeke both got ready to come with me into the rift, as Dani had suggested they take us there. It felt like a long time ago that I'd said I wanted to go into the rift, to go to the Tempest, and there I was, only now about to go. And yes, I still wasn't going to go north to the Tempest. It felt like I was bouncing from one problem to the next. Christopher's plan to keep me busy had worked.

As Ken was loaded onto a helicopter to begin his life of pain and misery, I waited outside with everyone else. Neb, Timo, Attia, and everyone else in Inaxia needed to know what was going on with the Guilds. As did anyone else that might have any kind of contact with them, including the Queen of Crows.

"They know that you're coming for them," Nadia said, giving me the world's most awkward hug. "The Guilds, I mean. Christopher all but guaranteed that. He told you that he was trying to keep you busy, doing so as a favour, which means that seeing how it didn't work, he knows that you are going to search for him. You need to be careful."

I nodded. "I will be as careful as I ever am."

Nadia stared at me for a moment. "That is not what I think being careful entails."

"If you need more help, you need to contact us," Ji-hyun said. "If there's a bunch of Guild members out there aiming to murder the remaining Ancients, you might need the help."

"Darice will help," I said. "Also, I have friends in Inaxia, people I trust. We'll be okay; besides, I'm not entirely certain that Neb can be killed. She's been around for so long and had so many people try, and not one of them ever ended up as anything but dust. If there's one person in the world, or the rift, who I think would probably survive an apocalypse, it's her."

Ji-hyun nodded agreement. "Try not to start an apocalypse."

"I'm not promising anything," I said with a smile that I didn't really feel. "Hiroyuki is going to find out what happened here, somehow he will, you know this. There's a good possibility he is going to find out where Ken is, and he's going to want to talk to him."

"I have already told him," Ji-hyun said. "Hiroyuki is heading to Moon Island tomorrow. Alone. I will deal with him when I get back there. He deserves answers, but he's been made aware that he is not there to execute Ken. Not unless we have no other choice. Right now, I think Ken probably has more information than he's letting on. Such as the names of people who aided him. I want those names, and then I'm going to find those people."

In any other circumstance, I might have felt slightly sorry for the anger that Ji-hyun was going to inflict on those responsible for the murders of their own Guild members. But they'd earned it, and I hope that their worlds burned because of it.

Ji-hyun gave me a hug, telling me to keep careful, and walked off to deal with yet another thing that was part of her job. Nadia offered me a fist bump, which I reciprocated, and she walked off to work with the RCU.

"You ready?" Dani asked.

"Let's go," I told her.

Dani opened a tear beside her and motioned for everyone to step through. "After you."

Zeke tossed the large bag through the tear before stepping through, with Drusilla and me only a short distance behind. The Tempest was going to have to wait a little longer. It was time to go consolidate our information and allies. But more importantly, it was time to get some answers.

CHAPTER ELEVEN

The Crow's Perch was originally supposed to be a prison town. It had been conceived by the Primes of Inaxia as a prison to send all of the people who rose up against them centuries ago. The Queen of Crows had turned it into a thriving community, all of whom would sacrifice themselves to keep her safe. Should she want to, the Queen could be one of the most influential people in the rift. And yet, she seemed content with ruling over her subjects without complaint.

There had been numerous attempts on the Queen's life in the past few years, all of which had resulted in dead assassins and angry residents of the Crow's Perch. It had fostered a them-versus-us attitude, and the majority of the inhabitants of the city didn't trust anyone from Inaxia. And rightly so, considering that the people of Inaxia thought the Crow's Perch nothing more than a prison, and that was if they thought about it at all.

I had found out not too long before that the Queen was the granddaughter of Neb, and that her real name was Darice. It had been a secret for centuries, if not longer, a way to ensure that the enemies of one didn't try to get to them through the other.

As a rift-walker, Dani could open tears and step through into the rift without the use of the embers. It made getting around a lot easier, but there were two big drawbacks to it. Firstly, she never used to have an awful lot of choice about where the tear went through to. She could manage a rough approximation of where we would like to go, but there was usually a lot of walking involved once we got there. She'd gotten better with that over time, until now she was pretty accurate with the tears that she opened.

Secondly, whilst she could take riftborn through, by bypassing their embers in the same way, it made those travelling with her exceptionally sick. It was only for a few minutes, but having thrown up every single time I went through one of Dani's tears, it sucked. A lot.

I'd been told that if I kept going through them, eventually, I would no longer feel the need to throw up. I'd had to go through them more than forty times or so until I reached the point where whatever was inside of me didn't evacuate in an explosive fashion.

Unfortunately, whilst Drusilla had been through a rift-walker tear enough times to ensure that she too was not violently ill, Zeke had not.

Upon setting foot only a few hundred metres from the Crow's Perch, Zeke turned green in a most unpleasant way before running to find the nearest bush so that he could do what needed to be done. The sounds were not pleasant.

Zeke returned after a few minutes, walking toward us as he used a small bottle of mouthwash to get whatever taste lingered out of his mouth. "I know that if I do this a lot, it will stop doing that," he said, pointing to the still-open tear behind Dani. "But I hate this and really don't want to have to build up a resistance to it by coming through time and time again until I stop."

"It doesn't really take that long," Dani said with what could only be described as a smug smile on her face. "You three take care of one another, and shout if you need help."

"You know where we are if you need us," I said, aware that Dani was going to be heading back to work with Ji-hyun. If anyone needed to be taken to or from the rift quickly, it was better she was there.

Dani gave me a thumbs-up as she stepped through her tear, which snapped shut behind her.

We turned and walked the short distance toward the city of the Crow's Perch. The recent attacks had resulted in more guards being stationed outside, all by their own little guard huts. The metal and stone walls of the city had been reinforced and built up until they were now fifty feet tall. Armed guards patrolled the tops of the walls, and several pointed in our direction as we reached a close-enough distance that one of the bow-using guards could pick us off with ease.

They continued to watch with suspicion as we walked up to the front entrance of the city, which now had two large stone pillars on each side and a portcullis between them. Several guards stood on either side of the pillars, with two from each side stepping into the middle, in front of the portcullis, and holding up a hand for us to stop.

"It's fine; they can go through," one of the guards said to whoever was operating the portcullis.

"How do you know they're not here to hurt us?" another guard asked, his hand placed on the pommel of his sword.

"That's Lucas," the first guard said. "He saved my life last time he was here. He saved the Queen's life, too. Seems pretty stupid to have saved her life only to come back and end it."

"Just here to talk to the Queen," I said. "Not here to fight or end anybody's life. There's been too much of that already."

"Yeah, we heard about the Ancients," the guard said.

As we reached them, I saw that several of the guards looked nervous about our being there. I wasn't sure if the nervousness was because we were newcomers who they didn't know, or if it was because they'd had so many people try to kill them all in the last few years that it was just a constant state of emotion for them.

The portcullis began to slowly rise; the sound of gears turning somewhere out of sight was loud enough that there was no point try-ing to talk to anybody.

When the entrance was clear, I said to the guard, "I assume no one else's tried to kill you or the Queen since I was last here."

"It's been pretty peaceful since that trouble with the Vipers," the guard said, referring to the fact that the Viper Guild had attacked the city in the hope of killing the Queen. Like everyone else who had tried, it hadn't worked out well for them. "Thank you for what you did." The guard offered me his hand, which I shook.

Zeke, Drusilla, and I walked into the city proper and started along a maze of cobbled streets, where dozens of people watched us from the windows of the houses that sat on either side. Most buildings in the city were at least two or three storeys high, and I wondered, as I always did when I came to the Crow's Perch, just how many people lived there. I doubted if even the Queen knew the full number, as there always seemed to be more houses, or more floors on houses than were there previously, as more and more inhabitants of the rift decided that they wanted to live outside of the rule of Inaxia. It was perfectly understandable; I wouldn't want to live under the Primes' rule either.

I'd been shown the way through the city to what passed for the palace, or at least the Queen's residence, which was close to a large market area, usually full of people selling, buying, or doing whatever shady things I wanted to know nothing about.

We reached the market and crossed it. The smell of food, of fresh bread and pastries, of cooking meats, of locally sourced fish from the nearby lake, which I wouldn't eat if you paid me, was intoxicating. The sound was less so. It was like a few thousand people all talking at once, all trying to get their point across. It felt a little bit like walking into a wall of sound.

"And you've done this several times?" Drusilla asked.

"Yes," I told her. "They have a particularly nice jam-and-custard doughnut, although I'm not entirely certain what the fruit is, or where they get the ingredients for the custard, or if it's even called a doughnut. But it tastes nice."

The doors to the residence opened, and the Queen of Crows stepped outside. The din of noise from behind us ended in an instant. You could've heard a pin drop. Because when the Queen of Crows makes her presence known, you pay attention.

The Queen of Crows was officially meant to be a prisoner, along with everyone else in the Crow's Perch. Unofficially, she was pretty much given free rein to do whatever she wanted. Since the previous attacks on the city, and the way in which she and her people had swept the attackers aside, that unofficially was starting to sound more like *Come and stop me.*

The Queen wore a long black cloak that was cut to resemble feathers, and a hooded mask that completely covered her head, designed to look like a black beak. I'd met her several times, and she'd always been in both. She also wore a black-and-red dress that stopped mid-thigh, long silver gloves that ended at her elbows, and black boots. It was probably the most colourful I'd ever seen her.

The Queen stopped before us, nodded slightly, turned to the crowd of people watching her from the marketplace, and shouted, "Your Queen loves you all."

The cheer that rose up from the people of the marketplace reverberated in my chest. It was akin to being in a football stadium when thousands of people cheer a goal being scored. The leaders of Inaxia should be thankful every single day that Darice didn't want to control the rift, because I was pretty sure that if she'd asked her people to take it for her, they would have done. And I was also pretty sure that there would be a lot of people within other towns and villages dotted around the rift that would join their cause.

The Queen motioned for the three of us to follow her back into her residence; she said nothing to any of us as she led the way through the building to the throne room. The room had changed since I'd last been there, with black-and-grey drapes hung across stained-glass windows, allowing a rainbow of colour to cascade across the marble floor.

The Queen took her seat on her throne, and said one word: "Leave."

There were approximately fifteen people inside the room when we arrived, mostly guards, several of whom I assumed were advisors or hangers-on, and all of them left the room without a word.

The Queen held a finger up before any of us could speak. She pushed the hood back over her head and unfastened the clasp of the mask at the back of her skull. She pulled the mask up and off her head, dropping it onto a dark wooden table beside the throne.

Neb had once told me that her granddaughter, Darice, looked a lot like her except with paler skin. It was a fair description. Darice's hair was dark brown, streaked with something closer to golden. Her skin was closer to olive in tone than Neb's, but she had the same slate-grey eyes, the same muscular tone to her frame, and the same commanding presence. I knew that she had become a riftborn when she was only twenty-two, but even so it surprised me to see someone, who for all intents and purposes, looked like a much younger version of Neb.

"If you are about to tell me that I look just like my grandmother," the Queen said with a frown, "you can keep that opinion to yourself. I am fully aware of who I look like."

"Actually," I said, "it's pleasant to finally see the face behind the mask. Who you do or don't look like isn't really the point."

"Wait," the Queen said. "Drusilla and Zeke, yes? We have met before; I'm fairly certain of that."

Both of them nodded. "We have," Drusilla said.

"Yes," the Queen said. "You are the one dating Lucas. You are also the one who Neb thinks highly of. Which, I assure you, is a very short list of people. And you, Zeke, are the one some people call Gunslinger."

"Yes, ma'am," Zeke said. "Your Majesty."

The Queen waved away the last words as if swatting a fly. "You don't need to call me that; I don't even like people who live here calling me that."

"What should we call you?" Drusilla asked.

"*Queen* is fine," she said. "*Darice* when we're alone. I think Lucas has earned the right, and I'll extend it to you two as well. I assume you are all aware that no one is meant to know my true identity, and considering the lack of assassins who have tried to kill me in the last year, I'm also going to assume that none of you have sold that information out to the highest bidder."

"You assume correctly," Drusilla said.

"Why only the three of you?" Darice asked.

"We have our own mess on Earth that is being dealt with," Drusilla said.

"Also," Zeke said, "Lucas has a tendency to get people to try and kill him when he goes places by himself. We figured this time, it would be easier if instead of letting him nearly die, we just stopped it before it happened."

The Queen laughed, the sound echoing around the throne room. "I have known Lucas for some time now, and every single time he visits, either someone is trying to kill him or someone is trying to kill me. Actually, thinking about it, usually both of those. Neb told me about the Ancients being killed in England, three of them in total, I believe; she heard about Noah, too. I liked Noah. He had principles; he was a good man. One of the few Ancients I didn't want to stab with a fork. Ahiram murdered by Callie; Saul and Asiah killed in Inaxia. That left Theoris, Callinicus, and Fǎ Zi, who were all killed in England, and now Noah in his compound. That means we're down to four Ancients in total in a short space of time. Neb, Timo, Attia, and Hesansh."

"Five," I said. "Eztli is still out there."

The Queen shook her head sadly. "He arrived here with the others but went his own way. I sent people to keep an eye on him. They found his body just inside the Vast Death."

"What killed him?"

"Someone cut his head off," the Queen said, "after fighting him. Several dead bodies, all with Viper Guild medallions. I'll say this for Eztli: he went out fighting."

"Do you know where Neb, Timo, and Attia are?" I asked, pushing down the sudden worry about the surviving Ancients. "Have they set off for Inaxia already?"

"Yes, why?" the Queen asked.

"The Guilds have turned on themselves," Drusilla said. "They murdered their own people and are going after the Ancients. Neb and the others need to be warned that it's not just the Vipers they need to watch out for."

The Queen remained silent for a moment. "Rogue Guild members. I assume that with Noah's murder, there are no Ancients left on Earth now."

I walked the Queen through the information we had about the rogue members, explaining that they had been waiting a long time to complete the task of making sure the Ancients were all dead. That would include those who thought that they were safe.

The Queen considered everything for a moment, looking between the three of us who stood before her, and said, "The three of them decided that it would be a good idea to go to the capital together. They aim to seek aid and allies who might be able to find out who are murdering the Ancients. I told Neb it was a terrible idea; she ignored me, because she ignores everybody and thinks that she is fucking immortal. It felt like Attia needed to get back there; I think she was worried about the state of the city the longer she wasn't in it."

"Did they go alone?" Drusilla asked.

The Queen shook her head. "I sent an attachment of people with them. Smart people who know how to stay out of trouble."

"How long ago did they leave?" Zeke asked.

"A day ago," the Queen said. "They were all quite insistent."

"We need to get to Inaxia and warn them," Zeke said.

"You'll have to catch them up," the Queen said. "They're probably already at the city."

"What would have happened after Neb and the others arrived in Inaxia?" I asked, incredulous. "Is she trying to gain allies? Or is she trying to get the assassins to show themselves?"

"Both of those, I think," the Queen said. "She's not immortal, although she certainly behaves like she is, but she isn't stupid. I imagine she's fully aware of the target she's putting on herself when she arrives in that city. I think Timo knows too. The pair of them are more than capable of taking care of themselves, and more than capable of bringing people out of the shadows so that the world can see what they are."

"I don't think she's going to need to do that," Zeke said. "These aren't the lurk-in-the-shadows kind of people anymore."

"I know you need to go to Inaxia," the Queen said. "But you need to pause for a moment. I think the three of you entering that place together would make it harder, not easier. From what my allies in the city tell me, the deaths of those Ancients who helped rule the place has had a troubling effect on the populace. People are scared, people don't know what will happen next, and even those of us who have lived for millennia balk at uncertain times. It doesn't help that the surviving five Primes are about as useful as a chocolate teapot. They appear to be more interested in discussing how they can take more of that power vacuum for themselves than they are in doing their damn jobs. But unfortunately, that was always the way with those people."

"You think that the three of us going in together might cause some people in charge to become nervous?" Zeke asked.

"I do," the Queen admitted. "But more than that, I think that they will see three powerful riftborn arriving in the city shortly after Neb and Timo arrived with the last surviving Ancient who lived in the city, all of whom are known allies, and fear might give way to panic. It is inevitable, given the circumstance; panic gives way to someone doing something stupid. Make no mistake: the Primes are close to panicking. And they have always been capable of doing something stupid."

I nodded in agreement. Having spent time in the company of Primes before, I found the idea of them doing something stupid because they were worried about a loss of power or control to be exactly what would happen. The possibility of them declaring martial law or arresting the three Ancients for simply arriving at their doorstep was a deep concern.

"I need to go north, too," I said. "To find the primordials, to get their help. It feels like instead of that, I'm being pulled in the opposite direction."

"We can go to Inaxia," Drusilla said. "Find Neb and Timo. You head north and try to get help. At least that way, you're not running around the rift, trying to do everything yourself."

"Oh, he does that a lot," the Queen said.

"See?" Drusilla said, gesturing toward the queen. "You do it a lot."

I held my hands up in surrender. "I get it, but right now, these Guild members are in the rift aimed at the Ancients, so that's where I'm going. They need to be warned. The people of Inaxia need to be warned. These Guild members murdered their own people; they won't stop at innocent lives who are in the way."

"You still have the problem of all three of you being a beacon the second you step into the city," the Queen said. "If Neb, Timo, and Attia have arrived in the city with Primes who are already paranoid, you three arriving isn't going to help."

"How about I go in alone?" I asked, raising my hands before objections. "I go in loud, asking to speak to the Primes. Demanding to speak to Neb, Timo, and Attia. Walk right up to the seat of power. While I'm doing that, you two behave a little more inconspicuously. Ask questions without raising alarms. There's a bar there I know; people inside will be with us. Wait for me to enter loud, and you two go in after."

"Are you sure?" Drusilla asked.

I looked around at the three other people in the throne room with me and nodded. "Taking the information we know, whoever is behind this has managed to get half of every single Guild to betray their own people. To kill their own Guild members. Their Guild brothers and sisters, who they have fought alongside, potentially for generations. The surviving member of the Falcon Guild said that Callie had been involved for a long time."

"You think she's working alone?" Darice asked.

"Sixty-forty in favour of it just being her," I said. "Basically, we have no knowledge of exactly what is going on. We only know that there are people who are dead, the Guilds have collapsed and murdered their own, and the plan was to make sure all the Ancients were dead once that was done. Inaxia is the target, and the people running it are too stupid, power-hungry, or incompetent, or a combination of the three, to actually work together and stop it."

There was a loud knock at the throne-room door; it managed to sound both urgent but also tentative, as if whoever was on the other side had important information to impart but also didn't want to piss off the people who were in the room.

The Queen commanded whomever was outside of the room to wait, and she replaced her mask, taking a second to fix it behind her head, before getting to her feet and brushing down her clothes. "We will discuss the details of what happens next once I have finished with whatever has happened that needs my attention. Enter." The last word was said with a booming sound, a command uttered by someone who was very used to people following her commands.

The door was pushed open without pause, a young female guard framed in the light of the doorway as it opened. She wore dark leather combat armour and matching dark boots. A sword hung sheathed at her hip, and she carried her helmet under one arm. She was slight of build and stature, probably no more than five feet in height, but she gave the impression that the sword was not for show. Her gaze was one of a soldier, someone who had seen battle, someone who had taken part in winning said battle. She bowed her head, her blond hair spilling over her shoulders as she did. "Your Majesty," she said without looking up.

"Stop bowing," the Queen said with the kind of tenderness I would not expect from a ruling monarch.

The guard stood up straight, proud of where she was, and you could see on her face just how much it meant to her to be in the presence of her Queen. "We were doing patrols in the ruins around the area, and we came across someone who said that he was friends with Neb. That he needed to see you and discuss the danger that Neb was in."

The Queen looked between the guard and the three of us before strolling across the floor toward the guard. "You had best bring me to them."

"We brought him to you," the soldier said slightly strangely, as if she wasn't entirely sure that she had brought him to her.

There was a pause where I was unsure how the Queen was going to react to that news; I got the impression that bringing strange men straight to her without any kind of checks taking place was not something they did very often. The first time I'd been there, I was only allowed to see the Queen because it turned out she'd been expecting me.

"Well, you had best bring him to me," the Queen said.

"We can't be this lucky, right?" Drusilla whispered.

"Are there a lot of strange men just wandering the rift?" Zeke asked.

I didn't have time to say anything as a middle-aged man was brought into the throne room by two large soldiers, one stood on either side of him. Before I'd left Noah's compound, Hiroyuki had shown me a photo of the man stood before us. He was tall, slender, and walked with the air of someone who knew they were important. He had a gaunt face with a large, waxed moustache, and short-cropped blond hair. The man had a large smile on his face, right up until the point that he recognised the three of us.

"Christopher Dubois," I said, followed with the kind of smile that suggested nothing good was about to happen.

"You weren't meant to be here yet," the man said in a French accent.

Christopher's expression did this weird melting thing, and all at once, his body decided that he should be somewhere else. He turned almost on the spot in an effort to run, but before I could reach out with my smoke and smother him, or drag him back to us, the Queen had reached out with one hand, grabbed the back of his shirt, and thrown him roughly to the ground.

"She said you wouldn't be here yet," Christopher shouted.

Drusilla stood over the prone Christopher and looked down at him with a grin. "In that case, this really is our lucky day," she told him.

CHAPTER TWELVE

Y ou know what, Christopher?" I asked as Drusilla dragged the man to his feet, pushed him up against the pillar, and held him there as Zeke pressed the barrel of his rifle against the man's head.

"Do not kill him," the Queen said, reminding all of us that we were still in her throne room and it was probably bad form to cut someone's head off without permission.

"I promise you he will be in the same condition he is now," I told her as she hurriedly pushed the three guards out of the throne room, closing the door behind her as she did.

"I'm going to assume that you used your gift to get those guards to bring you here," I said. "I'm also going to assume that you came here trying to kill the Queen. Or, at the very least, trying to see if the Queen could be turned to your side with your merest suggestion."

Christopher's gaze couldn't figure out which one of the three of us he should be looking at. It flicked between me, Drusilla, and Zeke with startling speed, and for a moment, I thought he might stroke out if he didn't calm down.

"We have questions," Zeke said in the tone of a man who expected answers.

"You will let me go," Christopher said locking eyes with Zeke. "And then you, Zeke, will murder your friends. And you both will let it happen."

Zeke's rifle waved just a little bit toward Drusilla, who stood and watched without moving. But whatever control Christopher was trying to have over all three of us vanished the second I punched him in the nose, breaking it and quickly covering his face and shirt in blood.

Zeke blinked, lowered the gun, and punched Christopher in the face.

Drusilla also blinked and then punched Christopher in the face too.

I smiled because it's not every day you manage to shatter someone's illusion about how powerful they are.

"I'm so sorry," Zeke said. "I wasn't certain what was going on; it was like it wasn't really me."

"I just stood there," Drusilla said, sounding somewhat astonished by that idea.

"I think that Christopher here isn't quite as powerful as he would like to believe," I said. "Ken told me you could manipulate people's thoughts. I guess it's hard to do to three people at once, especially when one of them has touched the power of the rift."

"I think you broke my nose," Christopher said, his words muffled by his hand which was over his face.

"Good," I told him.

The door to the throne room opened and the Queen stepped back inside, the female guard alongside her. The guard's expression was now hard and angry, and as she glanced Christopher's way, that anger only intensified. For a moment there, I thought I was going to have to step in front of Christopher to ensure that the guard did not tear him limb from limb. Not that he didn't deserve it.

"So, you came here to kill me?" the Queen asked with something approximating humour in her voice.

"How's that working out for you?" I asked him.

"I did nothing of the sort," Christopher said.

"That is fine," the Queen said. "Whatever your motives, you mind-controlled one of my guards—and for that, there are consequences."

Christopher looked up at that. The blood smeared across the lower half of his face gave him a ghoulish appearance, but he couldn't hide the fear that filled his eyes. "Aren't there rules about killing prisoners?" He looked between everybody in the room, as if seeking out an ally who might suddenly take pity on him. His face crumbled when he realised that he was in fact utterly fucked.

Drusilla crouched beside the defeated Christopher and said, "What rules do you think we should apply to someone who has willingly attacked our friends and us? What rules apply to someone who helped murder a good man? Death for you is better than you deserve. Meet it with some dignity."

"She said you weren't going to be here," Christopher snapped. "She fucking set me up. I did everything she asked. *Everything.*"

"Let me guess: Callie." I told him. "You should really pick your friends better. She'd screw her own mother over if it got her what she wanted."

Christopher grimaced.

"She let you come here to die," Drusilla told him. "Seems like she doesn't think of you as being as useful as you think you are."

"I think we can find somewhere more secure to have this conversation," the Queen said. "Besides, I'd rather he did not continue bleeding all over my nice, shiny floor."

Christopher was warned in no uncertain terms what would happen to him should he try to use his power on anybody else whilst he was a . . . guest of the Queen of Crows. The man was bloody and beaten, in both a physical and emotional sense. I've seen people who had lost their will to fight, who had accepted the situation they found themselves in, and were now trying to make the best of it. Christopher fell in that bracket. However, no one was an idiot, so he was bound and gagged.

He was taken through to the tunnels beneath the Queen's palace. They were tunnels I'd taken before, and I knew that they led outside of the city.

Instead of continuing on through the tunnel outside, Christopher was dragged down a second tunnel, at the end of which were several cells. One of the guards opened a cell, revealing nothing but darkness inside, and Christopher was tossed inside. He hit the floor hard with his knees and toppled over to the ground.

One of the guards stepped inside, and the second later, a blue flame inside a wall-mounted brazier lit up the cell. The cell itself was a hundred feet square at a push and contained a bed which I personally wouldn't have slept on if you paid me, a small toilet, and a sink.

Two chairs were brought into the room and placed in front of the prisoner, who had dragged himself up onto the bed and was rubbing his knees. One of the guards grabbed the steel manacles on Christopher's wrists, and attached them to a chain, which was, in turn, attached to two large steel hoops that were embedded in the stone wall. Christopher wasn't going anywhere unless he was able to tear himself free from metal and stone, and that didn't seem to be within his power set.

I crouched down beside Christopher, and he looked over at me, expecting the worst. "I'm going to make this very short," I told him. "I'm going to remove your gag. If you use your power, I will know, and you will die. But first, I will take your vocal cords. I will leave you here, forgotten about in a cell, to die slowly and painfully without the ability to even scream for help. I know that sounds rough, but I want to impart upon you just how much patience I no longer have. Do you understand?"

Christopher nodded enthusiastically, although the fear in his eyes was still there. Maybe he wasn't as stupid as I first thought.

I looked over at Drusilla and Zeke, the latter of whom still carried his rifle, and I could see it in his face that given the chance, he would've been happy to put a round between Christopher's eyes.

The Queen stood beside them, with the female guard who had brought the news of Christopher's arrival, as well as several guards who wore masks similar to her own. They were members of her elite force within the city, and all of them would most likely die for her, but they would definitely kill for her.

I removed Christopher's gag, and someone tossed a handkerchief in his direction so that he might use it to clean his face a little. His hands were still bound in front of him, but he was able to use them.

"What do you want to know?" Christopher asked.

"I already had a very nice conversation with one of your group," I said. "Do you know of the Falcon Guild?"

"Should I?" Christopher asked. "Do you know the names of every low-level grunt in the RCU?"

"Why did you try to distract me by threatening my friends?" I asked.

"I owed someone a favour," he said, "so I did as she asked. And now I don't owe them a favour. In fact, I have a feeling full well that you would be here waiting for me."

"What were you meant to say to the Queen?" I asked.

"It was a message to be passed along to you," Christopher said. "Callie asked me to come here and give the Queen a message to give to you. You are to go to Inaxia. Alone. You have two days. If you don't, she starts making people in the city disappear. She means that, by the way. She leaves that city full of nothing but corpses. Right now, she's . . . behaving herself, being quiet, letting everyone live their lives. She wanted me to impart just how much she will change that if you don't comply. Callie will meet you in the capital city, and any questions you have, she will give you the answers to. I think she genuinely believes that you might have some kind of rapport. I don't see it, personally."

"Neb, Attia, and Timo?" I asked. "The three who went into Inaxia. What about Hesansh?"

"No idea about Hesansh," Christopher said. "All I know is those three of the last four Ancients are in one city. That they went there to find help, but I don't think that was what they found. Inaxia is in lock-down; the people in charge have no idea that Callie is already in the city with her people, just sat waiting. I was supposed to go back there and help. I was supposed to be a big part of all of this. I should've been a big part of all of this. I am better than being used as the errand boy for an insane megalomaniac. And you should've just done as you were told. If you had, Noah would still be dead, but you might already have the answers you want. Instead, you decided to involve yourself, time and time again, and all you have achieved is nothing."

I stood and walked out of the room.

"Don't you want answers?" Christopher shouted. "I know things."

I shook my head. "I have all the answers I need. You were told to keep me busy, and you did so by threatening my friends and burning down my home. It didn't work, so you were punished by being sent here so that you could be grabbed by us. You already confirmed that it was Callie Mitchell who sent you. You already confirmed that Inaxia is under lockdown, that Callie hasn't attacked the city. The Ancients and remaining Primes aren't dead, as there's no way Callie would kill them and expect me to come peacefully. So, she's going to sit and wait, and she doesn't want to change the parameters of what she wants from me by doing anything stupid."

"I could tell you about your embers, about the shadows," Christopher said. "You don't know about that, do you?"

"That's a bit of a random leap," I said.

"What about our embers?" Drusilla asked. "Or is that just another line of bullshit from Callie?"

"The shadows in the embers," Christopher said. "The Ancients lied to us about them for centuries. The shadows make us stronger."

"And you know this firsthand?" I asked him.

Christopher's expression faltered. "No," he admitted.

"So, you're feeding us something you may have heard because you hope it'll save your arse," I said.

Christopher opened his mouth and quickly closed it again.

"More bullshit," I said with a dismissive wave of my hand.

"I have a question," Zeke said. "You guys are working with those who killed the two other Ancients from Inaxia, yes?"

Christopher nodded.

"Why kill them both first?" Zeke asked. "I understand the need to destabilise the city, but it was a long-enough time before the rest of your plan that it feels like someone jumped the gun a bit."

"I don't know for sure," Christopher said. "It's not like we had nice meetings where I got to sit down and discuss their plans whilst eating croissants. I did as I was told, and most of the time, I wasn't informed what was happening. I can only surmise that they killed them first because they wanted the rest of the Ancients to be afraid. To make mistakes."

"It's what I'd do," Drusilla said. "Turn the political cogs into one giant mess that filters through a population pretty quickly. No one has any faith in their leaders if their leaders have no faith that they can do the job. Or if they seem to be utterly useless at their jobs. Although, as we've all seen in life, there will always be people who follow those in charge no matter how ridiculous they might be. There are always lemmings who follow their leaders off a cliff, even while everybody else is telling them that their leaders are taking them off a fucking cliff. Sorry, I spent a lot of time in Ancient Rome; it was not always a great place where smart people were in charge."

"I think you might have issues," Zeke said, giving a sideways glance to Drusilla.

"No shit," Drusilla replied.

"We done here?" I asked.

No one had any more questions.

I looked back to the Queen. "Do whatever you need to do; I'm finished with him."

The Queen drew a dagger from a sheath against her hip, walked over to Christopher, and looked down at him.

Christopher stared up at her. "She sent me here to die because I failed to keep you busy for long enough. She said she knew I was going to fail. That I was always going to fail. You know what's stupid? It wasn't even her fucking favour."

"What?" I asked. "Whose favour was it, then?"

Christopher laughed and looked over at me. "Fuck you, I'm done here. You going to ask me my last words?"

The Queen slashed the dagger across his throat, stepping out of the way to avoid the torrent of blood as it gushed from the wound. "No," she said, cleaning her dagger on a piece of cloth as she looked down at a still-living Christopher as his life force left him.

When Christopher was dead, which didn't take long, the Queen turned to her guard and said, "Bury him somewhere up outside. Don't mark it; I don't want to know. Just make it deep; I don't want him coming back as a zombie or something equally ridiculous."

The guards nodded and set about their task silently.

"I hope you got everything you wanted," the Queen said to me.

I nodded, although I'd wanted to know what he meant at the end about it not being Callie who had asked him to involve himself in my life; I knew when someone was done being helpful. "I need to go to the capital," I said. "Looks like I have an invitation to see a psychopath before she decides to rain down horror on the people living there."

"You know this has to be a trap, yes?" Drusilla said.

"Definitely feels trap-like," Zeke concurred. "You don't even know *how* Callie is going to contact you."

"I know," I said. "She'll have people watching the ways in and out of the city; she'll know when I arrive, although I don't plan on going through the front door. She'll know that, too. I want to get a look at the city before I announce myself to Callie and anyone else watching. I won't be much help if I go in loud and have to spend my time avoiding the guards there. And I can't do nothing, because if I don't go, Callie will carry out her threat. No more innocent people die because of her."

"So, your plan is to go in alone and scout the place out?" Drusilla asked. "Alone. As in by yourself."

I nodded. "I get in, look around, make sure the city isn't rigged to blow up or something, and get word to you two before announcing myself to Callie."

"How are you going to do that last bit?" Zeke asked.

"That's something I was going to figure out on the way," I said with a smile.

The Queen let out a sigh and looked up at the sky as dusk settled around us. "We need to get you ready, then. It's almost dark. It might be wiser for you to travel during the night, but it won't be safer."

"Nothing about what I'm going to do by the time I reach Inaxia will be safe," I said. "Might as well start now."

CHAPTER THIRTEEN

Before the three of us could leave the Crow's Perch, we were each given a change of clothing so that we didn't stand out so much in our jeans and T-shirts. So, we all wore black trousers, a grey tunic with blue stitching down the centre, and black boots which looked somewhat similar to what the military wore on Earth. All three of us also got a charcoal-grey cloak to wear, each fitted with a hood. The cloak and hood were lined with the fur of a three-tailed shadow, an animal that had hunted me on more than one occasion, and I couldn't possibly imagine why you would want to go out and find one. On the plus side, the fur was remarkably soft and warming, and I do like a good cloak.

We were also given a cart and two oxforth to pull us to our destination. The oxforth were populous creatures in the rift and resembled something between oxen, camels, and horses, although they were larger and faster than any of those.

The massive animals had chestnut fur, which kept them warm in the winter but cool in the summer, and while docile in nature, they also had two huge horns on either side of their large heads that I'd seen used to great effect on anything stupid enough to think them prey.

I'd asked the Queen about using the tear stones to get us to Inaxia quickly, but she told me that they were heavily guarded near the city. And that there had been a standing order to destroy any found within a mile of the city itself. It was safer to go via cart.

It was always frustrating that I needed to use a tear stone to get out of the rift but didn't need one to get into it. But even more so now that we'd unlocked *fast travel* around the rift, moving between tear stones with relative ease, and were unable to use it to get closer to Inaxia.

"Be careful," the Queen said to all three of us as we climbed onto the cart. "Whatever is happening, it's bad, and it's almost certain that my grandmother is neck-deep involved. Even if she doesn't mean to be or want to be. Those clothes should let you pass through the city without too much attention, but the second someone knows who you are, it's all going to go to shit."

"We'll be careful," Zeke told her.

"As careful as we ever are," I said.

The Queen chuckled. "That's what worries me, Lucas. You should know, we have a few people who work outside of Inaxia who are loyal to our city. One of them, Cortez, is a good man. Officially, he's a black-smith, and he makes just enough weapons to not make that sound like a lie, but unofficially, he works for me. He's a spy, is what I'm saying. You can't miss his cottage; if you're going in through the east entrance, it is about a mile outside of the city. On the main road. There will be guards there; they all work for me too. Tell Cortez I sent you; he will either help you get into the city or put you up until you figure out what you're going to do. Don't ask him to make any weapons, because he's shit at it. At least in comparison to your good self, Drusilla. Either way, and whatever it is you decide to do, seek Cortez."

Despite the fact that it was still dark out, we set off at a good pace. It was a couple of days of riding at a normal speed, and while we all wanted to get to the capital as quickly as possible, we didn't want to tire out the oxforth.

Being out in the dark in the rift was a dangerous prospect. There were things that were a lot scarier than a three-tailed shadow that you needed to watch out for.

The cart had blankets and equipment in the back for staying out in the open for a few days. There was a cover across it, and it was large enough that one of us could sleep, while the other two sat up front. So, I sat up front with Zeke while Drusilla slept in the back.

"Do you think that one of the Ancients is working with Callie to do all of this?" Zeke asked.

I considered the question for a moment and wasn't entirely certain how to respond. "I don't know," I came up with. It wasn't much of an answer, but it was all I had. "Not Neb or Timo. Almost certainly not Attia; she's already terrified of what happened to the Ancients and Primes, and she barely got away with her life."

"Which is usually a good indication of someone being involved," Zeke pointed out.

"Valid point," I said. "And it's true that I don't know her well enough to give a definitive answer; it is possible that she is playing everyone and is working with Callie."

"What about the other one, Hesansh?" Zeke asked.

I considered the idea. "Hesansh always seemed to be far too lazy to do anything that didn't involve drinking. It's possibly either of them, or both of them, or none of them. I don't know any of them well enough to give an answer, though. You had any dealings with them that might lead you to a different answer?"

"Not even a little bit," Zeke said.

"There's only four of them left now," I said. "And it's improbable that of those who have died, they were all linked to one another, unless Callie knows which Ancient is linked to whom."

"Which is possible, considering she was linked to the rift," Drusilla said.

"Yeah, it's not great," I agreed. "Either way, it's more likely that at least some of the surviving four have lost their connection to the rift. If one of the Ancients is working to kill the rest of them, they'd be playing Russian roulette to do so. There'd be no guarantee of who was linked to who, and while it's possible that Callie knows and is advising someone, there's a lot we don't know. I'm beginning to get a little fed up of reacting to everything, of not being able to have time to deal and decide what I want to do. The last few days has just been one crisis after another with little time to figure out how to slow them down or stop them."

The rest of the journey was done with relative ease, and the three of us all managed to get some sleep and rest. It began to feel like just another trip, although I think all of us were aware that it was anything but. It's amazing how the human brain, even a rift-powered brain, sometimes allows you to forget, or at least suppress, the events you're currently living through. Probably some sort of coping mechanism from back when our ancestors were continuously worried about being eaten by something considerably larger than them, so that they didn't live in a constant state of panic and terror.

Inaxia came into view as dusk began to settle in on the second day. It was an impressive city and home to, at last guess, several million people.

Inaxia's internal structure was built within five rings. Guards and the military were in the outer one, merchants next, living accommodations third, with schools, libraries, and academia in the second ring, and the seat of power in the middle.

We passed by several farms as we made our way to the east gate. It was easy to spot the garrisons of varying sizes in the distance, and we made sure to never venture too close to them or the myriad of patrols taking place in the surrounding landscape. It looked like tensions had heightened since I was there last. Understandable, considering.

Inaxia itself had a hundred-foot-high stone wall, with half a dozen entrances around the wall and several ports to the south-east. The last time I'd been there, I'd used the canal to enter the city, and I'd considered its use again, but it was slower than the oxforth and cart.

While, in theory, each ring of the city stayed in its own lane, in practice, several of them merged. Merchants did work in the military ring, and there were people from the academies working all over the place. Apart from those in power, the only other professions that allowed anyone free rein to travel between the rings were the Investigators and medical personnel. Investigators were essentially the police, and they worked outside of the hierarchy of the rest of the city. I really wanted to avoid as many of them as possible, even those I considered friends. This wasn't a social trip, and the fewer people I involved, the better.

The centre of Inaxia was an enormous hill surrounded by a wall that was a few hundred feet higher than the outer walls. On top of the hill was a large complex where the Primes lived. Each Prime had their own lodge and area for their people to live and work. It was called the shield, even though it was no longer circular in shape and hadn't been for hundreds of years.

There were seven spokes coming out of the central ring, each one running until it reached the outer wall. Trains ran around the outer wall, stopping at stations where the spokes and wall met. The whole thing ran on rift energy. The trains were a big part of what made Inaxia run. Trains for people, trains for goods. Lifts that took goods up to the high walls. In theory, the city was a well-oiled machine, but peek behind the curtain and you'd see it was all held together with fraying string and more than a little hope.

We were nearly a mile outside of the city when we arrived at the idyllic cottage with the name CORTEZ written on the fence post.

I got down from the cart and looked around. It was two hundred feet from the road to the cottage's front door. And it was completely exposed between the two. The cottage itself was a single-storey building, with an abundance of colourful flowers in pots sat outside of each of the large windows. Off to the left of the building were several two-storey buildings, all of which looked a little bit like townhouses back on Earth. There were several men and women milling about outside of them, all of whom stopped what they were doing when we arrived.

A middle-aged man walked toward us, and I resisted the urge to rest my hand on the spear strapped to my back. The man was taller than me, with olive skin and a mass of dark curly hair which fell across his broad shoulders. He had a thick moustache and a gaze that told you he was in no mood for any stupidity that might be heading his way. He wore a simple white shirt, dark trousers, and old, worn leather boots, and carried a rapier against his hip, the pommel of which was intricate, in the shape of a snake wrapping around itself. He was a man who, I was fairly sure, had used that sword many times.

"And you might be?" the man asked with a Spanish accent.

"Lucas," I replied. "This is Zeke and Drusilla. We were told to come here and find Cortez, that he could help us. Just not for his blacksmithing skills."

"Who told you?" the man asked.

"Royalty," I replied. "I'm fairly sure you don't want me to say the name out loud. You are either Cortez or you can find him for me; either way, we were told to come here for aid. She said you were to be trusted, except with your blacksmithing; she said that was not your . . . forte."

The man laughed a deep belly laugh. "I am Cortez," he said. "And she said I was shit at blacksmithing, because I am. I can make a knife. I can make a nail. But I can't make anything of any real value or use beyond some simple carpentry. Bring your cart over to the barn; your animals will be fed and watered while we talk. I'm going to assume she asked you to come to me to get you into the city."

I nodded.

"Come on, then," Cortez said, nodding toward the cottage. "I have some tea and wine. I will be having the second of those options."

We took the oxforth and cart over to where Cortez told us to take them, and handed the reins of the animals to one of the workers there, before we walked back to the cottage and found Cortez waiting for us at the front door.

The interior of the cottage was as pleasant as the exterior, with comfortable furnishings and a very homely feel that I didn't get from the man himself.

"So," Zeke said as he looked around the living room we found ourselves in. "You like crochet."

The room had a dozen crocheted throws, of various shapes, patterns, and colours, some of which were quite intricate, and I imagined that whoever had made them had been an expert in such matters.

Cortez's expression sparkled slightly as he gestured for us to take a seat on one of the comfortable-looking purple velvet couches. "I love crochet. I am currently making a throw for a friend. Our mutual friend, in fact. Would you like to see it?"

We all nodded as we took our seats, and Cortez revealed a massive throw that was easily eight feet long by six feet wide. The exterior border of the throw was bright yellow, with the colour changing to a darker and darker shade of yellow before it incorporated dark blues and began to look somewhat like the night sky. It was an intricate and impressive piece of work, which I was certain had taken the man an exceptionally long time.

Cortez folded the throw and placed it on a chair before retrieving a six-inch-tall crocheted crow. The crow looked exactly like every other crow I had ever seen except in two places: it wore a silver crown, and it had a smile on its face. I had never seen a crow smile before, and I was pretty certain that if I saw one in reality, I would run. There are some animals that really shouldn't smile.

"You really like to crochet?" I said.

Cortez placed the smiling crow on the wooden coffee table between us, and after a few seconds of it smiling at me, I turned it around. Much to Cortez's amusement.

"It's creepy as fuck, isn't it?" Cortez said with a smile. "The Queen is going to absolutely love it."

Drusilla was the first to laugh, followed quickly by myself and Zeke.

"Before I became a riftborn, all I did was fight," Cortez told us. "Fight for my country, my people, my men, for those who used human life as if it were an infinite resource. I did terrible things for my crown and country, or at least I thought they were for my crown and country. In reality, they were for rich people so that they could be richer while everybody else suffered. Inaxia is full of people like that. So, I help the Queen and her people when I can: I spy, I trade in secrets, in rumours, and occasionally, I put up someone who will be going on into the city to carry out a task I need not know anything about."

"We're not assassins," I said. "We're not going into Inaxia to kill anybody. Hopefully, anyway. In fact, the opposite is true; I'm hoping to get into the city to stop anyone dying."

Cortez took a seat in a velvet chair that matched the sofa the three of us were sat on. A woman brought in a silver tray with four glasses and a pitcher of yellowy-orange liquid. She placed the tray on the coffee table, nodded to Cortez, gave a sideways glance to the rest of us, and then left.

After picking up the pitcher, Cortez poured four glasses, picked one up for himself, and sat back in his chair. "It's sweet tea," he said by way of explanation before taking a sip of the drink. "It's quite delicious; I grow the leaves myself, and then we make the tea. It is a way in which I can get in and out of the city without always having to bring my blacksmithing gear with me."

Drusilla poured herself a glass, took a sip, looked back at me and Zeke, and said, "This is really nice."

I poured a glass for Zeke, passing him his drink, which he took a mouthful of before exclaiming the same thing.

Despite a little trepidation, I took a drink and everyone was right; it was sweet and pleasant and refreshing. It tasted slightly of orange and lemons but with a hint of that green-tea taste.

"Why not just tell everybody you make tea?" I asked as I drained my glass.

"In hindsight," Cortez said, "that probably would've been the best idea. But I'd already told people I was a blacksmith, and as word got around that was what I was doing, it became harder and harder to change. Those first few years of trying my best to actually become a good blacksmith were deeply frustrating. I actually employ six blacksmiths on this land now. All of whom are considerably better than I am, which means I don't have to take part in blacksmithing myself. I can dedicate my time to my crochet and my tea. But we are not here to discuss pleasantries; you want into the city."

"We do," I said.

"That is not a problem," Cortez said, placing his glass back on the table. "I require only one thing for payment. I want to know why. Not a lie, because I can tell when people are lying. It is my gift. You will tell me why you wish to go into the city, and if I deem it safe for my people to take you, we will arrange passage. All three of you might be a problem, though. We usually only arrange it for one at a time."

"Is the plan still for you to go in alone?" Drusilla asked. "Because I would like to re-voice my opinion that it is a stupid plan."

"I second that motion," Zeke said. "I don't think we can just park up out here and do nothing. Judging by the number of carts we've passed and the number of patrols that are around, eventually we are going to meet the latter. And I'm not entirely sure that our story of *We're just waiting for a mate* is going to hold an awful lot of water."

"If Callie sees someone else coming in with me, she might not react well," I said. "I'll get word back to you within a few hours, hopefully. I go to the Primes and announce my arrival to Callie and her people, and that way, you can make sure we all have a quick exit. I'm going to assume Callie is either in charge of the city or is watching the Primes, so we can go from there. I'm going to head to a bar by the name of the Human Head. It's run by some friends of mine, Necia and Roseline. If anyone has their ear to the ground, it's them."

I'd considered asking Isaac, a revenant friend who had died in the line of duty for the RCU and arrived in Inaxia shortly after, but he was working with the guards, and I didn't want to get that close to anyone who might recognise me.

"That it?" Drusilla asked.

"If this all goes to shit," I said. "Scratch that; when this all goes to shit, we're all going to need to get out of here as quickly as possible. These oxforth are going to need to be rested and ready to get us as far away from this place as possible as quickly as possible. I don't want either of you to get spotted by one of Callie's people, to give her a reason to do something stupid. I'm already stretching the rules by going in quiet to scout out the place."

"Are we meant to just stay here and twiddle our thumbs?" Drusilla asked with a little irritation.

"Two of you can stay here," Cortez said. "Your oxforth will be rested, fed, brushed; basically, they will be well taken care of. As will the two of you who stay, although we will ask that you both help with matters around the ranch. There are blacksmithing jobs that require doing, and just general handy work. Are you both okay with that?"

Drusilla laughed, the tension leaving her. "Yes, I think I will be fine with some blacksmithing."

Cortez stared at her for several seconds before he said, "Drusilla as in the daughter of the Roman Emperor? If that is you, I have heard much about your abilities involving metal work. And judging from the spear that Lucas carries, that is not a normal steel spear tip. I think, if you are willing, it would be of great interest to our little ranch to have someone of your ability help with the blacksmithing that we need to have done."

"I can help," Drusilla said, folding her arms. "But I will need to make sure that Lucas gets into that city safely, and that if he leaves in a hurry, we will be ready to go."

Cortez clapped and stood. "Excellent," he said. "So, all I need from you, Lucas, is the truth of why you wish to go into Inaxia."

They seemed little point in lying or withholding information from him. He clearly had the trust of the Queen of Crows, and if we wanted to get in and out, we needed his trust. "Have you heard about the assassinations of the Ancients?"

Cortez nodded. "A lot of dead Ancients, several dead Primes," he said.

"He means the ones on Earth," Drusilla said.

The look on Cortez's face suggested that he had not. It was going to be a long evening.

CHAPTER FOURTEEN

Cortez said nothing as I told him about the events of the last few days. He occasionally shifted uncomfortably in his seat, but he thankfully allowed me the chance to explain everything without interruption.

When I was done, he let out a long exhale and said, "I really wish I still smoked."

"We pretty much feel like that all the time," Zeke said. "Can I assume you still plan to help us?"

Cortez nodded slowly, as if trying to decide whether or not he was getting himself into something that was more dangerous than stupid or vice versa. "We leave in two hours. It will be the dead of night; we can get you in, but once in, you are on your own. You will have to figure a way out yourself. It is too dangerous for us to loiter in the city. None of what you have planned can be linked to me or my people; not only our livelihood but our lives would be in jeopardy if it was. The Primes are not magnanimous when it comes to anyone interloping on their power base. If this is agreeable, prepare to leave."

Everyone agreed that it was.

Cortez motioned for us to follow him out of the room, which we did, continuing on through the cottage until we were outside again. He walked on toward a number of small buildings at the rear of the ranch, next to several dozen oxforth that were in an enclosed area.

We stopped by a paddock and Cortez turned to the three of us. "It is time for you to say your goodbyes. Only Lucas comes from this point forward. It is for our protection. And yours."

I kissed Drusilla and we held one another for a moment. "Be careful," she said. "Come back in one piece; I do not like the idea of having to wage a one-woman war against that city if something happens to you."

I smiled and kissed her again before removing my spear and passing it to her. "I will come back with my shield. Metaphorically."

"You're not taking this with you?" she asked.

"It's a weapon designed to kill anything connected to the rift," I said. "It might not kill them outright, but I'd rather not go into the city which is already full of dangerous and nervous people and make them more nervous. Nervous people do stupid stuff."

"I get it," Drusilla said. "It'll be here when you get back."

Zeke offered me a fist bump, which I reciprocated. "Be safe," he said. "I'm going to get Cortez to teach me how to crochet. I want to make an army of those crows and then just leave them around places to creep people out. I think I now have a new mission in life."

I laughed and slapped him on the shoulder. "Good to have a goal."

I followed Cortez through the paddock, waving goodbye to Drusilla and Zeke as we turned the corner and were out of sight. There was a small hut nearby that was impossible to see from anywhere except behind the paddocks. Cortez opened the door, revealing a set of dingy stairs that led down into a darkness below.

"We won't be long," Cortez said, stepping inside and motioning me to follow.

I continued walking behind Cortez and was several steps down the stairs when the door to the hut slammed shut behind me. After what turned out to be a fairly short descent, we ended in a lounge room, with a pier to the left of me, complete with a canoe bobbing gently on the water beside it.

"Am I about to go canoeing?" I asked.

Cortez looked over at the canoe and then back to me with a smile. "Do you get seasick?"

I shook my head. "As much as using the river to bypass the first few circles of the city is a great idea, I'm surprised that they would have such a glaring hole in their security as to let a canoe through."

Cortez laughed, the sound echoing around the small room. There was a scratching sound from the right of where I stood, and I turned to see a wooden wardrobe sliding to the side, revealing a second, larger room beyond. A young woman with dark skin and a bald head exited the room and nodded to Cortez.

"This is Zoe," Cortez said, motioning to the lady who had just entered the room. "She has worked for me for several decades; she is an expert at getting people in and out of that city. She will get you in, but she is not getting you out. It is too dangerous."

"You already told me that," I said.

"I know, but I am telling you again to make sure you understand that Zoe will not be staying around to wait for you." Cortez looked over at Zoe. "You understand that, yes?"

"Yes," Zoe said in Portuguese.

"You going to wait around long enough to get to the Human Head so you can report back what's happening?" I asked.

Zoe glanced over to Cortez and nodded.

"Excellent," I said. "You get back to Zeke and Drusilla and tell them what's going on, so if they need to come in to rescue me, they can."

"You know the Queen?" Zoe asked me.

I nodded. "You?"

Zoe moved her hand from side to side. "I've met her a few times; she's nice to me. Actually, she seems to be nice to everybody. Except when she's not nice. I want you to know that I feel very similar about people."

I wondered if the short Portuguese lady was attempting to threaten me. It certainly sounded like a threat, although the smiling that she did whilst speaking made it seem less threatening. Or more threatening. I'd spent a lot of time around Nadia, I realised.

Cortez chuckled. "She is trying to tell you that she will kill you if you give her a reason to."

"I don't plan on giving her a reason to," I said, and looked over at Zoe. "You take me into the city, and you leave. Whatever happens after that is my problem. But no one has told me how we're getting into the city yet."

"We canoe," Zoe said, passing me a map that she'd taken out of her pocket. "We need to get to the bank of the river closer to the city. Once there, we tether the canoe and use a hatch on the side of the city; it'll take us down into their sewer system. We follow that up and out to one of the rings, and from there, you go wherever it is you need to go. I will be with you until you enter Inaxia after the sewers; what happens after that is on you. Any questions?"

I studied the map. "This is sewers, I assume."

Zoe nodded. "Memorise it, because you don't want to get lost down there. If we get separated, you'll need it, and it'll be good if you need a quick, unwatched exit."

I folded the map up and placed it in my pocket. "Thank you very much for doing this."

Zoe shrugged. "The Queen asks, and we obey."

I didn't take long to get into the canoe, with Zoe picking up the only set of oars and pushing us away from the pier as Cortez watched.

"I will see you soon, Lucas," Cortez said. "Your friends will be safe here. Good luck."

I thanked him, and Zoe began to paddle softly, moving us through an underground stream, where I had to occasionally move my head so as not to smack it on one of the many rock formations that jutted out on all sides. I was sure that Cortez would be thinking of Drusilla and Zeke as collateral, should I aim to misbehave.

I sort of understood it. The rift is a dangerous place, full of dangerous people, and even those you believe might be working alongside you might have aims which harm those you care about. Finding someone like the Queen of Crows, who is open and honest about her alliances, and about what would happen to you should you cross her, is rare. Most people in the rift are at best duplicitous, keeping their secrets close to their chest lest someone discover something about them which could harm them.

Once out from under the cave system, we picked up speed as Zoe paddled quietly across the river, avoiding any of the normal traffic from merchants or guards who frequented the same stretch of water. It was a quiet and pleasant trip, allowing me to look around at the lights in the distance from nearby ships without fear that we were about to be spotted. The night sky was free from cloud, and the light from the strip that cut across the darkness illuminated everything in a cool glow.

I'd never quite gotten used to the lack of stars and moon in the rift; I used to wonder if there was a reason for it but never had the time to look further. Maybe one day I would.

As always, the city of Inaxia was illuminated from multiple sources both within and around the gates. No matter the time of day, it was a busy and bustling metropolis. It was easily the most populated city in all of the rift and the closest thing we had to the mega cities which existed back on the Earth side. Several million people all inside a city that you could easily lose yourself in; that's if you could get inside to begin with. The Primes had always ensured that entry into their city, as they saw it, was regulated, which meant it was almost certain that I would be discovered the second I arrived at one of the gates. Which was obviously Callie's plan. Which was also why I didn't want to do that. The idea of walking up to Inaxia and not being aware of what was going on inside, especially with Neb and Timo in there, didn't fill me with hope. I wondered if Callie knew I was never going to just walk up to the front door. Bit late now.

Zoe stopped the canoe against the bank and tethered it to a short pier. She looked down at me as I got out of the canoe and joined her on dry land.

"Thank you very much," I said as we walked along the dark trail toward the nearest part of the Inaxian wall.

There were tall reeds on one side of us, each one easily greater in height than I was, whilst on the other was the river we had just been paddling on. The cobblestone path was well marked although not well maintained, leading me to believe that it was not the main thoroughfare for guards or Investigators—the Inaxian police—to use on a regular basis. I hoped that the noise of guard boots as they walked along it would give us extra notification of anyone coming our way. That made me feel a little bit better.

Zoe stopped walking after about fifty feet and motioned for us to step into the reeds. She held a finger to her lips and gestured for us to stay low.

I dared not move as the sounds of voices filled the air, and it wasn't long until boots could be heard stomping along the path that Zoe and I had been walking on only moments earlier.

"You really think that we need to walk this long-since-forgotten-about path?" a rough voice asked.

"We have our orders," a second voice replied, this one seemingly belonging to someone younger, although that was difficult to tell with rift-fused, as appearance gave no indication of actual age.

"But these orders are stupid," a third voice said, this one higher in pitch than the other two and feminine in nature. "They're sending all of the guards out to patrol, and that leaves fewer inside the city to keep the peace. How does that make any sense?"

There was the sound of someone coming to a stop. "I said, we have our orders," the second person said. "Now if you two could stop bellyaching for the next half an hour, we can get this ridiculous routine done, and then we can go back inside and not have to do it again."

The other two grumbled, but neither spoke up, and the sounds of their boots on the cobblestone pathway started up once again.

I remained still. I had a lot of practice over the years of being still; it was one of those things that Neb had wanted me to master. "*Sometimes, you must wait for your prey*," she used to say. I always wanted to disagree, but she was usually right. Even so, kneeling in the reeds would have been a lot more pleasant had something not crawled over my bare hand.

I looked down at whatever it was that had decided my hand was a pretty good roadway to get from one piece of muck to the other. It looked like a small frog, although instead of having four legs, it had sixteen and moved a little bit like a centipede. I had absolutely no idea what it was, because I couldn't possibly know the name of every single animal that lived in the rift, in the same way that I couldn't know all the animals that lived on Earth. I knew one thing, though: that I did not want it on my hand anymore.

Zoe looked down at the thing on my hand and back up to me with genuine fear in her eyes. Her expression did absolutely nothing to make me want to continue having the creature remain on my hand. I considered turning to smoke to let the thing drop into the mud and hopefully scurry away to whatever hole or nest it lived in, but that might notify the three guards who were only a dozen or so paces away from where we were crouched. I was not about to shake my hand, because the sudden movement might well have pissed the thing off enough that it bit me. And I was almost certain that it could bite me. There was a zero percent chance that my luck was good enough that whatever this thing was, it didn't have teeth. Or venom. In fact, judging by Zoe's expression, it almost certainly had both.

I practically willed the small creature to fuck off and leave me alone, or at least for the three guards strolling beside us to hurry up. Because the world works like that, the guards stopped by the reeds Zoe and I were hiding in. I could see all three of them quite clearly; there was a portly older gentleman with a large beard and a perpetually scowling expression. A younger man, who I judged to be the second of the three who spoke, had chiselled looks and the appearance of someone who took a lot of pride in their armour. The third was a young woman who appeared to be no older than her mid-twenties but, as per usual, could be hundreds of years old. She had an intelligent expression on her face, and her eyes darted around, looking for anything out of place. I hoped that the darkness of the reeds was enough to keep Zoe and me hidden. I had no interest in hurting these people just out doing their job.

Thankfully, the three guards continued on, and after thirty of the most stressful seconds of my recent life, I was able to turn to smoke, and the monstrous miniature-frog thing dropped into the mud with a satisfying *splat*.

"That was a needle frog," Zoe said by way of explanation, as I watched the small creature scurry off into the darkness.

"Whatever further information you are about to give me, I don't want to know," I told her. "I am going to assume that whatever it could've done to me would have sucked. And I'm going to leave it there."

"Really sucked," Zoe said. "Really, really sucked. I know a few people who have been bitten by one; they did not enjoy the experience. And they were both riftborn."

"You appear to enjoy telling me that a lot more than I'm comfortable with," I told her. "We should hurry on before those guards make a second loop, or come back this way, or whatever the hell it is they're doing."

Zoe nodded in agreement, and I followed her out of the reeds, giving my body a quick pat-down to ensure that nothing was clinging to my clothes that had the word *needle* in its name. The sight of me brushing down my clothes made Zoe chuckle.

"I am glad that I am a source of amusement for you," I said without any real hard feelings in my voice.

"I'm glad you're not currently bleeding from your eyes and ears," Zoe said with a grin. "Would've made getting into the city unnoticed a little bit harder."

We reached the base of the city walls after only a short distance, and Zoe placed her hand against part of the stone, which shifted ever so slightly. There was a click from somewhere within the wall, and part of it slid open to reveal a staircase leading down into what was clearly, judging by smell alone, a sewer system.

Zoe looked back at me, and her expression of *ta-da* quickly gave way to one of horror. I followed her gaze behind me and saw the three guards on their return journey toward us. There was a lantern bobbing in the darkness, and it wouldn't be long before they spotted us. And then any hope of me doing this quietly was gone. Not to mention the fact that it would put Zoe in serious danger.

"Get inside," I said.

Zoe practically yanked me through the gap in the wall that led beneath the city. She pulled a lever next to the open piece of wall, which slid back in place before any of the guards spotted us. When the wall was in place, she rested her forehead against it and let out a deep breath. "The gods, I hate this place," she whispered, although the acoustics of where we were allowed me to hear her easily.

"You're more than welcome to go back out there if you like," I said, trying to make a joke of it, but as she turned and I saw her face, I knew that she had taken me seriously. "Just a joke. You're not going back out there; you're definitely not getting sent out to deal with the guards. We carry on with the plan, just as we agreed."

Zoe's expression softened, and she nodded as if in agreement.

"Any chance I can get a runner message to my friends to let them know I'm in the city okay?" I asked.

Zoe nodded. "I can sort that out for you."

Runners ran from city to city, delivering messages, post, whatever was needed. They were a mixture of the post office, security guards, and stagecoach workers, with offices throughout the city. It was a dangerous job, and more than a few had stories they could tell about bandits, marauders, or the wealth of dangerous creatures that lived in the rift. But it also paid exceptionally well, and the people who did it usually loved it, as they enjoyed being away from the city and seeing what the rift had to offer. A lot of them were also exceptionally loyal to those who ran Inaxia. As people are wont to do when someone makes them rich.

"Come on," Zoe said, pointing off into the distance of the sewer system. "Anyone you pass down here, you leave alone. No one in their right mind ever decided to want to work down here; most of them are just trying to do their day-to-day, to make money for whoever it is they owe. But some of the people who come to the rift are sent down here because they're too dangerous to stay up there or to have roaming the wilds."

"I know," I said. "I lived in the rift for a long time; I worked here too. For Neb, mostly. The tales of some of the people who work beneath the capital city are not pleasant ones."

When you come to the rift for the first time, having died as a human, your past is forgotten. At least in principle. Some of the people who arrive in the rift were the kinds of people who hunted humanity when they counted among its number. Serial killers, deviants, the worst of the worst, except now they had powers and were practically immortal. Not the kind of people you want to let loose on a whole new group of unsuspecting rift-fused. Most of them are dealt with quickly and quietly, sometimes by people like me. However, sometimes those people were too important to just dispose of and so were given jobs out of the way, drugged or chained, kept in place somehow, allowed to fester in their hate and need to prey on those weaker than them. The sewers beneath the city of Inaxia had long since been known as a place you do not go at night by yourself, or even during the day by yourself, and if you do have to, you let someone know where you're going. The people under the city might be chained or drugged, but they're still dangerous.

"Who are you?" Zoe asked after several minutes of getting used to the odours that accompanied our sojourn, as we walked among the pipes and noises of the sewer system. Occasionally hearing the noise of something or someone it would be best to avoid.

"I'm just someone who needs to make sure that people are safe," I told her. "How did you come to work for Cortez?"

"He's my uncle," Zoe said. "Not literal uncle, but we are related by blood. He's the brother of my mum's grandfather. So I think that's a great-uncle, it sounds like that kind of area. Mostly, I just call him Cortez. How do you know the Queen?"

"Neb introduced us," I told her as I ducked under a large green pipe, which had steam coming out of it.

Zoe stopped and looked back at me. "You know Neb?"

I smiled and nodded. "A little, yes."

Zoe's eyes narrowed as she tried to figure out if she'd heard about me. They opened wide. I figured she had remembered something.

"You are the ex-Raven," she said. "The Talon. The Queen said that you saved her life."

"I guess you could call it that," I told her. "Although I'm pretty sure it was a mutual saving."

"Interesting," Zoe said, continuing on her walk. "Very interesting."

"How do you figure that?" I asked, avoiding several more steaming pipes; it was a maze of unpleasantness beneath the city.

"Cortez told me about an ex-Raven who saved the Queen," Zoe said. "Said you burst into the city and fought two dozen men to get to her."

I chuckled. "That might be an exaggeration."

"The Queen said you were an exceptionally dangerous man," Zoe told me. "Is that something I need to worry about?"

"I don't know," I said. "Is Cortez in the habit of doing things that might piss off dangerous people?"

Zoe looked back this time. "He's not, but I may not deal well with figures of authority. And there may be a few people who work for him who may not be very happy with a Guild member turning up to our house. To some, the Guilds are a little more than an extension of the guards who live in Inaxia."

"The Guilds are gone," I told her. "They were killed, betrayed by their own people. You might not like them all, but there were good people who worked with the Guilds. They didn't deserve to die; they didn't deserve to be betrayed."

"And you're here to hunt them down and bring them to justice?" Zoe asked.

"No," I said. "I'm here to make sure more innocent people don't die."

Zoe stopped and looked back at me. "I figured you'd want justice or vengeance. You were a Guild member."

"I'd like nothing better than to hunt down everyone involved and send them to their deaths," I admitted. "But, right now, that only helps me. What I want isn't really why I'm here. This is Callie Mitchell's show, and the sooner I can get off it and figure out how to stop her, the better."

CHAPTER FIFTEEN

The sewers of Inaxia were a maze, and I got the impression that they were difficult to navigate, even for someone who had lived and worked within the city. I would have quickly gotten lost if not for Zoe's help. She moved quickly and quietly, avoiding the steam-hissing pipes and only occasionally needing to stop to consider which path she needed to take next. I was exceptionally grateful for the map that sat in my pocket.

We walked by people I knew not to stop and linger near, not out of fear for myself or for Zoe but because the look in their eyes suggested that if I knew the kind of things these people had done, I may have had to deal with them on a permanent basis. I was never of the opinion that who you had been in life made a damn difference when you got to the rift, but there was a limit to that. Some people didn't deserve a second chance; some people didn't deserve a life within the rift, even a piss-poor one.

"Do you happen to have a plan for when we get up to the city itself?" Zoe asked without looking back.

"We're going to go to a bar called the Human Head," I told her. "It's run by a revenant by the name of Roseline Vincent. I've known her a really long time, and as I told Cortez, that is where I'm going to take you and leave you. Do you know it?" I hoped that Necia Torres might also be there. Necia had been a friend of mine, and sometimes more, for many decades, and if there were two people in Inaxia I trusted, it was Roseline and Necia.

Zoe nodded. "I've known Roseline for a while. She's done some work for Cortez over the years, helping information get in and out of the city under the noses of everybody. I trust her, and she can get word to Cortez that I am fine before I make an attempt to get back out of the city again."

"Is it far from here?" I asked, not wanting to get the map out when I was concentrating on where I was putting my feet. All of the corridors were beginning to look the same.

There was a clang somewhere behind us, impossible to tell, considering how claustrophobic the sewer area felt at this point. Zoe immediately stopped walking. She turned to me, a finger against her lips, and stood still for several seconds.

Zoe visibly relaxed and motioned for us to continue, but we heard from somewhere in the darkness of the sewers, "They went this way." The voice was deep and seemed to reverberate around us as footsteps began to reach us, each one like a drum of war.

"Guards," Zoe whispered. "At least two."

There was no point in asking if she was sure; the expression on her face said everything.

"Hurry," she whispered as we set off once more, albeit at a quicker pace.

We stopped twice more in the fifteen minutes before we reached the exit, and both times, we heard people behind us. The footsteps were faster, more pronounced, and after both stops, Zoe hurried us along faster. We were being pursued. *Hunted.*

We reached the exit, which was hidden behind a stretch of wall in a dark alley somewhere off the beaten path of the city. I took a moment to relish the fresh air before Zoe pushed me away from the sewer exit, farther down the alley, and behind a brick wall.

The three guards we'd seen earlier exited the sewer a few minutes later; they all looked tired, as if they'd been running.

"You two stay here," the largest of the three guards said. "I'll go report this. We can't be having anyone using the sewers as a way in and out of the city."

"Move," Zoe said as the guards raised their lamps to illuminate more of their surroundings.

We continued on through the darkness of the city, avoiding the occasional guard patrol. Investigators didn't control the city, so we were unlikely to bump into any unless they were out already working on a different case.

We reached the Human Head in better time than I thought we would, and I rapped on the door twice, receiving no reply. I tried the handle, but it was locked, and no lights were on inside the establishment.

"That's a little strange," Zoe said looking up and down the street, as if expecting trouble at any moment.

I said nothing; there was no need to give voice to the concern that I felt. Instead, I walked down the alleyway and looked over the fence at the rear of the property, and found that it too was dark. If there was anyone in the building, they weren't using any light sources.

I went back to Zoe and told her what I had found. "Right, what's the plan?" I asked.

"I can't risk the sewers," Zoe said. "There don't seem to be many guards out and about, which means that they're probably on the gates. I'd rather not chance it. I'm considering breaking into the bar to wait for Roseline to return, but I don't think she would be all that happy to come back and find me sat having a nice drink. Or I go with you. And I'm going to assume that the last one is out of the question."

"I considered it," I told her. "I don't think Cortez would be at all happy with me if I brought you along. And I don't know what's going to happen when I get there; there's a chance that when I get up to the Primes, one of them tries to have me arrested. Or Callie's people jump me before I can get there. In theory, I have time before I'm meant to find her, but once she knows I'm here, she's likely to try and find me instead. It's very strange that Roseline isn't here. It is late, but I expected her to still be in her bar. Maybe she's off having a date, or just seeing friends or something. You're right; she would not like you to break in and wait for her here."

"The Eastgate isn't too far from here," Zoe said glancing down the dark road in the direction of the side gate. "How about we go and see how difficult it would be for me to get out, and we go from there?"

I was on a timer. I wanted to be able to find the three Ancients and talk to them before Callie got hold of me, although I knew it was going to be unlikely. The likelihood was that Callie's people were already aware I was there, although I had no idea how. Even so, get to the Prime residences and go from there. Hope for the best, plan for the worst. Although, in this case, they weren't that dissimilar.

"Let's go check the gate," I said. "You're an adult and I'm going to assume more than capable of taking care of yourself, but I told Cortez you wouldn't get in trouble, and I get the feeling he's going to hold me to that promise."

We set off at a jog along the streets of Inaxia as the majority of its populace slept or were out trying to ensure that they weren't noticed themselves. It meant that the journey was without incident, even when we had to occasionally wait for a patrol to pass.

The Eastgate was, frankly, a nightmare. There were, at a best guess, fifty guards all within the city limits. The number of people trying to get in or out of the city at this time of night was small, on account of the fact that travelling through the surrounding lands at night was not good for your long-term health without preparations.

Zoe and I found a good vantage spot behind a wall a few hundred feet away from the gate; it gave us a good view of the guards as they walked around the area. But more importantly, it gave an excellent view of the gate itself, and there was no way anyone was slipping out of there without being noticed.

"I could try to get back through the sewers," Zoe said with a grimace.

"You said you couldn't risk them," I pointed out.

"My only options appear to be bad ones," she said. "At least I know my way around the sewers."

"I don't think that's a particularly wise idea," I said.

Even without the guards now being aware of it as an entrance point to the city, I'd noticed how some of the people we passed down there looked at the pair of us. I saw the decision-making process in the eyes of a few of them—they knew they might be able to take one of us but not two. At least one of those people had a hunger on their face that sent a cold shiver up my spine. It didn't matter so much that Zoe was female or small as much as it mattered that she was alone. If she had retraced her steps through the sewers to get out, I was fairly certain she would've had to leave bodies behind. And that was a complication neither of us wanted.

"I think it best if you come with me," I said. "Although we also need to get word to Cortez that you are okay. Something that Roseline would've been able to do in her bar. You suggested we can find a runner to do it quickly. I assume you know one on the way. And besides, it's not like you're going to be out getting into fights with the guard of the city."

"Let's go," Zoe said.

I followed Zoe back along the way we'd walked only a few minutes earlier, cutting through alleyways, some of which I didn't even know were there until we started walking down them. Eventually, we arrived at a runners' station that was open.

I stepped away and kept watch as Zoe spoke to the hooded individual inside the small wooden hut. It took only a few moments before Zoe returned.

"All done," she told me, with a slap on my shoulder. "I asked if they could get me out, too, but the price was higher than I was willing to pay."

A cloaked figure emerged from the back of the hut and set off through the city at a high pace. They would need to go through one of the gates, but they were a runner and there was no guard who wanted to remain a guard who would dare to stop them.

"I hope you've got some weapons on you," I said, suddenly wishing I'd brought my spear.

Zoe lifted her shirt slightly, revealing the two daggers which sat at the top of her thighs and the throwing knives which sat on either side of them. "I'll be okay."

We made good time as we ran through the city, moving from circle to circle, until we reached the bottom of the hill that led up to where the Primes lived and worked, called the shield. There would be a greater number of guards as well as Prime Soldiers, the personal bodyguard of the Primes.

"We don't kill anybody unless we have to," I said, looking up the hill and trying to figure out the best way of getting up it without being exposed for several hundred feet.

"I wasn't planning on killing anybody," Zoe said.

I looked back at Zoe and wondered just how many times she'd been in a fight. I assumed that she had been in battle at some point; she was a riftborn and the likelihood was high. "If this all goes very badly, are you going to be able to defend yourself?"

"These knives aren't just for show."

"Just making sure. I never asked, but what is it that you can do?"

Zoe shimmered slightly before a second identical Zoe appeared next to her. "This," she said, nodding to the Zoe beside her.

"Nice to meet you," the second Zoe said.

"She moves mostly independently of me," Zoe said. "I give mental commands, and second Zoe follows them. Everything I have on me, she has on her. The knives on her waist aren't for show, either."

I looked between the two Zoes. "Wow. It's nice to have another pair of hands watching our backs."

"We should really get going," Zoe said as the shimmering began again and the second Zoe disappeared. "She doesn't stick around long."

We hurried up the hill toward the shield, a train line high above us, casting shadows over us which I hoped might help conceal us for as long as possible. Trains were a necessary part of life in Inaxia, and they were used to move both people and goods between circles. Powered by rift energy, they had a faint blue glow to them even after they were shut down for the night.

We got to the top of the hill without incident and moved through the outer rings of the shield until we reached the entrance, which gave the appearance of ancient Greece, with large pillars and several murals on walls painted in the style that would have been found in ancient Greece itself.

"Which Prime are we going to see?" Zoe asked.

"Roberts," I said. "I know he's still alive. I dislike him, and I figure if anyone has their finger in an illegal pie, it will be him. Besides, I already know he hates me, but I also know he doesn't want to lose the power he has here. I figure go knock on his door, get him to take me to Neb and the others, and explain that we don't have long before Callie tries to take over the city. I know he won't be working for her—she wants him dead almost as much as I do. If she hasn't already started."

"The place does feel off," Zoe said as we continued through the shield.

The plateau of the shield contained eight plots of land, each one separated by a six-foot-high stone wall. Each plot of land contained a mansion belonging to a different Prime and their most trusted followers. The colours of each Prime adorned a flag that was placed outside of each house. Prime Roberts, our first port of call, had a flag that was white and blue. The centre of the area, between all of the mansions, was adorned with large willow-like trees and colourful flowers.

The eighth house had been empty the last time I'd been in the city, used by the Ancients who had helped rule Inaxia. With another two murders, it meant three houses were now empty; black silk drapes lay over the doors and windows in what appeared to me to be an effort to be as ostentatious as possible. I was sure the Primes would find some way to fill them. Probably to their advantage.

I found it strange how few soldiers and guards there were up at such an important place within the city. The last time I had been there, the whole area had been awash with guards and soldiers. I motioned for Zoe to stop, and crouched beside the trunk of an exceptionally large tree.

"What's wrong?" she asked, her eyes darting around the area, expecting trouble.

"Nothing," I said. "And that is the problem. There are no guards up here. We have seen no evidence of anyone dealing with the security of such an important place. This is too easy. I do not like easy."

I searched each of the houses in turn, noticing that of the five surviving Primes, lights were only on in the homes of three. That itself wasn't necessarily a reason to be concerned, but something felt very wrong.

Zoe obviously shared my concerns, looking around suspiciously. "Well, we've made it this far," she said. "Do you want to go back?"

"No," I said. "If Neb, Timo, and Attia are all here, talking to the Primes and trying to figure out how to keep this place safe, it's possible they've taken the guards inside the buildings, keeping them close for safety. But still, something feels off here."

"Callie could have made a move before she said she would," Zoe said.

"That's my assumption," I told her. "But we're here now and something really weird is happening. I don't know what it is, and I don't like it, but I came here for a reason, and I'm not leaving without knowing what happened to Neb and Timo."

We continued on in silence, leaving the protection of the shadows afforded by the trees and bushes, and vaulted over the fence outside of Prime Roberts's property. Making as little noise as possible, we hurried to the side of the mansion, stopping to look through windows into empty rooms, until we reached the rear of the property, where voices could be heard.

I paused and reached out to tap Zoe on the shoulder; she stopped moving and turned back to me, a question on her face.

"I need you to stay out here," I whispered. "Before you argue—when I go in there, if something goes wrong, you need to get back to Drusilla and Zeke as quickly as possible and let them know what's going on."

"What about the guards?" Zoe asked.

"If it all goes to shit in there, staying hidden from the guards isn't going to matter anymore," I said. "Just get out of here as quickly as possible, and get back to Cortez and my people. Leave me here; whatever's happening, I'll be fine."

Zoe stared at me for several seconds before nodding once. "I will," she whispered. "How are you going to let me know if it all goes to shit?"

"You'll know," I told her. "Just stay out of sight."

Another nod.

I pointed to the garden at the rear of the property, where there were large bushes and more trees offering shade and shadows to hide within.

Zoe nodded that she understood and set off in that direction, keeping low and out of any light which spilled from the windows of the mansion beside us.

I waited for her to get some distance before I continued on around to the rear of the property, where I could see Attia sat inside what appeared to be a large study. I resisted the temptation to break the door down or turn to smoke and blow through the cracks, in case doing so might set off an alarm of some description. Instead, I tapped lightly on the glass pane of the door, but Attia didn't look up.

She was tied to the chair, and I saw bruising and blood around her mouth and nose. Her head lolled forward, and I forced myself to move farther along and check the room beside it. Attia would probably have been livid if I had broken into rescue her only to bring down an entire army of guards on our heads.

An open window farther along the house was an easy access for me to gain entry into a library after turning to smoke and blowing through the inch-wide gap before re-forming on the other side.

Once inside the house, I remained still, listening out for any impending attack that might be coming my way. When nothing happened, I moved quietly to the thick wooden door, which practically shone from its impressive amount of varnishing.

I pushed the door open and peered into the empty hallway beyond. There were several pieces of art on the walls, all of which depicted

Prime Roberts in various periods throughout history. Each one had him depicted in a commanding pose, including one of him atop a burning ship at the Battle of Trafalgar according to the little brass plaque below. Though I was pretty sure he hadn't been there.

I moved quietly along the hallway, coming to the door behind where Attia was. I tried the door, expecting to find it locked, and was surprised and more than a little wary that it opened without pause. I stepped inside the room, closing the door behind me, making sure that it was as quiet as possible when it clicked shut.

The study had the smell of blood in the air, and as I made my way over to Attia, I saw that her throat had been cut and she'd been stabbed in the heart. Her blood drenched her entire body, along with the floor beneath where she sat.

I scrambled back, trying to get my bearings, making it to the desk before the door opened and the masked man from Noah's compound stepped inside, dragging the dead body of Prime Roberts behind him by one foot. The Prime was topless, showing a plethora of bruises and cuts, and his throat was slit from ear to ear. A dagger, the handle in the shape of a dragon, protruded from his heart. I grabbed the office chair beside me and threw it through the window, smashing it totally, hoping it was enough of a signal for Zoe to run like hell.

CHAPTER SIXTEEN

The man I'd last seen in Noah's compound wore the same dark, unmarked mask that he had worn then. He strolled over to the body of Prime Roberts, grabbed the dead man by his hair, and tore his head clean off his body, tossing it toward me.

"That was unnecessary," I said.

The unknown man laughed. "Your weapons. On the table. Now."

"Absolutely go fuck yourself," I told him. "You'll find me a harder time than Prime Roberts."

"You do as you're told, or Neb dies," the man said, his voice filled with little more than hate at the name of my old mentor.

I considered whether or not to just keep the weapons and make him take them, but I got the feeling he was acting under orders—and if Callie wanted to talk to me, she wanted me alive—for now. If he was telling the truth, I wasn't going to gamble with Neb's life, and if he wasn't, well . . . he would find I didn't need any weapons to kill him. I removed the belt of throwing knives and my still-sheathed dagger, and placed them on the table beside me.

"So, is this the part where we fight?" I asked, looking around as I stepped back and the masked man picked up the dagger. "Or is this the part where you tell me where Timo and Neb are?"

The man's laughter increased.

"Where are Neb and Timo?" My words were clipped and full of anger.

"You should be more worried about yourself. I watched you and your little helper as you moved through the city. We had to install a curfew, you know? We knew you would come. We didn't know what day exactly. It was difficult to install the curfew over several weeks, but as soon as Neb arrived to investigate the Primes, I knew you would come." He gestured toward the body of Prime Roberts, which he casually pushed to the floor before dragging the chair across the floor and placing it a few feet from me.

"Am I supposed to sit?" I asked.

"That's not for you," the man said, taking a seat. He was completely confident in his ability to remain alive in my presence. The arrogance almost made me show him how wrong he was, but I held back. "I suggested we just kill you, Timo, and Neb. Murder all of you and dump your bodies in the river. Let the crabs and fish feast upon your corpses."

"But you are not in charge, are you?" I said with a sneer. "Your judgement was overridden. I bet that stings."

"I am perfectly happy with my position in life," the man told me as he stood and walked to the door that I'd entered through what felt like a lifetime before. "I got my way with killing Attia, though, and Prime Roberts. I assume that has your attention."

It took an awful lot of effort not to look down at the head of the man that used to be Prime Roberts. "I should let you know something," I said. "If you have hurt Neb or Timo, there's nowhere in the rift or Earth that you can hide where I won't find you."

The man's laughter boomed around the room, even with his mouth behind the mask. "You don't even know who I am."

"I'm making a wild guess . . . Hesansh," I said. It was the only thing that made sense—the only Ancient who had rejected coming to the conclave—and was known for his brash and egotistical nature. The power coming off him meant Ancient—and, as there were a limited number left, it was the only plausible option.

The man pulled his mask free and threw it across the room with enough force that it hit the side wall and smashed into a hundred pieces. He snarled, his face bestial, more animalistic than I had anticipated.

His eyes looked as though they belonged to a wolf, his hair long and flowing, falling over broad shoulders, his beard bushy and full, touching his chest.

"How did you know?" Hesansh asked with a crooked smile.

"There are only so many Ancients left," I said, rolling my eyes. "And there needed to be someone with considerable power helping. I figured that one of the Ancients was behind it all, but you're too stupid to be the one in charge. You are a blunt object, and Callie is the scalpel."

Hesansh laughed once again. "You are not as smart as you think you are."

"And you need to tell me what I'm supposed to be doing," I said, looking around the room without taking my eyes off the Ancient in front of me. "You killed your brothers and sisters. I assume you have Neb and Timo. Two Ancients who are meant to be your allies, if I needed to remind you of such things. You killed a Prime and Ancient here, and you have installed some sort of curfew throughout the city in the aim of capturing me. Although I don't think that last part is quite true, is it? I think you installed the curfew for other reasons. Me being here, that's just a little bonus."

"Callie didn't trust that you'd turn yourself in," Hesansh said. "So, she had eyes on every gate. You weren't meant to creep through; you were meant to be captured, then brought here. She doesn't like unpredictable behaviour."

"She's just going to have to learn to live with it, I guess," I said. "Where are the rest of the Primes?"

"You think we just killed Roberts?" Hesansh asked with a laugh.

"You killed them all?" I asked, hoping I was wrong.

"All who wouldn't adapt to the new order of things," Hesansh said. "Their Prime Soldiers were slaughtered like cattle. After the first few Primes, the rest became more interested in working with us. They are being re-educated at the moment."

"Tortured?" I asked.

Hesansh laughed. "No, they have agreed to work with us. They just need to understand what that means."

"And what does it mean?"

"We're going to go to the throne room," Hesansh said with a predatory grin. "Once there, you will see that Neb and Timo are both alive and well. You will answer questions asked to you, or they will not be. You will die last, bathed in the blood of your friends, and when we're done, I will find everyone who helped you, and I'll burn them alive."

"You will try," I said softly.

Hesansh motioned for me to leave the room, which I did without making comment. I felt completely safe with the Ancient behind me; he was obviously on a very short leash, and I wondered what Callie had offered him—or what hold she had over him, to keep him under such tight control. He was, at best, a moron, but that didn't mean he wasn't also a savage weapon used to kill and terrify in equal measure.

"I'd heard you were drinking yourself to death," I said as we walked down the hallway I'd taken not long ago. "I guess it takes a really long time for someone such as yourself to achieve it."

"My brothers and sisters used me as the blunt weapon of the Ancients," Hesansh said from beside me, his anger leaking into his words. "For thousands of years, I was only ever used to kill and destroy. It's what I was good at. Waging war, destroying all that stood in our way. I killed more than my fair share for Neb; I assume she never mentioned *that* to you. Or the fact that she used my talents to keep people quiet, to ensure compliance. She is not the figure of heroics you might believe she is."

I tried very hard not to laugh. "I've known for a long time what Neb really is. There is very little that she has done that would shock me. There is very little that I haven't done for her."

"Ah, yes," Hesansh said with distain. "Neb's little assassin. Or are you more her fixer? The person who she calls when there is a problem, no matter what that problem is, and she doesn't want to get her hands dirty. I used to play that role before you were born, boy. Except I did it for all of the Ancients. And they feared me so much that they insured I would spend centuries drinking and whoring myself into oblivion."

"Oh, cry me a river," I told him. "You had choices. You could have refused. But, let's face it, you *enjoyed* it. So don't give me that 'woe is me' crap."

Hesansh snarled and pushed me into the large throne-room doors before me, revealing the expensive throne room beyond. At the far end, placed in front of a huge stained-glass window, was a dais, upon which sat an ostentatious throne of dark wood and gold. It was the exact kind of throne I would expect Prime Roberts to own.

Timo knelt at its base; she had two masked assassins stood bracketing her, one of which held a blade against her throat. More masked men and women stood guard around the room, several of them with Guild medallions hanging around their necks. I spotted Hawk and Eagle Guild medallions, next to three people with Viper Guild medallions. Traitors. Murderers. If I had my way, they would all know what it was like to be hunted and afraid.

Sat on the throne, her legs dangling over one armrest, eating from a bowl of fruit that was on the table next to the throne, was Callie Mitchell. She wore a large, red, jewelled necklace around her neck, and matching bracelets on each wrist. They looked to be something akin to rubies, but the red was darker than I would have expected . . . It took me a moment to remember that she had taken Ahiram's blood when she'd killed him, and I really hoped they weren't made from what I thought they were made from. She waved to me.

"Well, it's good to see that you're enjoying the festivities," I said as I was marched in front of Callie and forced to kneel next to Timo. "I can't imagine why you need answers from me about anything. Don't you already know everything?"

Callie swung her legs back over the throne so that she was sitting properly; she placed the bowl of fruit back on the table and leaned forward toward me. "It has been too long," she said, her voice soft and inviting, as if she were talking to an old lover that she had not seen in some time.

"Not long enough," I told her.

Callie's laugh was silky, and I wondered just how far gone she now was. She had always been unbalanced, but touching the rift had left her completely insane.

"How long since you decided all the Ancients had to die?" I asked.

"Ah, I've wanted that for a long time," she said, tapping the side of her nose like she was revealing some grand secret. "Couldn't do it before I was reborn. Not enough power. Couldn't do it when the Tempest had control of me; it had its own agenda. But I've managed to wrest control of my mind back." She grinned at me conspiratorially and I saw the determination and drive of the woman I'd known before she had gone into the Tempest. But whatever was left of her was mixed with something else, something *unpredictable and dangerous.* "And now that I'm my own woman again, Lucas, I see so much. So very much. And the Ancients *have* to die."

"How'd you get the big dumb idiot to agree to that?" I asked, pointing my thumb in Hesansh's direction. "He's going to die too when he loses his link."

"He knows," Callie said. "He just doesn't care."

"I thought you were going to wait," I said. "That was what you sent Christopher to tell me. That if I came to Inaxia, you wouldn't hurt anyone."

"I lied," she said as she snorted gleefully, throwing herself back into the throne.

"Why?"

"I know something you don't know," Callie almost sang, followed by a laugh.

"I'm not entirely certain that that's how questioning your prisoner works," I said, looking over to my right at Timo, who, apart from a swollen black eye and split lip, appeared to be in reasonable health. She forced a smile, showing bloody gums.

Callie waved in her direction, as if giving her permission to speak.

"They put two shitty little devices on a necklace around my neck," Timo said, glancing up at Callie before continuing. "One cuts me off from the rift. The other makes me slower, like those little devices in the helicopter. It's like a bubble that Callie has control over. I can see everything outside of the bubble happen in real time, but inside it, I move so slowly."

"We found a few of those devices at Noah's, too," I said. "They stopped us from using our power to fight back against the attackers."

"And now Noah is dead," Callie said cheerfully with a wave of her hand toward Timo. "And that's the end of that chat."

"They didn't stop me from killing a bunch of them, though," I told her. "Where's Neb?"

"She is safe," Callie said. "Probably safer than anyone else you know."

"What does that mean?"

Callie motioned turning a key in front of her lips.

"I'm not interested in games," I snapped. It took a lot not to dive toward Callie and get retribution for all she had caused. Instead, I took a deep breath and let it out slowly.

Callie's expression turned to one of irritation. "If you're not going to play this game, then what is the use of you being here? What is the use of me keeping your friend here? I'm a very busy woman, and frankly, you should be happy that I have decided to take some time to see you."

"I think maybe having all that knowledge inside of you has melted your brain. You're the one who wanted me here. So, what did you want? I have things to do myself . . . including killing that lumbering dolt over there," I said, gesturing to Hesansh, who took a few steps toward me before smashing me in the back of the head with his fist. I assume it was his fist; it might have been a car. It's hard to tell when you're lying on the floor, blinking through the darkness that starts to swim in your vision as you try to figure out where you are.

Callie glared at Hesansh. "We do not damage my guests," she hissed at him. And he took a reluctant step back, glaring at me the whole time.

I lifted myself up from the marble floor and spat a glob of blood onto the ground. "You have tried to murder me several times at this point. You have tried to murder people I care about probably more times than that. You have murdered people I care about. You sent your thugs to kill Noah and his people, you have kidnapped Timo and Neb, you had your people kill so many Guild members, and Ancients, and innocent people. And for what? What is all this death and destruction actually achieving?"

Callie looked at me for a moment, and I could see her mentally turning things over in whatever was left of her mind; she obviously wanted to share, in some weird Machiavellian villainess way. "I may have suggested to other people that they needed to arrange those things to happen. I facilitated the possibility of a better world, and other people decided that I was correct. The only person I have actually killed with my own hands was Ahiram. And he deserved to die. Although I would admit that his death has set all of this in motion. And I will also admit that I knew it would happen, that I wanted it to happen."

Callie and I maintained a hard stare for several seconds.

"I will also admit, then," Callie began, "that I am responsible, in a way, for all of this happening; I'm just not responsible for individual actions. An architect isn't responsible for what happens inside their buildings."

"Everything that has happened over the last few days is only taking me further and further away from making decisions of my own," I said. "I've been running around, putting out fires that you created. And for every fire I extinguish, or at least temper, you light another one. I want to know why. Why are you playing these games? If you want to control the rift, or you just want to kill all of the Ancients, then why not do it?"

Callie leaned in close to me and whispered. "Because I need you to be here."

I held her gaze as she leaned back. "What does that even mean?"

Callie's smile made me feel as if something was crawling up my spine. "I need you to be here, because you coming here means you never leave, and you never leaving means I win."

CHAPTER SEVENTEEN

I f anyone would like to explain what the fuck you mean, that would
be great," I said, looking around the room.

"I told you the last time I saw you that I could see like your chained
revenant friend could," Callie said. "That I could see the chains of the rift."

"Are you telling me that you saw my future, and my future ends
with me coming to this city?" I asked. "That everything that has happened over the last few days has been designed to get me here so that
you can . . . win?"

Callie shrugged. "Not exactly. The Ancients all needed to die. And
they will. Even those who work with me."

"So, I have to stay in this city and all of the Ancients are going to
die." I looked over at Hesansh, who was staring at me with something
close to outright hostility. "And what is the plan here? I'm assuming
I'm here because you want to tell me what the plan is, because you
always were someone who needed everybody else to know how smart
you are. So, what's happening, Callie? What's your long-term goal here,
apart from the deaths of a lot of people?"

Callie got off of the throne and sat beside me. "Can I tell you a
story?" she asked as if I were a five-year-old child.

"Sure," I said, considering it wasn't like I had any choice.

"A long time ago, I was exiled to Earth when the Blessed were
stopped from carrying out their plan," Callie said, telling me things I

already knew. "The other members of the Blessed, the other practitioners, wanted more than anything else to be accepted, to have a role in the rift that didn't make them second-class citizens. They believed that the best way to do that was to overthrow the Primes and stake out a new world for themselves. It was horseshit."

I looked over at Timo and then back to Callie. "You had a better plan?" I asked with a shrug.

Callie cuffed me around the head. "Don't interrupt. Anyway, my plan was somewhat different. You see I wanted to *understand* the riftborn, the revenants, and the rift itself, but more than anything, I wanted to make us *free*. And you know when I found? That the Ancients had been lying to us for a long time. They portray themselves as the bastions of this place, as those who were gifted the power of the rift so that they might go forth and claim the rift for themselves. And the whole thing was a giant fucking lie. That is what I found out, Lucas. That your precious Neb and Timo lied to us all."

I stared at Callie for a moment.

"You may ask the question I know you have," Callie told me.

"Hesansh is right there," I said. "He lied too, so why isn't he dead?"

"Mostly because he is helpful to me, I need him for now," Callie said. "It's why Neb is alive, by the way. They are linked, and I can't have Neb die without losing a valuable ally in the process."

"Where is she?" I asked.

Callie cuffed me again, harder this time, making my ears ring in the process. "I am not done telling my tale. I assume you would like to know what the lie is. But before we get to it, I'm going to tell you what I told all of those Guild members who I got to join me so many decades ago, just waiting for their time to make the rift a better place. I set them free. Without the Ancients, the rift would be a better place; they took something that did not belong to them."

I nodded. "Yeah, yeah, I've heard—they took power from the rift—"

"I'm aware I've told you this before," Callie said, interrupting me. "Or possibly a version of it. Essentially, the Ancients took the power of the rift from the Tempest. They have used it to ensure their place in society. There used to be more of them, you know. And then they started dying, and there were wars; obviously, you know all of this. But what you don't know is that the Ancients didn't just accidentally take the power of the rift. They literally *stole* it.

"When the Tempest resurrected me, I saw what happened; I saw how they took this power. And the Tempest wanted that power back more than anything else, and from that moment, all I knew was that I had to allow the Tempest to reclaim their power. That the rift would never be right until it had. And with every single death of an Ancient, that power goes back into the rift. Except it doesn't."

"I don't understand," I said, risking another wallop.

Callie smiled instead. "I know you don't. You're not that much smarter than the lump of man meat in the corner. You see, because I was linked to the Tempest, because it resurrected me, the Tempest couldn't sever that link. So, I retained a large portion of the power it gifted me, even though my more human mind has gone back to what it once was, or an approximation of it. I am close to the Callie of old, although obviously you've seen yourself that I have little moments where my brain doesn't work as I would wish it to. Think that is a byproduct of me being able to see all of the chains. I honestly don't know how your chain revenant friend isn't a blabbering wreck.

"Every single time an Ancient dies, the power should go back to the rift. But while I was connected to the Tempest, I discovered a way to stop that, to take all of that power for myself and use it in a way that will actually benefit the people of the rift. With the Ancients, despite their own connection to the rift, the power only goes one way: from the rift to them. My resurrection and my subsequent murder of Ahiram allowed me to take his blood. You were there when that happened. I used that blood to tap into his connection to the rift. It was an odd sensation, to be able to see who he was connected to, to be able to see the past, to understand how when the Ancients took the power, it was done in such a way to ensure the Tempest could not reclaim it whilst they lived. The Tempest knew it needed that power back, and I knew I needed that power for myself."

"So, it cut you off," I said.

"It did," Callie said through gritted teeth. "I should have been the *herald* of a new age, and it decided I wasn't worthy."

"All of this is for more power for yourself?" I asked, shaking my head. "That's all this is about?"

"No, of course not," Callie snapped. "As I said, I theorised a way in which I could kill an Ancient and have their power become my power. It wasn't simple to do, and it required me to use the power the Tempest had given me in a way I don't think it had expected. I plan to claim the power that the Ancients stole, and use it to fix the rift. I'm going to make this place better. The Ancients squandered their power with petty bickering and unnecessary war; the more power I claim, the better. And when I am done, I plan on taking control of the Tempest and using that power to reshape the rift. To make sure that there are no second-class citizens. To make sure that the links between the rift and Earth are controlled by someone who knows what they are doing."

"I assume that means you," I said. "Your jewellery is made from the blood of an Ancient. Ahiram, to be exact."

Callie looked down as if seeing the bracelets and necklace for the first time. "Oh, yes, I forgot to mention these. They're pretty, aren't they? They're made from a mixture of his blood and the frozen waters around the prison. You remember that stuff, yes? It was meant to kill anyone who stepped into it, but because you've been touched by the rift, it had a slightly different effect on you."

I nodded that I remembered. "The water was pure rift energy; it healed me."

Callie nodded. "Do you want to take a guess at what these do?"

"They somehow connect you to the rift so you don't need the Tempest," I guessed. "Although, if the Tempest kicked you out, I don't know how it wouldn't realise. So, that means it's not the Tempest; it's something else. It's another source of power."

"That's almost right," Callie said, speaking as if I were a small child who got a question right at school. "They let me absorb rift energy. When an Ancient dies, their power flows back into me instead of going to the rift. Works with anyone with rift energy inside of them, so everyone in the rift, but the Ancients are much more powerful. Took a long time to get this working. Has the added benefit that while I'm wearing it, those lovely devices I made don't work on me. There's just too much rift energy inside of me for them to have much of an effect."

"How exciting for you," I said. "You've made jewellery that lets you absorb the souls of dead Ancients. Wait, if you're absorbing that power, it's not going to the rift. It's not healing; it's going to make things worse."

Callie smiled. "Short-term pain for long-term gain."

"You're going to kill people on Earth," I said. "Here, too."

"Oh, well," Callie said, with a dismissive flick of her wrist.

"So, you just absorb the power of the Ancients," I said, "and then what? What do you plan to do with all of that power?"

Callie smiled. It was an unpleasant gesture. "If you live long enough to see it, I assure you it's going to be amazing."

"You're going to use that power to do what? Take over the rift? Earth? Become a god?" I asked, raising my voice. "You're usually so chatty about how clever you are; what's stopping you this time?"

Callie's smile wavered. "This has been a pleasure. However, I really do think you need to understand just what the Ancients actually did. Do you know?"

I stared at Callie Mitchell, the woman who never really cared about who she hurt so long as she won.

"I asked you a question," Callie snapped.

"Timo told me," I said looking over at my friend. "They went into the Tempest, and none of them could remember what happened, but when they left, they were linked to it, linked to one another."

Callie got to her feet and jabbed a finger in Timo's direction before taking her seat on the throne. "These *Ancients* gave themselves the names of honourable birds, when in reality they are just scavengers. A murder of crows. No, that's not right; they should have called themselves the rats. Or cockroaches. For that is what they did; that is why Timo is kneeling beside you, a dagger at her throat. That is why I hunted them down and executed them. They took their power through murder, through theft, and I will bring about their ruin."

I didn't bother pointing out that Callie was doing the exact thing she was accusing the Ancients of doing. Instead, I glanced over at Timo, to see only regret in her eyes, which shook me more than anything else I had seen so far tonight. Whatever Callie had said had struck a nerve. "What happened?" I asked.

"I don't remember," Timo said, a tear rolling down one cheek. "I really don't. I don't have the link anymore; she saw to that."

I looked from Timo to Callie as the realisation of those words struck me. "Timo's no longer an Ancient," I said.

"Timo is correct; she is no longer connected to the rift. She still has her abilities, she is still riftborn, but she is no longer an Ancient." Callie told me. "She was connected to Noah."

"Why not just kill me and be done with it?" I asked. "Why all of the performance?"

Callie got off the throne and stepped down from the dais. Time froze around us as she moved so quickly that I saw three of her as if she were moving in stop motion. She leaned in so that her lips were close to my ear, and whispered, "You have to be here. You need to see what is going to happen next. You need to be a part of what is going to happen next. I win if you come here, if you understand. You will be the one to sever the last Ancient's link; you will kill Hesansh or Neb. I'm hoping the latter. You will be the one to gift me everything I want, and it's going to be glorious. And best of all, you're going to do it willingly.."

"Am I fuck," I snapped. I moved my head slightly to get a better look at Callie and the insanity that swam through her eyes. "You sound like a chain revenant who has gone too deep."

"I see everything," Callie whispered. "Not all possibilities of the future but what has to happen. And you, oh, sweet Lucas, you are not prepared. But you will be. I'm going to fix this world. I'm going to make it better for everyone. Well, everyone who gets out of my way. Anyone else can just die."

"So, you're telling me that I'm not going to die here?" I asked. "That you need me for something else? I am very tired of hearing cryptic shit."

Callie's laugh was manic. "Do you want to die? Because you can die. I can have Hesansh pop your head off and roll it across the floor like a bowling ball. And should that be what happens, this world and all the worlds that touch it will burn."

I glanced up at the masked person who stood behind Neb, holding the knife to my friend's throat. There was something about them I found familiar; maybe they had been one of the Prime Soldiers. It was hard to tell without any identifying marks that I could see.

The door opened and Zoe was pushed inside; she stumbled slightly as she was shoved by another mask-wearing person, this one with an Owl medallion hanging around their neck. Zoe stopped walking and was grabbed by another guard and marched over to stand beside me. My heart sank as I saw her, not just because I had hoped she had escaped to tell everyone at Cortez's Ranch what was going on but also because I knew that Callie would use Zoe to torture me. Because whatever game Callie was playing, apparently I was to be part of it. Once again.

Callie let out a long, world-weary sigh. "You are unexpected. I really dislike the unexpected; it brings me out in hives."

Zoe shrugged, and I saw just the hint of a shimmer across her face.

"You created the devices that slow time for those people in the helicopter," I said to Callie, hoping to bring the attention back to me. "It was the same writing that was at the prison. Made you feel like you were walking through treacle. You shrank it, put it inside the helicopter, and then made sure everyone was moving too slowly to access their embers when the explosion happened."

Callie grinned. "I did. I made them, and I made the ones that remove power; both of them use similar ideas. It's just the writing inside that's different. They both use the rift-infused water that was around the prison. I had to go back to retrieve some; actually, I had to retrieve quite a lot, as it turns out. The amulet around Timo's neck right now stops her from using her power, a modified version of the devices I used in the helicopter. Although I didn't put them inside. I didn't make the people die."

"Hesansh?" I said, looking over at the large Ancient.

Callie laughed. "Absolutely not. When you realise who did it, you're going to feel so stupid. Or you're going to be already dead; either option works for me."

"I really didn't think that you had the charisma to be able to ensure that so many people followed you," I said. "I guess I was wrong about that."

Callie shook her head. "No, you're not. It turns out that people don't like me. I don't think people ever liked me. They respect me, which is better. They definitely fear me, which, in the scheme of things, I prefer. But like me, no; I've never been someone who could say that I was likeable."

"So, who's doing all of this for you?" I asked, pointing a thumb back in the direction of Hesansh. "Because it's not that dumb motherfucker."

I ignored the growl that left the throat of the dumb motherfucker.

"Are you stalling for time?" Callie asked, and looked back at Zoe, who had said nothing. "Why are you just standing there? Can you do nothing? Can you say nothing? You are a very strange lady. I did not take you into the equation when I arranged this. Do you know how rare it is for me to be surprised these days?"

"That must really suck," I said.

"Not really," Callie said, and motioned to one of the mask wearers stood at the side of the room. "Kill her."

"Lucas," Timo said slowly, her voice sharp even then, a level of concentration on her face as she fought against the power that was used against her. "Asteria. Stop . . ." She never finished her sentence, as the mask-wearer behind her slit her throat, then pulled the dying Timo back a fraction to drive the blade into her heart.

Time seemed to slow all around me for a moment as Timo's murderer kicked her body down to the ground. I was already up on my feet, tackling the murderer, driving my fist into their stomach. I smashed my elbow into their mask, cracking the side of it slightly, but before I could do any serious damage, Hesansh kicked me in the side, sending me careering across the room. I hit the glass window behind where Callie had been sitting, and it spiderwebbed as it cracked.

One glance down at Timo's lifeless body, and I felt an overwhelming urge to kill everybody in the room. I charged back at Hesansh, who swatted me out of the air as if I were nothing. I hit the ground hard, went to turn to smoke, and nothing happened.

"You didn't really think that we would let you use your power whenever you like?" Callie asked with a wicked gleam in her eye as she stepped over the body of Timo.

It took me a second to realise what she meant before Hesansh punched me in the face, knocking me back to the ground. He kicked me in the ribs hard enough to lift me off the floor and dumped me back down a few feet away.

Before he could launch another attack, Zoe stepped in front of me, both daggers in her hands.

Hesansh laughed. He reached out to grab Zoe, but she ducked under his grasp and sliced one of the daggers across his stomach before dancing away as more of the masked people around the room advanced upon her.

I managed to get up onto my hands and knees, sucking in air. I was pretty sure I'd received a few bruised ribs, and my vision was still swimming. Callie was screaming at someone, or about someone; it was hard to tell, as my attention was more on the advancing mask-wearing assassins.

I realised that someone had slipped one of the devices blocking my power onto me, and I desperately searched for it, but time ran out and one of the mask-wearers came at me, a dagger slicing across my bicep as I tried to move out of the way. Two of the mask-wears advanced on me, forcing me back toward the broken window. Without my power, without my connection to the rift, there was no way I could beat so many. There was no way I could beat Hesansh, who had easily won whatever could've been called a fight between us.

One of the mask-wearers got through Zoe's defence and stabbed her in the chest. Instead of showing pain, she looked back at me and threw a dagger, which hit the glass window beside me and shattered it.

Zoe disappeared from view as I vaulted through the remains of the glass window, feeling something strike me on the back of my shoulder as I fell out into the garden. Blood trickled down my arm as I noticed the dagger that had cut through the top of my shoulder and was now stuck in the wooden window frame.

"Stop him," Callie screamed from somewhere behind me. "He can't leave the city."

Without glancing back at who was still inside the residence, I turned and ran into the night.

CHAPTER EIGHTEEN

Zoe was safe. It was the only thing that I could have considered good after what I had just seen. Her duplicate had been sent to cause chaos and try to help me escape. Unfortunately, Timo had been unable to join me.

I jumped the garden wall, catching my foot on the top of the wooden struts and planting face-first in the grass beyond. I had to find and get rid of the box that had been placed on me. But I didn't have time to stop while people were chasing me. I needed a place to go where I could hide for a short time and figure the best way out of the city to safety.

There were precious few of them. And even fewer people inside the city I now trusted. I headed toward the Human Head pub.

The alarm had gone up about my escape, and the shield, which had been devoid of any Prime Soldiers or guards when Zoe and I had first entered, was now beginning to fill with their number as they left the residences that surrounded it.

Avoiding all of them was nearly impossible. There was too much open space between the residences and getting away from the shield, back toward the main city. I knew that should I just make a run for it, I would be captured and killed. Whatever pantomime Callie had been playing was over. Her guards had tried to subdue me, but Hesansh had gone in for the kill once Timo was dead, all while Callie shouted that she needed me alive.

Timo was dead and Neb was gods knew where.

I felt almost panic build up inside of me as my brain struggled to understand what both of those things meant.

I kept to the rear gardens of the residences in the shield until I reached the final one, with a forty-foot gap between me and cover. It was still dark, and I was all but human, and judging by the sounds of those searching for me, they were getting closer. I couldn't remain in my spot, between two large bushes and next to a tree that gave cover from the residence, for long.

Escaping without my power was going to be impossible. There was no way I could get out of this city as something close to human, and with the dripping of blood from my fingertips as it ran down my arm, someone was going to be able to hunt me.

I patted myself down, checking every pocket and recess in my clothing. The cloak and garment that I had been given by the Queen of Crows had a surprising number of pockets, both visible and hidden within the folds of material.

I eventually found the small device that was stopping my power between my belt and waistband at the rear of my trousers. I stared at it for a second; I wondered how it managed to remove my power if it was made from the same water around the prison. I touched that water, it had healed me; it did not remove my power.

The metal amulet was only three inches long, and the sides glowed turquoise from the water within. I pried the amulet open with a knife, the water cascading over my fingers, feeling warm to the touch. Inside the amulet was a small, circular piece of red wax, about the size of a ten-pence piece. It had tiny symbols inscribed upon it and had been hardened. I had no idea what any of the symbols meant. It was gibberish.

I tried to turn to smoke and found that I could with ease. I pocketed the wax, turned to smoke, and billowed across the open ground. Escaping the city was going to be easier, but I had told Zoe to go to the pub if things got worrying. I needed to check that she hadn't gone there before I left. There was no way I could leave her in the city while those who hunted me might find her.

I moved up over the shield, spreading the smoke thin so that it didn't catch the eye as easily. I sped across the ancient Greek columns and wondered if the view of the city in all of its glory would have been more impressive if I hadn't been trying to evade capture at the time.

Moving toward the rail tracks, I kept to the shadows, avoiding patrols, which had increased in number as I assumed they would. Occasionally, I could hear shouting in the darkness behind me.

I managed to get up on top of a stationary train and re-formed as I dropped down to the track beside it. It was some distance from where I stood to where I needed to be. It would be a night of dodging guards and worse.

I set off with all urgency, moving across the train tracks high above the city. Nothing was running, and the only things out at night were enemies, so it was easy to be unconcerned about the possibility of innocent lives becoming embroiled in what was happening. Everybody out hunting me had lost any right to be considered innocent.

Even with my power intact, it took me the better part of an hour to get through the city to the pub. The morning was just beginning, the scar across the night sky receding. It had been hours since I had entered the city, and it was likely to be several more before I could get out safely. Daylight was going to make it even more difficult. Hopefully, we would be able to hide out at the pub until such time as night fell again. Although I was fairly sure that by the time it had become dark enough that I could leave, those hunting me would tear apart the city in their search.

As there were no tear stones inside the city, accessing my embers to escape the situation was out of the question. I had a decision to make about how to leave, and there were no good answers.

I stood outside of the front door of the Human Head and peered through the window, trying to find a flicker of movement within. I tried the door but found it still locked. Not wanting to be seen stood outside of the bar for any length of time, I took the alleyway to the left until I reached the rear of the bar. I quickly scaled and vaulted over the wooden fence, landing in the back garden.

The garden had seen better days and was now mostly consumed by wild grass and whatever animals considered that to be home. There were old chairs sat on the patio-type area, along with a table that was rotting from the middle outwards.

I stopped by the back door and tried the handle, finding it unlocked. I pushed the door open slightly, the smell of death lingering in the air. I stepped into a small room with coats and cloaks hanging on one side, and several boots lined up on the opposite. The only other door in the room was open, revealing a kitchen area beyond.

The pub was still dark, and as I moved through the well-stocked kitchen and into the bar area, the smell of decay intensified. There were glasses shattered all over the floor behind the bar, along with bottles of various alcohol. The smell mixed with that of death until it was overwhelming, and I had to place my hand over my mouth and nose as I moved through to the rooms adjacent to the bar.

A living area that was usually immaculate was now the scene of a battle. Upholstered chairs had been torn apart, the stuffing and metal springs thrown around the room, the former making it look like it had snowed inside. At the far end of the room was Roseline. She was slumped on the floor with a broken bottle in one hand and a war hammer in the other. The war hammer was rift-tempered and would kill a rift-fused with a well-placed strike to the head. It looked like she'd never gotten the chance to deliver such a blow, as the weapon was still clean.

Roseline hadn't fared so well. Her neck had been opened from ear to ear, and she had multiple stab wounds across her bare arms and hands, from when she must have defended herself from her attacker.

I crouched down beside her and closed her eyes with my fingertips. She had been a good friend and one of the few people in this cursed city that I liked. And trusted.

Footsteps approached. I went to grab my spear, and remembered that it was with Drusilla. I picked up the hammer, finding the weight of it to be unusual. Fighting with a hammer was a skill I had never bothered to master.

The masked assassin who had killed Timo stepped into the room, their cracked mask telling me which assassin they were, although their true identity was still a mystery to me. They stood in the doorway, and said nothing, but they repeatedly looked down at the body of Roseline.

"Did you kill her?" I asked.

They looked over at me and nodded once. "She would not listen."

The voice behind the mask was immediately known to me, and my heart broke a little, knowing that someone I had loved was working for people like Callie. That someone I had loved had murdered Timo in front of me.

"Necia?" I said, hoping I was wrong.

Necia Torres removed her mask, throwing it to the side, her body shrinking to its normal size.

"That's new," I said. "I knew that you could manipulate the power of the rift to create weapons, but I didn't realise you could use it to change your appearance."

"Callie taught me," Necia said. "Make myself bigger using rift energy. I really wish it had never come to this."

"You murdered Timo," I said, my voice quiet.

"The Ancients were a cancer," Necia said. "They took and took, and gave nothing back. She, like all of the Ancients, deserved her fate. Her death was cathartic."

"Was Roseline's?" I asked.

Tears filled Necia's blue eyes. "I said she would not listen. I tried to explain that Callie was right, that the rift needed to be cleansed of those who take advantage of it. Who have taken from the rift and never given back. The Ancients."

"You sound like you're about to fight a holy war, for fuck's sake," I snapped.

"This is a war for our home," Necia snapped back. "Our very lives have been pulled around by the machinations of the Ancients for thousands of years. Making sure they always stand to gain, where everyone else loses."

"Hesansh is an Ancient," I pointed out.

"And eventually, he too will lose his power and cease to be," Necia said.

"And how does he keep his power when all of the Ancients are dying?" I asked, before realisation dawned on me. "Neb. She's linked to Hesansh. That's why she's somewhere safe, until he finishes whatever work it is he's doing. And then she dies, and he loses his power, and all the Ancients will be done. You were going to kill me back at the residence. I always thought I was owed being killed face-to-face."

"Callie said you can't leave the city," Necia said. "It's important to her plan."

"She also said I have to take the life of Neb or Hesansh," I replied. "Didn't do that, either. So, maybe she's not as good at looking into the future as she thinks."

"You will come with me back to the Prime residence," Necia said. "You will do as you are told, or Callie will start having the people of this town executed until you do."

"She had her people kill Noah," I snapped. "I watched Hesansh murder him. She can go fuck herself, as can the rest of you cult-like pricks."

"You were meant to stay out of this until we could bring you here," Necia shouted. "I called in favours to try and get you to stay out of way."

"Christopher did the favour of blowing up my house and threatening my friends on your orders?" I said, trying to keep my anger from bubbling over.

"We couldn't risk you doing something stupid," Necia said. "This could have all been so easy. You come here, you end Hesansh, and you bring about a better world. Hesansh is ready to die, although I doubt he will make it easy. I think he wants to see how the man who replaced him in Neb's life does against him."

"I don't care," I said, meaning every word. "You've joined forces with a monster. She is responsible for the deaths of thousands of people over the years. She manipulated the Guild members to turn on their own people and murder them in their beds. The Primes are either dead or have joined her out of fear, and I have lost friends. People I care for. And you helped that happen."

"This is why I never asked you to join us," she said sadly. "I knew you wouldn't; I knew that you would stand fast in your need to hate Callie Mitchell."

"I don't hate Callie Mitchell," I said. "She died years ago when she touched the rift. Whatever is walking around masquerading as her is some weird version of her. She is obsessed with stealing the power of the Ancients at any cost."

"They never should've taken the power," Necia said. "It was not given; it was stolen. Do you know how they did it?"

"And she's doing exactly the same thing! How can you not see that?" I demanded. "The Ancients went into the Tempest and took it but didn't know what they were doing," I said. "The primordials hate them for it. Which is more than fair." In truth, I wasn't entirely certain how they had taken the power for themselves; it was something I always meant to ask, but the constant fighting and trying to survive had meant it was a question I kept putting off.

"Callie told us that your Ancients killed the primordials," Necia said. "Butchered them and took their bones, making weapons like that spear that you use. Timo might not have remembered, the others might not remember, but that's what happened. The Ancients murdered the primordials to gain power."

"This is the first time I'm hearing about the butchering of primordials," I said. "It seems like something the primordials would have brought up when I spoke to them. Besides which, Callie wanted to experiment on the primordials not that long ago."

"Callie has realised the error of her ways," Necia said. "She is going to fix the mistakes of the past, and we can move on with a stable Tempest, a stable rift, where life is better."

"The primordial bone used to make that spear was given freely," I said. "I asked the primordials if it was okay. I would not have taken it otherwise. It helped me stop Callie from destroying the Tempest, killing untold numbers of primordial and rift-fused, from creating a permanent tear between the rift and Earth. Do you have any idea what would have happened to humanity? It would have been a slaughter. Millions of people would have died as Earth changed forever when the power of the rift flooded over it."

"You have been lied to your entire life," Necia said. "Neb kept secrets from you. About her past, about your own power. Your embers. Do you even know that the shadows inside them are meant to be a way to gain more power? No, because the Ancients made sure that riftborn didn't know. They told us that the shadows would hunt us, would kill us."

I remained silent, not wanting to say that Christopher had mentioned something similar, although I'd dismissed his claim as bullshit. I wondered if Callie was just spouting nonsense to get people on board with the promise of future power. It was worth looking into if I ever had the chance.

"*You'd* know all of this if you had just let Callie explain it all," Necia continued. "If you had just pushed aside your own arrogance, your own need to win, and just accepted that she knew what was best."

"And what happens once you've all achieved your unlocked potential?" I asked.

Necia smiled. "We will make this world and any linked to it better."

"What does that mean?" I asked. "'Any linked to it'? You mean Earth?"

"I meant what I said," Necia replied.

"And all of this will be done by force," I said.

Necia's smile didn't fade, but a hardness settled in her eyes. "We will do whatever is necessary."

I stared at the woman I had once loved, someone who I always thought was one of the best of those living in the rift. Someone who made the rift a better place. I stared at her and realised with horror that she had been seduced by a cult. There was no other word for it; the gleam in her eyes as she spoke about Callie said everything I needed to know.

"You murdered Roseline because she would not join Callie Mitchell," I said. "She would not listen to you as you tried to explain the virtues of a woman responsible for the murders of hundreds, if not thousands of people. You tried to indoctrinate her into your cult, and when it didn't work, you killed her."

Necia's expression hardened. "We are not a cult," she said, her words sharp and full of anger.

"That is exactly what someone in a cult would say," I told her. "You are murdering people, Necia."

"We do what must be done," Necia said.

"You work with a monster," I shouted, letting the anger I felt into every word.

I did not want to fight her. I knew that a fight between the two of us would end in the death of one of us. She would not walk away from this, and neither would I. I glanced down at the hammer in my hand; it was not my preferred weapon of choice.

"You cannot be allowed to leave this place," Necia said. "You will never join us; we both know that. And you will do everything in your power to ensure that our vision never comes to fruition. You will die here. If there is any part of you that still loves me, you will let this happen; you will let me kill you quickly. I do not wish for you to linger in pain; I want this to be quick and over. I will mourn you."

"I thought Callie wanted me alive," I said.

"You have outlived that right," Necia said. "Outlived your usefulness."

I sighed; this was going to get worse fast. "You're right; I did once love you," I said. "But as for everything else, go fuck yourself. I'm going to make this as difficult as possible, and I guarantee that if you do manage to kill me, you're going to remember this fight for the rest of your life."

Necia threw one of the hatchets directly at my head, forcing me to dodge to the side and allowing her to close the distance quickly. The second hatchet was brought up toward my groin, a killing blow if it had struck. I deflected her arm with the hammer and drove my fist into her jaw, knocking her sideways, spinning the hammer over my hand and bringing it down toward her knee.

Before the weapon struck, Necia kicked up, catching me behind my own knee and forcing me to retreat, putting several feet of distance between us. Necia still held one of her hatchets, but the other was embedded in the wall behind where I had been originally standing, next to Roseline's head.

Necia rolled backwards, getting to her feet, as purple mist swirled around her hand, forming a large razor-sharp claw and gauntlet upon it. I'd seen her use such a weapon to devastating effect, and I did not wish to get caught by it.

I kept a wary distance as Necia moved towards me, spinning her hatchet over and over in her hand whilst flexing the claw gauntlet, making the finger blades slide against one another. She darted forward, slashing with the claw, trying to force me to the side so that she could bring up the hatchet toward my ribs.

Instead, I stepped into her guard and slammed my elbow into her face, kicking her in the chest as hard as I could, sending her flying back. The idea of hurting Necia would have been unthinkable only a short time before. If the cult that she belonged to had killed her, I would have hunted down each and every person involved and ended their lives. But now I was fighting for mine, and Necia would not stop until I was dead at her feet.

I turned to smoke and billowed toward her, avoiding the swipe of her claw, which, as it was made of a rift power, would have caused me significant pain, and wrapped myself around her gauntleted arm, yanking it back as hard as I could. I re-formed, and, still holding on to her arm, yanked so hard that it dislocated her shoulder. I stepped down on the back of her knee and drove my elbow into her ear.

Necia spun around, catching me in the knee with her hatchet. It was a glancing blow, but the blade sliced through the flesh above the kneecap, causing incredible pain and forcing me to hobble back, putting some distance between us once again.

Purple mist once again enveloped Necia's body, and the wounds that she had received began to heal. I turned to smoke, quickly moved toward her, re-formed, and brought the hammer down on her knee. This time, she was unable to move quick enough to avoid the weapon as it smashed into her kneecap, shattering the bone with an unpleasant crunch.

Necia screamed in pain but quickly regained her senses and slashed across my stomach with the claw, cutting through my clothes with ease. Blood poured out of the wounds that I'd received across my stomach, and I moved back quickly, my hands on my stomach, trying to assess whether or not she had cut through the muscle. I was grateful to feel that my insides had not gone outside of my body.

Necia dragged herself upright as we stared at one another in silence. Neither of us was walking away from this unscathed, it seemed. I wondered if I could kill her. Not emotionally, but physically, if I was good enough to kill her. If I wasn't, I was going to die.

As my body began to heal, I took a step toward Necia, the hammer down by my leg. Necia threw herself at me, an unexpected attack, leaving me with no option but to turn into my smoke form. She sailed through me, slashing at my smoke with her claw, causing pain to explode across my form. It is hard enough to maintain myself in smoke form at the best of times. Doing so when an attack causes every nerve and sinew in my body to roar in uncontested agony is beyond difficult.

I was forced to re-form, crashing to the floor close to the door, the hammer skittering out of my hand. Necia took the opportunity and attacked, the claw coming down toward my neck and face. It was a blow that would have killed me if I had not turned my arm to smoke and wrapped it around her legs, pulling as hard as I could, tripping her. She fell back with considerable force and smashed the back of her head on the ground behind her, hitting it so hard that I thought she might have crushed her skull.

I gingerly got back to my feet to find that Necia had remained still.

I walked over to her and looked down; blood was coming out of her ears, and her nose. She blinked and looked up at me. "I cannot feel my hands," she said.

I looked down where the claw would have been to see only her normal hand. The hatchet was long since lost inside the battlefield of a room that we were in. She would heal, in time. A broken neck, a fractured skull, neither were killing blows. She had gotten terribly unlucky, and I had very little time before she would be able to fight once again.

"I do not wish to die on my back," Necia said.

I picked up one of the hatchets. The blade was rift-tempered just like the hammer. "Did you use these on Roseline?"

"She would not listen," Necia said, as if it were her mantra. "Will you give me a warrior's death?"

"I will give you the same death you have given everybody else," I told her sadly. "A pointless one." And I drove the hatchet into her head, killing her instantly.

CHAPTER NINETEEN

It went without saying, but I did not hang about inside the pub. I left quickly via the same way I'd entered, and moved across the rooftops of the buildings in smoke form. Getting out of the city was now my only option.

I'd told Zoe to go to the pub if things got bad, but considering she hadn't yet turned up, I had no idea where she was. I had to hope that she had found a way out and was already free. I considered finding other allies, but I would be putting them in terrible danger just by being near them, and who knew who I could trust now.

Instead, I found an empty building a few streets away from the west gate and settled down to wait for nighttime. Going up and over the wall in smoke form during the day would have gotten me spotted by someone, and I did not wish to have any more fights if I could get away with it.

While the fight with Necia and the need to get out of the city as quickly as possible had ensured that I didn't linger on the loss of someone so important to me, the time I spent in that building alone, with nothing but my thoughts for company, would have either been considered cathartic and healthy, or dwelling and unhealthy. Depending on which doctor you had asked.

Timo was dead. I'd known her only a relatively short time, but I'd come to like her, trust her. She was one of the few Ancients who didn't seem to be looking out for themselves. I was going to miss her a great deal.

By the time night rolled around, I was ready to leave. I hadn't made my peace with Timo's loss, nor with Neb being in the clutches of a deranged psychopath. Nor had I made my peace with how quickly all of this had come about.

Unfortunately, death rarely comes with additional time attached. Even when you have been given a time scale and you can set your affairs in order, and you can spend time with the ones you love, it is never enough. The end result always comes too quickly. There is never enough time to say everything you need to say. But that doesn't stop you regretting being unable to say those things. Even more so when the death is quick and unexpected.

I wondered whether or not I'd ever get the chance to tell Neb how I felt. That she was important to me. That she was the closest thing I might have had to a parent, besides my own. My parents had been good people, but after I had died and become resurrected in the rift, Neb had been the first person to make me feel like this new life had potential. That I had potential.

There was a possibility, one that sat within my heart, that made me ache, in which Callie's half-truths, her lies, were actually the truth. The idea that the Ancients had claimed their connection to the rift, their power, by abject slaughter of the primordials, explained more than I wanted to consider. Neb did not like to go to the Tempest, and the primordials had always been wary, if not outright hostile, to anyone entering their territory. Occasionally, the hostility would cause one of the primordials to attack a rift-fused settlement. I had connections within the primordial community, but I wondered just how my kind were viewed when the Ancients, those of us with the biggest connection to the rift, the most potentially powerful of our kind, had possibly achieved such a thing by murder.

If I was honest, I'd known Neb to do a lot of shady things over the centuries, but the idea of her murdering primordials for power wasn't something I figured she'd do. Timo and Noah too. Something felt off about it all, and I now had more questions than answers.

Only Neb and Hesansh remained alive. So, while Hesansh wanted to maintain his connection to the rift, Neb would be safe; at least, I hoped so.

I left the building once darkness had settled in, turned to smoke, and flew up over the rooftop, keeping to the shadows of the nearby city wall. Every now and again, I got close to a set of guards and found that they carried those damnable devices that Callie was so proud of. I could feel my smoke form vanishing the closer I got, and I had to return to my normal form more than once when guards got too close.

Eventually, I found a spot in the wall where there were no guards nearby, and passed through in smoke form. I moved out and down the side of the city wall, passing over the river, trying to keep as low as possible so as not to draw any attention from patrolling boats, which appeared to have increased in number since the previous night.

I made it to the bank opposite the city, re-formed, and sat down at the edge of the long grass that surrounded it. I was a few miles from the Cortez ranch, but it wasn't a long way to run, and in smoke form I was able to move even quicker. Even so, I refused to let myself feel safe. That was a good way to relax, and relaxing out in the rift when people are trying to kill you is a good way to get dead.

I'd made it a mile, getting closer and closer to a set of ruins on my right. I slowed, wondering if anyone could have gotten inside them, waiting to ambush me. I'd re-formed into my usual human appearance and was jogging along the road when I saw the glint of something in the night. I quickly turned to smoke as the arrow passed through where I had been, clattering off the stone road, and cartwheeling into the nearby long grass.

My nerves roared out in pain where the arrowhead had touched my smoke form, and I found myself immediately turned back to human, whereupon I rolled off the side of the road into the ditch beside it. Doing so probably saved my life, as a second arrow whizzed just above me, where my head would have been only a second earlier.

Necia wasn't lying when she said that Callie was done with trying to keep me alive.

I turned back to smoke and moved along the ditch, until I was fifty metres farther up, shrouded by several large trees on my right, with long grass on my left. I turned back to human again as I crouched behind one of the trees.

I counted to ten and returned to my smoke form, billowing across the road and re-forming behind an equally large tree on the opposite side. There had been no more arrows, and I wondered if the archer responsible had lost me, or if they were unable to get a shot and were waiting for the right time.

I moved around the tree, the ruins giving me good cover from whoever was inside. Whatever the ruins had once been, they were now mostly just a collection of pale stone walls of various sizes. The remains of a large building, two of the walls having collapsed in on themselves, sat at the rear of the ruins. The top of the building gave a good vantage point over the surrounding area, although you would've had to be an excellent shot with a bow to be able to catch someone from the distance between the ruined building and the road I had been on.

Moving slowly along the remains of the wall, I eventually reached the end and was about to turn to smoke and move up over it, to get a better look at the area beyond, when the wall exploded outwards. I was caught heavily in the shoulder, sending me sprawling to the ground as pieces of masonry and dust covered me. A large piece of stone struck me on the side of the head, and for just a second, the world went dark.

Thankfully, I recovered in time to roll aside from Hesansh's attack as he launched himself at me with terrifying speed. I was unable to move quickly enough to avoid the second attack as he darted toward me, kicking me in the ribs before bringing his opposite knee up toward my face. I managed to get my hands up in time to block the blow, but the force of it was enough to lift me off the ground.

I turned to smoke and billowed toward Hesansh, re-forming and putting all of my energy into the punch that connected with his jaw.

Hesansh took two steps back and kicked me in the chest so hard that it broke my ribs and sent me flying back across the ground.

I couldn't breathe—pain laced up my chest, and it felt as if it were on fire. No one had ever been able to take such a punch. I'd only just been able to learn how to perform it without breaking my own hand, such were the power and force that the blow contained.

Blood trickled down from Hesansh's cut lip; he dabbed at it with a finger. He stared at the blood as if surprised that it was there, and then a cold fury crossed his features. Purple mist moved up from the ground, wrapping around his legs, up his waist, across his chest, and down his mouth. He inhaled the mist deeply, shuddering after doing so.

He took two steps toward me as my body fought in vain to heal itself quickly enough so that I would not die. I had never been hit as hard as Hesansh had managed. Not even those monstrous creatures that Callie Mitchell had created had been strong enough to do the damage that one kick from Hesansh had achieved. I knew he was strong; I knew that his power was to draw energy from the rift and use it to increase his own strength, speed, and physical attributes. I'd always been led to believe that his power was dangerous, not that he was capable of the level of strength he had just shown.

I needed to use a nearby tree to ensure that I could stand upright, although *stand* was probably not the right word. It was more of a controlled swaying.

Hesansh watched me for a moment, as if finding the whole thing amusing. He picked up one of the large pieces of stone belonging to the ruin. It was big enough that even the strongest of riftborn or revenants would have had trouble with it; it should have needed at least two hands to even move it. But where he grabbed the stone, his fingers tore into it, creating a new grip. He lifted the stone up for me to see, placed it in both of his hands, and crushed it like a beer can.

Brick dust covered him, and I used the opportunity to run into the ruins. I needed to get away, but I needed time to heal my myriad of wounds before I could turn into my smoke form, where I would be quickest. I made it five feet before Hesansh covered the distance between us, crashing into me, grabbing my cloak, spinning me around, and throwing me headfirst back through the ruined wall.

I landed roughly, the air knocked out of me, my head swimming from the impact with parts of the ruins, but I had enough where-withal to know that I had absolutely no chance of beating Hesansh and needed to leave. Now.

"Callie has us all out looking for you," Hesansh said. "Apparently, you needed to stay in the city. Callie said that it was really important you didn't leave. I think she was really hung up on the idea of you kill-ing Neb, and frankly, it's something I'd like to see. I don't think you'd do it, though."

"Necia said Callie put out an order to kill me," I said. "Apparently, I'm not *that* important."

"She told Necia to kill you?" Hesansh asked with a raised eyebrow.

"Ah, Callie is giving different orders to different people," I said. "What did she tell you? All part of her plan, I assume."

"Necia is dead?" Hesansh asked.

I nodded.

Hesansh smiled. "Didn't think you had it in you."

"You'd be surprised," I said. "So, Callie is telling you one thing and other people something else. Always trying to get people positioned into the right places. She thinks she can control the future, doesn't she?"

"Maybe," Hesansh agreed. "She said if you survived the night and escaped, you were no longer part of her plan. She spends too much time looking into those . . . chains of hers. Always trying to find the best circumstances for her plans to work. She's angry you keep chang-ing them."

"Is that how you knew I was here?" I asked.

Hesansh laughed. "Someone saw you turn from smoke to your human form earlier. You got a little too close to some of the guards Callie supplied with her devices, didn't you? I figured you'd come out over the river. Once Callie said if you made it out you were game, I made sure there were no guards where you escaped, made it look like the perfect point."

"Superb," I said, hoping the pain that was lacing through my body would go away.

"You cannot run," Hesansh said. "You cannot hide. I have given you as much of a chance as I am willing to. That is over; I no longer have to put up with your existence. Neb replaced me with you, and look how that worked out. I am strong and powerful, more so than I have ever been. And you crawling in the dirt at my feet. I never have to worry about holding back. Callie no longer needs you alive, and that's something I aim to provide."

"You know, Neb never mentioned you," I said. It might not have been particularly wise to anger the person who was kicking the living piss out of me, but if I was going to go out, I wasn't going to go out pleading for my life.

"Do you think that hurts me?" Hesansh asked as he looked down at me.

I stared into the eyes of an Ancient and saw the rage and hate inside, but there was something else. Hurt. "Yes," I said softly. "I think that hurts you very much."

Hesansh screamed in incandescent rage and kicked me in the chest, sending me spiralling back across the road; I hit the edge of the ditch and rolled down it. My body was healing as much as possible, and I wished that I had the capability to draw power from the rift that Hesansh appeared to have. Was that just his natural ability as an Ancient, or was it something more? Had Callie taught him? Had she given him access to more power of the rift?

"Get back up here and die with honour," Hesansh shouted from atop the side of the road.

I got to my feet and spat out a mixture of blood and dirt before looking up at him. I noticed movement out of the corner of my eye; maybe this wasn't going to be such a one-sided fight after all. "You are accessing the power of the rift," I said. "This isn't what you could do as an Ancient. Neb would have mentioned it. She would have mentioned how strong you were. I can feel the rift energy flowing into you. The purple mist, that's what Necia dragged up too. Didn't help her. Won't help you."

"Do you think that this is the time for a chat?" Hesansh barked.

The bullet that hit Hesansh in the neck was the first of six that struck different parts of his body. Hesansh threw himself to the ground as blood poured out of the wounds, until all of a sudden, it didn't. The purple mist that I had seen earlier was back, covering his body and allowing him to heal almost instantly. He really had been given a massive upgrade.

Zeke came out of the darkness, using his Winchester rifle to fire over and over at Hesansh, who ran for the safety of the ruins. He might've been able to heal quickly, but judging from the screams, he was unable to stop the pain from racking his body.

Drusilla stepped out of the ruins, a huge spear in hand with a wicked curved blade that shimmered with the rift-tempered power. She drove it into Hesansh's chest, twisting it, tearing it out, and driving it back in again.

Hesansh brought his arm down across the haft of the spear, snapping it in two, the purple mist still surrounding his body, and he turned and ran back toward the city, moving at a speed none of us would have been able to keep up with. Any normal riftborn would have been killed by now, but with his connection to the rift and obvious power increase, he was a much more difficult proposition than an Ancient with that connection removed . . . like Timo and Noah.

Drusilla rushed over to me, helping me up the ditch and hugging me after checking that I was okay. She passed me my short spear, which I didn't realise I'd be so happy to see again.

"I've never seen anyone move like that," Drusilla said. "Nor have I ever seen anyone take that much damage and just shrug it off."

"At least three of those bullets managed to keep the rift-tempering," Zeke said as he reloaded his rifle. "Hesansh shouldn't be moving. He should be very, very dead, which is actually a little bit what you look like."

"I'm fine," I said, feeling anything but. "Did Zoe get back to Cortez okay?"

Both of them nodded. "Zoe said that they had Timo," Drusilla said. "Is she okay?"

I looked between them and shook my head. "They killed her. They killed Timo and Attia, and they have Neb."

No one spoke for several seconds, until Zeke said, "We need to get moving. Grieve later; live now."

Drusilla and I agreed with him, all three of us running through the night toward the Cortez ranch. Once there, and after Zoe had come over to check that I was okay, I explained to everyone what had happened.

When I'd finished, Drusilla said, "We need to go tell the Queen of Crows."

"Agreed," Cortez said. "I am not sure how she will take it."

"Neither am I," I said. "But it needs to be soon. She can't find out from rumour or innuendo about what happened. I need to get back there and let her know. We also need to get back to Earth and let everyone there know what we found out. We could kill two birds with one stone."

I saw the expression on several faces and winced inside.

"Okay, bad choice of phrase," I said. "We go back to Earth, tell everyone, and come back through to the rift closer to the Crow's Perch. We might be a bit tired, and I definitely didn't want to do it that way to get to Inaxia, but it'll be quicker than taking the oxforth. Besides, I need to properly heal, so embers is it."

"Sounds like a plan," Zeke said.

"What about Hesansh?" Cortez asked.

"Hesansh had more power than I've ever seen from a riftborn. I saw him drag the power of the rift into himself. He healed almost instantly; he was stronger than anything I've ever fought. I think that maybe Callie is responsible. I think, somehow, she's let him access to the rift. I don't mean like the Ancients did originally; they couldn't just tap back into that power when they wanted to. This was like he accessed the actual power of the rift itself. Necia mentioned something about their embers and the shadows. I need to talk to Casimir and Maria to see if they know anything about it."

"It could take you some time to get back to the Queen," Cortez said. "If we can get word to her about what happened, we will. Sooner is better with things like this."

"Thank you," I told him.

"Didn't you say something about you being able to access the rift too?" Zoe asked. "Like sense stuff?"

I nodded. "Mine is more about being able to tell where things are; I am stronger, but not to the degree that Hesansh has become. And speaking of which, I couldn't tell where he was. Nor Necia, nor any of the people inside with Callie. I'm wondering just how many people she is allowing to have access to the rift. And if that's the case, I don't even understand how she's done it. I think I need to go to the Tempest. I need to talk to the primordials; I need to know what she's doing and how she's doing it."

"You mean Valmore?" Drusilla asked.

"Not just him," I said. "I need to talk to them all. I need to know if what Callie said is true. Did the Ancients murder the primordials in order to gain power?"

"If they did, I'd certainly understand them holding a grudge," Zoe said from the corner of the room. "I'd be pretty pissed off for a long time too."

"I think you all need to move north," I said. "I have no idea what Callie has planned, but before Timo died, she told me that I needed to go to Asteria. If that's where Callie is planning to go, then that's where I need to be. It must be where they're holding Neb."

"The city across the water?" Zoe asked.

"Why would she need to go there?" Cortez asked. "That's Theoris's city."

"With her dead," Zeke said. "There's a possibility that the city is in complete chaos. Maybe Callie aims to take advantage of that."

"Why?" Drusilla asked. "What is there that is so important? It's days of travel by sea; there's no other way to get there. Despite Lucas uncovering our ability to teleport between tear stones, they don't seem to work to get there."

"Theoris had them disabled," I told her. "Timo told me about it. Apparently, Theoris didn't trust the idea that people could just turn up uninvited. She sounds like she was more interested in isolationism than actually being part of the rift. Timo said she was a strange lady who never really fit in with most of the others. She went there the first opportunity she got and never came back, except for occasional meet-ups."

I shrugged. "I have absolutely no idea what Callie's going to do next. She appears to have lost her mind. She told me I had to be there in the city, that I had to be the one to end the connection between Hesansh and Neb. If I were you, I would move to a place that could be better protected and defended; if anyone has a bone to pick with you or your people, they might use this as an excuse."

We all left Cortez's ranch and made the short journey to a nearby tear stone, which would allow us to open our embers and step through. Now that we no longer cared about Callie knowing what we were doing, we no longer had to stay away from using the tear stones closer to Inaxia.

After Zeke went through, Drusilla said, "I'm not okay with you going there by yourself. I saw what that Ancient did to you. Without our help, you would've died."

I nodded in agreement, reached out, and took her hands in mine. "You being in the Tempest with me will get you or me killed. Valmore is tolerant of me, even friendly, but he is one primordial of an unknown number. We would not be able to stop the others if they decided to kill us. At least alone, I'm hoping I have enough sway, having been touched by the rift, that they might allow me to speak. I do not plan on lingering there. I will be safe. As safe as I can be anywhere."

Drusilla stared for a moment, leaned toward me, and kissed me gently on the lips. "You have not convinced me, but I also don't wish to argue here. We'll argue later."

She opened a tear and stepped through into her embers, the tear snapping shut behind her. I opened my own tear a second later; I wondered if there was anywhere I could just hide for a few days to avoid the inevitable conversation that I was going to be having with more than just Drusilla when I told everybody about my plan to go to the Tempest alone.

CHAPTER TWENTY

When I'd given my Raven medallion to Nadia, I expected that when I needed to use it to return to Earth, I would find myself in her home. It isn't an exact science as to how close you return to the object or place that you feel a draw to, but usually it is within a few feet at most.

I looked between the pair of them. "My shadows," I said, looking around at the number of them who were living their lives as if they were real.

"What about them?" Maria asked.

"Necia and Henash mentioned using them to gain power," I said.

"How are you supposed to do that?" Casimir asked. They had changed into the form of a bearded dragon and were happily clinging to my other shoulder.

"I don't know," I said, as I stopped by a large shadow who was chopping wood that wasn't there. "Can I touch them? I've tried before and I just walked straight through them. But then at night, they try to tear me limb from limb. I don't think there's ever been a time when there's been an option to absorb my shadows. Should there be an option?"

"First time I've heard of it," Maria said.

I explained everything I'd seen about Callie and the necklace, and what Necia had said about increasing her power, and how the

Ancients had caused people to fear the shadows because they didn't want competition.

"We can look into it," Maria said. "And by *look into it*, I mean we can study them and see if we can figure out how Necia managed to absorb them."

After bringing both of them up to date about what had happened while I was in the rift and hoping that I hadn't spent too much time in my embers healing, I found myself walking back through to Earth and ended up on the beach at Peddocks Island.

It was windy and overcast, and there was nobody else on the beach except for Nadia, who was sat on a blanket, a wooden box beside her, as she held my medallion in her hands.

"You okay?" I asked.

Nadia looked up at me and nodded. There was a deep sadness on her face, and it appeared as if she had been crying. "I knew it was you. I knew you'd come here when you came back. You haven't been in my chains for a long time, and then a day ago, you just were. It was as if you had always been there. And every path I looked at led to this moment. Sit, please." She patted the blanket beside her as if for emphasis.

I sat down, opening the wooden box as she motioned toward it. It was full of the Raven medallions. She placed my medallion inside the box, removed the one she had been wearing, and put that beside it.

"What's going on?" I asked.

"You've been gone a little while; Zeke and Drusilla arrived back about four hours ago," Nadia said, avoiding the question. "You must've needed extra healing. They told us all about what happened, about Timo. Attia, too. I'm sorry."

"Thank you," I said, keeping my voice barely a whisper.

Nadia reached over, placed her hand atop mine, and squeezed slightly. "Drusilla told me about how Callie said that the Ancients stole their power from the Tempest. That true?"

I shrugged. "Timo said she couldn't remember what happened under the mountain. She just knew that they walked out from the Tempest with its power. I would think that if they'd been up there slaughtering a lot of primordials, the primordials themselves might have mentioned it. They dislike the Ancients, some more than others, but I've known Valmore a long time, and he's never once mentioned that his kin were eaten by the Ancients."

"So, what is Callie's plan, then?"

"She wants the power of the rift for herself," I said. "She thinks she's the only person who can fix it all, make it all better. I saw that hunger in her eyes. She *needs* to be the one to take control. She thinks she's better than everyone else."

"She's going to kill a lot more people to get that wish," Nadia said.

"I have to go to the Tempest to find out how to stop her, how to take away her connection to the rift, if I can," I said. "Because I think that's how we stop Callie. She wants to take the power of the Ancients and keep it all for herself, which she believes she can control. She's allowed herself to delve into the rift. To see the . . . chains, as you do. She speaks like a chained revenant who has spent too much time in their chains."

"It's like a drug," Nadia said, as she looked over to me. "Once you get a little taste, you just keep wanting more and more. And before you know it, you've spent six months delving into the chains, and now you can no longer tell the difference between right and wrong, or between what is true and what is possibly true, maybe, in another reality or dimension. Or if there even are other realities and dimensions. It's a bit of a mind-fuck."

"How long have you been sat out here?" I asked.

"Hour or two," Nadia replied. "There's a seagull just out there who has been trying to grab a crab off of one of those rocks. I've been watching it, mostly watching it fail over and over. The tenacity of a seagull has kept me entertained while I hoped the crab escaped."

"Anything else?"

"There are tears all over the place," Nadia said. "They're littering the world, hundreds and hundreds of them. None near here at the moment, but the RCU agents and surviving Silver Phalanx people are out there, trying to stop anything too nasty from causing problems."

"Do you know how this ends?" I asked.

Nadia sighed. "There's never enough time. You have led me from a place where I was lost, to friendship and loved ones. I do not know how this ends, but I do know that I can no longer be the caretaker of the Raven Guild. The Guilds are dead, Lucas. All of them. Something new has to be reborn from their ashes. I don't know what it is, but I do know that while the Guilds have done a lot of good throughout their existence, they have been corrupted, destroyed from within by those led astray by Callie's dogma, and now they go after anyone who is against them."

"They've been attacking RCU agents?" I asked, feeling anger bubbling up again inside of me. They had ruined something that was meant to do good, and the idea that I had carried around my own Guild's medallions for so long only to have had it become meaningless was difficult to take.

Nadia nodded. "They are little more than cult members; that's what Gabriel called them. Ji-hyun has other words for them, but once she starts, she keeps cursing in Korean, and I can't quite keep up with the filth that is being spewed forth."

I couldn't help but chuckle myself. "She does do that. I'll take the medallions with me. At least then I know that they will be put to good use; I'll give them back to the primordials as a peace offering, see if they can help get the primordials on our side. Or at least, if not on our side, not against us."

Nadia nodded and brushed sand off of her ankle-length black dress. "Callie is right, at least in a way. I know you probably don't want to hear that, but her wanting the power that was taken to be replaced is the right thing to do. She just doesn't care who's hurt in the process. She wants it done quick and nasty so she can control it all herself in the end. I believe, with what you have said, that she has spent too much time in the rift and is causing as much harm as possible in the process."

"Callie is a monster," I said. "She's not done yet."

Nadia shook her head. "She envisions herself as judge, jury, and executioner of everybody in the rift. Of everybody connected to the rift. Everything you have told me about what she said and did in Inaxia makes me think she wants to control the access people have to the rift. When a chained revenant goes too deeply into their chains, that's what they try to do. They try to eliminate everything that will stop the most optimal chain from taking place. To stop the most optimal timeline. Usually for them. That is why I believe Callie will do the same thing. Everything that is not optimal for her has to go. She wanted you in Inaxia. She saw you there, and that led to you killing Hesansh or Neb, that led to her gaining more power, that led to her winning. It's all dominos, and by escaping the city, you've removed one of them. She's going to be mad now."

"Angry or insane?" I asked.

"Both," Nadia said.

"A lot of people are going to die," I said.

"Yes, they are," Nadia said. "I'm going to stay here for a while, and then I'm going to go and help stop the Guild members who are working for Callie. It's a full-time job. I'm not entirely sure I will see you again. That this won't be the last time I am able to stand with you like this."

I stood and stepped toward Nadia, who turned toward me and hugged me tightly. "I will see you again," I said. "I promise."

Nadia pulled away, tears in her eyes. "Don't promise things you can't keep. Lucas, it has been an honour."

"This is all sounding a little too final for my liking."

Nadia smiled. "I just mean that we're both about to go do a dangerous thing. You're going to figure out how to get the Tempest to stop Callie, or try to. The same Tempest that grabbed her in the first place. I have no idea what's going to happen, Lucas."

I'd been trying not to think about it too much, but I guessed going to the Tempest, to try and see if whatever it did to Callie could be reversed, or stopped, or anything, well, it really was stepping into unknown territory. "How about this? I'll do everything in my power to come back, no matter what happens in the Tempest; if I can get here, I will."

Nadia smiled. "I know you will. And that is all any of us can ask. There are other people who would like to see you; make sure you speak to them. Good luck, Lucas. You changed my life, and no matter what happens next, I will always be grateful. Find Callie, stop her."

"I will," I told her.

Nadia looked at me for several seconds, and eventually she said, "Thank you for everything."

"It's been my pleasure," I told her, and picked up the box of medallions, and left Nadia on the beach.

CHAPTER TWENTY-ONE

I carried the medallions with me back to Drusilla's home, finding her sat outside, waiting for me. She placed the book on the table beside her.

"Apologies for the delay," I said, lifting the box to show her. "Nadia had a thing that I needed to pick up." I put the box on the floor and stepped toward Drusilla, who got up and kissed me.

"She worried because she doesn't know what's going to happen next," Drusilla said, returning to her seat. "It must be hard on her."

"She mentioned it," I told her, sitting down in a chair next to her. "And I told her that I will do everything I can to come back. A lot of things have tried to kill me over the years, centuries. Nothing's managed it yet."

"And you won't let me come with you," Drusilla said.

"I figured you weren't done telling me why I was wrong," I said with a smile, although I felt that the joke hadn't landed. "And while I would normally agree with you, on this occasion I have to do this by myself."

"Nadia said you had to go alone too," Drusilla said, obviously bothered about it. "I do not like doing what I am told. I do not like doing what I am suggested to do. I certainly don't like it when the possibility of something happening is supposed to dictate what I do. I have never paid any attention to a chained revenant's ramblings. They are more often than not wrong, or at least partially wrong, about their visions. But on this particular occasion, she said that just once, I should listen to what she says and let you do this alone. She told me that if I go, you will not return." Drusilla took a drink of water and wiped her eyes with the back of her hand.

I reached over and squeezed her hand. "I've been to the Tempest before; I've spoken to the primordials before. This is no different, although I'll admit to some trepidation about actually trying to figure out how to stop whatever connection Callie and the Tempest have. It's what needs to be done."

Drusilla leaned over and kissed me. "Go see Ji-hyun," she said. "When you are done with everything, come back here. You can leave the medallions; they're not going anywhere until you get back."

I gave her a kiss and got to my feet. "I won't be long."

I left Drusilla and went to the main offices, where I found Ji-hyun, Dani, and Gabriel talking just a short distance away from the empty reception area. Zeke was sat on a nearby chair, polishing his Winchester rifle. He looked up at me and nodded.

"Has everybody told you that no one is happy about you going back there by yourself?" Zeke asked.

"Now it does appear to be the topic of conversation," I said. "It sounds like there's enough going on here to keep you all busy."

Zeke nodded and continued to clean his rifle, using the nearby table as a place to keep all of his polishes. "I was going to do this somewhere private, but Ji-hyun said I could just clean my guns here. You heard about the large number of tears?"

"Nadia told me," I said. "Sound like it's mostly in hand, though."

"Mostly," Zeke said. "Nadia had a lot of stuff to say. She never said you were going to die, Lucas. Just that she couldn't see what happened on your journey."

"The chains are all over the place at the best of times," I pointed out. "Look, I don't plan on staying in the rift permanently. All the doom and gloom seems unnecessary."

"You're going to have to do something to make sure the primordials listen to you," Zeke said. "Nadia told me about the medallions. No doom and gloom; I'm just tired, Lucas."

"I'm going to see if handing them back might put our relationship with the primordials on the right path," I said.

"If what Callie said was the truth and the Ancients murdered a bunch of primordials, well, there ain't no putting that right," Zeke said. "You can't put right the eradication of an entire group so that a different group can gain their power. If that's genuinely what the Ancients did, then it was evil. No other word for it. And then they kept a secret for thousands of years, because . . . well, they either knew it was wrong, or they just didn't want anybody else to do it. That's if Callie was being truthful."

"Big *if,*" I pointed out.

"You're not kidding there, my friend," Zeke said. "You got a plan to deal with Hesansh, what with him being linked to Neb?"

"I'll do what I need to do," I said, giving all the answer that I was capable of giving. "I'm going to go and see those three over there; you going to be okay?"

Zeke got to his feet and offered me his hand, which I shook. He pulled me into a hug, and we stood like that for several seconds. When he pulled away, he smiled and nodded. "I choose to believe that you are too fucking stubborn to go out without a fight. And I know that you will keep fighting long after everybody else has given up. So, I doubt very much this is the last time that we will see one another. I'm not saying goodbye, but I will say good luck. Not just with the Tempest and primordials but with the Queen, too. By the time you get back to her, she will have heard something. You were in the embers awhile; you must have needed more healing than you thought. Also, news travels slowly in the rift but not quite at a tectonic pace."

We shook hands again, and I walked over to see Gabriel, Dani, and Ji-hyun; they all turned to greet me as I reached them. Ji-hyun looked as though she needed a rest and a big glass of wine, not necessarily in that order. She was always the strongest person that I'd known, and best placed to deal with whatever shit was currently going down. She gave me a hug.

Gabriel, who often wore his heart on his sleeve, smiled and hugged me, with Dani pushing him aside to hug me after.

"Guys, I'm not dying," I said.

"I know," Ji-hyun said with complete confidence. "Because if you were, I would have to kick your ass. So, you better not. Because I will get a Ouija board, and I will bring your ass back here, and then I will kick it."

I laughed. It felt good after the last few hours. "I promise no dying. Nadia appears to have freaked everybody out a little bit with her 'I can't see Lucas in my chains' spiel."

"Ravi called while you were gone," Dani said. "They finished their initial investigation into the helicopter crashes in England. And you'll be surprised to know that they identified the bodies of all the riftborn involved. However, Theoris wasn't on board that helicopter."

"Theoris is alive?" I said.

Dani nodded. "Or at least not killed on board that helicopter. It's weird because there was a device in the helicopter, stopping them from being able to use their embers, so I don't know how she managed to flee."

I thought back to when I'd seen her. "The necklace," I said. "She has the same necklace as Callie is wearing. It's a blood-red teardrop. It's made from Ahiram's blood, I think; I'm not sure if Callie was being truthful about that. It allows the wearer to be connected to the rift in a huge way. Callie told me that the necklace stops those devices from working. She had bracelets, too, and she told me that's why the power of the Ancients goes to her rather than the Tempest. I'm going to guess that Hesansh is wearing one too. It's why he was so powerful."

"So, Theoris is working with Callie?" Ji-hyun asked.

"By now, she must have lost her link to the rift," I said, wondering which Ancient she'd been paired with and how long it had been since she'd started to lose her connection. "She'll be slowly losing her power. Why would she even start working with her, though? What does she get out of it?"

No one had a good answer for that.

"I'll see if the primordials can shed some light on it," I said. "It's a hell of a way to make everybody think that you're dead, though. Maybe so that everyone is kept guessing as to which Ancients have lost their connections. This isn't just about giving back to the rift; once an Ancient loses their connection, they will have a dwindling amount of power. Yet nearly all of them have been killed. Several by their own people who have been brought over by Callie, or Theoris; still a lot of questions. Maybe I can get some answers."

Ji-hyun let out a small sigh. "You will come back. This is not open to suggestion. Are you sure you want to go alone?"

"No," I said. "I don't want to go alone. But the primordials aren't exactly friendly, and I can't risk them thinking that I am there to do something the Ancients did. But I know Valmore, and at the very least, he trusts me . . . hopefully."

"I can't believe Timo is dead," Ji-hyun said, the change of subject abrupt and jarring. "It's just . . . she was one of the good ones. I can't believe she would be a part of anything like what Callie was suggesting."

"I know," I said. "Be careful out there whilst you're dealing with the people stood against us. They are fanatical; I had to kill Necia. She was beyond saving. She murdered Timo without a second thought, she murdered her friend, and she would've murdered me. Two of those were because we said no to her cult of Callie Mitchell. I don't know how long this has been brewing, but my guess is these people have been slowly moving over to the dark side, so to speak, for a long time. It's quite possible that Christopher's ability to persuade people started to bring a few of them over to the cult. Or at least put the idea in their head. But he's dead now, so we can't ask."

"Oh, shit, Lucas," Ji-hyun said, her voice quiet. She reached over, grabbed my hand, and squeezed it slightly. "This whole thing is so goddamned fucked."

I squeezed her hand back and gave a small smile at her gesture.

"They have to be stopped," Gabriel said. "They are causing problems all around the world. Eliminating those who would stand against whatever it is Callie has planned."

"The level of organisation is actually quite impressive," I said. "Or would be if it weren't aimed at us."

"They believe that anyone who stands against Callie no longer deserves to live," Ji-hyun said. "We've had more than a few taken captive, who have then tried to take their own lives rather than be questioned. Dealing with these people is an exercise in exhaustion. Good luck."

I looked around the room, and Zeke gave me a short salute, which I returned. Gabriel, Dani, and Ji-hyun hugged me, and I left, heading back to Drusilla's, where we spent the next few hours holding one another as we watched the sun come up.

"I love you, you know," Drusilla said as she lay across my chest, her hair falling over my naked torso.

"I love you too," I told her. "I plan on coming back. Just because Nadia can't see me in her chains doesn't mean I'm going to die. Whatever is going to happen in the Tempest isn't going to keep me from coming back."

Drusilla chuckled. "I don't think you're going to die. Dying isn't really the issue here. While we were in the rift, everyone here had their plate full of traitors and fiends. I don't think that's going to stop anytime soon. Everyone is on edge. I don't know what's going to happen, but just be safe. Or as safe as you can be."

"Theoris wasn't killed in the helicopter," I said. "Ravi called; there's no trace of her."

"Any chance Theoris is stuck, or hiding in her embers?" Drusilla asked.

I considered the idea for a moment. If she had been injured in their helicopter crash, there was a chance that she was stuck in her embers, healing. A riftborn with bad-enough injuries could spend years in the embers healing until they could leave. There was no real way to know, unless someone could go into the embers to check. But I wasn't even sure that that was a thing that was possible.

"I want to say no," I said. "I didn't really know her, but Timo said to go to the city Theoris rules. At the conclave, she was wearing the same kind of necklace—albeit a smaller version—that Callie wore. I'll find out. One way or another."

I glanced out of the window at the rear of our home, expecting to see more of the beautiful sunrise, and instead seeing a gigantic tear across the sky above us.

Drusilla turned to see what I was looking at, and her mouth dropped. "That is the largest tear I've ever seen," she said. "It must stretch from here across to Boston. We're going to have a long day."

Alarms began sounding across the island. Fiends were coming.

CHAPTER TWENTY-TWO

Drusilla and I ran out of our home, getting dressed on the way, weapons in hands, and almost ran into Dani, who was coming toward us.

"We have a lot of problems," Dani said, her words all jumbled together.

I pointed up to the sky. "No shit."

"Not just that," Dani said. "Shitloads of tears all across the East Coast; the emergency calls are coming through fast from every state. These things are in the ocean, too; they're everywhere. Hundreds of tears. There's a huge one that stretches out from Rochester all the way to Boston. None of the others are as big as that, but they don't need to be big to let through some pretty horrible stuff. They're elder fiends, Lucas. Dozens and dozens of them."

Fiends were animals on Earth that touched the energy from the rift and transformed into something monstrous. They came in three types: lesser, greater, and elder. The former two were both dangerous if you didn't know what you were up against; the latter were dangerous even if you did.

Elder fiends were created a little differently from the lesser or greater ones. When a tear happened and an animal on Earth went through, just as an animal in the rift went through, an elder fiend was created. It merged the two creatures and, considering animals in the rift are considerably more dangerous than most of those on Earth, it didn't end well for anyone coming across it. Elder fiends were hyper-intelligent and aggressive, but they were rare and they didn't ambush and then wait a bit. They burned out quickly and left a lot of bodies in their wake.

The tear that lit up the sky became full of lesser fiends, all of which flew around like bugs the size of sedans. The fact that there were more tears, all around the island, all across Boston, and that those created elder fiends in their dozens was terrifying. Each one capable of causing untold damage to everything they came across.

"Ji-hyun is getting everyone available to get to the East Coast, and we're lucky that we have a lot of good agents," Dani said. "But we can't deal with all of these and have traitors trying to stop us, trying to kill us."

"This is because the Ancients are dying and their power isn't going back to the rift," I said. "This is what Callie told me would happen. Short-term pain, she said. I need to get to the Tempest."

"You were both touched by the rift," Dani said. "If she can do all this shit, then why can't you?"

"She went into the rift," I explained. "It took her years to come back and make herself known. I was only touched by it; she actually walked into it. Or, rather, was dragged into it screaming."

Drusilla speared a bluebottle the size of a wastepaper basket with a weapon picked up from the blacksmiths, cleaving the creature in half. "I guess this one is finished," she said, flicking ichor off the end of the blade. "You are not walking into the rift. That is insane."

Beyond Drusilla I saw Nadia using her chains to bring down three more of the bugs, several of which looked like overgrown mosquitoes. She appeared to be enjoying herself. Everyone needs a hobby.

With Nadia joining our ranks, as more and more agents flooded out of the buildings around the island, the sounds of gunfire and battle filled the air. We reached Ji-hyun, Gabriel, and Zeke as the latter was shooting bugs out of the sky with pinpoint accuracy for every shot.

The sky above us became awash with flame, and huge spikes of fire ripped out of the tear, impaling everything unlucky enough to be close to it. The dead fiends fell to the ground and melted. Ji-hyun looked back at us with the determined look of someone who wanted to find the person responsible and feed them their own hearts.

I shot a piece of smoke at a fiend, turning it into a hardened bullet before it reached the creature. The impact was both disgusting and satisfying.

"That's new," Zeke said.

"Just thought of it," I said, looking at my hand. "Not entirely sure why. But since I left Callie's presence, I've had a hankering to try a few new things. The old tricks aren't going to work against these people. Need to find some new tricks."

I looked around the island at the dozens of agents who were killing the swarm of fiends which had descended upon them. Most from the sky, birds and bugs that had been close to the rift's power when the tear opened, but there were several creatures crawling out of the ocean to wage war against them. It was going to be a long day.

By the time we were done killing the vast array of creatures, everyone had the look of someone who was absolutely done wading through the remains of fiends that had once been insects and fish.

I sat down on the hill above where a contingent of agents were mopping up the remains of fiends. No casualties, but everyone was going to have long-lasting memories about the day we'd just had.

"Not the best day ever," Dani said as she sat beside me.

"Nope," I said. "That's quite the understatement."

"Where is Hiroyuki?" I asked Ji-hyun, who joined us. Like pretty much everyone else, she was covered in fiend remains. "Has anyone had any contact with him since he went off to wage war against any surviving Guild members?"

"I spoke to him a few hours ago," Ji-hyun said. "It was not a fun conversation. He's being stubborn, and he's hurt, and he doesn't really know what he's supposed to do with himself except find the people who hurt him and hurt them. You can't tell him otherwise."

"Yeah, that sounds like him," I said.

I picked up the box of medallions from where I had left them nearby, and jogged back over to the group, all of whom were busy dealing with a large number of lesser fiends who had gotten close to them. The ground was slick with pieces of monstrous bugs, and I spotted Ji-hyun as she immolated fiends in quick succession, letting them fall to the ground where they melted. She spotted me, and I tossed over her phone, which she caught in one hand.

Drusilla spotted me and ran over. "I think we're going to be busy here for a while; if there's anything you can do inside the Tempest that will help, you should do it. Just push all of the buttons and see what happens."

"That's the plan," I told her. "Keep safe. I'll be as quick as I can."

We kissed, and when we pulled away, I opened a tear and stepped into my embers.

Despite several reservations, mostly based on Nadia's beliefs, I had every intention of returning. I had every intention of seeing my friends again. And I had an even greater intention of coming back to Drusilla and spending however much time we had left together with her.

I stopped walking and stared at the small dormouse who ran up my arm and sat on my shoulder. "Raven Guild medallions?" Maria asked.

I nodded. "I need to get to the Tempest. I'm going to use the forest."

"Not a great idea," Casimir said, after the small sparrow landed on my other shoulder.

We stopped at the entrance to the forest. It was dark and foreboding, the trees swaying slightly in a breeze that did not exist. I had walked through it a handful of times, and each and every time, it was an unpleasant experience that I swore would be my last. I should probably stop doing that.

I looked back at my two eidolons, who had both jumped off my shoulders and now settled on a nearby fence post.

"Maybe you should just be more careful than usual," Maria said.

"Not you, too," I replied.

"We are here if you need us," Maria said.

"Thank you both," I said, and stepped into the forest and whatever was going to await me on the other side.

CHAPTER TWENTY-THREE

The forest is a deeply unpleasant place. Every time I've entered it, I've seen different visions. People I couldn't save. People who didn't want to be saved. People I've lost, people I loved. The one thing that I realised walking through the forest is that every time I do it, it gets a little easier, and I forget that until I'm back inside the forest. It's as if the place wants me to forget that it's getting easier, so that I don't use it too much.

The darkness didn't bother me; the mists that swelled around my feet, occasionally giving me glimpses of my past, changing colour as I stepped, were not frightening. Despite my initial hesitancy, I knew that I was doing the right thing.

I stepped out of the forest and found myself next to a large lake filled with midnight-blue water. A forest of huge trees towered all around me, each one of them hundreds of feet tall, creating a canopy of leaves that made everything below it live in perpetual darkness. The lake was called Lake Spirit, and was home to a primordial by the name of Pru, who I was almost certain was watching me. We'd never met, and it appeared she was perfectly happy with that arrangement.

There were still four metal huts that had been built back from the shore, close to the bottom of the mountain, next to a gentle-looking slope. The huts were in a horseshoe shape facing the lake. Each one was on stilts, with a ramp going from the forest floor to the door itself.

Each of the huts looked old and was covered with rust, pieces fallen off, and moss and grass had grown over those that had touched the ground. Callie Mitchell had brought them there, back when she had been human, monstrous and evil but human. Barely.

"Pru," I called out, watching the ripples across the still surface of the lake. Pru didn't much like people; she didn't much like anybody, from what I'd been told, but she also hadn't been outright hostile toward me. I wondered if she might have some knowledge of where Valmore was.

When it became pretty obvious that Pru was not going to be cooperative, I set off toward a large clearing to the west of where I stood. It didn't take me long to find who I was looking for. A massive animal that looked like a cross between a stag and a wolf lay on the ground, its black-and-crimson fur shimmering as the wind whipped across it. Each of Valmore's four paws was the size of my chest, and he had a thick, bushy tail, which flicked from side to side as he saw me. The antlers that sat atop Valmore's head were each longer than I was tall, and as he got to his feet, it was obvious that he was graceful and quick but also pure muscle and overwhelming power.

Valmore looked down at me with his ice-blue eyes and smiled. At least, I hoped it was a smile. He padded over toward me and nudged me with his massive muzzle. "Lucas," he said, my name reverberating through my chest. "It is good to see you again. And you have brought a gift?"

"I've missed you, my friend," I said, looking up at Valmore and smiling. "But this isn't so much a gift as it is recompense for a crime that I hear was done against you." I opened the box to reveal the medallions inside.

Valmore stared at the medallions for several seconds before slowly looking up to me, curiosity and question written cleanly throughout his expression. "I do not understand. What are you telling me?"

"I need to talk to the primordials," I said. "Not just you but all of you. I need your help before Callie Mitchell tears the rift apart in an effort to take control of the power of the rift and turn herself into . . . well, essentially a god. She's killing the Ancients and taking their power.

"But she's behaving like a chained revenant who has spent too much time in their chains, and she has no intention of healing the rift. She wants the power only for her. She wants to rule and shape this place as she sees fit, and that means destroying anyone in her way. At some point, she's going to come to the Tempest, going to try and, I don't know, destroy it . . . take whatever power remains to it . . . Whatever she does she will not care that the primordials are here."

"Why should we worry about some puny human?" a voice boomed from nearby. A huge creature lumbered around the corner, slowly walking toward me, each of its four legs taller than any man I'd ever met. It was twenty feet long, with a large, scaled black tail with foot-long spikes on the end. White and charcoal-grey fur covered its torso and legs, each massive paw tipped with deadly claws. It had a face that reminded me of an enormous deerhound, but the mouth was too large, the dozens of razor-sharp teeth too long for it to close properly. The fur around the top of its face was long and swept back down its neck, passing two huge antlers covered in burgundy velvet. The fur covered a jagged scar down the side of its neck that I knew from experience was there. It was missing one eye. An eye I'd taken in battle. Prilias.

Valmore stepped in front of me and faced the newcomer. "You will not hurt him," he said, his voice full of threat.

"I have no intention of hurting your pet," Prilias said. "You have brought back some of what was stolen so long ago. Yet you only do so to gain our favour in your battle against someone who has also taken from us without any form of recompense. You still wear a blade of primordial bone."

I removed the spear from my back and glanced at the tip before looking up at Prilias. "This was given freely."

"By Valmore," Prilias said, looking over at his brother. "I concede that fact. You did not kill the primordial that that was taken from; no one did. Its bone was ripe for harvest. It is correct and proper that nothing goes to waste in the Tempest. But what is contained within that box was stolen."

"I want to understand what happened," I said. "What did the Ancients do?"

"Not all of them," Valmore corrected. "Two of them."

"They all benefitted," Prilias snapped. "They were all happy to take the power and do as they would with it. To conquer the rift and make themselves its rulers."

"What happened?" I asked.

"Lucas is not responsible for the crimes committed against us," Valmore said. "He has tried to help us. He stopped the mountain from exploding worse than it did. We are supposed to be the keepers of the Tempest under the mountain; if it had been allowed to rupture, we would all be dead, and the power that flowed out would have left the rift a ruined place."

"He is a small cog in the large machine that has taken so much from us," Prilias said, his eyes squarely on me. "I will not kill him; I will not feast upon his bones. But if he wants the help of the primordials, he will need to go deeper into our territory; he will need to seek out those of us who remain hidden. Val, you will need to bring us all together once again; he is your pet, so this is your responsibility. The conclave of the primordials will need to begin. He will have to prove to all of us that he is true to his word."

"Callie Mitchell and her followers are causing devastation both in the rift and on Earth," I said. "I need to find a way to stop it. If we can't, then it's not just everybody else that gets hurt; the primordials and even the Tempest will not be left unaffected."

"Does he know what will happen should the conclave decide to allow his request of aid?" Prilias asked.

Valmore looked back at me, a pitying expression on his face. "I do not believe he does."

Prilias's laugh was loud and unpleasant, the sound ringing in my ears and my chest.

"What does he mean?" I asked.

"If the conclave decides that they wish to aid you," Valmore said, "there will be a test. You will have to go into the mountain and allow the power of the Tempest to touch you to see if you are worthy."

"Didn't I already do that?" I asked.

"No," Valmore said. "The Tempest allowed you to link to the rift. To feel its heartbeat, to feel the world around you, but this will be a connection unlike any other. If you fail, you will not get a second chance at anything."

I looked between the two primordials. "Meaning what? That the same thing that happened to Callie will happen to me? That I'll be vaporised and reborn at some point in the future?"

"No one knows," Valmore said. "The Tempest's power could vaporise you, it could destroy you altogether, it could bring you back, it could do any number of things. The primordials cannot enter the chamber; our entire bodies are made up of rift energy, more than any other creature in the rift. If one of us entered the chamber under the mountain, we would be killed, almost instantly, and our rift energy would be consumed by the rift itself."

"Is that like what Callie is doing with the Ancients?" I asked.

"Yes," Prilias said. "Their rift energy is not being put back into the rift. We can feel a building-up of power throughout the rift; it is isolated in the south of this world. She is storing power. If she pours all of that power, the power of twelve Ancients, back into the rift at once . . . we don't know what will happen. Currently, the power is flickering across the rift, causing an unknown number of tears. Whatever she is doing, it will eventually have catastrophic consequences."

"Such as?" I asked.

"If she is manipulating rift energy in a way to cause all of these tears, she might cause one that does not close," Valmore said.

"Or," Prilias said, "she would merge the Earth and the rift. I am fairly certain that would be cataclysmic for both of us."

"So, why haven't you stopped her?" I asked.

"We cannot leave our land," Prilias said.

"I understand that you hate us," I said. "But I don't think any of us wants this sort of destruction. If all of us die and only the primordials exist, what is the use of being the last things in the world where there is nothing else?"

Prilias and Valmore shared a glance. "I will take him to the conclave," Valmore said. "We will ensure that he speaks to the primordial elders and that he is given a fair account."

Prilias stepped up toward me, his head only a few inches from my own. Should he have wished it, there was a good chance he could've killed me before I was able to react. "You took my eye," he said, his breath warm on my face.

"You were attacking settlements within the rift," I said. "People had died."

"One of your Ancients was there," he said. "The one who took from us."

"What was their name?" I asked.

"I did not discover it," Prilias said. "I did not care to. I do not care about your kind, I do not like your kind, but I do not kill innocent people without reason. The people I killed had arrived at that settlement with the Ancient. I wanted to kill just the one person, and everybody else was just in the way. Except you. I am less than pleased that you stopped me, but if we are to stop the destruction of my world, I will not stand in your way."

"Thank you," I said.

"It seems, Lucas," Prilias continued, "that Valmore considers you to be a good man. A man of some integrity. You raced to stop me from killing innocents and only succeeded in stopping me from killing an Ancient."

"If it helps, there are only two, maybe three left," I said, wondering if Theoris was truly alive, or if it was just Neb and Hesansh now. "I don't know if any of them are the ones who stole from you, but in the long run, the power brought them only pain and suffering."

I kept eye contact with the much-larger creature and tried my best to ensure that no emotion could be read on my face.

"If you turn out to be anything like the two who stole from us," Prilias said, "I will feast upon your flesh myself. There is nowhere you could hide that I would not find you. Do you want to know how many of our kind your Ancients killed?"

I wasn't entirely sure how I was supposed to respond to that. Part of me desperately did not want to know; the idea that they could kill at all to take the power of the primordial was horrific. If it turned out that it was ten, or a hundred, or even a thousand, would it make any difference? One was too many. The taking of just one primordial to satisfy their need for power was too many. "How many?" I asked, never dropping eye contact with the larger creature.

"I don't know," Prilias said softly, sadness etched in every word. "There are several hundred of us remaining where there were once several thousand. But I don't know the exact number. I'm not entirely sure that anyone does. But the fact that you would not shy away from it leads me to hope that my brother over there might be right about you. Do not fail him. Do not fail my kind. The wrath of a primordial is a terrible thing, and many of us have been looking for someone to release it upon."

I walked past Prilias without another word. The conversation was getting us nowhere, and I began to feel like it was going round and round in circles, with Prilias desperately wanting to get out all of the pent-up anger and resentment that he had felt for so long.

"If you fail," Prilias said, as Valmore dipped his head so that I could climb upon his back, nestling against the thick, warm fur, as I knew to hold on, based on prior experience, "I will kill you, Lucas. That much I promise. Valmore, I will see that any primordials in the area arrive at the conclave. Good luck."

"Are you ready, Lucas?" Valmore asked me.

"Yes," I said. "Are they all going to be as hostile toward me as Prilias?"

"Oh, no," Valmore said as he set off at a gentle run. "Some of them will be much more hostile toward you."

CHAPTER TWENTY-FOUR

After what felt like hours of riding across tundra, I'd seen a vast amount of land in the Tempest that I wasn't sure anyone else had ever seen, beyond the primordials themselves. There were plants and animals that I had never encountered before, and lakes of aquamarine and turquoise, the power of the Tempest itself almost coming off the surface of the water in waves.

Valmore had told me to rest, had said that I would not fall from him whilst I slept. At first, I tried to resist the temptation to fall asleep on the back of the running primordial, but the firm grip of his fur kept me in place, and I eventually succumbed to sleep.

I didn't know how long I had been asleep when I woke to see a clearing the size of a football pitch, green grass fluttering with the strong wind that moved across the plain. To the right of me was the foot of the mountain under which the power of the Tempest resided. I could feel it calling to me, telling me that it could give me what I wanted. It was as if it were a pressure in my head that was trying to soothe me, to make me feel that it would all be okay if I just accepted it. I continuously pushed the thoughts aside as Valmore strolled across the clearing.

Beneath the shadow of the mountain sat a mound. It was at least fifty feet long and sat thirty feet above the rest of the clearing, with steep slopes on all sides that I could see. It appeared to be the kind of place where someone would stand and command those below.

Directly in front of us, on the opposite side of the clearing, was yet another forest; the trees seemed much less dense than in the one that I'd seen when I first arrived, the leaves all autumnal colours. To the left was open tundra as far as the eye could see. Occasionally, I caught a glimpse of something moving across it, although whatever it was made sure to keep away from coming close to the clearing.

"I call a conclave," Valmore shouted, letting loose a roar which shook the ground as I dropped to it from his back.

"Do you think they heard you?" I whispered, with a smile that quickly vanished from my lips.

"Do not speak," Valmore said without looking down at me. "I am unclear as to how some of the primordials will react to your presence."

I took his words to heart and made sure to keep my mouth shut.

Nothing happened for several seconds, until roars came back from the depths of the forest. At first it was one or two, but it was soon a cacophony of noise as it crashed over me and met similar noise coming from the direction Valmore and I had ridden from.

I turned to look as at least fifty primordials ran across the tundra, and spotted several leaving lakes that we had ridden past not long before. Some of the primordials had a similar appearance to those that I had met so far, a mixture of wolves and deer, with thick fur of various colours. But some had the appearance of large frogs with scaly skin and bone ridges around their heads, which reminded me of dinosaurs. At least one of them actually looked like a stegosaurus, albeit mixed with an arctic fox, a combination that I would never have considered in a million years had I not seen it with my own eyes.

Trees snapped behind me, and I turned to watch another primordial, this one with the appearance of a triceratops mixed with that of a buffalo. It looked like something that could be used as a battering ram against a castle. The three spear points of bone that protruded from its head were each at least three feet long and, like the rest of it, jet black. It turned in place, showing bright blue stripes across its stomach and side. Not a single creature there was coloured for camouflage or for needing protection from predators. The only predators the primordials ever had were apparently the Ancients.

Prilias has said that only two of the Ancients had committed any crimes against them, although which two, and what crimes, remained to be discovered.

Several of the primordials flew down from the top of the mountain, some looking like bugs, some like birds, and some in the same dinosaur style as several of their kin. One gigantic primordial flew toward us, a creature I'd recognised as watching me the last time I'd been under the mountain. I was surrounded by creatures that were not only massive and towered above me but had also been done wrong by my own kind. I kept thinking of the Ancients as a separate entity, as something that I could distance myself from, but they were riftborn just like me. Maybe the primordials would not see that their predators had finally gone but that one stood before them, with a box of their bones in hand.

Judging from the amount of noise that was made by the primordials, not all of them were pleased to see me; in fact, several of them didn't even seem pleased to see Valmore. They roared and hissed in his direction, and he replied in kind.

I stood still and remained silent as Valmore ensured that I was neither eaten nor stamped into paste. If any of the primordials had decided to do either of those things, there was very little I could do to stop them. There was very little Valmore could do to stop them.

After several minutes of ear-splitting shouting, Valmore motioned for me to move toward the mound in the shadow of the mountain.

"You are to talk to them," Valmore told me as he picked me up in his mouth and placed me atop the mound.

"You know I could have just turned to smoke," I said, brushing myself down as I landed.

"I do not think it is wise for you to show your level of power at this exact moment," Valmore said. "You will tell them what you told us earlier; they will have questions."

"Who's in charge?" I asked, looking around at a sea of faces belonging to ancient creatures who had been done wrong by people I had considered friends. I let out a little sigh.

"The triceratops with the blue marking," Valmore said without looking back at his people. "His name is Tasicus. He leads the conclave. He is . . . I guess you could call him an historian. Or keeper of knowledge of our people."

I looked beyond my friend and easily found the primordial called Tasicus. "He looks really mad."

"He always looks like that," Valmore said. "But he is fair and honest. And he has no love for Prilias and his wish for violence against your kind. He is the oldest of us, possibly. It is hard to tell, but he is the one you have to convince to get us to help. His opinion carries a lot of weight; the opinions of several others too, but his the most."

"Anyone else I really need to keep an eye on?" I asked.

"Lavis," Valmore said. "The stegosaurus. She is smart and capable, and beloved by a large number of my kind. She will often decide with Tasicus, but she is her own primordial, with her own mind, and if she does not believe you, there is a very large possibility it will split the vote. And not in your favour."

"Lavis and Tasicus," I said making sure to keep an eye on both of them; they stood at opposite ends of a large crowd of primordials, both of them staring directly at me. I have never had something that looked like a dinosaur become that interested in me; even if they were herbivores back on Earth, it didn't make it any less intimidating.

"You will be fine," Valmore said. "But you should know the last of your kind to stand there and talk to us betrayed us and started killing us when we would not give over our power."

"One of the Ancients?" I asked, already knowing the answer. "Which one?"

"Ahiram," Valmore whispered. "His name is best left unspoken."

"Who was the other?" I asked.

"Theoris," Valmore said. "I would not say her name, either."

I turned back to my old primordial friend. "Just those two?"

Valmore nodded.

I watched Valmore walk away and take up a seat just beyond the clearing, next to the frog primordial that I had seen earlier. I wondered if that was Pru.

"Riftborn," someone said, the word echoing all around me.

I turned to look at the crowd before me, still unsure which one of the primordial had spoken.

"You come bearing *gifts*," the triceratops, Tasicus, said, making the word *gift* sound like anything but.

I looked down at the box of medallions at my feet. I opened the box and stepped back aside. "These do not belong to us," I said. "We were not told how they were taken from you. We were not told about what happened to your people, I cannot fix the past, but I hope that by bringing these back, it shows that I want to try to make a present and future."

"Valmore tells us that your spear was a gift," Lavis said. "You are welcome to keep that; none of us would have it said that we would want our bones to go to waste when we have died naturally. The bones that were taken from this place to make some of those medallions did not belong to primordials that died naturally."

"Some were offered freely?" I asked.

Lavis nodded. "Not all of us hold all of the Ancients responsible for the crimes of a few, but all of us distrust them because of it. They used the power given to them; they never sought to return it, even if it meant their deaths, but some primordials forgave. Some offered their bones to be used as medallions. I cannot tell you which medallions would have been given freely and which taken by force."

"Those responsible hid their crime for millennia," I said. "There were two of them, the people you know as Ancients. One is dead, and the other is . . . I don't know. I spoke to one of the Ancients, Timo; she did not remember committing crimes against your people. If she had known what had happened, she would have tried to make it right."

"Are you here to make amends?" Tasicus asked.

"Eventually, I hope that is something that I can do," I said honestly. "If I'm truthful, I'm still unsure what they did. None of the other

Ancients appeared to know. I understand that it is a difficult thing to talk about, but I wish to know the truth."

"Depending on how this conclave goes," Lavis said, "there's a possibility that you will regret those words."

"We are not here to discuss old wounds," Tasicus said.

The triceratops had a point. A sentence I never thought I'd think. "There is a person by the name of Callie Mitchell who was gifted a part of the Tempest's power. I believe that her own mind may have fractured in the process, or maybe that whatever the Tempest did to her has stopped and she is reverting to her previous personality. Whatever is happening to her mentally, she is murdering the Ancients."

"Yes," Tasicus said.

"Their power is meant to go back into the rift, back to the Tempest," I said. "But she's keeping it for herself. She's allowing others to tap in to that power, making them stronger, more dangerous.

"Tears are happening all over, and I suspect that's due at least in part to the chaotic nature of what Callie is doing. She wants to take the power of the rift and reshape it as she wills. She wants to *control* the rift, and anyone in her way has to die. I need to know how to stop her. If she continues on this path, the death toll will be unimaginable. She has already killed so many. People I cared about. I would not wish more to feel the grief that I feel."

"And you are here for vengeance?" Tasicus asked.

I let out a long breath. "Originally, yes."

There was a lot of roaring as many of the primordials tried to talk at once, until Tasicus let out a roar of his own and everybody fell silent. "Continue," he said.

"I know you feel that because of the actions of two Ancients, all Ancients were responsible," I said. "They took the power and used it to advance themselves, accepting what had happened. Maybe some of them knew what had been done here, maybe not, I don't know. But I do know that there were Ancients who used their power for good.

There are people alive today who wouldn't be without them. There are primordials who are alive today because they helped me stop Callie from taking control of the Tempest only a few years ago."

More roaring, and once again, Tasicus calmed the crowd.

Once the crowd noise had subsided once more, I continued. "I met Callie in Inaxia, and she was surrounded by Guild members whom she had persuaded to turn on their own people, and they revered her. A woman I had once loved had fallen under her spell. Callie has created a cult. If the woman I just spoke about was being honest, or had been told true information, Callie plans on getting the riftborn to absorb the shadows in their embers, making them more powerful. When that is done, they're going to conquer this world and Earth; actually, Necia said all of the realms linked to this world. I don't know what that means, but I assume she means Earth."

There was a general low-level murmuring that happened throughout the crowd, but eventually, Tasicus spoke. "There are more worlds than Earth that are linked to the power of the Tempest. Earth is linked to the rift, but the Tempest is linked to everything. If Callie has the inclination to conquer all of those worlds, then we should all be deeply concerned about her. It appears that the power of the Tempest bestowed upon her in order to carry out its wishes has been corrupted. Or maybe it was always corrupted; it is difficult to tell. So few people ever even see the Tempest core itself, let alone are given a portion of its power. The fact that she is telling riftborn about the shadows in your embers is a deeply concerning matter."

I felt the eyes of hundreds of primordials on me, but I was unsure what I was meant to say to that. Eventually, I figured I had to say something; otherwise, I was just going to be stood before them and things were going to get weird. "What are the shadows?" I asked.

"They are your power, held back," Lavis said. "They hunt you at night because by tearing into you, they become one with you. Occasionally, a riftborn accidentally allows this to happen; they are usually mentally unprepared for what follows. There have been several lost to their embers because of this. The Ancients knew what they were; I assume you were always told that they were to be feared, that the shadow should be avoided at all costs."

I thought back to the time when I had first become a riftborn. Had Neb warned me off the shadows? Had I decided to avoid them myself? Had the eidolons taken my fear of them and assured me that I was correct? I couldn't remember. It was possible that someone had told me to fear the shadows; it was possible that it had been Neb. It was just as possible that it had been someone who had been told by someone, who had been told by someone, et cetera, all the way back to whichever Ancient started the rumour. And now Callie was correcting that lie. She was telling people she could give them power and then proving it by giving them the power that they had all along. The Ancients, if they hadn't already been murdered, would have brought about their own downfall eventually, just because people would have realised that they had been lied to their whole lives.

"So, what do you want to do about her?" Tasicus asked, starting a murmur of agreement that ripped through the crowd at his question.

"I want," I started, before pausing a second to consider my words. "I don't know. I need to stop her, and the people following her, before more die. I need to stop Earth being ravaged by fiends because Callie decided to play fuck-around-and-find-out with tears. I don't know how to stop her; I don't even know where she is.

"If we do nothing, a lot of people are going to die. Not just humans and the rift-fused but also the primordials. If Callie plans to conquer this world, you are all in her way. She needs the Tempest; I'm pretty sure that that's what her ultimate goal is."

"Is it true that the power of the Tempest also touched you?" Lavis asked.

I nodded. "I can sense things, I'm stronger, I'm . . . I feel more at ease in the rift than I did before. I can sense power, although I couldn't sense Callie's allies. She seems to be able to freeze time, or move too fast for the time to understand her. Look, I want answers. And I'm pretty sure the only way I'm going to get them is to go to the Tempest under the mountain. And I know for a fact that the only way that I'm going to get there is with your permission. I don't know how to get into the mountain without your help, and honestly, I don't want to make enemies of the primordials by doing it without permission.

"Too many things have gone that way already. We crashed a part of it down the last time we were here. Can you help me stop her? Can you help me speak to the Tempest? If we can remove the power she has, we might be able to stop more people from getting hurt."

"We will consider your request," Tasicus said. "Thank you for your honesty."

Valmore walked back over to me and picked up the box of medallions in his mouth; he carried it into the throng of primordials and placed it down among them. I stayed where I was as I watched one of the primordials smash the box open, the contents spilling over the grass. They all stared at the box and medallions for several seconds, before one of them let out an anguished howl. It was quickly followed by more and more of the primordials, until the entire area was awash with howls of pain.

I remained where I was on top of the mound as Valmore returned to me. "You did a good thing today," he said. "Whether they agree to help you or not, you did a good thing."

"I'm sorry I didn't know," I said. "Why didn't you tell me?"

"I judged you on who you were; not other people's behaviour you were not aware of," Valmore said. "If I had told you that your whole world was wrong, was based on lies and death, would you have believed me? Besides, every interaction that we have ever had, we have been dealing with more important things. Usually involving the deaths of innocent people. I was wary of you for a long time, Lucas. But you are my friend, and by the time you became my friend, I was unsure how to tell you the truth. I should have done. Maybe the death and destruction facing both of our worlds would have been lessened if you had known the truth; maybe you could have directed things to go in a different way. We will never know."

Valmore led me away from the mound and the primordials as they considered their decision about my request. I had absolutely no idea what I was going to do if they refused. I had no idea how I was going to get into the mountain. I had come there to ask the primordials for aid, but I hadn't really been sure what that aid was supposed to be until I'd spoken to them. It just felt like the right thing to do.

We sat away from the rest of the primordials as night fell, and my stomach began to growl. Valmore kindly showed me several types of berries that I could eat nearby, and I was allowed to start a fire, as the wind began to pick up and the temperature plummeted.

It wasn't until the break of dawn the next morning that Tasicus and Lavis approached me, each of their footsteps causing the ground beneath me to shake.

"We will help you get to the Tempest under the mountain," Tasicus said. "But in return, the medallions from the other Guilds will be returned to us. Is this agreed?"

I considered the proposal for a moment, but in reality, there was nothing to consider. "All of them I can find," I said.

Tasicus smiled and nodded. "Lavis will take you under the mountain. Valmore will stay here and await your return. You will be tested, Lucas. The Tempest will know who you are, and it will know what you want. You cannot lie to it, or it will consume you. I understand that it gave you a fraction of its power before, but this will be unlike anything you've ever experienced.

"I believe that is why it gave power to Callie; she knew who she was and what she wanted. The Tempest is not a living thing in the way that you believe something to be alive. It is pure power, pure energy, emotion and nothing else. There is a possibility that you will die. Are you willing to take that chance?"

I got to my feet and brushed myself down before looking between the three large primordials and nodding. "Thank you for agreeing to this. Let's get it done."

CHAPTER TWENTY-FIVE

As the vast majority of the primordials went back to wherever it was they lived, I was left alone on the grassy clearing with Valmore, waiting for Lavis to return, ready for our departure.

Prilias padded over toward us, a confident swagger in his movements. "I didn't think you would do it," he said to me. "I thought they might eat you. Part of me was hoping that they would eat you."

"Sorry to disappoint," I said. "I believe I would be a little bit stringy, anyway."

Prilias laughed; it was a somewhat disturbing sound. "I still might get to eat you. If you screw this up, and if anything happens to Lavis, the rest of the primordials will hunt you down. I think that might be quite fun."

"Just go home," Valmore said, sounding as though he was deeply tired by the whole process.

Prilias turned and left without another word. I watched him go and looked up at Valmore, who was also watching him.

"Is he going to be a problem?" I asked.

"One day, he will try to claim the primordials," Valmore said sadly. "He wishes that he had the influence that Tasicus has. Or was as beloved as Lavis. He will never achieve either, and he knows this, and it makes him bitter."

"Are you going to go home now?" I asked.

Valmore looked up into the distance. "I believe I will spend some time with my people. It has been many years since I have lived here, among them. You brought me back to them, sooner than I had expected to. I do not believe that everything happens for a reason, Lucas. But I do believe that sometimes in your life, you will meet people who will have a profound effect on you and your world. I believe that you are one of those people. And I thank you for it."

"It has been a pleasure," I said. "I hope, once this is all over, that I can come back and do more than just bring a box of medallions."

"That would be something I would look forward to," Valmore said as Lavis strolled toward us. "I will leave you in her capable hands. Metaphorically. Go safely, Lucas. I wish you luck."

Valmore nodded to Lavis as they passed one another, and I stood where I was and watched my friend walk away, only for the view to be replaced with another primordial.

"You are a convincing speaker," Lavis said, her voice soft and full of kindness. It was in contrast to several of the other primordials I'd heard. "Shall we?"

I followed Lavis out of the clearing and around the foot of the mountain for several miles. It began to get colder and colder the farther we went, until within only a few hours of leaving the clearing, we were walking through ankle-high snow.

"Do you require a lift?" Lavis asked, looking down at me with what I was pretty sure was a smirk on her face.

I stared up at her for a moment, considering how to answer the question *Do I want to ride on the back of a half-stegosaurus half-fox?* It wasn't something I'd ever considered before. "That would be lovely," I said with a slight bow of my head.

Lavis lay down in the snow so that I could use her rear leg to climb up onto the fur that adorned both of her flanks before it changed into the plate-like armour that would have been more expected on a stegosaurus. I walked along her back using the plates, each one the size of me, until I was at her neck, where I sat down. Like Valmore, the fur around her neck and head was soft, and whilst it looked white from a distance, it was more of a creamy grey up close.

I sat down, my back up against one of the rigid plates, and Lavis got back to her feet. "Are you comfortable?"

"Yes," I said. "Thank you very much."

"You should hold on," Lavis said, with some humour in her voice. "Grab the fur at the base of my neck."

I wrapped my hands inside the soft fur, and it moved as if to hold me in place, much like Valmore's fur had. Unlike Valmore, whose running was smooth, Lavis ran like she was about to bulldoze through a door. Every pound of her feet was power incarnate, and I saw trees shake from the sheer strength that she could put into her run. If Valmore was akin to a sleek motorcycle, Lavis was like riding on top of a train, and I wondered if the metaphor would last if she had to stop suddenly for any reason. Because I got the feeling that that was not an option.

It wasn't long until we were moving at high speed, much faster than even Valmore had run, but Lavis was incredibly agile, moving out of the way of trees and rocks with ease and grace. It took several more hours of riding before she began to slow, and even then, it was some time before she came to a stop.

"This is where you get off," Lavis said.

I turned to smoke, blowing back to the ground and re-forming.

"Could you have done that the whole time?" Lavis asked.

I nodded. "Valmore told me to not use my powers. I wasn't entirely certain when that request ended."

Lavis chuckled before her face grew serious, as serious as a stegosaurus's face could ever look. "You should know a few things," she said. "You cannot lie to yourself; you cannot lie to the Tempest. You will die if you do. I don't know what you will see, but if you come out of this on the other side, you may have knowledge beyond what you currently have. You may have power more than you have. You may have both. You may have neither. Whatever the Tempest decides is final. You do not get a second go. Good luck. You will need it."

"Can the primordials help with Callie?" I asked.

Lavis shook her head. "We cannot leave this place. The mists surrounding it make it so. Occasionally, they disperse and one of our kind, usually Prilias or someone like-minded, goes out, but they are inevitably pushed back."

I thanked Lavis and strolled toward the large tunnel mouth beside me. There was no light inside and no way of knowing how long the tunnel was or how deep it went. I looked up at the mountain; there was a possibility that the tunnel went spiralling up to the peaks of the mountain itself. I looked back to ask, but Lavis was already running back the way she had come.

I took a deep breath and began to walk into the mouth of the tunnel. After a hundred feet, tiny pinpricks of light adorned the stone: rift power. It was enough that it bathed the whole area in turquoise that would have looked almost pleasant under other circumstances.

There were several times when I thought that the tunnel went back on itself, taking me in gigantic circles as I moved deeper and deeper beneath the mountain. But it was difficult to know whether or not that was the case. Or if I was just unable to gather my bearings when there was nothing to see but rock and tiny holes of light. I noticed no creatures in the tunnel, and no sound except for the occasional whipping of the wind as it blew in from outside. I didn't know if that was from back the way I'd come or from somewhere else within the tunnel, but every time it happened, it made the hairs on the back of my neck stand up. I let out a long breath and continued on toward whatever the tunnel was leading me to.

By the time the tunnel began to glow a brilliant white-blue, I'd been walking along it for several hours. After another hour of walking, whereupon the tunnel became brighter and brighter, until it was almost too much to look at, I stepped out into a large chamber, and the sense of awe that I'd felt the last time I was there crashed back over me.

I stood at the top of a city-sized basin that was thousands of feet deep. The basin was pale blue, with swirls of indigo, red, blue, and moss green at the top, and more and more purple the farther down it went. The blue glowed so brightly, it hurt to look at.

The basin itself was made of primordial bone. The last time I'd been there, I'd been unsure if that was true; this time, I knew it for a fact. It was just something . . . I knew. Unlike the last time, the basin was no longer smooth all the way around, and big chunks were taken out where parts of the mountain above had crashed down upon it. The last time I'd been this close to the Tempest, Callie had been swallowed by it, and I thought I would never see her again. It had been a happy thought.

Just like the last time I'd been there, in the centre of the basin was the Tempest. A massive swirling vortex of blue and purple power. Energy shot up out of it through an opening at the top of the mountain high above us. The energy continued on into the sky and exploded in lightning and thunder. Also just like last time, there was no sound when the power was ejected straight up. Despite the winds being ever ferocious, there was no noise as it passed over me; it was both calming and terrifying.

Unlike last time, when the whole place had given me a sense of peace, this time I felt a constant state of unease. I didn't know what was going to happen next, and the idea of being swallowed up by the Tempest only to be spat out sometime later, my personality no longer only my own, was a terrifying thing to consider.

I stared at the basin and remembered that it was a map of the rift. Callie had tried to control it once, trying to find out where and when the tears would happen, to control them, to control who was turned and when. The idea of someone having control over that was terrifying. There are some things which should not be controlled.

"I need to talk to someone," I shouted, feeling more than a little foolish at the idea of shouting at energy.

The wind continued to whip around in its ferocity until I heard above it, "Lucas."

I looked around, expecting to see someone descend from above, but there was no one. "Who spoke?" I asked.

The wind whipped by once again. "You have come to see me."

"The Tempest?"

"The last time you were here, you left with a small part of my gift; you have returned. What is it you require this time?"

"How can I talk to you?" I asked. "I know that's not the most important thing right now; I just sort of don't know what to do or where to look."

There is nowhere in this world or any other that I could imagine where the idea of energy chuckling is something you get used to. It was weird.

"Just talk," the Tempest said. "I can see who you are, into your soul, I can see your truths and possible futures. So many possibilities. It's like your friend, the chained revenant; I see everything she sees but with complete clarity and crystal understanding of what will happen next. And I'm not driven mad by the knowledge."

"Did you foresee Callie using your power to kill all of the Ancients?" I asked, more than a little irritated. "Or that she is going to use that power to conquer this world and every other world linked to it? And I didn't even know there were other worlds until a few hours ago. It's been a long day."

"I saw her plans to reshape the rift, to make it a better place," the Tempest said. "I did not consider the *how* to be as important as the need to do it. I have since learned that was a mistake. One of many I made. Wait a moment."

Bright blue energy snapped out of the Tempest, leapt up toward me, and re-formed directly in front of me, taking the shape of Drusilla. "Is this form pleasing?"

"It is, but I'd rather you pick another," I said. "I'd rather not have this conversation with someone who looks like a loved one."

The Tempest looked confused but changed their shape to that of an actor I had seen with Drusilla in a TV show only a few weeks previously. One of the perilously few times we were able to have an uninterrupted evening, where nothing was trying to kill us or destroy part of Earth or the rift.

"That's your choice?" I asked.

The Tempest looked down at itself, taking in the exquisitely tailored black suit, before looking back up at me. "I think I will just stay with this one," the Tempest said with a smile. "You can call me . . . Vincent."

I wanted to tell the Tempest . . . Vincent that this too was very weird, but honestly, I just wanted the whole thing to move forward. "Fine, I need your help. I need to know how to stop Callie. I can't believe that you would have given her part of your power so that she can conquer and destroy."

"I gave her my power to fix the rift," Vincent said, his tone soft but with an unsaid violence behind his eyes that made me feel uncomfortable. I didn't think that the Tempest was violent, but the character that the actor was playing had been, and it was unnerving to have that character stare at me. "I did not expect her to murder all of the Ancients. They took the power of the primordials, murdered them, ate them, stole their bones and flesh, and then used it to rule the rift. It was time for that rule to come to an end. But no, I did not wish for her to murder them all and keep all the power for herself. She was not meant to behave without thought or care."

"If you can see into my soul and heart, why didn't you stop her?" I asked. "Why give her that power?"

"Because she was certain she could make the world better," the Tempest said. "I believed her. I still believe her. She can make the world better; she just chooses to do it in a way that will make it much worse for a lot of people. Also, it had been a long time since I'd spoken to anyone; there's a possibility I *wanted* to believe her."

"She doesn't care about how she gets the power," I said. "Just that she wins."

"Yes," Vincent said. "That is exactly what I thought of her. She is ruthless; that is why I gave her the power. She was honest about who she was and what she wanted. Unfortunately, while she had part of my power, she also retained part of her old personality. Personality is hard for me to control, especially when someone is strong-willed. I can tell when someone is dishonest, I can see what someone desires in a broad manner, I can see possibilities of what a person might do with my power, but I cannot read minds. By the time I stopped using my power to control her, it was too late. Another mistake on my part."

"No shit," I said before I could stop myself.

"The Ancients took what was not theirs to take," Vincent said. "They came here as a large group, and two of them, Ahiram and Theoris, discovered that the primordials were a source of rift power. That it fed their very blood and bones. They murdered one, feasted on it, poisoned the others, dragged them in here, and used the blood of the primordials to take power, linking them all together in the process.

"It was long before I'd gained what you might call a personality or even the ability to communicate. The rift was newer back then, and I was less evolved. I think that their behaviour may have led to me gaining sentience, in a weird kind of way."

"So, those two Ancients conspired to use the blood and bones of a primordial to take power from all of this?" I asked. "How did they know how to do any of this?"

"Not all of the primordials at the time were happy staying in this land," Vincent said. "Some, just like humans, wanted more. Wanted power. They conspired with the two Ancients to ensure that when the power was gifted to them, they would help the primordials leave this place and gain more power for themselves. I believe that they killed the primordials who helped them to cover up their crime. Who gave them the information they needed to understand how to take that power in the first place. The primordials blame all of the Ancients, even though they know that not all of them took part in what happened. Most of them weren't even conscious; they were unwitting pawns in whatever plans that the pair had for the rest of them."

"What plans were they?" I asked.

"I have no idea," Vincent said. "They'd already taken their shadows in their embers. Already become more powerful than any other of their kind. The rift was changing rapidly, and with it my power and influence, my . . . personality. They came and stole their power at almost the exact right time to do it."

"What is this shadows stuff?" I asked. "Not the first time I've heard it in the last few days, but no one has ever mentioned it to me before."

"The Ancients must have kept the knowledge secret," Vincent said. "You will have to ask them. Taking your shadows is the first step to taking the power of the Tempest. I hoped that because Callie was human and had no shadows to tame, it would make her . . . easier to control. I am not omnipotent, Lucas. I can admit I was wrong."

"What can we do to stop her?"

"If the unstable tears could be stabilised, then there is a possibility that the Earth and the rift could coexist in a more symbiotic nature. Unlike now; things are not equal."

"Were the rift and Earth always meant to be linked?" I asked.

Vincent nodded. "The rift exists throughout. This one part of this rift is linked to Earth, but there are other links within the rift. And those links link to other rifts and other worlds. A stabilised rift and Earth would have led to this rift becoming symbiotic with another rift; that is how it is meant to work. The Ancients ensured, by accident, I assume, that would never happen. The length and breadth of the domino effect from what they did could forever change how the rift works. Callie was meant to be a scalpel; instead, she was a sledgehammer. Actually, she was more akin to a nuclear bomb."

"How do we fix it?" I asked.

Vincent laughed. It was genuinely more unnerving than when the primordials had laughed. "We?"

"You sent Callie out there to fix something and she only made it worse," I said. "Is there not a way for you to bring her power back?"

Vincent considered it for a moment. "If she dies, the power will revert to me, or it will revert to the person who killed her, depending on how she dies. However, at your current power level, you would be unable to kill her. You have not even gathered the power that you could acquire from your own shadows. You need to do that."

"I don't have time," I said.

"Time is relative here," Vincent said, pointing behind me.

I turned and saw my body talking to Vincent exactly where I entered. A streak of Tempest energy had torn through my body, starting at my hip and coming out by my neck. I didn't look like I was in pain; I didn't look like it was bothering me. Although I was pretty sure it wasn't doing me any favours. I looked down and saw that I was hovering hundreds of feet in the air.

"Like I said," Vincent told me, "time is relative here. There are things we need to do before I can make a decision about the kind of man you are."

"Okay," I said. "What do we need to do?"

Vincent raised his left arm and a tear appeared beside us. "You need to walk through."

I looked into the tear, expecting to see Earth or a part of the rift. I did not expect to see my embers. I paused.

"Are you afraid?" Vincent asked.

"I would be a fool if I were not," I said, looking between Vincent and the tear. "I don't know what you want from me or what you need me to do."

"Yes, you do," Vincent said. "You just don't want to admit it to yourself. Lavis told you: you need to be honest. Honest with yourself, and honest with me. If you can do neither, then this conversation is going to be very short and will end with your death."

I stepped into my embers and stood looking around as Vincent joined me, the tear snapping shut behind me.

"Interesting architecture," Vincent said as he studied the buildings around us. "Carthaginian, some modern, some sixteenth-century French. Very interesting mix. And I believe these two coming toward us will be your eidolons."

Maria the hawk and Casimir the stag arrived soon after we had. Maria landed beside me, whilst Casimir stood between me and Vincent, looking between the two of us as if wondering what they were meant to do next.

Vincent walked over to Casimir and stroked him on his flank. "Your eidolons love you."

"We have been through a lot together," I said.

"They have individual personalities," Vincent said. "That is rare; it is rarer still that a riftborn and his eidolons have bonded in friendship. They are, after all, made from the same energy that I am. Obviously a much more diluted version; no offence. But it's still rift energy. A small piece that you could have absorbed into yourself. Several have done that; some of the Ancients did that."

"Why would anybody do that?" I asked.

Vincent walked toward Maria and stroked their head. "When someone is looking for power, they take every chance they get to try and win. They believe they are in competition with everybody else, you see. The truth is they are not, but they cannot see beyond the need to win an imaginary race."

Looking beyond Vincent and the eidolons, I saw that the shadows were milling around at the end of the road. They began shuffling toward us, not fast, but with a need that I could sense upon them.

"Are you doing this?" I asked Vincent.

"They know that I am not supposed to be here," Vincent said. He found a chair from somewhere that I hadn't seen earlier, placed it on the floor, and sat down. "You know what you need to do."

I stared at the increasingly large number of shadows moving toward me. "I have to let it happen."

"Let what happen?" Maria asked.

"He's going to let the shadows attack him," Vincent said, as if that were a perfectly normal sentence. "Only very few riftborn can achieve this. We can't have every single one of your kind doing it; it would be chaos."

I expected Maria and Casimir to argue with me, to tell me that I was stupid, to tell me that I had just met Vincent and there was no way I could tell if he was being truthful. They didn't. "The shadows will need to be tamed," Casimir said.

"It is the only way," Maria told me.

Both of them were speaking as if they were far away; it was almost like they were a recording or reading from a book.

"I will wait for you," Vincent said. "Whilst we are here, time will cease to exist outside of here. The embers, as you know, have a different way of dealing with time. With my manipulation, I can stop it. The process that you are about to go through is not a fun one. It is not a short one. I do not have feelings, or emotions, at least not in the same way that you have. But I do believe that I shall pity you."

"You are very bad at doing a sales pitch," I said.

"You should probably take off your shirt," Vincent said. "It won't survive."

I removed my jacket and shirt, draping them both over the wooden fence beside Maria. She nuzzled her head against my hand as I did, and whispered, "We will be here when you are done."

I nodded a thank-you, did the same to Casimir, and ran toward the shadows. As I reached the first of them, it was like hitting a wall of limbs all trying to grab me at the same time. Eventually, I was dragged into the mass of shadows, and my world became one with pain.

CHAPTER TWENTY-SIX

Absorbing one shadow was not how I expected it to go. Each of them arrived in turn as they grasped and tore up my flesh, drove themselves into my chest. The first left no mark on my body, save a little redness. With every bloody tear along my arms and stomach, my body immediately healed itself, leaving only a red soreness in its wake. This happened over and over again, until each and every one of the shadows had driven itself into my body. What had started with a little redness had left my chest raw and bloodied by the time the final one had completed its task.

I stayed on all fours, sweat pouring off my face, as I sought to breathe through the agony that continued to lace through my body. It felt as though I had been placed through a woodchipper, healed immediately, and then passed back through the other side. And this had gone on for hours.

Vincent stood beside me, looking down with what appeared to be indifference. "It is done," he said.

I opened my mouth to speak, but all that came out was a raw and ragged sound. My throat burned, and my head swam, and whilst I wanted to tell Vincent to fuck off, I wasn't even able to look at him for more than a few seconds before I crashed to the ground.

"You'll be okay soon," Vincent said in that same passive tone he always used.

I gave a thumbs-up. And then I flipped him off because I was in pain and it sucked.

Vincent laughed. "I am beginning to like you. I see why your eidolons became friends. I see why they trust you. I see why the primordials trusted you. There are many people out there who are good, Lucas. People who want to do the right thing, people who do the right thing. I have to ask: what if doing the right thing isn't nice? What if it would hurt a great number of people? What if the right thing and the good thing are not the same? Is doing the right thing in the long term the best course of action if it would hurt people in the short term?"

I left out a long breath as I began to feel a little bit more like me. "I think you might need to be a little clearer," I said as Maria, now a dormouse again, ran over to me and sat on my hand, studying me intensely.

"You okay?" Maria asked.

I nodded and got slowly to my feet, letting Maria jump off my hand onto a nearby fence. My embers were beginning to change, many of the buildings vanishing, leaving only a few in the small village that had been created there. In their place were open fields, and a river, as the mist there had been a hallmark of my embers, vanished. It was as though I were watching a film that had started in black-and-white and now turned to colour. It was both stunning and unnerving.

"I wish to make a deal," Vincent said. "If you agree, the power that you have just taken from this place will be amplified by my own. You will be able to do what you need to do. You'll be able to stop Callie, to take back the power that was taken from this place; you'll be able to stop those on Earth causing trouble."

"What's the catch?" I asked.

Vincent looked around. "I offered a similar deal to Callie. I believe that is why she is now trying to create an army of people who have all unlocked their potential. I believe that is why she has kept some of the Ancients back, allowing them access to the power that I had bestowed upon her."

"How?" I asked, unsure I wanted to know the answer but knowing I needed to know.

"There are secrets inside her head that she should not have," Vincent said. "She is trying to absorb the power the Ancients took. It is making her more unstable and having effects on the rift."

"She said she needed me to kill Neb or Hesansh," I said. "Why?"

"She probably believes it," Vincent said. "She has seen the chains of the rift, seen how things will end for her. From what I know of her personality, she has picked the most probable course of action that will result in her getting what she wants. She has foreseen that you killing one of those two Ancients is what brings about her winning."

"So, that means I can never kill Hesansh," I said, "for fear that it would give Callie what she wanted? And it would sever the link with Neb, who would slowly die without it?"

"No," Vincent said. "She is only picking the most *probable* outcome. There will be countless others that are less probable but still possible."

"What's the bargain?"

Vincent looked around my embers, and when he turned back to me, there was genuine warmth in the smile on his face. "The rift is meant to have a Guardian. The Guardian does not just keep the rift safe; they are meant to be the *Herald* for when one rift unlocks into another. The Herald is tasked with travelling through the various rifts that are interconnected, spreading their power and ensuring safety in the other rifts. They should be the first thing seen by the early settlers of those rifts, someone who can explain what is happening, someone who can watch over them until they are ready to set out on their own.

"Not just that. Every rift must have a Tempest, it must have a source of power. The Herald is the keeper of that power, the protector of that power. I offered that to Callie in my mistaken belief that a human would be easier to control, would be more willing to give up their life to become the Herald. I was wrong."

"Wait, Callie said something about being the *herald of a new age*," I said. "Is this what she meant?"

"She wanted more than I was willing to give," Vincent explained. "The Herald is far too important a task to give to someone like Callie."

"And I have to die?" I asked, not entirely keen on the idea.

"No," Vincent said with a chuckle. "You would have to give up your life on Earth and the rift. You would live within the lands of the Tempest. You would be its protector until such time as a second rift is founded, and then you would move on. And on, and on, and on, and on, for all eternity. You could come back to one of the rifts that you had been to before, but there is no way of knowing how much time would have passed since you'd left. With every rift you go to, with every Tempest you find, you would help create a new protector for the rift. Just like you will help find the protector of this rift for when you leave."

"Let me get this straight," I said. "If I agree to this, I will get the power that I need to stop Callie, to fix the rift and protect the people of both the rift and Earth. In exchange, I have to find a protector of the rift, and as the Herald, I then have to leave into another rift and do the same thing over and over again. Forever."

"That is roughly what you would be doing, yes," Vincent said. "However, there is one more thing. Upon fixing the rift and its relationship with Earth, it would mean reverting the rift to what it was supposed to be. The number of tears would dwindle; they would become more powerful but controllable, and that would mean the number of rift-born would decrease. It also means that revenants would come straight through to the rift to live forever as they were meant to. Revenants were never meant to live on Earth; they were meant to be brought through to the rift to live out their lives. This will be the case."

"So, what happens to all of the revenants currently living on Earth?" I asked.

"They would have to come through," Vincent said. "There is no other way of fixing the problem that was created."

"There are thousands of revenants on Earth," I said. "People with families, loved ones, people who work, people who have lives. They would all vanish to be populated within the rift. That seems to cause more problems than it solves."

Vincent considered this for a moment. "You are correct. An influx of that many revenants at once would become an issue. Do you have a way of fixing this problem without such a drastic act?"

"When all of this is done," I said, "the revenants living on Earth should be given a choice. They could either come through to the rift immediately or live out their days on Earth as they were meant to, with the option of coming through to the rift at any time. It would help stop a mass influx of people. And it would give those with lives on Earth a chance to say goodbye."

Vincent nodded immediately. "We will do it your way. If you agree to become the Herald of the rift, I will grant you the power that comes with that position. You would have access to all of the power I possess."

"Is this the deal you offered Callie?" I asked. "Does she have access to your entire power?"

"No," Vincent said. "I offered her the position of Guardian. It seemed more in keeping with her power set. I believe that the position of Herald should be held by a riftborn; the power that you will have will take some time to settle within you. You might feel a tingling."

"A tingling?" I asked.

"Your body might be pulled apart and then pulled back together again," Vincent said. "I was trying to make it sound more appealing than it will be. I have never given my power over to another being. Not totally. I may be a being of pure energy, but this is new to me, too."

"Why do you sound concerned?" I asked, looking between Vincent and the two eidolons, both of whom shared my expression of confusion.

"There's a possibility I will cease to exist," Vincent admitted. "I am not alive in the sense that you are, but I have come to enjoy existing."

"If you give me all of your power, and you vanish," I asked, "what happens to the power under the mountain? And more importantly, will I still be me?"

"You will still be yourself," Vincent said. "I have no need to destroy you and rebuild you. This is done with our mutual cooperation. As for your first question, the Tempest is still the source of the power of the rift, but it is also the source of your power. You can, should you wish, absorb it totally. Or portion it out to whoever you feel deserves it. Or make a big dome around it and sit on it. I have never had the imagination to do any of those things. I am, after all, just energy. My personality comes from watching so many of you for so long. A bit like your eidolons. I knew that at some point I would have to create a Herald, and that they would need to create a Guardian, and I was okay with this. I have not spoken to many of your kind over the millennia, and have met none, until now, that I would consider to be worthy of the position of Herald. Primordials are incapable of becoming such a person, but I had many conversations with Lavis and Tasicus over the years. I hoped that one day I would find the person I was meant to pass on my power to; I thought that I would be okay with that. But now I am not. I find that to be unnerving. I do not like it."

"Whatever happens," I said, "I will make sure that in some way you are remembered and that you live on. I promise you that."

Vincent took my hand in his and placed his other hand against my cheek. "You are a good man, Lucas Rurik. Despite all that has happened to you, you have always maintained your morals, and that is why you will make a great Herald. You will change the world. All of the worlds. And it will be glorious."

The world burned bright white, my eyes searing, my skin feeling as though it were aflame. It was as if I was being immolated on a continuous basis. There was nothing but heat and pain, and it appeared to last forever, encompassing my past, present, and future. At some point, and I had no way of telling when this was, the pain stopped. It was replaced with a realisation that I was becoming something more, that there was a very large world all around me, which was shrinking toward me at an alarming rate. It was as if my mind had been opened and knowledge had been poured into it. It didn't hurt, but it was an odd sensation, as though I was being stuffed full of something.

As the brightness decreased and the world swam back into vision, I saw Maria and Casimir alone before me. We were no longer in my embers but under the mountain, the power of the Tempest thrumming beneath me as I sat on top of it. The basin below me flared with incandescent white light, which was not painful but was distracting.

The light immediately dimmed, until I was the only one sitting in the centre, with Maria and Casimir hovering in the air beside me.

"This looked weird," Casimir said.

"I don't see Vincent anywhere," I said. "Are you both here, or are you still in my embers? Do I need to go into my embers to go back to Earth? Or can I just open a tear and do this myself? What function do my embers serve now?"

The second I spoke each question, the answer came to me. The eidolons were both in my embers and also in front of me. My embers were now a refuge, a sanctuary, where I could recharge and relax. I could bring people into my embers without consequence. Time moved the same there as it did on Earth, and I no longer needed to use them to heal. I simply healed as soon as I touched rift energy. Travelling between Earth and the rift was a simple matter now; I had the powers of the rift-walker. It was all deeply strange.

After several seconds, Vincent appeared before me. He looked around as if in some confusion.

"You know, Vincent," I said, "I've been thinking of you as a he because of the appearance you've taken. But you're no more he or she than any other entity made from pure energy. What would you like me to call you? You don't have to stay looking like Vincent now."

"I wish to stay in this form," Vincent said. "I like the name Vincent. I believe I will keep using it. *He* is fine. It sounds right. If I change my mind, I will let you know. I expected to disappear. What have you done?"

I stood and stretched. "I thought it unfair that you should vanish after giving me the power that you have. So, instead, I took a piece of that power, a piece of you, and placed it within my embers. It is your home. Along with Maria and Casimir, my embers are now yours. You may change them as you see fit; feel free to redecorate. They are there for you to live as long as you wish. If you ever require more company, I'm sure I can accommodate it. I've never taken a primordial into my embers before, but there is a first time for everything."

Vincent stared at me for several seconds. "Thank you. I did not expect this level of kindness. I did not expect anything. I believe I have made the right decision. Callie will know that I have given up my power to someone else. She will not be pleased. It may accelerate whatever plan she has."

"I will deal with Callie and everyone working for her," I said. "But first, I'm going to fix the tears that are causing havoc on Earth. I know I can do that; I know what my power can do. I understand why you have waited so long to give this power to someone. In the wrong hands, they would make themselves a god."

"It's a good job you're not a god, then," Maria said. "And that you have us here to make sure you never get too big of a head."

I laughed as Vincent and my two eidolons disappeared back into the embers. I looked around at the basin. Power crackled all around me, and while the Tempest was considerably smaller than it had been before I'd arrived, I knew I could not take all of its power. I did not need all of its power, and I believed that taking more than I needed could lead me to use it in ways that would be unhealthy for me.

I looked up at the sky high above my head, the gap in the top of the mountain letting me see the beauty of what passed for night in the rift. Dealing with Earth first would undoubtedly let Callie know what I was capable of, but that was fine. Let her know; let her panic. Let her be aware that I was going to come for her. And that I was bringing with me the full power of the Tempest. There was nowhere for her and her friends to run; there was nowhere for them to hide. They were all dead; they just didn't know it yet.

I exploded up out of the top of the mountain, casting my smoke self across its peaks and infusing each and every molecule with the rift power that I had absorbed from the Tempest below. I brought all the power back toward me at once and caused an explosion so large that it lit up the night sky for hundreds of miles in all directions.

I hovered above the mountain, aware that I had just made my intent clear to the rest of the rift. I was here. And I was coming to deal with anybody who crossed me. There was a new sheriff in town, and I aimed to put things right.

CHAPTER TWENTY-SEVEN

I flew down from the top of the mountain, gliding inches above the grass below, letting it cascade through my hands as I soared across the landscape at terrific speed. I'd never felt anything quite like it. I was capable of covering miles in moments; I soon found myself hovering above where the primordials had heard me speak.

I landed softly and looked out across the forest and tundra around me as several primordials poked their heads out of lakes and the tree line, all staring at me. I was unsure if it was in fear or curiosity, or maybe a mixture of the two.

Lavis was the first to leave the safety of the tree line; she strolled confidently toward me, stopping and lowering her head so that I might place my hand upon it.

"You have taken the power of the Tempest?" she said, looking back up at me as I removed my hand.

"I have," I said. "The energy that resided there called itself Vincent. He now lives in my embers and would be pleased to see you again. I have things to do, but when I am done, I will open my embers so that you can be reunited."

More and more of the primordials were entering the clearing, each of them staring at me. I could feel their concern mixed with awe. One of them whispered, "The Herald is here," which was soon picked up by others, until the word *Herald* was being chanted throughout the night.

I felt deeply uncomfortable and understood how some people could allow such adulation to go to their heads. To make them believe that they really were capable of godlike acts. But I was not a god; I was a man who had become a riftborn and was now responsible for fixing the mess that some of my kind had made thousands of years earlier. The responsibility hung heavy.

"I was unsure if it would accept you," Lavis said. "When you are done, this will be your home. The Tempest. The land that you stand on."

I nodded. "I know. I will make this my home until such time that I have to leave. And when that time comes, I will ensure that every species in the rift is left in a better place than it is now."

"Thank you," Lavis whispered.

I looked around and saw Valmore, who smiled at me and nodded. I returned the smile and nod, and promised myself that I would come and see him once all of this was done. "I have to go. Thank you for your help. For all of you." I shouted the last part, letting my power carry my voice across the clearing so that everyone there could hear what I said.

As the murmurs of *Herald* began once again, I opened a tear beside me, and stepped through onto Prospect Island, next to an exceptionally freaked-out Gabriel as the tear snapped shut.

"Hello, Gabriel," I said, somewhat enjoying the moment of shock on his face. "I need you to get everybody together. Because things are about to change in a very big way."

Within ten minutes, I'd been hugged and warmly greeted within an inch of my life. Nadia, being the last to arrive at Ji-hyun's office, saw me, ran over, and hugged me tightly.

"I've never been so happy to be wrong in my life," she said.

"I've never been so happy that you were wrong either," I said with a smile as I pulled away.

"What is so important that you need to speak to all of us?" Ji-hyun asked.

I gave them all a lowdown of what had happened since I'd left; there were several gasps and a lot of questions that I had to not answer, as I went on. When I was finished, Drusilla was the first to walk up toward me.

"So, you'll be stuck in the rift?" she asked tentatively.

"I will," I told her. "The duties of the Herald are to wait until I can find a protector of the rift, and until the rift opens into another rift, and then you go from rift to rift, and world to world, finding and protecting new people."

"How long do you have?" she asked.

"I don't know," I admitted. "Months, years, centuries. I have absolutely no idea how long any of this is going to take. I'm still getting used to the power that I have inside of me."

"But once you fix everything," Nadia said, "the revenants will have to move into the rift?"

I nodded. "Those of you who want to. Revenants were never meant to be on Earth. It was fallout from what the Ancients did. Once that has been fixed, they will no longer be created on Earth. Or, should I say, created to stay on Earth. Those who are already here can choose to come into the rift, or choose to stay here and live out their days. The longer you're here, the longer it takes for the rift to be completely fixed, though."

Nadia raised her hand. "Rift, please."

I smiled. "You don't have to decide right now. But, Ji-hyun, I think someone needs to put out a video, or a news article, or something explaining what is going to happen. Because once the rift is fixed, it's going to happen really fast, and a lot of people are about to get asked to make a large life choice. And I don't want anyone being surprised by it."

Gabriel remained quiet, sat at the end of the table, staring into space.

"Are you okay?" I asked him. "Gabriel?"

"I don't know what I'll say," he said, his voice barely above a whisper. "My whole life as a revenant, I have waited until the time that I was taken into the rift to live the rest of my life there. But there was always a chance this wouldn't happen. Knowing that it will, knowing that it was always meant to happen, feels like someone took something from me and is only now giving it back. I don't like that feeling."

Dani placed her hand on Gabriel's and squeezed slightly. "You've got time."

Gabriel looked at her, nodded, and smiled. "That I do."

"What are you going to do next?" Ji-hyun asked. "You're, what, a god?"

I shook my head. "I am deeply uncomfortable with that suggestion."

"Uncomfortable or not, that's how some people are going to see you, Lucas," Ji-hyun said. "Some people might think you have all the answers, or that you could fix their problems. We can't put you on film saying everything you've said. It needs to be someone else."

"Not for one second did I suggest it should be me," I pointed out.

"I know," she said. "I'm just wanting to make sure that you know."

"I'm sure you'll all figure it out," I said. "I closed the tears. I hope that casualties weren't too large."

"We don't know yet," Drusilla said. "Numbers are coming in all the time. Seems like we may have lost a lot of good people but even more civilians. Estimates are in the tens of thousands. But until we can get out and find out for ourselves, it's all guesswork."

"Callie will be made to pay for this," I said.

"Good," Ji-hyun said.

Everyone filed out after, with Drusilla giving me a kiss for good luck on the way; I stopped her from leaving for a moment and asked her to take a seat.

I explained about the shadows in my embers and told them both that they should go into their embers and do what I did if they wished to unlock their full power. I also explained that this information still needed to be kept from the masses of riftborn, at least until we could figure out a way to ensure that a whole bunch of people would not try something that might either kill them or turn them into exceptionally powerful beings. Let's not add to the current crisis.

"The Ancients really kept all of this shit from us for all these years," Drusilla said with more than a touch of anger.

I nodded. "They were scared what would happen if a whole lot of riftborn tried it at once. And I actually agree with them. A lot of riftborn aren't ready, might never be ready. It would kill too many, and there are some who really should never have more power."

"I don't like this," Ji-hyun, said pointing at me.

"I didn't think you would," I told her. "But this is happening. This is the new reality. I am imbued with the power of the Tempest, and it's not going away, and you, as a riftborn, have choices to make. I came here to tell you what was going to happen; the rest is up to all of you."

"We can let everybody know," Ji-hyun said. "But make sure that when you do meet Callie, you end this once and for all. No more mystical returns, no more get-out-of-jail-free; this whole thing needs to be done. For good."

"I will," I told her, and looked between Ji-hyun and Drusilla. "This isn't goodbye, because I'm not dying. I think we've all figured that part out. I'm not actually sure if I can die anymore, or if I would just go back into the Tempest. But I need to fix things, things I didn't even know needed fixing. And you might not see me for a while, depending on how long it takes. I don't know what's going to happen when everything is fixed, either. It turns out that whilst the Tempest is an incredible amount of power, it does not know everything. I kind of hoped it would. I think Vincent hoped it would too."

"Vincent?" Drusilla asked.

"Oh, the Tempest took the form of Vincent D'Onofrio but dressed as the Kingpin," I explained.

Drusilla looked surprised. "I never thought someone would say that sentence to me. Seriously?"

"Yes," I said. "It was both unnerving to talk to him and a bit cool. It was a weird day. It has been several weird days. At this point, this might actually be the weirdest year of my life by some margin."

"And Vincent, the Tempest, told you everything?" Ji-hyun asked.

"It's not omnipotent," I said. "So, neither am I. Anyway, I need to go back. The longer I'm here, the more time Callie has to prepare. It's almost certain that she is aware of what I can do. I'm pretty sure she wants this job, and I know for a fact she should never get it. I don't think her cult or followers are going to be particularly happy with my arrival."

Drusilla kissed me again. "It feels like I keep saying goodbye to you. I don't plan on doing it again. I'll see you soon."

"Yes, you will," I told her, and looked over to Ji-hyun. "Good luck. I know you never wanted this job, and I know you never wanted the responsibility that comes with it. You're the best thing that's ever happened to the RCU, and quite possibly the best thing that's ever happened to the rift-fused who live on Earth. With you backing them, they have someone in their corner they can trust. I'm sorry that I'm about to make your job harder. But in the long run, it needs to happen. Earth and the rift can't keep going the way they are; too many lives are lost, and too many more are given leeway to behave badly."

Ji-hyun walked around the desk and offered me a fist bump, which I reciprocated. "There's no point in telling you to be careful, because even without the power of the Tempest, you never were. But if everything you say needs to happen, then I trust you. We will be ready for whatever happens. All of us. I'll make calls to other RCU offices around the globe, and we'll put out a joint statement. We'll make sure people are aware about what is coming, and will clear out any fiends that are left. Be safe, Lucas. Go do what you need to do."

I opened a tear into the rift and stepped through, wondering if it was the last time that I would be able to go from Earth to the rift or vice versa.

CHAPTER TWENTY-EIGHT

The tear that I'd created was meant to take me to the city of Asteria. It would've meant a quick trip to the island across the ocean from Inaxia. Unfortunately, it appeared that I was unable to create a tear directly to the city. Instead, I stood on the beach of the island of Astra, upon which the city lay.

I looked around at the deserted beach, the water lapping against its dark sand, and set off in the direction of Asteria. It was a day's walk to the city itself, and I wondered why I hadn't just arrived where I wanted to go. Maybe, despite the power that now coursed through my body, there were some things I just couldn't do.

After a few hundred metres, I took to the air and flew the rest of the way, speeding over the rocky terrain below, and across a wide-open plain, ignoring the shouts of anyone beneath me. When I reached the forest that sat outside of the city, I landed at its edge, close to the moat which encircled Asteria. There was a drawbridge, which had been pulled up, leaving a hundred feet of empty air between myself and access to the city.

I stood at the edge of the moat and looked down at the deep water in front of me. I saw the swishing of tails and the occasional fin; I was unsure exactly what creatures lurked in its depths, but I had neither the time nor inclination to find out.

I turned to smoke and billowed up and over the moat, over the hundred-foot-high city walls. I moved across tall, dark stone buildings with thatched roofs. I saw no movement below; I saw no signs of life, so I continued on until I reached the city square.

I landed, re-formed, and looked around at the open area which I stood in the middle of. There was no one there. It was, I had to admit, a little bit of a surprise. I expected people running at me with pitchforks and, possibly, burning torches. I did not expect nothing.

Many of the buildings around the square were adorned with signs showing them to be shops of varying descriptions. All of the doors were closed. I wondered if I had somehow walked into an exceptionally strange trap. I sent pieces of my smoke out across the city, moving quickly, aided with the power of the rift. I saw what they moved past, and saw nothing. No signs of life, not even a rat, or whatever other vermin lived within the city.

I brought all of the particles of me back and looked up at the hill in front of me toward the palace where Theoris lived. It was an opulent building with bright white walls and golden peaks atop. Stained-glass windows adorned almost every wall, and I imagined that living inside of it must have been like living inside of a kaleidoscope.

Returning to smoke, I moved across the city, across more houses, which got larger and more impressive the closer I got to the palace. The city was huge, and the fact that it was surrounded by large walls made me wonder just how long all of this had taken. As I flew over the houses of the rich and powerful, and across large parks adorned with flowers of nearly every colour of the rainbow, I still saw no movement.

I landed just beyond the Palace Gardens, which were an especially beautiful piece of horticulture, and looked up at the monument to excess in front of me. I'd always known that Theoris liked to live an opulent lifestyle, that she had left the mainland because she could no longer feel like she was under the yoke of someone else, but I hadn't expected her to build something that wouldn't have looked out of place in eighteenth-century Russia.

I strolled up the stairs and pushed open the large wooden doors, each one covered in intricate pieces of art showing a mural of what appeared to be someone stood before a tear and taking its power. It was needlessly opulent for a front door.

With the door opened, revealing the fifty-foot-long and -wide entrance beyond, the smell of death was immediate. I stepped into the palace, the sound of my boots on the marble floor echoing all around.

I walked across the floor and opened the door directly opposite the entrance, revealing a long hallway that snaked around to the left and right after forty feet of doors on either side. I stopped by each door, pushing it open to reveal the skeletal remains of an unknown number of people. The skeletons were piled up on top of one another, as if people had been jammed in there and then left to die.

At the end of the hallway, I felt the tug of rift power to the right of me, so I took that path, following it around and finding more dead, all of whom were skeletal, the stench almost overwhelming. I pushed open a large white door and stepped into a throne room, which looked like something out of ancient Rome, with eight fifty-foot-tall white marble pillars and a mural painted on the ceiling, depicting a map of the rift. Windows lined one side, all of which had been shattered, the colourful glass spread across the red stone floor.

At the far end, on top of a stage, with steps leading up to it, was a gold-and-silver throne. Theoris sat upon it, but unlike the young and full-of-life woman I had met in England, this version of Theoris was old, her hair white and falling out, her skin greying. She stood, using a walking stick of dark wood, and began to descend the stairs toward me. There was no need for me to offer her any help; I didn't much care if she fell down the damn things.

"I knew you would come," Theoris said, her voice raspy. She reached the bottom of the steps and coughed for a few seconds, her chest wheezing. "This is what happens when you lose your connection to the rift."

"Good," I told her. "I hope it fucking hurts. I know what you and Ahiram did. You killed the primordials, took their power, poisoned your own people, and forced power into all of you. Why? Why not just you two?"

"We were worried that if it had just been the two of us, we'd have been hunted down for the rest of our lives," Theoris said. "The more of us who underwent the transformation, the less likely it was that we were singled out. The more likely the others would protect us. Didn't think we'd all be linked in pairs, though; that was unexpected. Didn't realise that Ahiram and I would be linked, either; I do wonder if the Tempest did that on purpose."

"You were the first to lose your power," I said. "When Ahiram died."

Theoris nodded.

"I don't understand why you helped Callie do all of this," I said, gesturing around me. "You are getting nothing. You are withering and are going to die alone. You gained nothing."

"I was going to die," Theoris said, breaking into a laugh, showing the rotten teeth within her mouth. "Callie told me she could reverse it. That the rift power she took from the lives of the other Ancients could be used to keep me alive. To keep my power."

"How long before you figured out it was bullshit?" I asked.

Theoris laughed, a wet, unpleasant sound. "Long enough that by then, it was too late. I told myself it didn't really matter that they were dying; it wasn't like I liked them to begin with. Any of them. I came here because I was done with their squabbles, their need to try and make the rift a better place, the angst. Do you know, after all this time, not one of them ever went back to the Tempest to find out what really happened? They were scared, I think. Scared what they would find, scared what they would have to do to fix a problem they had benefited from for thousands of years. Now there is no longer a problem. I felt little pleasure in their deaths, although there were a few I was happier than others to hear had died. At the end of the day, while I didn't get the power I was promised, this all needed to be done.

"The rift is chaos incarnate. Callie aims to tame it. I knew her when she was a part of the Blessed. I knew what her plans were; I knew that she wanted to control the rift and, to do that, had to control the Tempest. You stopped that from happening, and in return, Callie got what she wanted, and when she went after Ahiram, I thought she was finally going to revive him after all the centuries, and she killed him instead. I don't think there was much lost there. Any feeling I had for the man died when he decided he wanted to conquer the known fucking world."

"So, you just let her kill countless people because Callie told you she had a power to tame all of this and keep you alive?" I asked. "She's going to burn the rift to the ground; she's going to burn the Earth as well. She's taking power that doesn't belong to her and keeping it. And every time another Ancient dies, that power becomes more unstable. The tears are happening with more frequency, and they are becoming greater in strength."

"She doesn't want to wield power for herself," Theoris said. "You still have no idea what she's really doing. I guess you're going to find out."

"Where are the people who lived here?" I asked.

"Gone," Theoris said. "I spent a long time cultivating the people who lived here to Callie's vision. Just like she did back on Earth with the Guilds. When the time came, they were willing to lay down their lives for her. For her vision. They went across to the mainland; they've been waging war ever since. Some went back to Earth to aid the Guilds. Some decided not to join our ranks and had to be disposed of. Of a hundred thousand people, nearly seventy thousand loyal soldiers remained. They will be a bane against any place who stands against Callie, who stands against progress."

"When I spoke to the Tempest, I had to be truthful, or I would die," I said. "The Tempest didn't force me to be truthful, but it could've done. It could've taken the rift energy inside of me and twisted it until I said what it needed me to say. I can still sense the embers of rift energy inside of you. You're not human; you are a riftborn who has lost their access to the Tempest. It is aging you quickly, and you have lost most of your power, but it is still there. A tiny spark inside of you. I can see it. I can see that you do not wish to die yet. You are not afraid of dying, but despite all of your bravado, there is fear in you. You fear being forgotten."

Theoris's expression turned serious, and she clutched her cane to her chest. "You can't," she said, her voice a whisper, but the fear it held made it feel like a shout.

"I can take it," I told her. "I can make you die here and now, a bag of bones in the middle of your palace. A palace that I will burn to the ground, along with your city, along with any traces that you ever existed. No one will remember your name; no one will remember the Ancients who lived across the ocean. You tell me where Callie is right now, or I will erase your existence."

Theoris's eyes went wide, and she stammered for a second. "Tunnels beneath the city. The rift energy is strongest down there."

"Where are Neb and Hesansh?" I asked.

"Both are with her," she told me. "They are linked to one another. After your escape from Inaxia, where Callie admitted to Hesansh that you were going to kill him or Neb, she saw a new vision. A new way forward. She is going to spare Hesansh from what comes; he will remain by her side forever more. Neb will be entombed."

"Where are all of her followers?"

"A lot of them died in the city," Theoris said. "Most of them are still in Inaxia, causing trouble, making sure that whatever happens here isn't noticed. Some of them went with her. After you killed Necia, Callie was livid, sent her people out to destroy the city, burn it to the ground, kill anyone who tried to stop them. They are waging war against the civilians of Inaxia. Considering how much they are outnumbered, I imagine that they do not plan on winning that war, just wanting to take as many as they can before they die."

"I haven't been back," I admitted. "It's on my list. Why the helicopter? Why go to all of the rigmarole of such an act?"

"I didn't want anyone coming here," Theoris said. "Figured that with everyone thinking I was dead, no one would suspect my involvement. Not until it was too late. I wanted to go to England, though, needed to see the other Ancients before they all died. I wanted to be reminded why they deserved their fates."

"What does Callie want from me now?" I asked. "I ruined her plan."

"I don't know," Theoris said. "She was really quite angry with you."

"And what is your plan?" I asked her. "You're just going to sit here and die?"

Theoris nodded. "I will sit upon my throne, the death of a queen. No one took my city from me; it still stands."

"A city of nothing," I said. "Congratulations. How do I get down to Callie?"

"There is a building at the rear of the palace," Theoris told me. "There is an elevator inside it; it will take you down to an underground chamber. A river of rift water sits there. No one is allowed down there to see what she has been doing, but it's going to be spectacular. And you can't stop it."

I walked past Theoris toward the broken windows. I stopped and turned back to her. "That little piece of power inside of you. I cannot take rift energy from a person; we all have it in us. It is theirs, and I can do nothing about it."

Theoris let out a barking laugh. "You lied to me."

"No," I told her. "I cannot remove rift energy. That is true. But the energy inside of you is stolen from the Tempest. Despite the fact that you have been cut off from the rift, I have to wait for your death before all of your power reverts to the Tempest. I am not a patient man." I threw a dagger at her, catching her in the heart. There wasn't even enough time for her to scream in defiance as a look of shock quickly vanished and she collapsed onto the ground. With a wave of my hand, I absorbed the rift energy into myself as Theoris collapsed into a pile of dust.

CHAPTER TWENTY-NINE

I followed Theoris's instructions, knowing them to be true, and was soon stood in a wooden lift powered by the same rift energy that powered most of everything else in the rift. It rumbled down, a cacophony of noise, any semblance of stealth gone, but Callie knew I was coming, and I wanted to conserve energy for whatever I was about to find at the bottom of the lift shaft.

On the several-minute-long journey the usual stone walls were occasionally replaced with vast open areas covered in mining equipment and veins of periwinkle and turquoise rift energy which appeared to pulse inside of the rock. They were mining it. Mining rift-energy-filled rock. A lot of people died there. I didn't need to see the skeletons to know this. I felt it. Vast numbers of people who came to mine never went home.

Eventually, the lift settled at the bottom of the shaft, and I stepped off into a gargantuan chamber. A river of rift water ran along the left-hand side, the water moving quickly, occasionally lapping up onto the stone path beside it. Anyone walking down there who was not already touched by the Tempest was taking their life into their own hands.

I walked along the path for several minutes, until I arrived at a second chamber. The water ended there, where it was being collected by a metal device the size of a hatchback car. It took water in and pumped it out into a glass chamber attached to it. The chamber had a Tempest's core inside. The spinning core pulsated with power, and I knew with complete certainty that this was how Callie planned to conquer everything. It wasn't pure rift energy, hence the periwinkle tinge to it, but it was powerful.

Callie herself sat on a chair a little ways away from the rift energy, at a desk covered in paper and parchment. There were rift-powered lights all around her, illuminating the whole area in purple. Neb sat caged a dozen feet from her, her hands and feet bound by shackles, her head bowed low. Defeated.

"Lucas," Callie shouted from across the chamber. "Theoris is dead, I assume?"

"She is," I said. "You are creating a second Tempest power.

"The jewellery helped you to absorb the Ancients' power, but it also lets you access the power you'd collected. It's why Theoris was wearing some. She'd lost her connection to the rift when Ahiram died, but you let her connect to *this* rift energy because you needed her alive. But it didn't quite work, did it?"

"No," Callie admitted. "Apparently, you need to still have that connection to the rift to be able to access that power. The rift energy kept her alive, slowed her death, right up until I took the jewellery back from her. After that, it was like she aged at speed. A mild miscalculation on my part, but it did enough to help me. It was too much energy for one person to absorb, unfortunately; otherwise, I'd have just let her die long ago."

"It's why you're working here so far away from the mainland. Can't risk people finding out. It's why no one could find you after Ahiram. You came here; you were starting the creation of the core. I assume a lot of the people in the town above who weren't on board with your plan were sacrificed to you."

"In one way or another, yes," she said. "This place is rich with rift energy; it's the perfect place to start anew."

"You've done a lot in a short time," I said. "How did you keep all of your plans from the Tempest when it took control of you? I doubted it would have been thrilled at the possibility of being replaced."

"The Tempest can't read minds," Callie said. "It only saw that I wanted to make the rift better, to heal it. It didn't care how. I imagine it told you as such."

"It did," I admitted. "I just wanted to hear it from you. What happened to the necklace and bracelets?"

"I fed the power into the core," Callie said. "I am now linked to it in body and soul. I do not need baubles to allow me to control its power. I *am* its power."

I took another look around the room. "You've been planning this for a long time."

Callie clapped. "I have been building this for a while now. When I first came back, I wasn't really myself. The Tempest lingered in my head, making sure I behaved; I wanted you to think that it was still there. That's why I did the little trick of slowing down time back in Inaxia. I wanted you to think I wasn't all together with it. Unfortunately my ruse didn't really work, did it?"

"For a while it did," I admitted. "And then I remembered that you were a lying sack of shit. Lots more things clicked into place after that."

"You have absorbed the power of the Tempest," Callie said. "We are the same."

I shook my head. "I am the Herald of the Tempest. We are not even close to being the same."

"*Herald*," Callie spat.

"Yeah, you wanted this job, didn't you?" I asked. "You sound mad it's not you."

"I was," she said, surprising me with her honesty. "But I got over it. I'm something much more now."

"Where is Hesansh?" I asked. "I heard that you let him live so that he could be the last Ancient to die; I assume that's some kind of inside joke on the rest of the Ancients."

"I did," Callie said. "And also, I knew that you wouldn't kill him whilst Neb still lived. She's my little insurance policy; you don't want her to wither away and die. But then, that was before you found out what they did. The slaughter, the butchery, the mass murder is quite a lot to take in. I assume you have a very different view on the Ancients now that you know the truth."

I looked over at Neb, the defiance still in her eyes.

"I know the truth, yes," I said. "That Ahiram and Theoris conspired to steal the power of the Tempest. That they decided to poison and use the other Ancients as a way to mask what they'd done for themselves, but it didn't quite work and they quickly discovered they were all linked to one another. They couldn't risk killing the other Ancients because they didn't know who they were linked to."

Callie laughed. "The other Ancients aren't innocent; they didn't try to find out what happened. They just accepted the tale as truth, moved on with their lives."

"I know," I said, looking back at Neb. "They all kept secrets that led to this moment. They kept secrets that have hurt people, but those responsible for starting it are dead. I wonder, did Hesansh know? Was he clued in on what Theoris and Ahiram did?"

As if on cue, Hesansh stepped out from behind a curtain at the far end of the chamber. He was shirtless and had seemingly grown in size. His muscles bulged, and there was a purple glow under his skin. "I did," he said.

"You look like someone inflated you like a balloon," I told him.

"I allowed him to connect to my power," Callie said. "The energy will eventually kill him, and he knows it, but not before he kills you."

"I thought I had to be the one to kill him," I said. "Wasn't that your plan?"

"Plans change," Callie snapped. "It seems like I no longer need you. I have everything I want right here. Doesn't matter what you do, I win."

A thought came to me. "You can't see me in the chains, can you?"

The flash of anger across her face told me I was right.

"It's because I'm the Herald," I said. "You can't see me in the chains, because I'm not connected to the rift in the same way as everyone else. I am connected to the heart of it, the core of it. There is no Tempest, not in the same way you saw it. You should just give up, because you can't win here."

I looked back to Hesansh, who was walking toward me with the confidence of a man who knows what to expect in the coming confrontation.

"Neb, I am sorry that this is how you lose your connection," I told her, and looked her way. "I wish it wasn't."

Neb smiled and nodded.

I felt a weight lift from my shoulders, knowing that Neb was prepared for what was going to happen.

Once Hesansh was close enough, he threw a punch, which I stepped back from, pushing his hand to the side with my own, thinking that his attack was slow and ponderous, only for his free hand to come up and catch me under the chin with speed and power. It took me off my feet and sent me flying up into the cavern ceiling. I'd underestimated his power and speed, and as I dropped from the ceiling, followed by a ton of rock that collapsed onto me, I knew that Hesansh was no longer just an Ancient; he was now even more of a monster than whatever he had been when we'd last met.

I turned to smoke, moved out from under the rock, and re-formed beside it, only to be caught in the head with a kick that sent me flying back into the wall behind me. More rock collapsed, and I fell to my knees, my head swimming.

Hesansh darted toward me with incredible speed, throwing punch after punch that I was barely able to defend against. He was faster and stronger than anything I'd ever fought in my entire life, and even as the Herald, I was finding his onslaught difficult to defend against.

I caught his wrist in my hand and smashed my elbow into his face, knocking his head back but keeping hold of his hand and pulling him back toward me to hit him again. I let go this time, and he flew across the chamber, impacting with where the new Tempest was being created. He smashed through it, spilling the water across the ground, as Callie screamed out in rage and frustration.

The small but powerful core that Callie had been creating exploded across the room, bringing down huge chunks of rock. The power washed over me, and I felt the coldness of something alien and wrong. This power should not exist; it was barbaric.

Hesansh strolled through the ever-expanding wash of power, his body absorbing more and more of it with every step. I turned to smoke, moved around him as quickly as possible, and caught a glimpse of Callie running out of the chamber. I re-formed, tore the cage door free, and grabbed Neb.

Hesansh charged toward us, but as I held on to Neb, I snapped back to a particle of myself that I had left near where the rocks had collapsed earlier, teleporting both of us across the chamber, only to watch Hesansh crash into the cage, disintegrating it.

"Hold on," I told Neb.

Neb did as she was requested, her arms around my neck, as I flew up into the ceiling, where part of it had been destroyed, using the rift energy to burst through the rock in front of me as though I were Superman. Rock parted for me as if it were paper as I smashed through hundreds of metres, until I came out at the top, next to the palace. I put Neb down, and she fell to the ground, pieces of rock and dust falling off of her.

The ground beneath my feet rumbled and moments later erupted as Hesansh burst out, landing fifty feet away from Neb and me. He was even larger than he had been down in the chamber, his entire body pulsing with stolen rift energy. His ability had always been to be able to pull rift energy into himself, making himself more powerful, but this was beyond anything I'd ever heard of before.

With a roar of hate, Hesansh threw himself toward me, almost galloping on all fours as he closed the distance between us in an instant. He was pure power, and there was so much of it inside of his body that it would eventually burn out to nothing, but that wasn't the problem I was going to have. And unless I could find a way to stop him, there was a possibility he would kill me or delay me enough that Callie would be able to escape. Neither of those options worked for me.

I went to grab my spear and found that it wasn't there. It had removed itself from the sheath on my back during the escape from the chamber below and was embedded in the grass fifty feet away. I managed to duck a swipe of Hesansh's now-taloned hands, and they tore through the wall behind me like it was nothing. I hit him in the stomach with a rift-powered blow, sending him staggering back, and followed up by flinging pieces of smoke at him, which I imbued with rift energy, each one causing a small explosion as it tore into his skin. Pieces of him were ripped away and immediately healed.

Hesansh closed the distance between us and kicked at my chest. There was no finesse or skill to his attack; he was just power and rage. I easily avoided the kick and slammed my hand up under his knee, unleashing more rift power, which caused him to fly up and land several feet back.

I walked toward Hesansh as he got back to his feet, and punched him in the side of the face, knocking him back to the ground. He slashed up at me with his talons, but I avoided them easily. I stamped down on his elbow, breaking his arm, and punched him again in the head. I unleashed punch after punch of rift-power-enhanced blows down on Hesansh, but with every hit I connected with, he almost instantly healed. With every healing, he became more and more consumed by the power that was inside of him, the purple flooding out of him as if he were a colander. There was nothing left of the man now.

Hesansh managed to catch me in the chest with his palm, and the resulting shockwave sent me flying back across the side of the palace. I smashed through a large stained-glass window, the glass raining down above me as I hit the opposite wall inside the room.

I walked back through the ruined window and out into the garden beyond. Hesansh was already running toward me, purple light pouring out from every part of his body. He was halfway to me when he suddenly stopped. He just stopped. He looked confused for a moment and then collapsed to the ground, screaming in pain.

He was still screaming in pain when I reached him a few seconds later and looked down at the pitiful form of a man who thought that he could take power without consequence. More power than his body could handle.

I couldn't absorb the Tempest energy that was inside of him, as my own energy found it to be unpalatable. It was why I had been unable to seriously hurt him; we were opposites, in a way. I had more power, I was able to maintain my old self, but my own power had no effect against the amount that he had absorbed.

I dragged Hesansh back over toward Neb, who I found sitting on the ground. For a moment, I wondered if Hesansh's current state had been because Neb had taken her own life; I was glad to see that that was not the case.

Hesansh whimpered as I dropped him on the ground. "It needs to happen," I told Neb.

Neb glanced between her old comrade and me. "Do it."

I looked down at Hesansh, his body back to its normal size, his power having eaten him alive. He was almost dead. The Tempest that Callie had created had hollowed him out. He looked up at me, pleading in his eyes. I ignored him and walked over to my spear—which was only a short distance away, thankfully— picking it up from the ground, and turned to see Hesansh on his knees, his eyes closed, awaiting death. I was happy to give it to him.

Hesansh's head was quickly removed from his body with a swipe of my spear. I put more strength into it than I've ever hit anything before, and it moved through him as if he were not there. Any semblance of Tempest power was drawn into me a moment later as the remains of his body fell to ash.

I dropped the spear at Neb's feet. "Just in case something else comes," I said, and burst into smoke, covering the whole area in seconds, seeking out Callie. There was no point in waiting for the lift, and I was soon diving down into the mines, moving through their winding narrow corridors in search of my prey.

I found her sat in a large room among hundreds of shining bright crystals, each one full of rift power; purple and blues of different hues shimmered, some of them so bright, they illuminated the rest of the room. They had been piled up in the corners to await transport or to give to Callie as she continued her experiments creating a new Tempest far below.

"You could've changed the world for the better," I told her.

Callie looked up at me with burning anger in her eyes. "What did you think I was trying to do? You remove the Ancients, you remove anyone who's causing a problem, and then you control everything. The Tempest was never going to give me the rest of its power, so I was going to take it. I would've ruled this place like a benevolent god. I would've made it safe, I would've made the Earth safe, I would've made every rift that connected to ours safe. Instead, I was hunted down like a criminal."

I stared at Callie for a moment. She had been responsible for so much death and destruction, her machinations for power and knowledge had done untold harm to so many people, that it felt wrong that it would end in such a fashion. Captured in a room full of crystals with the rift power inside them, no more allies, no more friends, no one she could turn to.

"I was told you were going to have people down there with you," I said.

"It turns out that the Tempest I created required more energy than I had expected," she told me without a single hint of remorse.

I picked up one of the crystals, crushing it in my hand, feeling the rift energy trapped inside flow back into me. "You were always a monster, Callie," I said, dropping the crystal back to the pile.

"And I am linked to the power of the new rift core," she snapped back, standing up straight and proud. "What can you possibly do to me?"

I turned to smoke and flew back down toward the core as Callie screamed something behind me. I landed next to where the new rift core was spinning. The power inside of it called to me; it was power that the Tempest should never have lost, and Callie wanted to claim it for her own. To corrupt it, to make it something monstrous, like her.

Callie landed beside me, a thud on the ground. "I am *better* than you," she snapped. "I'm better than all of you. I'm the only one who can control the rift."

I pulled open the chamber door that housed the core and took a step to the side. "You said that you were one with the power of the new core, but I think that's a lie," I said. "If you were *one* with anything, you wouldn't have sent Hesansh to kill me alone. You'd have made sure the job was done properly. So, what's the problem? Can you control it or not?"

"I can," Callie shouted.

"Control it, then," I said, motioning toward the core. "Take the power from that core into yourself. You're still linked to it, even without the jewellery. So, do it."

Callie eyed me suspiciously.

I took a step farther away from the core. "Be my guest."

"And then what?" Callie asked.

"You're constantly saying that you'd be the best person to have control of the rift," I said. "Prove it. Take that power and do what you say you're going to do. You still have rift energy inside of you, but you're not linked to this. Why?"

Callie hesitated.

I removed a primordial-bone dagger from the sheath on my hip. "You can go in there and do what you say you can do, or I'm going to kill you."

"I can't be killed," Callie said, charging into the rift core. She looked back at me, triumph on her face as the power of the rift flooded into her. "I am a god."

I watched as Callie began to glow, the power quite literally flooding her body, until she stepped out of the chamber, illuminating the whole area around her.

I sheathed my dagger. I wasn't going to need it.

She walked up to me and laughed. "Bow to me, little man. I am your better."

"I don't think so," I said.

She pushed me, forcing me to take a step back, but her eyes widened in horror as she saw that it left a trail of rift energy connecting us.

"I was curious about the rift energy," I said. "You cultivated it, stored it, poured it into yourself, but it was never really yours. It belongs to the rift, Callie. It belongs to me. I could have gone in there and taken it, but I wanted to see your face when you understood."

"No, no, no, no," Callie stammered.

The power continued to flood into me, the link growing in size and intensity as Callie ran toward me, throwing a punch, which I easily avoided. I levitated off the ground, just out of her reach, and let her scream obscenities at me.

Within moments, Callie's glow was fading, and she dropped to her knees. She began to panic as her breathing laboured; she could no longer breathe the air of the rift. I took one piece of my smoke, loaded it with rift power, and fired it at Callie's head. It had the same effect as being hit with a sniper bullet, covering the rocks behind her in blood as she collapsed onto them.

I waited a few minutes as the rift energy continued to flood out of Callie, turning her to dust. A deserved fate. I flew back up through the mineshaft to the outside and found Neb still sat on the ground, the spear at her feet.

"Did you expect me to take my own life?" she asked me.

"I figured it was worth giving you the option," I told her. "You will die within a year or two, Neb. I know the truth of the Ancients; I know the truth about my shadows. I understand why you kept the latter secret, but you should have trusted people. Should have trusted me."

"I trusted Hesansh once," Neb said. "Trusted Ahiram, too. I really didn't know what he and Theoris did, not until it was too late. You know they wanted to kill us after forcing the power into us; they figured we'd be easier to kill to gain our power. The Tempest linking us stopped that. We all, well, most of us, tried so hard to make sure the rift was safe. No one knew that our very existence was what made it unsafe."

"So what's the plan, Neb?" I asked, taking a seat beside her.

"The Ancients are dead," Neb said. "I have maybe two years before my power completely vanishes and I die. I'd like to use that time to help put things right, if you'll accept it."

I nodded and got to my feet. "I will. I'd be happy to."

"So, you're the Herald?" she said. "Never heard of that before."

"Join the club," I said, offering Neb my hand, which she took. "You want to go see your granddaughter?"

"You going to fly me there?" she asked.

I smiled as my feet left the ground, Neb suddenly holding on to me tightly. "Let's go make the world better," I said.

CHAPTER THIRTY

I sat outside the entrance to the centre of the mountain, which I had created upon my return from Asteria. The basin in the mountain was still there, but having absorbed all of the power within, I saw little reason to continue keeping people out. Instead, I changed it to become a destination where new riftborn and revenants walked through. Their first stop on the road to a new life.

I built a cabin on the shores of the lake farther north of the mountain, several hours' walk away from the clearing where I had given my speech to the primordials. The cabin was made from the dark wood that inhabited this land, and furnished with items from friends who had brought gifts once it had been built. There was a forge beside it, which Drusilla used when she came to visit. She still enjoyed her time on Earth, but staying in the rift with me had become something she did for longer and longer as the years went by.

I occasionally missed not being able to go back to Earth, not having to sit in the rift and live out my days, but I honestly didn't mind. Most of the revenants who had been given the chance to come straight to the rift had taken it. Nadia had practically jumped through the tear as soon as it was open. Gabriel had declined, which I'd expected he would.

Instead of being at my cabin, enjoying the relaxing views, drinking wonderful coffee that Ji-hyun had brought me, I sat at the edge of the basin, waiting for the next inhabitant. Whereas the basin had been thousands of feet deep when I'd absorbed the energy contained within, I'd created a new portion where people would arrive. I didn't wish to have people climbing thousands of feet up the side of the basin to get out. It felt like a cruel sport.

The basin was now guarded by a garrison of soldiers, including people that I had handpicked, people who had lived within the rift already, and several primordials who wished to be part of the new world that we were creating. Valmore led the garrison, something he had been proud to do when asked. Some of the rift-fused had initially been wary of having a primordial in charge, but four years had passed without incident, and it was now a model that was being utilised throughout the rift.

I used Callie's science and notes to make a necklace of my own power and gave it to Neb. It wasn't going to keep her around forever, but it would slow her eventual death, giving her maybe a decade of life. She no longer had any power, and if she ever chose to take it off, she would die quickly, but I knew she wanted the chance to help. I knew that she would like to go out on her own terms. Well, now she had that choice.

The mist that had stopped the primordials from travelling farther south was gone. Lavis was the first to leave, wanting to travel the rift and see its sights. She'd met up with Neb, who was now helping fix Inaxia, a job she'd never wanted but had come to accept.

From what I heard, the conversation between Neb and Lavis had healed some old wounds, and while Lavis wasn't going to speak for all of the primordials, she was grateful that Neb wanted to make things right. I hoped it was a precursor to helping people heal. I'd spoken to Neb twice since the fight at Asteria and managed to hash out a lot of the issues I'd built up over the years. When her power was finally gone, I was going to miss her a great deal.

The last time I'd spoken to Lavis, she'd been in Plainhaven, Timo's old city. The people there had accepted her as if she had always lived there. She seemed happy.

Inaxia was still the capital city, although everyone who had sided with Callie had been arrested, charged, and sent to the new prison colony that used to be Asteria. I hadn't wanted to create such a thing, but it was deemed necessary when several of her most ardent followers had decided that a guerrilla-warfare campaign was the best way forward. I'd been loath to kill them all, creating martyrs for a new generation of dickheads, so they were sent to live where they could be watched. I hoped one day that Callie's influence could be broken, but not everybody shared my optimism.

I'd made the rift energy inert in Asteria, transferring it back toward the rest of the rift. It had taken a lot out of me and had been several weeks of tireless work, but it was now safe to live there. No longer would anyone there unconsciously absorb rift energy.

Much to Ji-hyun's dismay, she was given a new title and placed in charge of the worldwide RCU effort. It had been Ravi's idea, who'd been promoted to the head of European operations in what I was pretty sure Ji-hyun considered to be a retaliation. For someone who had never wanted any roles of responsibility, she sure was good at them.

Her first act had been to make Dani head of the Boston RCU, an act few disagreed with. She was good at her job and well respected. Dani, of course refused but had finally relented a year before when she decided that her experience now matched the position. I was happy for them all.

There was a tear at the side of the basin, close to where I sat, and Gabriel appeared. He looked over the side of the basin down into the massive area below and then over to me. He smiled, walked over, and hugged me tightly. "It's been a long time, my friend," Gabriel said warmly.

"Welcome to the rift," I said. "It's been quite boring without you."

Gabriel laughed as we left the basin and stepped out into the land known as the Tempest. "You know, it was always a little confusing that the land was called the Tempest and the Tempest was called the Tempest."

"I didn't name it," I told him. "If you wish, you can live here. Or you can move south, or west, or really, you can go everywhere. I will advise not doing it at night. There are still things out there that will eat you. No joke."

"Where is Hiroyuki these days?" he asked.

"Do you want to go see him?" I asked with a playful smile. "Grab hold."

Gabriel did as he was asked, wrapping his arms around my neck as I took off at speed. I flew across the land faster than I'd ever managed when I'd first become the Herald. It turned out that I needed at least a year to get used to the power that I had absorbed. And even now, there were new things that I found out I could do.

A few hours later, we landed in the square in the Crow's Perch. There was a little commotion as the people recognised me, several of whom started to chant my name. I told them all that if they didn't stop, I was going to open a huge tear right above their heads until they did. They stopped pretty quickly after that.

Darice stepped out a moment later, without her mask. She smiled at me and clasped me warmly on the shoulders. "You have brought a friend?" she asked, looking at Gabriel.

I introduced the pair as Hiroyuki walked out of the palace. He wore dark armour with a red crow emblazoned on the chest plate. He looked every inch the warrior I knew him to be, right up into the point that he saw me and Gabriel and let out a yelp of happiness. It sort of ruined the image.

I spent a few hours with Gabriel and Hiroyuki, enjoying their and the Queen's company, and Gabriel asked if he could stay and help with the city. The Queen was more than happy to have that happen, as I knew she would be.

After several hours of me trying to say goodbye, I found myself on the mound behind the city, a place where there had once been a great deal of violence. The Queen had known nothing about what her grandmother and the rest of the Ancients had done, and together, we had talked through our emotions and feelings about the whole situation. It was nice to have someone in a similar circumstance to my own.

"I keep thinking every time I see you will be the last time I see you," the Queen said with a wry smile.

"Apparently, you are not to get rid of me any time soon," I told her. "Hiroyuki and Gabriel will be great assets to your city. Which, by the way, I see is extending out; the walls are coming down."

"We no longer have to pretend that we are a prison," she told me. "Things are changing, thanks to you and those who helped you. A lot of people's lives are better. There are less tears, for one. Things are stable. I think this might be the first time in my entire life that I've ever had stability for more than a few weeks."

Anyone remaining at Neb's old city of Nightvale had moved into the Crow's Perch, and I heard news that several of the villages in the area were doing the same. It was going to double the size of the city. The Queen seemed perfectly at ease with the whole idea.

We sat and chatted for a while longer, until Hiroyuki appeared and bid the queen to return, as more and more of her guards were asking where she was.

"He's very good at his job," Darice told me. "It keeps me in check. Do not be a stranger, Lucas. I enjoy our chats."

I watched her walk away, and Hiroyuki walked up to me. "It's been a few months," he said.

I nodded. "I don't like to flutter around and bother people," I said. "I know you were trying to integrate the rest of the Silver Phalanx members into the city. How's that going?"

"Good," he said. "This place feels like home, which is something I never thought I would have again after what happened at Noah's. Thank you for bringing me here. You gave me purpose."

I shook my head. "You gave yourself purpose; I just pointed you in a direction."

"Did you always know that Gabriel was going to come here?" he asked.

"I had a pretty good idea," I told him. "Gabriel needs something to do, and this city is going to become one of the most important in all of the rift. There's potential for it to become the largest in all of the rift. It will need people like Gabriel. You and the Queen will also need people like Gabriel."

"You still haven't picked who's going to be the Guardian," he said. "Are there no candidates?"

I chuckled. "There are many candidates. The Guardian needs to be someone who not only protects the rift and its connection to Earth, and its people, and its land, but wants to do all of those things. Someone who can inspire and terrify. Because sometimes you need someone who can do both."

Hiroyuki offered me his hand, which I shook. "I wish you good luck in your search," he said.

I watched him walk away before I took back to the skies and flew north again to my little cabin. Drusilla was sat outside of it and smiled as I landed.

"You know, I've never quite gotten used to the fact that you can do that," she said, waving to the air.

"Sometimes, I still can't believe that I can do it," I told her. "There's a lot of stuff I do that I still can't believe."

She stepped down from the cabin porch and kissed me. "It's getting late, and you are very old; I think maybe you should retire for the night."

"I do feel like I need to be rested," I said to her with a smile of my own. "This all takes so much out of me."

Drusilla's smile turned mischievous. "Not too much, I hope."

We retired to bed after that, and I left her to sleep, as I was woken in the night. I left my cabin and stepped out onto the grass outside. The air before me shimmered, and I knew what was coming. And part of me was very excited, and part of me hated it.

"You have to go, don't you?" Drusilla said from behind me. "The rift is connected with another rift?"

I nodded. "I'm sorry."

Drusilla moved quickly toward me and embraced me tightly. "Never be sorry for who you are," she whispered into my ear. "You do know that I am not going to live here and pine away, waiting for your return."

I laughed. "I would not expect you to." We'd discussed this several times over the years, and we knew that it would have been stupid to suggest that we should stay together when there was a distinct possibility that we'd never see one another again. We'd had many years together, more than most get, and it had been wonderful.

"You need to go speak to Nadia," Drusilla said. "She's had a year."

"I know," I said. "I'm going to go and do it now. I'll come back; whatever has happened hasn't happened yet, but soon it will. I don't know how much longer we have together, but I'm looking forward to spending the rest of my time here with you. So long as you're still interested."

Drusilla let out a laugh as she wrapped her arms around me. "Well, I'll have to check the vast line of interested suitors standing before me. And if they're okay with it, then I guess I'm okay with it."

I promised to be back soon, and set off toward Lake Spirit, where Nadia had been cleaning out the huts and equipment left behind by Callie and her people during their first visit into the rift many years earlier.

Nadia was sat at the water's edge, looking across the still lake. She didn't even look up as I landed beside her. "I assume you are here because you want an answer?"

When I'd told Hiroyuki that I hadn't decided upon a Guardian of the rift, that had been a lie. I'd asked Nadia a year earlier, and she hadn't been able to give me an answer. She asked for time to think about it, and I told her she had until the rift found another.

"I am," I told her. "I think there's about to be a tear into another rift. I'm about to leave and do whatever the hell it is the Herald does. I'm still not entirely certain. I guess I'll figure it out as I go. But it could be a while before I come back, and I chose you because I know you will do a good job. And because I know that you are the best of us, Nadia."

Nadia shook her head. "No, "she said with a little anger, which surprised me. "I'm a terrible person. I have done terrible things. And the only reason that I've changed is because you came into my chains and flipped my world upside down. You made me a Raven, and then we discovered that actually, the Guilds might be better off no longer existing.

And now they don't. Most of the surviving members live in the rift, working for one of the big cities, helping people. I was so proud when I became a Raven. If I say yes to this, is it going to be taken away from me? Am I going to find out that being a Guardian of the rift is based on some sort of horrific act?"

I sat down beside her. "I have absolutely no idea. I doubt it. Being a Guardian is what you make it, not what other people who came before you made it. Besides, no one has ever done the job before. You would be the first Guardian of the rift; you would be able to help so many people. Protect so many people. I understand if you don't want to do this, and I will find somebody else, but I don't think I will find anyone as good as you."

"That's a hell of a sales pitch," Nadia said. "I've had a year to think about it, and every time I think, *This is excellent; I would love to do this*, my brain just tells me that it could all go wrong in an instant. I don't know what to do."

"We'll do whatever you want," I told her. "But I do need an answer."

She turned to me. She'd been crying; her eyes were puffy and red. "I don't want you to go."

I put my arm around her and hugged her against me. Her chains flicked around wildly for a moment before settling and wrapping around me. "Okay," she whispered. "I'll do it."

I took her to the basin, landing just outside, where we were greeted by Valmore. He looked down at Nadia. "Have you said yes?" he asked her.

She nodded.

"Good. The primordials will always be here to help you," Valmore told her. "You have become a figure of fondness for many of my kind. You will have whatever help you need."

"Thank you," Nadia said, her voice quiet. She turned to me. "So, how do we do this?"

I pointed to the entrance to the mountain. "We go to the basin, and I grant you some of my power."

We both walked in and down the steps into the basin. Nadia took my hand, and I pulled her toward me into a hug. We floated down toward the bottom of the basin, and part of the basin opened, revealing a glowing purple sphere about the size of a football. I picked it up and passed it to Nadia, and she took it from me.

"You stay here," I told her. "I'll be back when it's done."

Nadia nodded and stared at the sphere in her hands. I left the basin, making sure it was cleared out of anybody else, as bright purple light tore out of the entrance, covering anything within a few hundred metres of its opening.

It lasted for a few minutes, and when the light dissipated, I re-entered the mountain and dropped down into the basin, next to a kneeling Nadia. She looked up at me, "I know kung fu," she said, and laughed.

I brought Nadia back out of the basin. "Are you okay?" I asked.

"Yes," Nadia said. "This is like nothing I've ever felt before. I can feel so much. I can see so much. Did you know that Hiroyuki and the Queen of Crows are a thing? It's not the power showing me that, I just wondered if you knew."

I laughed. "I did," I told her. "They don't know that I know that."

Nadia smiled. "Drusilla is going to miss you so much, Lucas."

Sadness pinged at my heart. "I know," I told her. "I'm going to miss her too. I'm going to miss you all."

"Our new Guardian," Valmore shouted as we left the basin.

His words were repeated by the dozen men and women who guarded the basin. It made me incredibly proud to see Nadia accept who she was and the potential within her. She was going to be a great Guardian, and I knew I was leaving the rift in good hands.

I said my goodbyes, which were somewhat more tearful than I had anticipated, and returned to my cabin, where I spent the rest of the night sat on the porch with Drusilla, watching the shimmer before us become more and more pronounced. We did the same thing day after day, knowing it might be our last together.

Within a week, the shimmer was now a tear. It was too small to see what was beyond, but I knew that it was unlike anything or anywhere that I had been before.

Drusilla held my hand and pulled me into a deep kiss before pulling away. "I'm really going to miss you," she said softly. "Come back when you can."

I kissed her again, and part of me wished that I could just stay there with her forever. "I promise."

I stepped off of the porch, walked toward the tear, and waved my hand in front of it. It opened up massively, revealing a place I'd never seen before. Rolling hills of orange and yellow grass made it appear as though it were aflame. I looked back to Drusilla and said, "I love you."

"I love you too," she told me.

I turned back to the rift and stepped inside, and it snapped shut behind me, leaving me in a place I've never seen before, and I had no idea what was going to happen next. I smiled and looked around at a place I was going to get to know very well. I opened a tear into my embers, and Casimir and Maria left them, Casimir a large wolf, while Maria was now in the shape of a condor. They both remained at my side as we took the first few steps into the strange new land.

"It's time to search the cosmos," I said to them both. "Let's see what the universe has to offer."

ABOUT THE AUTHOR

Steve McHugh is the bestselling author of the Hellequin Chronicles. His novel *Scorched Shadows* was nominated for a David Gemmell Award for Fantasy in 2018. Born in Mexborough, South Yorkshire, McHugh currently lives with his wife and three daughters in Southampton.

JOIN THE FELLOWSHIP

follow us on our socials

 podiumentertainment.com

 @podiumentertainment

 /podiumentertainment

 @podium_ent

 @podiumentertainment